Our Story began in...

The Kind of a Girl...

as Lorraine Innis, a man in disguise trying to avenge the death of his girlfriend, accidentally foiled the assassination attempt on Russian president Kropotkin.

It continued in...

The Girl in the Diamond Studded Heels...

as Lorraine, now famous, became an international symbol of peace!

Now, learn what forces turned an average guy like Chesney Potts into the beloved heroine of the world in...

The Girl in the Aubergine Sandals!

ALSO BY G.C. Allen

The Kind of a Girl
The Girl in the Diamond Studded Heels

Coming Soon...

The Girl in the Lime Green Wellies
The Girl in the Saffron Espadrilles
The Girl in the Blood Red Stilettos
The Girl in the Sky Blue Plimsolls

Visit www.iLorraine.com

The Girl in the Aubergine Sandals

G.C. Allen

The Third Book in the
Lorraine Innis Series

Daley•into•Print LLC
Mundus Est Vestra Locusta

For
Cindy
Margaret,
and Sarah,
Three Ladies Who Exemplify
the Brains, Strength, and Heart of Aunt Elinor:

and

for Elby,
who most enjoys
the story of Chesney's childhood.

"He will not allow your foot to slip;
    He who keeps you will not slumber.
Behold, He who keeps Israel
    Will neither slumber nor sleep."

Psalm 121:3-4

The Girl
in the
Aubergine
Sandals

- 1 -
The Semi-Silent Retreat

Are you going to say something," Valerie Fierro asked, "anything?" Another milepost silently marked their progress; another exit untaken; another off-ramp passed by. The pattern of tail lights rippled onward ahead of them through the night like a scarlet serpent, winding northward on I-95 through Maryland. Another mile of one-sided communications as Valerie labored to extract a response out of Lorraine Innis. Normally, after an hour of such frustrating silence, Valerie would have slapped her. This was ill-advised for two reasons: first, Lorraine was behind the wheel of the rental car, one demolished car that day was enough; and, second, Valerie's left arm was in a plaster cast hindering the slapping capabilities of her right arm.

"Did Liverot say anything," Valerie asked after another half-mile. She had asked that question twice before on their journey, once on the Washington Beltway, and again just after the Baltimore tunnel. Lorraine was nothing if not consistent. She didn't answer those previous times, and she didn't answer now, at least not out loud.

Did Peter Liverot say anything? Lorraine thought. He said plenty. He said too much.

Wrong! How could I have been so wrong; wrong about Peter Liverot, wrong about everything?

Liverot could have been lying, reasoned Lorraine. The thought had occurred to her repeatedly since leaving the banker's deathbed. But why would he? Liverot had summoned Lorraine for a final confession. He knew he was dying. He was unburdening his soul; giving his earthly tent one last shake to rid it of its debris before breaking camp for eternity. Having made a clean breast of his disgusting existence, why would he backtrack to toss on one last lie? Was it habitual? Was it impossible for him to tell the truth, even in his final breath? And if it was a lie, what did Liverot hope to gain through it?

The banker had been surprised when Lorraine mentioned Martina Fergus. As far as Liverot knew, there was no connection between Lorraine and Martina. Then there was that other name he'd never before spoken to her.

"There's a rest stop coming up," said Valerie trying to mask her frustration behind a façade of concern. "Are you hungry? Thirsty? You've been going all day. Maybe a cup of tea? Do you want to pee?"

Lorraine just stared at the road ahead.

"Fine!" snorted Valerie. She tried to fold her arms disdainfully but only slammed the heavy cast against her other wrist with a painful thud.

Eckner, Lorraine thought. Why would Liverot mention Albrecht Eckner? Liverot had no reason except that it was the truth. That led to another problem: if Liverot had told the truth, how could she have been so wrong? That wasn't like her? Or was it?

"The doctors said he was still alive when he asked to see you," said Valerie.

Her tone was now nonchalant. Lorraine almost responded pedantically that Valerie's last sentence made little sense since corpses don't ask for visitors. But there were more pressing matters on her mind beyond correcting illogical statements.

Albrecht Eckner had been Liverot's right-hand man in Delaware, now he was the director of Fourth Fiduciary Trust's Gibraltar subsidiary. Why would Liverot bring him up? She would have preferred Liverot utter any other name rather than Eckner. She never felt comfortable around Eckner; that is her alter ego, Chesney Potts had never felt at ease around Eckner. Thankfully Lorraine Innis had never met him.

"So are you going to say anything," snapped Valerie returning to belligerency. "I do have a right to know."

A right to know? Lorraine had a right to know if her entire reason for being was founded on a faulty premise. She had a right to know how wrong she had been. If Peter Liverot was innocent of Martina's death, then had Lorraine caused his death? If there hadn't been a Lorraine Innis, she reasoned, Liverot never would have been at the White House in the direct line of that bomber. So instead of bringing Liverot to justice for his part in the death of an innocent girl, it was Liverot who was innocent. If that was the case, then Lorraine had his blood on her hands. Or did she? She had to know. Her worse fears had come to life. She had scrupulously checked her motives every step of the way. She had wanted justice, not revenge. What good would result if she defeated Liverot only to emerge as a bigger villain than he had ever been? Now, not only had she destroyed Liverot, she had done so without cause. That made her worse than Liverot. How could she have gotten it so wrong?

An eighteen-wheeler blew by on their left, pushing their car in its updraft as if it had been a dingy in the wake of an ocean liner. Lorraine adjusted for the car's swerve, and continued on in the center lane.

The center lane; wasn't that always the best course? Right up the middle. Didn't that offer the best opportunity to observe and react to either side? Would a more cautious approach have saved her from her current quandary? Or perhaps a more radical tactic would have brought the entire situation to a swifter resolution. Neither approach could have been any worse. Her thoughts returned to Peter Liverot's deathbed.

He had asked for Lorraine in his dying moments. Liverot saw her as the one person qualified to offer him absolution. How could she? It was she who should have been confessing to him. It was she, revered around the world for her goodness and purity, who needed forgiveness from that scoundrel. A quotation from Isaiah intruded on Lorraine's stream of consciousness:

"All our righteous acts are like filthy rags; we all shrivel up like a leaf, and like the wind our sins sweep us away."

A tiny sneer formed on her lips directed at herself. She had deluded herself. If she had any advantage over the likes of Peter Liverot, she reasoned, it was that her filthy rags had a few more patches, and a few less stains. That, apparently, was enough for the world; enough to make her a "saint" and Liverot a villain. Now, however, she wondered if there was much difference between them.

Still, she thought, she had to sort it all out, if only for the sake of poor Peter Liverot. Poor Peter Liverot? She smirked at the irony of pitying that ruthless bastard, but she did. She had to sort it out and set things right as best she could. Could she? Could anyone? She shrugged her shoulders.

"What? What?" said Valerie observing Lorraine's subtle gesture. "Damn it, will you say something? If you don't, I'll go nuts!"

Lorraine barely heard the outburst.

If only she hadn't asked Liverot to confess. He would have died, and Lorraine would have believed she had won justice for Martina. Lorraine could have ceased to be. Still, it wouldn't have been true justice.

"Hey! Can you hear me?" Valerie screeched.

Lorraine needed to know how wrong she had been. Until then, she would have to shut out everyone, even Valerie. She didn't want to burden Valerie with the knowledge that she had been wrong, as well. Valerie had been positive that Liverot was responsible for Martina's death. It wasn't Valerie's fault. No, Lorraine had accepted the evidence too readily. Evidence? It wasn't even evidence, it just had the appearance of evidence, and while it looked good, ultimately it was a mere a shadow of the truth.

As Lorraine drove across the Susquehanna River bridge, the wind began to gust from the north. Lorraine tightened her grip on the wheel and kept focused on the road ahead. By the time they reached the opposite shore, large dollops of rain were falling on the windshield.

"Oh, great," said Valerie. The change in the weather was just another excuse for something to say. Lorraine turned on the windshield wipers. The rhythm of the blades squeaking across the glass seemed to be chanting.

"Eckner, Eckner," they thumped, adding "Albrecht Eckner," on each third pass.

"Eckner, Eckner, Albrecht Eckner..."

Albrecht Eckner. She should have known that his loathsome presence was somewhere in this mess. She hadn't considered Eckner. He was thousands of miles away. She had concentrated on Liverot. Now, it seemed that Eckner was culpable in Martina's death. But why had he...

"Eckner, Eckner, Albrecht Eckner..."

"Bean Clerk Retch," that was the anagram of his name. Fitting, she thought. He had an accounting degree: a bean counter. And he had the ability to turn the strongest of stomachs. Still, you couldn't condemn a person for his name, much less the rearranging of its letters. It did fit though but was only admissible in the court of her mind. If she could just get Eckner in court, thought Lorraine, not a real court, he was too crafty, too oily ever to be convicted of... whatever he was guilty. Unfortunately, creatures such as Albrecht Eckner were not the types who were called to account in courts of law. Justice, with its heavily swaddled eyes, was blind to the deficiencies of character that were obvious to ordinary people. No, Lorraine had little doubt that putting Eckner in the dock would only enhance his reputation as a scoundrel and only frustrate those who tried to deal fairly with their fellow human beings.

"Eckner, Eckner, Albrecht Eckner..."

"Brethren Cackle," nodded Lorraine thinking of another rearrangement of the name. Eckner loved to laugh at his brethren or anyone else in the human race. Mocking was one of Eckner's favorite leisure activities. Give Eckner a corner table in a busy restaurant, and he would whisper snide comments on everyone in view. The worst thing, she recalled with a shudder...

"Are you cold," said Valerie, looking for any way to insert herself in Lorraine's train of thought. "I can turn on the heat..."

Lorraine reached over and turned on the car's heater, then switched it to defrost as the windows began to fog up.

No, the worst thing about Eckner was that he cloaked his malice in a veneer of charm and innocence. Having a conversation with Eckner was like being invited to a party in a cesspool disguised as a mineral bath. Inch by inch the unwary participants would wade deeper and deeper, only to realize too late, that they were up to their nostrils in the vilest filth. It was then that he would break his spell with that laugh - that brethren cackle - from the throat of ...

"Eckner, Eckner, Albrecht Eckner..."

She should have known, but he was an ocean away by the time Lorraine had been created. It was also worse that it was Eckner. Peter Liverot was disreputable by upbringing, but at least he came by his dishonesty honestly. Eckner, on the other hand, not only wallowed in the entrails of humanity, but he enjoyed it so much. With Liverot, it was survival. To Albrecht Eckner it was sheer pleasure.

How could she have been so wrong?

So, what would she do now?

"Hey, Zombie," shouted Valerie, now trying insults, "this is our exit; unless you plan on driving to Maine!"

Lorraine jerked the car up the exit ramp. How could she plot her next move when she couldn't even drive home? No, she needed to think. Think? That's all she'd been doing for the last...she glanced at her wristwatch...for the last eight hours. And in that time she'd only managed to spin in the same spiral of questions, adding more along the way, tightening the loop until it threatened to strangle her like a noose around her mind.

They stopped at a light a few miles from Valerie's townhouse when she saw it. She been at that intersection a hundred times before and had seen that shabby law office sitting in the strip mall, without ever noticing it.

A lawyer: that was what she needed. Not that lawyer, one who advertised bankruptcy and divorce work in large tempura letters on his plate glass window. There had to be other lawyers.

Another name slipped into Lorraine's mind: Jaggers. He was an attorney. Jaggers was usually right. It was his habit to be. She would look up Jaggers when she got home, and then, following his approach, she would organize the facts into a case. She would prosecute the case. She couldn't trust it to anyone who might be too lenient.

Lorraine pulled into Valerie's driveway and yanked the parking brake with an assertive ratchet. For the first time since they'd entered the rental car, she turned to face Valerie. Valerie gave a start; apparently, something in Lorraine's expression was disturbing.

"Uh," Valerie said, "I, uh, thanks. How am I supposed to..."

Lorraine squinted.

"I'll, uh, I'll call my insurance company tomorrow," said Valerie, referring to her mangled car last seen on the back of a flatbed truck in Washington. "Never mind." She climbed out of the car and then looked back at its driver.

Lorraine nodded, and said in a deep, though still feminine voice: "I'll call you after the trial."

Valerie's eyes widen. "What trial? Whose trial?"

"Mine," said Lorraine. She reached over, shut the door, and drove on into the night.

- 2 -
You May Look Like Yourself But You're Not Nearly as Nice

Lorraine drove to her own row home in one of Wilmington's more fashionable neighborhoods. She passed through the remote-controlled security gate and into her garage.

Plodding up to the first floor, Lorraine shed her coat and opened the closet. They were still there in the back; still locked tight: the old suitcase and the battered trunk. She pulled out the suitcase, carried it to the kitchen, set it on the counter, and poured a glass of water.

"Oh, shoot," said Lorraine as she looked at the reminder taped to the refrigerator door. "It's the fifteenth!" She had thought about it the previous morning, but so much had happened since then it had slipped her mind.

"It's that time of the month," she said with a sigh. Normally, she didn't dread her mid-month responsibility, but today she didn't feel up to it. Maybe she could do it tomorrow. She paused a moment, chewing on her lower lip with its last residue of her signature Lorraine Innis lipstick. Then she looked at the clock. It was late, she reasoned. But not that late, she thought.

"After all that's gone on today…" she said aloud.

"But that's just why you should, you know how she is…" she replied.

"Yes, you're right…"

Having resolved the debate with herself, Lorraine climbed the stairs to her bedroom, removed her clothes, put her feminine accouterments away for the night, and stepped into the shower. She scoured every trace of her makeup from her face, as was her ritual the fifteenth day of every month. Then, after drying off and putting on her most unisex nightshirt and robe, she combed back her hair severely on her head, deliberately parting it on the left, as she had years ago and tucking her wet hair behind her ears.

16

Lorraine surveyed the results in the mirror. It helped – a little - at least psychologically.

"I guess it's the best I can do anymore," she said. "I don't look like myself, anymore, and like this, I don't really look like anyone. It will have to do. It will have to do. It will have to do…"

Lorraine repeated this last sentence as a vocal practice. Each time, she tried lowering her pitch, while at the same time projecting her voice in a more masculine timbre.

"Hello, hello," she said as she paced the room, her hand cupped over her ear to accurately hear her own voice. "Hello, it's me. How are you?" Was it her imagination, or did this exercise grow increasingly difficult each month? She really needed to keep in practice, if only for the few minutes she needed her old voice every thirty days.

"I suppose that's as good as it will get," sighed Lorraine. It would have to do. Lorraine returned to the living room, sat down on the couch, picked up the phone and dialed. While waiting for the other end to pick up, Lorraine noticed the demure way she had crossed her legs and shifted to a looser, more masculine straddle.

"She won't see how I'm sitting," she scolded.

"No, but she may hear it in your voice," she replied.

The phone rang three times before the other end picked up.

"Hello?" said a woman's voice.

"Hi, Mom, it's me," said Lorraine in the deepest voice she could muster after almost a year of speaking in a light contralto.

"Who?"

"Chesney, your son," said Lorraine, pushing her voice even lower.

"Chesney! Your voice sounds odd. Do you have a cold?"

"It's nothing, just sinuses," said Lorraine. "Either that or it's a bad connection."

"Oh, my, you'd think your sinuses would have dried up now that you're out of the country."

"I guess not, Mom, at least not in the monsoon season." Lorraine hopped off the couch and crossed into the kitchen to turn on the faucet. "In fact, it's starting up again."

"I can hear it," said Mrs. Potoski. "I wish you were home, Son, where it's safe, except for the bombs, that is."

"Bombs? Are they bombing Florida?"

"No, Chesney, not Florida. I'm fine. Haven't you heard the news, all about the President?"

Despite almost being caught in the attack on the White House, Lorraine had missed the reference. She'd better play innocent for the sake of Chesney Potts' cover story.

"What happened to the President?"

"Some crazy person walked into the White House and blew up the President and another man. They haven't released the crazy person's

17

name yet, but as I said, they killed President Merton and another man. I think it was the Secretary of Banking."

Lorraine shook her head. "There is no Secretary of Banking, Mom."

"Well, it was somebody who had something to do with money," insisted Mrs. Potoski.

Poor Peter Liverot, Lorraine thought, blown to pieces and only remembered as "somebody who had something to do with money." Perhaps, that was how he'd prefer to be remembered. If the media knew the full story, he'd go down in history as "the biggest small-time crook on the East Coast."

"And that's not the worst of it," continued Mrs. Potoski.

"No?" said Lorraine wondering what could be worse.

"No! They were probably trying to kill Lorraine."

"Lorraine," muttered Lorraine with a shake of her head.

"Lorraine Innis! Don't you have Lorraine Innis where you are? I thought everyone has Lorraine!"

Lorraine sighed. Mrs. Potoski was talking about Lorraine Innis as if she was some television program or dishwashing liquid. Perhaps that was closer to the truth.

"Yes, Mom, we've got Lorraine Innis," she replied in her deepest voice, "Sometimes we have too much Lorraine Innis."

"Too much? Oh, no, I think she's wonderful."

You would, thought Lorraine. It was amazing to her that the only person in the world who seemed to have had their fill of Lorraine Innis was Lorraine Innis.

Mrs. Potoski seemed to take offense at his silence.

"Chesney, don't you like Lorraine?"

Lorraine forced herself to grin. "Sure, Mom, what's not to like? She's terrific."

"You're not fooling me. When you were a little boy, and you pretended to like something you didn't like you'd say it was 'terrific.' You used to say that about my tuna casserole. Remember?"

"How could I forget?" Mrs. Potoski's tuna casserole featured impenetrable slabs of Velveeta sanded with canned bread crumbs then baked until it resembled an incinerated terrapin.

"And you haven't changed since you were a boy," continued Mrs. Potoski.

Lorraine looked down at her manicured nails and shrugged her shoulders to debate that point.

"You still use 'terrific' in the pejorative, as if it was a bad word," said his mother, before pausing. "What were we talking about?"

"The terrific, sorry, the wonderful Lorraine Innis."

"Oh, right. Well, she's the kind of a girl you should meet," said his mother.

Lorraine burst into involuntary laughter.

"What?" asked Mrs. Potoski. "Lorraine Innis is a lovely person."

"Sorry," said Lorraine. The only place Chesney Potts and Lorraine Innis could possibly meet would be a cloning laboratory. "I just don't think..."

"I didn't mean it would happen," said Mrs. Potoski. "After all, she's not in your league, is she?"

"Thank you," said Lorraine. So, his mother thought he wasn't good enough for his own company.

"Nothing against you, dear, but, I mean, Lorraine Innis is a brilliant internationally beloved, woman." The inference, of course, was that Chesney Potts was a dull, provincial, drone. "Still, I doubt you'd meet Lorraine Innis up the Hoogli River, would you?"

"No, I don't think I'd bump into Lorraine here in India."

"I still don't understand why," said Mrs. Potoski, "why they sent you to the remotest corner of India to help start a bank."

"Banks work in mysterious ways," said Lorraine, "their interest to compound."

"Are you coming home soon, Son?"

Lorraine ran her fingers back through her long hair and sighed.

"No, I doubt it."

"They should let you come home, at least for a visit."

"Yes, well, it wasn't so easy to get here," said Lorraine recalling the process of self-recreation, "and it's not so easy to get back again. I guess I'll be here until I'm not needed anymore."

"Well, at least you like the work you're doing. You do like the work you're doing, don't you?"

"Well, it's rarely dull."

"Your father always said it was important to love what you do. If you love what you do..."

"...you'll never work a day in your life," said Lorraine completing the aphorism that was repeatedly heard in the Potoski home.

"It's true," said Mrs. Potoski, wistfully, "your father lived a very fulfilled life, except when it wasn't so fulfilling, at least not for everyone. But he worked hard, and he loved his work, and so it wasn't 'work.' That was his philosophy."

Ironically, his work had led to his early death. Lorraine stopped in mid-thought and stared into space.

"It's odd," continued Mrs. Potoski, "How your father was essentially a homebody, and now you're on the other side of the world. Your aunt, his sister, she couldn't stay in one place either. That's who she reminds me of!"

"Who reminds you of whom," said Lorraine, jarred from her reverie.

"Lorraine Innis," said Mrs. Potoski, "she's very much like your Aunt Elinor. Don't you think so?"

The question plucked at a deeply-rooted nerve.

"What? No, no," said Lorraine, before adding, "in what way?"

"I mean that she looks very similar to your aunt," said Mrs. Potoski. "In fact, they could be mother and daughter."

"No, they couldn't. That's ridiculous."

"Why not?"

"For one thing, Lorraine Innis' maiden name is Ammaccapane. Aunt Elinor was never married, and as far as I know, she didn't know anyone by the name of Ammaccapane. And even if she did, Lorraine Innis was born in Morristown, New Jersey. Aunt Elinor hardly ever went to New Jersey, and if she did, we probably would have seen her, and if we'd have seen her, we would have noticed she was pregnant, wouldn't we? Well?"

The prolonged silence on the other end of the line indicated to Lorraine that she had been ranting.

"I'm sorry I've upset you, dear," said Mrs. Potoski.

"I'm not upset," said Lorraine, though her voice trembled.

"I thought you said you didn't like Lorraine Innis," she continued. "For someone who doesn't care for the woman, you certainly seem to know a lot about her."

"I, uh, I must have picked all that up in some magazine. There's not much to read here."

"I know all those things about Lorraine," Mrs. Potoski continued. "That's not what I was talking about. I didn't say Lorraine was your Aunt's daughter. I said they looked enough alike to be mother and daughter. Aside from that, they're as different as night and day."

"Really?" said Lorraine, "I would say that they're really quite similar... looks aside, that is. I'd say they definitely came from the same...moral stock."

Lorraine nodded her head, satisfied with the comparison. Mrs. Potoski responded with a derisive snort.

"What?" said Lorraine. "Did I say something amusing, Mother?"

"Moral stock? Just because a person looks like another person doesn't mean that they possess the same character traits."

"They don't look anything alike," argued Lorraine.

"They're almost exactly alike...on the surface," countered his mother. "Other than that, they're as different as night and day. Lorraine Innis is honest, truthful, inspiring..."

"And you're saying Aunt Elinor wasn't?"

There was a pause, followed by a tone that bordered on the condescending. "I knew Elinor longer than you did, dear."

"But all her kindness, her deep spirituality..."

"Traipsing off to Tibetan monasteries on a llama..."

"You don't exactly traipse into Tibet," Lorraine pointed out. "It's not like going down to the corner for a quart of milk. And she didn't ride off on a llama, she was going to a lamasery."

"Still, enjoying wandering around the globe doesn't make one a heroine, not like Lorraine." Having made her point, Mrs. Potoski softened her tone. "I loved Elinor, Chesney, despite…well, everything. If it wasn't for her, I might not have married your father, or, then again, maybe I might have. I suppose that's not important since it happened anyway. And I know you loved her very much. But she wasn't exactly the most… well, the most admirable person, and as for…well, it doesn't matter. But she certainly isn't in Lorraine Innis' league…"

Again, his mother was choosing players for the Lorraine Innis League.

"…Except in their looks."

Lorraine winced. Of course, they looked alike, but she was loath to admit it, lest his mother somehow deduces that her youngest son was now the most famous woman in the world.

"They're nothing alike," sighed Lorraine half-heartedly.

"Maybe you're right. After all, Lorraine is so open, while your Aunt Elinor was always so mysterious."

"Mysterious? In what way?"

"Well, she always was thinking about things, and you never knew what they were. And besides that, she was always disappearing."

"Disappearing? Aunt Elinor didn't disappear."

"Yes, she did," said Mrs. Potoski. "You wouldn't know about that, especially since she reappeared eventually. She was good at reappearing, too, but better at disappearing."

"Mom, visitors have a way of doing that. It's what most of us call 'arriving' and 'leaving.'"

"She was like that her whole life. Never knew when she'd turn up, though not so much anymore."

Lorraine winced. It was a good thing that her aunt had given up her habit of popping up unannounced…especially since she was now deceased.

"Still, they could have been mother and daughter," said Mrs. Potoski.

"I give up," sighed Lorraine.

"Wouldn't that have been interesting? Lorraine Innis part of our family?"

"Terrific," said Lorraine, aloud, but to herself. "But I think you're mistaken." Mistaken? Lorraine recalled her pressing issue. "Mom?"

"Yes, Chesney, dear?"

"I was wondering…"

"Yes, dear?"

"Uh, have I, have I always made mistakes?"

"You?" She sounded confused with the question. "I don't recall you making mistakes. No, you never made mistakes."

Lorraine grimaced. "What about that day?"

"What day?"

"You know," said Lorraine gingerly, as if she were easing into a scalding verbal bath, "that day, that Saturday, back when I was twelve, you know…golf Saturday."

"I don't know what you're talking about," said Mrs. Potoski. Her denial sounded like an amateur actor playing an unreliable witness in a bad courtroom drama. "I don't recall anything about any Saturday, golf or otherwise."

Had she really forgotten, wondered Lorraine, or, as was more likely, had she resolved not to remember it?

"Besides," Mrs. Potoski added, "that wasn't your fault...even if it had happened...which it didn't."

Lorraine sighed; her mother remembered.

"Everyone makes mistakes, Chesney," said Mrs. Potoski, as if he were five-years-old and just been caught drawing outside the lines in his coloring book.

"I know, Mom," said Lorraine, "but I made a lot of mistakes...when I was growing up."

Mrs. Potoski laughed again. "Honey, everyone makes mistakes. That's how we learn," she said, her voice suddenly becoming serious, "are you in trouble?"

"No, Mom..." Chesney wasn't in trouble. Lorraine Innis, however, had more trouble than a chicken stumbling into a weasel convention.

"What I mean," Mrs. Potoski paused, "did you get a girl in trouble?"

Lorraine sat silent for a moment. Did Chesney get a girl in trouble? Well, in as much as Chesney Potts had created Lorraine Innis, and Lorraine Innis was up to her plucked eyebrows in trouble, yes, Chesney Potts had gotten a girl into massive amounts of trouble. For all the problems revolving around Lorraine, being pregnant was not one of them.

"No, Mom, I haven't gotten anyone pregnant."

Mrs. Potoski breathed a sigh of relief. "Then I wouldn't worry about it."

"But, Mom, did I make mistakes when I was growing up?"

"You never got a girl in trouble," said Mrs. Potoski, stuck on the topic of unplanned pregnancies, "you were just a little boy. Now, your brother..." She quickly returned that thought to her mind for safe-keeping. "No, you were a good boy."

"Thank you," said Lorraine, "but did I get things wrong?"

"You were a perfect child," said Mrs. Potoski with a conviction that only a mother could deliver, let alone believe. "All my boys were perfect. And I love you both very much."

"I love you, too, Mom," and then said goodbye, hanging up the phone with a sigh. There was little of value to be gleaned from the selective recall of Prudence Potoski.

- 3 -
Scissors Cuts Crate, Crate Crushes Shelf Paper

It was years since Prudence Potoski had slept through the night. It started with the birth of her first child, Stosh. He was a demanding baby. That fact, coupled with Prudence's new-mother jitters, meant that every time Stosh stirred, she jumped out of bed and ran to see what he wanted. Soon it was normal for her to be at Stosh's beck and call. And he did a tremendous amount of becking and calling. Her second son, Chesney, wasn't as needy, at least not intentionally. As an infant, Chesney was subject to all sorts of odd mishaps that invariably occurred at night. They were just one more factor that made a good night's sleep a rarity.

Then there was the last baby, but Prudence forced the thought of it out of her mind. Life had enough tragedies.

By the time she reached middle-age, Prudence had given up on the concept of normal sleep. She survived on just a few hours, here and there, and used the hours in between for reflection, playing solitaire, and reading. The death of her husband only intensified her erratic sleep patterns. She would fall asleep watching television, wake up, go to bed, read, fall asleep with the light on, wake up, turn off the light, think a bit, fall asleep, wake up, fall back asleep, and so on until dawn.

This night, in the midst of one of her waking bits, Prudence sat up in bed, turned on the light, and cried:

"No! You're wrong! There is a resemblance!"

Her outburst was in response to Chesney, and the similarities between Lorraine Innis and her sister-in-law, Elinor. Scrambling out of bed, Prudence threw on her robe and padded into the living room. There, beneath two-year's worth of *Ladies Home Journals*, she pulled out the faded copy of her college yearbook. Flipping through it, she found it: there in the "P"s, between Wilber Posner and Mary Beth Potter: Elinor I.A. Potoski. She looked at the previous morning's paper. The front-page story described how Lorraine Innis was going to be honored by the president. Next to the story was a large photo of Mrs. Innis. Prudence admired Lorraine Innis ever since she first burst on to the media radar; looking upon her as the daughter she'd never had, or the girl she wished one of her sons would marry. Comparing the newspaper photo and the yearbook, Prudence understood the feeling more fully. Lorraine Innis bore an uncanny resemblance to her sister-in-law. Chesney had dismissed it over the phone, but being in a remote corner of India, he didn't have access to the high-quality photos of Lorraine. Prudence picked up the latest issue of *Redbook* magazine which featured yet another photo spread on Lorraine. It also featured an article by Lorraine's cousin, Valerie Fierro entitled: "World Peace and Great Sex – You Can Have Both!" She was grateful Lorraine hadn't authored such a piece. Prudence preferred to think of her surrogate daughter as eternally virginal. The yearbook photo of Elinor was fuzzy, but Prudence Potoski saw it clearly in her mind.

"She wasn't exactly a beautiful girl," said Prudence looking at the picture of Elinor. She used to call her sister-in-law's looks: "handsome" or "interesting," but now, seeing her through a Lorraine Innis lens, Prudence could say that the faces of both women had a certain quality, though there was the major difference of the eyes, of course. No one she had ever met had eyes like Elinor.

They had first met in Prudence's junior year. Prudence was a transfer student to Eastgate State College, officially studying to be a teacher of English grammar, but with an unspoken ambition for something else.

She closed her eyes and was there as if it were only yesterday, or perhaps the day before that. The street lined with majestic elms, the old Victorian houses, once home to well-to-do families, now given over to fraternities, and sororities. In the early 1950s, the college was basking in the boom begun by ex-servicemen studying under the G.I. Bill. And there on the corner, its gingerbread work painted in complimentary shades of evergreen and ochre, sat the Rho Delta Delta sorority.

It was a Friday afternoon, or perhaps a Thursday, recalled Prudence, she couldn't remember exactly, but she was reasonably sure it was one of the days of the week. She did remember the most important detail: she was lining her drawers and shelves with fresh shelf paper. The paper was lovely: small blue and yellow flowers, growing from dark green vines on a pink background. She was sure of that. Shelf paper was important. She had been raised by a shelf paper mother in a shelf paper house. Even during the Depression, Prudence remembered her mother changing the shelf paper every spring. To Prudence, the Great Depression was about dime movies, favorite radio programs, and shelf paper. The annual changing of the paper represented her mother's opinion that the world should continue for at least another year. It was her yearly renewal of the covenant with the rest of civilization. Now Prudence was entering into the same pact: to cover every bare surface in every closet, drawer, and pantry with a layer of paper. As she carefully cut another length off the waxy roll, Prudence felt that in so doing, she was now indeed an adult. The ritual comforted her, as no doubt, it had her mother and grandmother before her, and other noble women back to the invention of shelf paper.

"Man on the floor," a woman's voice shouted down the hall. Prudence jumped, though she didn't know why. She was fully clothed, and her door was closed. Men were forbidden past the front parlor of the sorority. In the first few days at the start of the term, however, it wasn't uncommon for fathers, uncles, brothers, and boyfriends to receive a special dispensation to lug boxes, trunks, and suitcases upstairs to the bedrooms of their daughters, nieces, sisters, and girlfriends.

Through the door, Prudence heard a girl's voice directing someone up the hall.

"I'll take it from here," said the girl's voice stopping outside of Prudence's door. Then an indistinct reply in a deeper voice, then the sound of a kiss, and then another one - longer and juicier. Prudence turned away, though she couldn't see them through the door nor could they see her.

"You'd better hurry up," said the girl, "or else you'll run into him. I don't want you running into him. Not here. Not now." The boy grunted his agreement. "I'll see you later, you know where," she added. Prudence diverted her eyes as if she were intruding. She felt odd whenever she became involved in anyone else's intimate moments. Sometimes she felt that her shyness came from her name as if that ordained her personality.

"Don't be such a prude, Prudence," she had often been chided.

"Prude is just a shortening of prudent," was her pedantic response. She thought it was a good one and well-suited to a future English teacher. "It means to be discreet or judicious in practical affairs, and that's a good thing, isn't it?"

She won few arguments with classmates, but great admiration from spinster teachers, themselves being prudes of longstanding. Still, she hadn't had a lot of boyfriends in high school or in the first two years at the other college. It wasn't for lack of yearning. More than anything, Prudence wanted to be married and have a family. She daydreamed of meeting a boy at a dance and being swept off her feet just like in a movie. Sitting in the dark of the theater, Prudence would imagine that it was she up on the screen, gliding across the dance floor under the elegant direction of Fred Astaire, or the athletic guidance of Gene Kelly. She did some of her best dancing in her imagination. In real life, she wasn't particularly graceful. None of that had mattered to her first dancing partner. That had been her father when she was five-years-old. And it wasn't really dancing when you're standing on top of your partner's shoes. Even so, she loved to shuffle along atop his brown Oxfords as the radio played. For some reason, it was always The Ink Spots on the radio that inspired him to lift Prudence out of her seat for a dance. As she grew older, Prudence's self-consciousness prevented her from letting loose on a real dance floor with a real boy. Instead, throughout high school, she fulfilled her fantasies alone in her bedroom with an oversized ragdoll. But this wasn't at all satisfying. The doll wasn't a very accomplished partner, and she always had to lead.

Her dancing opportunities improved somewhat when she went away to college, but still not as Prudence may have hoped. At her previous school, she had danced with her roommate, Phoebe. Phoebe was as outgoing as Prudence was reserved. Phoebe was a theater arts major, very lively, very theatrical, always "on," short for "on stage," to use Phoebe's own description. One day Phoebe caught Prudence, red-faced, doing a clumsy solo rendition of the Lindy Hop to the music on the radio. Rather than laugh at her, Phoebe grabbed Prudence and led her through the rest of the dance.

Prudence glanced over to the framed photo on her desk of the two of them together backstage after one of Phoebe's shows. It had been a parting gift from Phoebe, delivered with drama and many tears, some of them even genuine. Now Prudence had a private room; no roommate; no boyfriend; no ragdoll; no hopes of doing the Lindy ever again. As she heard the boy's heavy footsteps trudge back up the hallway, Prudence let out a deep sigh and returned to the comfort of her shelf paper.

She was lining a bureau drawer when a knock was heard on her door. A knock wasn't entirely accurate. It was more like a rap, and at first, Prudence mistook the sound for someone accidentally bumping into the wall out in the hallway. It was only the second rap, which was louder, but still not a knock that made her wonder. The third attempt went beyond a bump to a thud, as if someone was trying to knock down the door.

Prudence took a step away from the door and flinched when the next thud escalated into a full-fledged thump. This time the sound was accompanied by a woman's voice. It sounded like the same one that had been whispering and kissing a few minutes earlier.

"Hey! Help me! Will you?! What are you, deaf in there?"

Brandishing a roll of shelf paper as a shield, Prudence took a deep breath and opened the door. A large wooden crate pushed into the room under the momentum of what probably was a final attempt at a knock. Prudence hurried backward to avoid being trampled. The crate seemed to be moving under its own power, the only evidence to the contrary, being a pair of legs behind it rushing by in short, furious steps.

"Watch out, will you!" said the voice from behind the crate.

With this, the woman dropped the crate on Prudence's bed. The springs groaned, and the slats emitted a pained creak, but thankfully, the bed held up. A less favorable report could be given for the rolls of shelf paper that were lying on the bed. These were crushed and crinkled beyond redemption.

"My beautiful shelf paper," Prudence whimpered.

The girl, now slumped atop the crate, either didn't hear or didn't care. Instead, she just rested there, reviving herself with several deep breaths.

From her vantage point, Prudence guessed that her uninvited guest was her own age, but several inches taller than her.

"Crap! That was heavy," said the girl, though as much to herself as to Prudence. Her next comment was directed to Prudence, though it was tinged with sarcasm. "Thanks for opening the door… finally."

"Oh, my pleasure," said Prudence out of politeness, though it hadn't been a pleasure at all. "That must have been heavy."

"I almost knocked your damn door down!"

"Oh."

The girl stood up straight, and arched backward, to stretch her muscles. She was indeed about five-foot-six. Prudence still couldn't see her full face, though what she could see in profile were a rather striking nose and one brown eye. Next, the girl rolled her shoulders and rubbed her neck, while scanning the part of the room not occupied by Prudence. She stopped at a paint-by-numbers picture of a country lane that Prudence had hung over her bed and shook her head.

"Sorry to bother you," said the girl, her scrutiny now on Prudence's desk. "Hmm… but I had to get that out of my room… quick."

"Quickly," said Prudence softly, "adverbs modify verbs." She doubted if the girl heard her, and said it more to restore grammatical balance to the universe than to correct her visitor.

Having examined the bottles, brushes and other items atop the dresser, the girl finally turned to face Prudence. As she turned around, Prudence started to smile, but then felt the smile freeze on her lips as she took in the girl's full face. The effect was jarring. It was her eyes. She had seen the brown eye that complimented her shoulder-length brunette hair and just assumed that the other eye was a match of its mate. Instead, she found herself gazing into a mismatched pair of irises; for, while the first was a rich brown, the other was a vivid blue.

Prudence had never seen anything like them. They were two different colors. She tried to look away, feeling that ogling a stranger at point-blank range was the height of impoliteness, especially a stranger she didn't even know. But try as she might, Prudence was unable to get more than a few inches beyond those eyes. It was as if they were magnetic. She tried glancing up at the girl's eyebrows, but her attention snapped back to those eyes. A peek down at her nose proved similarly futile. And as she looked at them, they seemed to change hue, ever so slightly. The blue eye grew darker, to a storm cloud gray, while the brown seemed to warm up with tiny flecks of gold. And Prudence felt the smile that she had been wearing broaden into a foolish grin, like a child captivated by a magic trick. As she continued to stare at the eyes, she began debating with herself as to how long she'd been gawking. Part of her thought it was at least two minutes, while another part of her reasoning it could only have been seconds.

The girl was talking to her, but Prudence couldn't quite comprehend what was being said. The girl could have been telling Prudence her name, or perhaps something about where she was from, or what was in that crate, or the weather report for Fond Du Lac, Wisconsin. Whatever it was Prudence couldn't focus on anything else but those mesmerizing eyes.

The eyes began to narrow as if the girl were making some sort of judgment or forming a conclusion. Then, finally, as the girl's lips moved, she turned and pointed at the bed, breaking the spell.

"...so, if you could just hold it here for a while, I'd appreciate it."

"Hold what?"

The girl turned around again, and Prudence cast her gaze downward to avoid meeting the eyes again.

"The crate." The girl put her hands on her hips as if to punctuate some mild annoyance. "Are you okay?"

"Why?" Prudence asked.

"Well, you're looking at me kind of funny..."

Prudence felt her mouth go dry. She couldn't very well tell this person that she had mismatched eyes, could she? Though she was sure the girl knew it; still, it was terribly rude. It was like informing a giraffe of its surplus of neck, or an elephant that it had a trunk. She would cover the awkwardness with a compliment.

"Funny? Oh, no, I was just admiring your..." she groped for a word that would fit. "...your, uh, your beauty!"

"My beauty?"

"Oh, yes. I, uh... I admire beautiful girls, um, that is, I like them." Fearing that she was staring at the eyes again, Prudence forced herself to look down at the girl's breast. Then conscious that this too was rude, she felt compelled to offer a new excuse. "Oh, yes, and what lovely, um, I mean what a lovely sweater; purple, isn't it?"

The girl gave Prudence a strange look. "Actually, I always called it 'eggplant,' dark purple, it's my favorite color."

"Ha, oh, yes," stammered Prudence. "Yes, beautiful girls look beautiful in beautiful, um, colors."

"Right..." said the girl, as she turned her head. Something on the desk seemed to have caught her attention, for she stared in that direction for a moment, and then turned back to Prudence, but not before first nodding her head and taking a step backward.

"Okay, then," said the girl, a forced smile now on her lips, "well, it takes all kinds."

"I suppose," said Prudence agreeing, although to what she was uncertain.

"Well," said the girl, nodding toward the bed, "if you want me to take that back out..."

Prudence felt she had offended the girl by staring. She had so wanted to make a good impression at this new school, and now she was in danger of getting off on the wrong eye, that is, the wrong foot with the first girl she met.

"Take it back? Oh, no, please, I'll be happy to keep it here. I, I can watch it. How will I be able to get in touch with you?"

The girl's eyes narrowed as if she doubted Prudence's sanity. She pointed to the door across the hall.

"I live there," she said. "I already said that. Remember? I think you'll bump into me now and then."

Prudence craned her neck and looked across the hall.

"Oh, so you must be…" She paused, not knowing who the girl must be, but hoping that the girl would complete the sentence.

She did, but only after an exasperated sigh, like one gives to a dull-witted child. "Elinor. Elinor Potoski. Remember?"

Prudence extended her hand. "I'm Prudence Hoover. No relation."

"I think I'd have remembered you from any family reunions," said Elinor giving her hand a reluctant shake.

Prudence laughed nervously and patted Elinor's arm, and then rubbed it vigorously. "No, I mean no relation to the famous Hoover."

"The vacuum cleaner people?" Elinor pulled her arm back.

"No, I meant Herbert Hoover, the former president."

"Oh."

"But I'm not related to the vacuum people either, as far as I know."

"What a coincidence." Elinor nodded as she leaned out the door and glanced down the hall. "I'm not related to Herbert Hoover, too."

"Or Eleanor Roosevelt, either," said Prudence. She realized the comment was inane, but she felt the need to say something.

"No, I'm not related to Eleanor Roosevelt, either," her head was still out the door. "For one thing, I spell it differently."

"Oh, how do you spell 'Roosevelt?'" asked Prudence.

"R-o-o-s-e-v-e-l-t," she said, drawing back into the room. "I meant 'Elinor.' Mine is spelled differently. Look, I hate to rush this, but I'm expecting a visitor any minute…"

"Man on the floor!" called the voice of the house mother.

"In fact, that's him," said Elinor hurriedly, "and I don't want him to see that." She pointed to the box and started to leave. "Thanks for keeping an eye on it for a while."

For a while? That seemed awfully indefinite for such a big crate.

"Hey!"

Elinor stopped and gave her a piercing look in two hues. "It's okay, isn't it?" She spoke forcefully. "Because if it isn't, I'll take it back, but he'd be very upset, and he doesn't really need to know about it. And even though we just met, you have to do it for me, because you are a sorority sister, aren't you?"

"Uh, I mean," flustered Prudence, "I mean, of course. I just wanted to know, how, um, how long do you want me to keep it?"

"A while! Until I come back for it. You don't mind, do you? See ya, bye!"

These last three words came from the other side of the door after Elinor had slammed it shut. A moment later, Prudence could hear Elinor directing the other boy who, from the sound of his shuffling, was carrying something heavy.

"Well," said Prudence "she certainly seems to know what she wants." Prudence gnawed on her thumbnail, ruining her pale pink polish in the process. What a strange girl, but a nice girl, wasn't she? Was she a nice strange girl or a strange nice girl? Prudence hoped that she was nicer than she was strange. Strange wasn't the right word. She wasn't really that strange, aside from her eyes, and her alternate spelling of Elinor. Still, neither of those were her choice. Prudence looked at the box on the bed. It certainly looked innocent, even nondescript. Nondescript: she stopped and wondered; could you really use "nondescript" to describe anything since doing so made the object being described defined even with a vague definition.

There was something mysterious about the crate on her bed. It was almost as if the box had powers similar to the eyes of Elinor Potoski, both attracting and repelling at the same time. She approached it several times, each time drawing away, afraid to touch it.

"This is ridiculous. You can't stay there on my bed," Prudence said as if the box had a life of its own. "I have to sleep there. And even if she comes back for you before bedtime, I have things to do, and you'll only be in the way. I'm moving you, okay?"

The box didn't respond. Prudence put her arms around it and lifted the box by its sides. She was surprised by its weight. It was one thing to hoist a heavy box and another thing to know what to do with it once it was in your arms. If she put it down on the floor, it would probably take two people to lift it again. This became a moot point in the next moment as the bottom of the crate burst open; its contents went crashing to the floor in a hail of thuds and clatters.

Prudence stood there, open-mouthed. Looking down, her surprise grew to shock as she saw the books, pamphlets, and film reels the container had held. Though she tried to respect Elinor Potoski's privacy by pretending not to notice the contents, they were impossible to ignore. There was only one possible conclusion. No wonder Elinor didn't want anyone to see them.

"My neighbor," gasped Prudence, "my new sorority sister...she's a communist!"

– 4 –
The Three Ds:
Dense, Dopey, and Distracted

E ven the shelf paper had been robbed of its joy.

For Prudence settling into a new school while hiding a box of communist propaganda was next to impossible. It was the fifties. Ike was in the White House, and the only acceptable red was that next to the blue and white on the American flag or the vibrant shade on the decade's most popular lipstick. Being a communist was perhaps the worst thing a person could be accused of being, at least in polite company.

Prudence managed to repair the crate and hide its seditious contents. Half of the materials were in that scary-looking Cyrillic alphabet, the others in English were ardently pro-communist. Hidden behind Prudence's empty boxes, the crate seemed to pulsate. It was as if the contents were sending out covert radio signals to Moscow, saying: "we're in place, comrades, awaiting your further instructions."

Elinor Potoski had seemed like such a nice girl. Potoski: what kind of name was that? Was it a communist name? That was ridiculous, Prudence told herself. There were no such things as "communist names." Oh, well, maybe Marx, or Lenin, or Stalin. Still, Potoski wasn't an American name, not like Hoover, was it? There wasn't a President Potoski or even a Potoski vacuum cleaner. That didn't automatically make someone an anarchist, though it may give them a head start.

Elinor seemed so very wholesome. She had nice teeth, clean clothes, well-kept hair, and didn't speak with an accent. On the other hand, they wouldn't send a crooked-toothed, sloppy girl with a Moscow drawl to incite insurrection. That would be too obvious. Nice looking girls weren't villains. Elinor didn't look like a girl who would overthrow the government. She looked sweet, except maybe for those eyes. Elinor's eyes were definitely different, particularly from each other. Prudence had found them compelling, even hypnotic. Perhaps that's why Elinor was recruited into the international communist conspiracy. Or maybe she had joined the cause and then had her eyes surgically altered behind the Iron Curtain to make them more mesmerizing. Perhaps if she been alone with Elinor a little longer, Prudence would have been transformed into a mindless pawn.

The carousel of doom revolved through Prudence's head at least four times an hour. The only distractions came from the start of the fall term. She had to register for classes and familiarize herself with the campus. She tried to decorate her room but arranging her clean, American belongings in the same space as the Communist carton was like trying to decorate a formal sitting room around an overweight orangutan picking its nose.

Conditions outside her room weren't much better, as Prudence discovered the first evening down in the parlor. She had gone there to be alone with her thoughts away from the crate.

"You're the new girl, aren't you, the transfer student," said one girl.

"Hmm?" said Prudence looking up. There was a tall, pretty girl standing there.

"I said, you're the new girl, right?"

"Oh, yes, I am."

"Ruby," said the girl, and she stuck out her hand. On her finger was a ring with a purple stone.

Prudence looked at it quizzically and then looked up at the girl. "I would have thought it was an amethyst."

"It is an amethyst," said the girl looking back at her ring just to make sure.

"Then why did you say it was a ruby?"

A second girl, this one short and round sidled up to the first girl and giggled through her nose.

"Ruby is her name," giggled the short girl.

Prudence glanced back and forth between the tall girl, the short girl, and the ring with the purple stone. After two round trips, it became clear.

"Oh...you're Ruby," said Prudence. "I'm sorry, I was thinking about... that is..."

"I'm Myrna," said the short girl extending her hand.

Fortunately, she wore no rings and "Myrna" was not a gemstone.

"And you're Prudence," said Myrna.

"Yes, I know...I mean, yes, I am, I'm sorry, I'm just a little preoccupied, I'm not usually so, uh, so, what's the word, oh, it begins with a 'D'..."

"Dense?" offered Ruby.

"Dopey?" suggested Myrna.

"Uh, no, distracted; I was going to say 'distracted.'"

The two girls nodded. There followed an uncomfortable moment in which no one said anything but everyone wished someone else would.

"So you came here from someplace else," the short girl said, breaking the silence.

"Uh, yes, I did," said Prudence, "I did, Verna."

"Myrna."

"Oh, yes, forgive me, Myrna," said Prudence. She could feel herself blush. "I went to a school downstate for my first two years…"

"So, you're a Junior," said Myrna.

"Yes."

"And you were a Rho Delta, there, too," said Myrna.

"Yes, I was."

"And, you…" started Myrna.

"Will you shut up," said Ruby cutting Myrna short, though she was already quite short already. "You're asking the dumbest questions. Not that you should even be asking her questions. I mean, you're not exactly Sergeant Joe Friday, and she isn't some criminal suspect."

"What do you mean: 'dumb questions?'"

"For pity's sake, Myrna, do you listen to yourself when you open your mouth? 'Did you come from someplace else?' Well, do you think she was born in the parlor? You've been here for two years. Have you seen this girl here before? She tells you she's completed two years of school. Of course, she's a junior. What did you think that made her a Rear Admiral? For pity's sake!"

"I was just making conversation," said Myrna.

Ruby looked like she was girding up for a second round of Myrna abuse when Prudence interrupted.

"I haven't met many people here, yet," she said.

"Yes, and let me apologize for some of the ones that you have met," said Ruby.

"What's that supposed to mean," asked Myrna.

"You figure it out, genius," said Ruby.

"I…I met…Elinor," said Prudence.

Both girls stopped and looked at her. Prudence wondered if she had hit a nerve. Maybe the other girls in the sorority had noticed things about Elinor, too.

"…uh, Elinor, I met…her…Elinor."

"Elinor Potoski?" asked Myrna.

Ruby exhaled. "How many Elinors do we have in the house, Myrna, for pity's sake? Of course, she means Elinor Potoski."

"Yes, that's it, Elinor… *Potoski*," said Prudence trying to say the name in a way that invited deeper interpretation.

"So, you met Elinor," said Myrna.

"Didn't she just say that, Sherlock Holmes?" said Ruby.

"She's got the room across the hall from me," said Prudence.

"Oh?"

"Yes," said Prudence, "I was just settling in, you know, decorating when she…" Prudence thought of the way they had actually met. She couldn't mention that. "…when Elinor came in and introduced herself."

33

Prudence paused, hoping that in the ensuing silence, her new sorority sisters would fill in the blanks. Instead, they just stood looking at her, and the blanks grew wider.

"Elinor is..." Prudence groped for something to say that was subtle. She didn't want to ask a direct question about Elinor's political leanings. There wasn't much that Prudence knew about the girl beyond that. The only other things that came to mind were her unique eyes. She couldn't very well bring up those, not without appearing rude. That left her with only one vague observation.

"Elinor is pretty."

Ruby looked at Prudence for a moment and then at Myrna, and then back at Prudence before agreeing that Elinor could be described as attractive, though she'd never really thought about it before.

Another pregnant silence ensued.

"So..." said Prudence, trying to think of a way to learn more about Elinor.

"So..." said Ruby, glancing towards the doorway.

"So, what's your major?" asked Myrna.

"Major, what a good idea," said Prudence brightening.

"Good idea," muttered Ruby, "we all have majors."

"I meant, what a good question," said Prudence. "I'm an English major."

"I'm a home economics major," said Myrna proudly, "and so's Ruby."

"I'm business and economics, not home economics," corrected Ruby. There was an edge to her voice and a look suggesting this was not the first time Myrna had failed to appreciate the distinction.

"What's Elinor's major?" asked Prudence, trying to sound nonchalant. She didn't want to appear too curious, even while asking a question.

"Elinor?" said Ruby, "I don't know, why don't you ask her?"

"Oh," said Prudence, realizing she was not being very subtle. "I suppose I'll do that, thank you."

"We don't see much of Elinor," explained Myrna.

No, of course not, Prudence thought. Elinor probably had little time for socializing. She was out organizing subversive activities.

"That's a shame," said Prudence. Ruby and Myrna just stared at her. It was as if they were awaiting an explanation of why it was a shame they didn't see more of Elinor. "Uh, I mean, she seems like such...uh...a pretty girl....Elinor does..."

Ruby knitted her brow suspiciously. Myrna simply looked confused. Another painful paused ensued.

"Do you have your courses yet?" asked Myrna breaking the silence. "What are you taking? Who have you got?"

Prudence said that she did, and rattled off her courses from memory. Most of them were in her major, save the last one.

"Oh, yes," said Prudence, "I've got World History, too. It's a requirement."

"Oooh," said Myrna, who up until this point had shown little excitement in Prudence's course load. "World History! Who have you got?"

"Pardon?"

"Who's teaching it? What professor?" Myrna was practically leaning into Prudence's face.

"Uh, I forget," said Prudence, "is there a professor Bacon?"

"Bacon? You don't mean 'Bascomb,' do you? Is it professor Bascomb?"

"Um, I suppose, yes, that could be it. It did start with a 'B.'"

A wide grin spread across Myrna's mouth, and if she hadn't known better, Prudence could have sworn that the girl licked her lips. Maybe it was the mention of bacon. Her absence of a waistline indicated she was a girl with a healthy appetite.

"Professor Bascomb is the only history professor whose name starts with a 'B,'" observed Ruby. Her eyes narrowed slightly, and a smile crossed her lips. "It has to be Bertie."

"Yes, you'll like Bertie," agreed Myrna.

"Bertie?"

"Professor Bascomb, Bertram Bascomb," said Ruby. Prudence noticed a gleam in her eye, or was it just the light?

"But we all call him Bertie," said Myrna, "at least the girls do."

"To his face?" asked Prudence. She had never called a teacher by their first name in her life.

"Some do," said Myrna.

"Some of us," said Ruby.

"Has Elinor taken his class," asked Prudence trying to switch the topic back to the one weighing on her mind.

Ruby stared at Prudence long enough to make her feel that her ploy hadn't been at all subtle. She felt her cheeks redden.

"Uh, Professor Bascomb…he must be more…informal," said Prudence backtracking.

"Oh, he's wonderful," said Myrna.

"Incredible," said Ruby.

"He really makes history come alive, then?" Prudence asked.

"He makes everything come alive," noted Ruby.

"What does he cover?"

"It's not what he covers," giggled Myrna, "but what he uncovers."

Ruby gave Myrna a censorious look.

Another girl entered the lounge. She was very attractive and was introduced as Yolanda.

"What are you talking about?"

"They were just telling me about Professor Bascomb's history class."

"Oh, yes," sighed Yolanda, "Bertie."

"So, he's really in depth?"

"From the Assyrians to the Balkans," said Yolanda.

"Remarkable depth, I heard," giggled Myrna.

"Does he do the Greeks?" asked Prudence.

"Fluently," said Ruby. She closed her eyes. Prudence imagined she must be recalling a lecture.

Prudence shrugged her shoulders. She'd never met a group of girls so enthused about ancient history.

"He must really make his history come alive," said Prudence.

"Oh, yes, history, and many other subjects," said Yolanda.

"He sounds like he really cares."

"He really makes himself available to his students," said Ruby.

Perhaps, Prudence thought, if this Professor Bascomb was so caring, he might have some advice about Elinor Potoski, the crate, and everything.

- 5 -
Keepers of
Zee Box

He didn't look like a Bertram Bascomb. By the sound of the name, a history professor called "Bertram Bascomb" should be old and stuffy; as musty and creaky as the subject they taught. This Bertram Bascomb was young.

Based on the glowing remarks of her sorority sisters, Professor Bascomb must be a good teacher. At least Prudence kept telling herself that while she tried to stay awake in his evening class. She hadn't had a good night's rest in a week. Alone in her room with that crate, sleep became nearly impossible.

The first night, with the lights off, and tucked under her quilted counterpane, Prudence could swear the crate was glowing as if it were radioactive. She almost would have preferred a box full of nuclear waste, as long as it was good old American nuclear waste. Prudence turned on the bedside lamp. The glow seemed to stop. She turned it off again. The glow resumed. Finally, Prudence realized the glow was coming from a street light outside her window. She pulled down the shade and closed the curtains.

Then the noises started. Spending the first night in an old house, Prudence reasoned she would hear all sorts of unfamiliar sounds. The problem was she didn't know what noises were from the house and which were emanating from the crate.

When she did drift off to sleep, the most fantastic dreams invaded her mind. They were even weirder than the wild thoughts that troubled her during the day. She dreamed of spies and plots to overthrow the American way of life. Elinor Potoski was in all her dreams, too, plotting against her. Upon waking, Prudence felt like she had just gone twelve rounds with the heavyweight champ of the USSR.

Now, sitting in the World History class of Bertram Bascomb, Prudence wished that the room wasn't so warm, the professor's voice not so soothing, and her body not so weary. She was sure, in between head nods, that she must be missing something good. After all, her new sisters had praised Bascomb so effusively.

Professor Bascomb was saying something about some dead group of people, which seemed to be a favorite topic of history teachers. In spite of Prudence's best efforts pay attention, she felt her eyelids drooping, and even shutting momentarily before she forced them open again. At least every other sentence was lost as the tomb of some obscure potentate. She tried to focus on what he was saying, but ultimately, it was to no avail.

Prudence took a stick of chewing gum from her purse and slid it into her mouth. That might help keep her awake. Or maybe it would help if she wrote down every word Professor Bascomb said. She looked down at her note tablet in shock. She had been doodling. Sketches of crates covered with hammers and sickles filled the paper. She flipped to a clean sheet, and tried to write, but wound up debating with herself instead.

What would you do, Prudence asked herself, if the crate hadn't broken open, and you hadn't found out what was inside?

I'd have left it in the corner, she answered herself and waited until Elinor came back for it.

For a moment, she sat there, satisfied until her mind posed the follow-up question: But you do know. Now that you know that she's given you a box of traitorous material, what are you going to do with it?

Maybe, I'll just ignore it.

Oh, really? What if she had given you a box of poison? Would you eat it?

No, of course not, she told herself. And I'm not eating, that is, I'm not reading that material. Nobody's reading it. And I doubt many people around here could read it. Half of it is in Russian, at least that's what it looks like. It has all those crazy backward letters. No one I know can read it.

And that makes everything all right?

Prudence thought a moment. Yes, perhaps it did. Maybe ignoring it was the right approach to the crate. In fact, she reasoned, it's safer in the corner of my room than anywhere else in the world.

Anywhere?

Well, maybe perhaps it would be safer locked up in a vault.

Or behind bars? Like at the police station? Or at the FBI?

The FBI? Prudence bit the end of her fountain pen. Her mind had a point. Maybe someone in authority should know about this. Someone else might know what to do with this.

But if she took that box to the FBI, they would arrest Elinor. Elinor's reputation would be ruined, maybe over circumstantial evidence.

Again, Prudence nodded to herself. She was satisfied with the reasonableness of her conclusion and turned her mind back to the history lecture... for another fifteen seconds. Professor Bascomb was saying something about the Babylonians.

But, Prudence asked herself, if that box of Russian contraband was so innocent, why was Elinor hiding it?

Prudence slumped in her seat. For more than a minute, she was incapable of forming a single logical answer to that last question. She started numerous responses beginning with words as "but," "maybe," and "if," but none were followed by anything that approached a complete sentence. Instead, her imagination was taken over by government raids, scandalous trials, and probing questions from Senate sub-committees.

After several minutes of paranoia, the warm room, the professor's soothing voice, and her own lack of sleep left Prudence with eyelids too heavy for the rest of her to support. Several times she felt her head lurch forward, only to be jerked back up by her neck and caught on the rebound by her shoulders. She looked around, hoping she had not been noticed. Fortunately, she hadn't. Even more fortunate was the conclusion of the class. Prudence rushed out into the fresh air. The effect of the cool evening breeze upon her skin was invigorating. Perhaps it was the contrast with her previous stupor or the first promise of autumn's crispness, but whatever it was, Prudence felt light and airy. Her arms swung effortlessly at her sides as if they were supporting her torso, rather than the other way around.

Prudence found that her mood extended to her surroundings. The whole campus was painted with a fresh coat of optimism. Her worries melted away. Worries? Had she any worries? Wait, yes, she was worried about someone, and something. But it didn't matter, not at least until she turned the corner and saw that the someone was standing there next to the something.

"Elinor," gasped Prudence, for indeed it was Elinor Potoski. Prudence quickly realized this was a waste of breath since Elinor knew her own name.

The face which had seemed so very All-American now seemed altogether foreign, and anti-American. Instead of the full plaid skirt and sweater that was the unofficial uniform of the co-eds of Eastgate, Elinor was wearing a tight, long gray skirt that accentuated her curves, making them at the same time enviable and dangerous. Her blouse, also gray, was tailored after a deadly fashion and was cut from puissant silk rather than homey cotton. Completing the ensemble was her make-up, which was also darker than she had worn when first they met. Elinor's lips were painted in a dark red, the color of blood; as if she had just devoured a slab of raw meat and its juice still stained her mouth. Her face was powdered in a striking pale tone that almost glowed from the shadows. And those multi-colored eyes, now seemed even more compelling, though now in a way more forbidding than fascinating.

"Purple and gray," gasped Prudence, trying not to look full into Elinor's eyes.

"Yes," hissed Elinor, though now her voice was tinged with traces of an un-American accent.

"They've changed."

"I can do that," said Elinor, who now was waving a long cigarette holder in her hand, "at will. Any color I like."

"Now they're purple and gray," said Prudence, though she felt stupid for repeating the obvious.

"Yes," hissed Elinor, taking a drag on a foreign-looking cigarette that was nearly as long as its very long holder.

Prudence looked down at Elinor's side and pointed to it. "The box!" She slapped her forehead for yet another statement of the obvious.

Elinor looked down at it as if she were admiring her pet boa constrictor, and then looked back at Prudence as if she were to be its chipmunk dinner. She raised a black eyebrow with amusement.

"But it was in my room."

Elinor blew a jet of smoke that went up Prudence's nose, causing her to snort.

"We can get in rooms," remarked Elinor nonchalantly.

"You can?" Prudence winced. Of course, they could. Elinor had just said they could. What a stupid thing to say. She was reacting even more foolishly than the simpleminded heroines in those one-dimensional spy serials.

"Ve can."

"Ve?" said Prudence, this time noting that Elinor's accent was thickening quicker than the plot of this espionage melodrama.

"Yes, all of us. Keepers of zee box."

"Yes, the box! What's that all about?" Prudence asked, pointing at the crate.

An amused look spread across Elinor's lips. "Do not play zee innocent. Vee know zat you know, vot's in zee box."

"I do?"

"Yes, but you don't know vot vee do to schnoopy little girls who know zat vee know vot is in zee box." Prudence strained to understand the thickening accent.

"Vat, I mean, what are you going to do to me?" asked Prudence.

"Not me, veeee." Elinor gestured with her cigarette holder in such a way as to indicate that Prudence was about to be introduced to a group of previously unseen henchman.

Prudence almost repeated Elinor's last words, but she caught herself. She decided it would be better to scream at the top of her lungs. Towards this goal, Prudence Hoover, threw her head back, open her mouth, and was about to scream, when she felt a hand grasp her shoulder and a foreign object being forced down her throat.

– 6 –
Cubs 2, Shalmaneser 5

The foreign object in Prudence Hoover's throat wasn't foreign after all. It was a wad of Doublemint chewing gum manufactured by the William Wrigley Company of Chicago, Illinois. It was the same stick of gum she had put there three-quarters of an hour earlier before falling asleep.

It was that gum that disturbed Prudence's already disturbing dream, causing her to choke. As she awoke, coughing up the gum, Prudence realized she was back in the safety of the classroom, a classroom now empty. The encounter with Elinor Potoski and the hand gripping her shoulder had been a horrible dream. Prudence sighed before tensing up once more. There was still a hand upon her shoulder.

"Miss…Hoover?" said a man's voice.

She clutched the edge of her desk.

"Are you all right, Miss Hoover?"

At least the voice was American, she thought. She had heard it before, not saying "Miss Hoover," but other names, less American names, names like Nebuchadnezzar and Tiglath-Pileser.

Like the voice, the hand was also less than menacing. In fact, it was caressing her.

"Miss Hoover?"

Prudence turned her head. "Professor Bascomb," she said, "I…I must have fallen asleep."

He smiled warmly. His eyes seemed even warmer. He removed his hand, gently brushing Prudence's shoulder as he did so.

"It's quite understandable," he said, leaning on the desk behind her.

"Understandable?" Prudence repeated as she turned to face him.

She looked up at him in his tweed jacket. His dark brown hair tousled, but in an orderly manner, like one would see on a devil-may-care leading man in a Hollywood movie. She had never seen a teacher who could wear tweed and not smell musty, whose mussed hair looked neat,

41

and most of all, who could sympathize with a student that he caught sleeping in his class. No wonder all the girls at the sorority liked him.

"I know World History is a pretty dry subject," he said. "You can take my word for it. This is only your first class. I've been kicking around with these jokers for years. Think of it! Years amidst Nebuchadnezzar, and Sargon..."

Prudence looked at her notes. "...Shalmaneser five, and Tiglath-Pileser three." She wanted to prove she had been paying attention before dozing off.

He laughed, revealing once more those beautiful teeth.

"What? Did I mispronounce their names?"

"Pronunciation impeccable," he said. "But they're Babylonian kings, not baseball scores. It's Shalmaneser the Fifth, not 'five.' Besides which, old Tig-Pileser was all glove, no bat."

"Excuse me?"

"Nothing, just a historical joke, and not a very good one at that," he said, somehow making the reference witty by his dismissal of it. Prudence still didn't get the joke. "You'll have to forgive me," he continued, "but I'm bored, I suppose. You see, I have this talent, not only for remembering all these old fossils and facts, but then inflicting them on poor unsuspecting students who cough up the tuition to sit through it."

"You shouldn't say that," said Prudence, "it's all very interesting."

"Oh, yes, it's absolutely fascinating. I suppose that's why I had to awaken you from a Babylonian-induced stupor."

Prudence felt herself blushing and looked down. When she looked up, he was staring at her with a benevolent smile.

"Never mind," Bascomb finally said, rubbing her shoulder, this time quickly and briefly, as if to brush aside some anxiety from her psyche. "It's not your problem."

"Oh, but it's very educational," Prudence blurted out, offering a justification for why the class was boring, "I'm positive it must be."

Bascomb laughed and then his teeth disappeared behind a more satisfied smile as if some pleasing thought had just crossed his mind. As he mulled over this new thought, his gaze began to drift from her face, down to her torso. After waiting several moments for him to reestablish eye contact, Prudence looked down. There on her sweater, over her left breast, was her sorority pin.

"Oh!" she said, dislodging his stare, "my sorority pin!"

His gaze moved slightly to the left where she was gently fingering her pin.

"I'm a Rho Delta!"

"Ah...Rho Delta Delta...hmm?"

"Yes, I just moved in, I'm a transfer student. English major. I was a Rho Delta at my other school. Our house is over on Elm..."

"Yes, I know, that is, it's a small campus. I...know some of the other members of your sorority."

"You do?"

"Yes, I do."

"Of course," nodded Prudence after a moment's thought, "you've had them before..." A brief look of concern clouded his expression. "...in your class, right?"

"Yes, in class. That's why I was staring at your... your pin," he explained. "I'd seen it before, and I was trying to recall where. So, you're new at Eastgate? Well, I'm sure you'll soon be into the swing of things. I'm positive you'll enjoy our campus as well as the other...extra-curricular diversions available."

"Like athletics?"

His one eyebrow rose slightly. "Athletics? Yes, I suppose. Do you enjoy...sports?"

"Not really," said Prudence. His expression fell. "But I do like games."

Professor Bascomb smiled, more with his eyes than his mouth. "You enjoy games, do you, Miss Hoover?"

"Very much so."

"And what sort of games do you enjoy?"

She thought for a moment. "When I was just a little girl, I was very good at beanbag."

"Beanbag?" He pulled in his chin as if recoiling from a noxious odor.

Prudence mimed an underhanded throw. "Yes, you know, tossing the beanbag at a target or into a hole. It's like horseshoes, but not as heavy. I haven't done it in years. I won several prizes at school field days. Of course, now I'm interested in much more adult games."

"I see." He leaned forward.

"Yes, I adore Scrabble," said Prudence closing her eyes to savor the thought of the word game.

Bascomb was silent long enough for Prudence to open her eyes again, wondering if somehow he had crept out of the room. He was still there.

"Scrabble," he said with a slow nod of his head, "yes, of course, you would like that, as an English major. I'm sure you're quite excellent at it. Are you interested in any other games, adult games?"

She thought a moment. "Do you mean like Anagrams?"

"Anagrams," he repeated, though with less enthusiasm than she had said it.

"Yes, rearranging letters...such as in a name. I'm not terribly good at them, but they can be a lot of fun, too. For example, if we took your name, 'Professor Bascomb...'"

"Please, call me Bertram..."

She felt herself blush. "Oh, I couldn't call you by your first name. You're a professor. Let's see, if we rearrange the letters in 'Bascomb' we get..." Prudence jotted down the letters in her notebook. She looked up in triumph 30 seconds later. "And we get… 'mob cabs!' See? Anagrams are an excellent mental exercise, besides being fun. Maybe someday I'll teach my children to do them."

"Your students…"

"Students?"

"You're planning on becoming an English teacher, correct?"

"Well, I suppose, yes," said Prudence, "I guess I meant when I'm a mother. I want to have a lot of children."

Bascomb's smile froze into an almost pained expression.

"Word games are fun," said Prudence. "Would you like to try? They're not that difficult."

"I'm terribly sorry," said Bascomb with an affable shrug. "I'm good at history, not at words. I guess you'd say I crave, well, action, not just talk."

He leaned closer. Prudence wasn't exactly sure why and just sat there. After a moment, he leaned back.

"That's okay," she said, "I'm sure you're too busy with all the responsibilities that come with being a professor to play silly games."

"Actually, I'm only an associate professor," he admitted. "That's sort of like being a Junior G-Man. I'm not boring enough to be a full professor, though I seem to be well on the way."

"Oh, you're not boring yet. I mean, you're not boring, not at all."

He shot another glance toward her doodle-filled notebook.

"I just have a lot on my mind," she said, shutting the book.

He placed his hand on her shoulder. "I'm a good listener."

"You mean like a guidance counselor?"

He removed his hand. "Uh, sure, I suppose you could call it that if you like."

Prudence brightened. Perhaps Associate Professor Bascomb was just the person to advise her on what to do with the crate. He did, after all, have the advantage of being a history professor. As such, she reasoned, there must be some example from antiquity…some king who was stuck with an unwanted sarcophagus or a pharaoh with an inconvenient crypt. If there were a historical precedent to her dilemma, he'd know about it.

"I think I would like to talk to you sometime about, well…things," she said.

The engaging smile returned to his lips. "Oh, yes?"

"Yes. It sort of a history question, I guess," she said. It was best to introduce the topic hypothetically, Prudence reasoned. "May I come by your office?"

He began to open his mouth, but then his smile faded, and suddenly he looked much older and more professorial.

"That would be fine," he nodded as he began to stand.

She glanced at her wristwatch. "Maybe if you had a few minutes now…"

For some reason, his eyes darted back down to her sorority pin.

"…we could talk."

He looked up at her eyes again, as if searching for something, then tossed his head to one side. "Unfortunately, I…I can't right now." He looked at his own watch. "You see I have company, my sister is coming for a visit, and I have to pick her up at the railroad station. In fact, I'm already quite late." He said, starting for the door.

"Perhaps I can stop by your office, some afternoon," said Prudence as she scuttled towards the door, balancing her purse and her books.

"Afternoons, well…no, I'm quite busy in the afternoons. I have private…tutoring."

"Some morning perhaps?"

"Yes, yes," he said, ushering her into the hallway, "stop by, better yet, stop by and make an appointment with the secretary…"

Bascomb guided her until he'd reached the building's exit.

"Yes, see the secretary," he said, looking over his shoulder. "She'll schedule you…"

"I'll say hello to the girls in the sorority for you," she called after him as he went out the door. It was hard to tell through the glass, but she could have sworn he grimaced as he disappeared from sight.

She was about to exit, when she heard a door open down the hall. The door opened towards her, and she saw Elinor Potoski. Prudence almost called out her name, but then stopped as she heard the words Elinor spoke to someone in the room she was exiting. What Prudence heard made her change her mind about calling out. Instead, she hurried toward the nearest exit.

- 7 -
The Broom Closet Affair

If Prudence Hoover had heard Elinor's remark in their full context, she wouldn't have run in fear. She may have left out of modesty, but not from fear.

Earlier, while Prudence was wrestling with drowsiness and ancient emperors, Elinor was involved in her own struggle, which was more pleasurable and more intense. At that moment, sorority sisters and history professors were the furthest things from her mind. At that moment, her entire world revolved around her left earlobe that was being nibbled by her boyfriend. The warm, moist breath emanating from his nostrils and condensing in her shell-like earhole only heightened the experience.

"Oh, yes," Elinor panted.

"Mmm, you like that?" He whispered, which was quite loud thanks to his proximity.

"Oh, yes," she replied. Elinor arched her back in ecstasy. In one swift jerk, she pulled off his clip-on necktie, undid the two middle buttons of his shirt and started clawing at his chest. Had he turned up the heat any higher on her thermostat, Elinor would have ripped apart his flesh and claimed passion as her defense. She would hate to hurt him, but at the same time was wishing he would drive her over that slender edge.

"Oh, Paul, Paul, Paulie," she gasped. Most of her pleas were genuine, at least seventy-five percent true. The other quarter was for effect, to urge him to stimulate her more.

"El, Ellie..." he said, now almost biting her earlobes, then in one lunge he pushed aside her long brown hair and slid down to her neck.

"Oh, Paulie, oh...SHIT!"

Her last expletive came right after the sound of a dull metallic clang.

"What?" said Paul, now removed from her ear, though still whispering. "What's wrong?"

"What's wrong?" Elinor spat. "Didn't you hear that?"

"Like a bell?"

"A bell?" she said, sitting up. "A bell? What did you think that was? The start of round two?"

"What? No..." His body was no longer touching hers. "I mean, what was it?"

"Turn on the light," said Elinor, "never mind, I'll do it!" She groped above her head for the string dangling from the room's solitary bare bulb. After a few futile swipes, she caught the string in her fingers and yanked flooding the small space in the harsh light of a 100-watt bulb.

"That! It was that!" Elinor jerked her thumb over her shoulder at the metal air duct running down the wall.

Paul studied the duct while rubbing his chin. "You must have hit your head on that duct in the dark," he concluded.

Elinor sat up and touched the back of her head, then examined her hand to see if she were bleeding.

"Do you really think so?" she said, trying to temper her sarcasm, while still conveying a good deal of annoyance. Then she sighed. "Oh, what's the use? What do I expect when I make out in a utility closet?"

"We could go back to the one over in the math building," he suggested. "That was roomier, and their storage room was pretty comfortable."

She shook her head. "No, thank you," said Elinor, "not after that shriveled little calculus professor caught us. It's a good thing I finished all my required math courses. I couldn't go back there."

"I don't think he got a good look at your face, Flash," said Paul, edging closer.

Elinor pushed him away.

"If he didn't see my face that's about the only thing he didn't see, the little voyeur."

A thoughtful look crossed Paul's face, and he shook his head. "You can't really call him a 'voyeur.' I don't think he came into that closet hoping to see a couple in the throes of passion."

"Well, that was his little bonus for the day, then, wasn't it?"

"So, it really isn't fair to label him a 'voyeur.'"

"Fine, he's not a voyeur, he's a peeping tom," she said.

"Oh, that's even a less accurate description," said Paul.

"Shut up," she said, and then noticed at his crestfallen expression. "I'm sorry, it's not your fault. It's mine for dating a pre-law major."

"It's no one's fault, Flash."

Elinor sat up and tugged down on the hem of her skirt, which had ridden up during the necking session. "And I wish you wouldn't call me 'Flash.' It sounds like I'm exposing myself to faculty perverts, like that math teacher."

"Calculus professor..."

"Glorified math teacher," she said, folding her arms across her bosom.

He nuzzled closer and put his arm around her.

"You're probably right," he said. He was patronizing her, but Elinor didn't mind. Even if he didn't think she was right, he was giving in to her, and that was just as good. She liked that about Paul. She had known him since childhood. He had always been that way towards her. It was one of the best things about him.

Paul leaned over and gave her a sensual kiss. Elinor closed her eyes and yielded to his lips. That was another thing she liked about him: he had great lips, and she knew how to use them. Elinor let out a gentle moan, partially for effect; the rest was unavoidable.

He released her slowly, then came in closer again, this time playfully kissing the tip of her nose. She opened her eyes and smiled. He smiled back.

"There, that's better isn't it," he said rhetorically before his mouth broadened into a grin, and he added: "Flash."

"You're a jerk," she said, and pulled back, hitting her head again on the metal ductwork. "OW! Shit!"

"Shhh," he cautioned.

"Don't tell me to be quiet!"

He put his arms around her and caressed the back of her head.

"Don't be mad at me," he cooed in her ear. "I only call you that when we're alone."

"We weren't alone the first time you called me that," she reminded him as if he needed reminding. It was his favorite reminiscence, and he repeated it often, though only to her, and then only in private.

"You were the prettiest little girl at St. Simeon's."

"Noticing little girls," she snorted, "you're as bad as that calculus professor."

"It's okay, I was a little boy at the time."

"You were a year older than me."

"I still am," he said. "And you were on the playground, and you got mad..."

"Don't say why," she pleaded. It was the part of the story she didn't want to be reminded of as if she needed to be. It was the main reason she was making out in a closet.

"You got mad, and I first noticed your eyes."

"Everyone notices them," she said. "It's as bad as having a limp, or a hair lip."

"I don't think so," he said.

"You don't have two different colored eyes," said Elinor. "You didn't get teased about having a head like a railroad signal, or constantly having some idiot ask you: 'do you know your eyes are two different colors?'"

"I think they're beautiful, especially now, right now, at this moment."

"What's so great about now?"

"You're angry," he said, "and when you're angry, they turn vivid. The blue almost goes violet, and the brown gets all warm, almost like molten gold...Flash."

Elinor looked at Paul's eyes. They were each the same color, and they didn't flash, blink, roll over, or do any other tricks. But they had that look in them. It was a look they'd had before. It had first appeared several years ago. It was a look that bothered her and scared her.

"Don't..." she said, turning her head aside.

"What? I didn't do anything."

"Good, don't," said Elinor.

"I'm not even touching you."

"That you can do," she said. "Touch me all you want." She meant it. At the moment, he could do anything he wanted with his hands or any other part of his body, just as long as he didn't use his tongue; at least not for talking.

"Huh?"

She turned back to face him. He was scratching his head, the big dope. He didn't even know what was on his own mind. He hadn't a clue as to what was on the tip of his tongue even though he often broached the subject at times like this.

"Never mind," she said. "Just skip it, okay?"

Paul shrugged his shoulders. "Okay." He smiled warmly. She reached over and grabbed the back of his head and pulled him forward atop her. They kissed. The danger was past. The crisis averted. She enjoyed several minutes of heavy kissing accompanied by some moderate petting. Elinor almost forgot she lying on a concrete floor in a utility closet.

After several minutes of recreational snogging, he rested his head on her breast and sighed. She played with his close-cropped hair, twirling the longer, curlier bits atop his head.

"I can hear your heartbeat," he said softly.

"Shhh."

That quieted him down for a few minutes at least, and Elinor tried to enjoy the final few minutes of pleasure until the dampness of the concrete floor would leech into her back. Her momentary bliss was soon interrupted.

"You know, El," said Paul. His head was still on her chest, and she could feel each syllable reverberating in her ribs.

"mmm..." was all she said. She didn't want to encourage him further. She had already warned him, so she hoped he wouldn't say anything foolish. She hoped he would announce he was hungry or had to go to work, or something...

"We should get married..."

"Damn it," she said, shoving his head off her chest and sitting up in one swift motion, banging her head on the duct again. This elicited another strong curse from Elinor.

"Are you okay, sweetheart?" asked Paul, reaching to rub the point of impact.

She slapped away his hand. He just stared at her with a confused expression. Really, thought Elinor, as many times as they'd had this fight, she expected he'd no longer be surprised at her reaction.

"What?" asked Paul. "What did I say? What's wrong?"

"We've been through this before!"

He looked at her for a moment, his eyes searching hers, and then he spoke.

"We've known each other, for…well, nearly forever. I've always been on your side. I've always been there for you. Even when we were just children, and I didn't know anything about love or passion, even back then, I knew you were special. And now, well, we're just so good, no, great together: we like the same things. We share the same things, especially each other. And you know I love you, El, and, well, I don't know what else qualifies a man to ask a woman to marry him and spend the rest of their lives together. But I know that I want to be with you."

Then he reached down, took her hands, squeezed them together, and kissed them. It was almost enough to melt her heart, almost. This was the fourth time he had delivered his argument for marriage; technically, it was the fifth time. The first time, the very first time Paul was only seventeen, and she was only sixteen. They couldn't have gotten married without parental consent, so she didn't count that. That was practice. Elinor grudgingly admitted that he was getting better. She wasn't sure how much longer she could deflect his proposals.

The truth was, Elinor confided to herself, she did love him, if you could call it love. Paul was right about their relationship. There was no one she liked more, no one who had been on her side. As children, they had been... conspirators? Yes, that was as good a term as any. And when they grew older and hormonal changes provoked them to natural curiosities, they had conspired to do that together, too. That physical relationship had been compatible as well. She hadn't been close to any other boys, nor had she felt the need to be either. Love him? Well, there wasn't another person she liked more, but still, that wasn't enough.

Paul knew what he wanted. He had known from an early age what he wanted to do. He had that annoying confidence of a person who is fortunate enough to be good at something and wants to do it. Elinor admired that, but at the same time was jealous of it; hated it, and feared it. She was jealous of him because she didn't know what she was best at, and had even less of an idea what she wanted to do. She feared it because she didn't know if she'd ever learn that about herself.

Paul just assumed that Elinor's talent was being the final piece to his own puzzle. She was there to complete him. He had his career, and her career, he thought, was to support his goals. She couldn't blame him, not too much. Most of the boys she knew thought that what women were for: to be their lovers, bear and raise their children, and provide a comfortable home life. And most of the girls she knew were okay with that, too. More than half the girls in her sorority were just there to land a husband. Even that new girl, the one across the hall, had seemed that way at first glance until Elinor had realized her real inclinations.

It didn't matter to Elinor what all the other girls wanted or would settle for. She felt like she was at an ice cream shop with only one flavor: vanilla, because vanilla was all anyone ever wanted. And that one flavor might be okay if that's all they had and you really wanted ice cream. But Elinor wasn't even sure that she wanted ice cream, and if she did, she wanted more choices than vanilla.

Most girls would have grabbed Paul at his first clumsy proposal. Part of Elinor felt guilty for not accepting him, but it wasn't too large a part of her. Still, she wondered how long she could keep turning him down before he'd give up on her altogether. She didn't want to drive him away, not totally, at least she didn't think so.

Elinor looked down at his hands holding hers, and then up in Paul's eyes. They were waiting for an answer. There was an uncertainty in them, while at the same time the confidence that sooner or later she would accept his proposal. Elinor liked that first look and resented the second.

She glanced down again at their hands. He wore a school ring on his. Hers were naked. He would love to slide a ring on her finger. Then she looked beyond their hands, a few feet beyond was the concrete floor. She noticed a small, greasy oil stain.

"No," she said, looking at the floor. She didn't say it cruelly. That wasn't her intent. But still, it was a "no," and that was a rejection. She looked up at Paul. Disappointment and the mute expectation of an explanation clouded his face.

"I can't say, yes," she said, "not here, not...not...not sitting on a dirty, cold floor in some closet."

He glanced around and nodded in agreement.

"Sorry," he said, "I guess I just got..."

"Carried away," she offered.

"Carried away," he agreed. His face brightened. "If that's all, let's go out. We'll find someplace else, someplace nice, and warm, and comfortable, and..."

She smirked at him and shook her head. "It's no good, Paul," she stroked his cheek. "It's not just the floor, dear." He smiled at being called "dear," which is why she added it.

"It's isn't where we are at this moment," continued Elinor. "Where else could we go? It's where we always are, having to hide, having to find little spots to meet, never being able to be who we are in public as if we had something to be ashamed of."

"We wouldn't have to hide if we were married."

She shook her head.

"For how long?" she asked. "Until we said, 'I do?' Would we have to find a secret place to hold the wedding?"

51

"We could always elope..."

"And that would just delay the inevitable. One of these days you're going to have to face it..."

He stood. "I'm ready. I'll settle it this minute."

She knew he would, and she knew she didn't want him to. Elinor pulled him back down.

"Let me rephrase that," said Elinor. "We, we are going to have to find a solution. It's more complicated than just the two of you. If you want to have lasting happiness, we're going to have to figure a way out of this. We have to find a way out of hiding. How can you expect us to get married when we can't even be seen in public?"

A smirk spread across Paul's face, and he nodded.

"It's something to work towards," he said.

"I'd like it, too," she said.

"Really?" he said.

Elinor nodded. He meant marriage. But she just thought it would be nice after all these years to actually have a date in public. Still, she didn't feel like correcting him at the moment.

As if to close the topic, Elinor leaned over and gave him a quick hard kiss, and then used his shoulders to pull herself to her feet.

"I've got to go," she said, pulling down to rearrange her clothes and then running her hands through her hair. "Do I look okay?"

"You always look great," he said, looking up at her from the floor.

She smirked. "Thank you, but I mean to do I look like I've just been rolling around in a closet?" Elinor didn't wait for an answer. She pulled a compact mirror from her purse to see for herself. After making sure she was presentable, Elinor picked up her belongings and went to the door.

"Give me a few minutes head start," she said, turning to Paul who was sitting cross-legged on the floor. Her instructions weren't really necessary. It had been their routine for as long as they'd been dating.

Elinor opened the door and looked out into the hallway. It was empty. The last evening class ended thirty minutes ago. She was about to close the door behind and nonchalantly walk away when Paul called her back.

"Yes?" she asked, standing in the doorway.

"Did you mean it," he asked, "about figuring something out? I mean, you want to, don't you?"

Elinor looked at him. He looked so cute sitting there. Paul was usually so sure and confident. She was the only piece of his life that made him uncertain. It was good for him, she reasoned, it kept him sharp.

She smiled at him. "Of course, I want to," she said. "Leave it to me. We've been hiding long enough. Soon we will have everything we've been waiting for."

– 8 –
The Benzedrine Marx Brother

Prudence ran into the cool evening air, across the quadrangle, and ducked around the side of a building. Actually, it wasn't a run. It was more like a scurry, like that of a frightened rabbit. Her heart was pounding, not from her sprint, but from the words she overheard.

"We've been hiding long enough," Elinor had said. "Soon we will have everything we've been waiting for."

Prudence hoped that somehow there was an innocent explanation for why a seemingly nice girl would dump a load of communist propaganda on her. Now that hope was shattered by Elinor's own words.

Prudence cowered against the home of the English department. Her body was as still as the statue of James Fennimore Cooper standing in front of the building. Compared to her, James Fennimore Cooper had it easy, she concluded.

"You didn't have to deal with boxes and communists while trying to get an education," she muttered. "All you had to worry about was Indians, and that's a lot less complicated. There's very little vaguery in a savage rushing at you with a tomahawk!"

"And I bet you never had one of your sorority sisters dump a consignment of rifles and firewater on your bed and run away."

The statue offered no reply.

"Did you even have to deal with rampaging braves, or did you just write about them?"

Prudence couldn't recall much about the man other than he had written *The Last of the Mohicans*. Just that title itself indicated that the biggest threat to Cooper's person was an old toothless chief boring people to tears with his recollections of long-ago raids and hitting them up for a loan until his pension check arrived.

"Indians! That would be easy," she continued. You try having an international conspiracy plopped on your best roll of shelf paper! And you got a statue for whatever you did. That's nicer than a dagger between the shoulder blades followed by a shove out a window!"

"At least," she told herself, "I know the truth about Elinor. That's what I get for trying to think the best of her and give her the benefit of the doubt."

Her anger only lasted a moment.

"Still, I guess it's better to think the best of someone while you wait for them to prove they're a rat."

After waiting for a few minutes, Prudence started back to the sorority house. As she walked, it occurred to her that now she had to do something about it. Prudence no longer had the luxury of inaction. Now she knew that a bona fide rat lived across the hall and was using Prudence's room to hide her droppings.

Her first impulse was to confront the girl. As she walked across campus, Prudence imagined herself picking up the crate, and dumping it back on Elinor with the same boldness with which it had been foisted on her. She imagined slamming it against Elinor's door with the same reckless disregard that Elinor had displayed when nearly pushing down Prudence's door. Prudence pictured the shocked look on Elinor's face as she realized that the jig was up.

"Elinor," Prudence could hear herself say, her mezzo-soprano voice dripping with acid, "Elinor, I know all about what you're doing."

No, that was too friendly. It would have to be something more like: "Potoski, you and your Commie pals are through. I know all about you, and I'm telling!"

Yes, that would work she thought as she paused under a street lamp. She felt empowered and decisive until she looked down and noticed she was wearing her cute pink sweater set, and suddenly felt less empowered. One didn't barge into communist cells wearing pink angora. Prudence mentally reviewed her wardrobe and concluded that she had too many cute clothes. She had nothing suitable for clearing out a nest of subversives.

The realization that she hadn't any racket-busting ensembles made Prudence feel anemic. Not only that but confronting villains rarely made them surrender, no matter what you were wearing. She had seen a movie where the heroine discovered the bad guys and told them: "You're criminals. I'm going to tell!" For all her bravado, Prudence remembered that the dopey girl was bound and gagged and taken to a remote cabin. It was only the frantic efforts of the hero that saved her life. Prudence realized that her plan was even more insipid than that dopey girl. For one thing, she didn't have a hero that would rescue her.

No, the best thing would be to tell the authorities. Prudence stopped on the path. Who exactly were the authorities? In her life, authority could mean anyone from the house mother at Rho Delta Delta all the way up to President Eisenhower. The one was too low, the other too high. It would have to be someone in between. The FBI would be a good resource, but she had no idea where the nearest FBI office was. That left the local police department. If the town police thought it necessary, they would call the FBI into the Potoski case. The Potoski case? Prudence thought a moment and nodded to herself. Yes, that's probably what they would come to call it. Prudence recalled seeing a police station in town on the main street. It was between the campus and the train station, the opposite direction from the sorority house. She turned and headed back in the direction she had come. Glancing up at the watch she saw it was nearly 9:00 p.m. She hoped the police department was still open. Prudence quickened her step.

The campus was dark and deserted. All the classes were over for the day. A line of lampposts illuminated the path ahead of her, like giant fireflies standing in single-file. Prudence counted the lights leading to the edge of the campus ending at Main Street nearly a half-mile away. She passed from light to darkness, darkness to light, firm in her new resolve. She knew what she had to do, and she was doing it. Nothing would stop her now; nothing except the figure now approaching on the path.

There, between Prudence and edge of the campus, between her and the police station, there was Elinor.

A wave of paranoia swept over Prudence. She froze in her tracks and looked up. She was in the dark between lampposts. She took a step backward from the path. Perhaps Elinor hadn't seen her. Now Elinor was between the lights but coming toward her. Prudence took another step back and nearly fell over a low hedge. She started to gasp but caught herself not wanting to make even the slightest noise that would give her away. Prudence held her breath and waited another moment. Elinor emerged from the darkness as she approached the next light. Under its illumination, Prudence could see Elinor walking at a steady pace. Her expression was enigmatic. She could have been wearing a scowl, a look of determination, or it could have just been the average expression one wore when one was walking and thinking of something else. Was she thinking of Prudence? Had she seen Prudence?

Prudence froze. She couldn't go any further without walking into the light. Was Elinor out looking for her? Now Elinor was back between the lights. What if she was searching for her? Maybe Elinor wanted her crate back. That would be fine, but why would she be out hunting her down? Why wouldn't she just wait at the sorority house? Maybe she needed it in a hurry. Maybe there was going to be a meeting that evening of her Red cell. Perhaps she had gotten into Prudence's room, noticed the crate had been tampered with and was now out to silence her for good.

How did communists polish off their enemies? Didn't the Russians ship dissenters to Siberia? That seemed unlikely. The train through the college town only ran three times a day, not counting the milk train, and none of their routes went near the Soviet Union. The area bus line had even more limited range. No, if Elinor were out to silence her neighbor, it would be swift and deadly. Prudence recalled reading that communist agents often shoved their enemies off of buildings, letting gravity do their dirty work. It was clean and looked like an accident. That wouldn't have worked back at the sorority. Prudence's room was only on the second floor, and the house was surrounded by hydrangea bushes that would cushion her fall. If Elinor sharpened the branches, they could impale her. No, someone would surely notice a sorority girl honing the hydrangeas to a lethal point. She could drag Prudence to the bell tower atop the administration building and shove her off of there.

Up ahead, Elinor walked under the next street light. She was now five lights away from Prudence. Her walk seemed determined, and her arms swung purposefully, not in the manner of a person out for a leisurely after-dinner stroll, but that of a young woman with a nefarious deed to do.

For a brief moment, Prudence's more rational side caught up with her thoughts run amok. Communist agents? Bus lines to Siberia? Death by hydrangea bush? Really! It was such utter nonsense! Wasn't it?

Now Prudence could just make out the sound of Elinor whistling. Was that *The Internationale?* As she neared, Prudence saw something in Elinor's hand that looked like a club. It was indeed some sort of weapon and that she was waving it, impatiently, even belligerently, at her side, as if she was spoiling to bring the club crashing through the skull of the nearest enemy of the revolution. Whatever tune she was whistling, her chipper attitude only seemed to underscore that Elinor relished using that club. Prudence tried one last appeal to reason but was swiftly overruled by her fears.

Turning tail, Prudence started scurrying up the path, away from Elinor, but then stopped short before the next street light. Not wanting to be seen, Prudence dove headfirst through the boxwood hedge. She emerged on the other side with just a few scratches on her arms and legs. She reasoned that a few scratches were preferable to a stiff pleat down one's skull. Behind the hedge, she could now hear the footsteps of Elinor as she approached. Should she stay put or make a break for it across the lawn? She noticed a small brick building approximately fifty yards away. The building's back faced her, but from the side, she could see that lights were on inside.

Deciding this was her best chance, Prudence slipped off her Bass Weejuns and starting running towards the building. For the first ten yards, thinking it made her less conspicuous, Prudence crouched at the waist as she ran, looking like Groucho Marx on Benzedrine. Deciding that speed was preferable to stealth, Prudence rose to her full height and took off like Harpo in pursuit of a blonde. As she ran, her arms began to pump furiously, each hand holding one of her loafers, like the batons in a double-shoe relay race.

Fearful of looking back, Prudence listened for any indication that Elinor was chasing her, but the pounding of her own heart drowned out all other sounds. With one final lunge, she reached the brick building and darted around the corner. There she stood gasping for breath, her shoulders rising and falling in rhythm with her bosom.

She waited a moment, listening for the sound of Elinor in pursuit: nothing. Elinor hadn't seen her. Prudence could go to the police station.

Prudence looked at the shoes in her hand. She would put her shoes back on and hurry to the police station. Prudence put her full weight against the side of the building and lifted her right leg to put on her right shoe. As a rule, the left shoe should have gone on in similar fashion, as it had throughout her whole life, but Prudence discovered, there were exceptions to every rule. Suddenly, as she pointed her toe into the loafer, Prudence felt as if her rear end were suspended in mid-air. This sensation of posterior weightlessness lasted less time than it took to describe it. A split-second later, Prudence felt her backside plummeting downward, and, in perfect accordance with the laws of physics, her entire body followed. Had she been holding a tea kettle, instead of a size six-and-a-half shoe, it could be said that Prudence fell ass-over-tea-kettle. As it was, all that could be asserted was that she fell-ass-over Bass Weejun. Tea kettles and shoes were the furthest things from her mind, however. Instead, all she thought off was screaming.

As she screamed, however, everything went dark. A thick piece of cloth was tossed over her head. She let out another shriek, this one even louder, but muffled by the fabric.

As she flailed her arms, Prudence realized that she had been caught. Elinor Potoski had maneuvered her into a trap, chased her right into her hideout, right into the clutches of her henchmen. Now, having fallen into their grasp, they were stuffing her into a sack. Where, Prudence wondered would she next see the light of day? Moscow? Siberia? Or perhaps they would just weight the sack and dump her in the murky depths of a nearby lake. Why did she transfer to a school with so many convenient bodies of water nearby? If only she had transferred to a school in New Mexico, or Arizona, or Sub-Saharan Africa.

Then, as she struggled, Prudence flinched as she heard a loud bang, followed by a crash, and a blood-curdling scream.

In the dark Prudence couldn't tell what had caused the bang or the crash, but the scream was unmistakable: it belonged to her.

- 9 -
When a Girl
Needs a Beard

She thought she saw someone on the path ahead of her, and then it was as they had just disappeared. That was fine with Elinor Potoski. She didn't want to be seen, at least not to be seen by *him*.

But it wasn't him. Even from a distance, Elinor could see the approaching figure was a girl, so it didn't matter. She didn't worry about girls. Elinor had a bigger problem. She and Paul had been a secret couple for more than five years. At first, their clandestine relationship had been exciting. Now it was boring. She liked Paul, and she knew he loved her. He treated her as well as he could. Still, Paul couldn't lavish much attention on Elinor. She envied the other girls in the sorority. She watched them preening for dances, receiving flowers, or going out for dinner, and imagined herself doing those things. Hell, at this point she would feel spoiled just being taken out for a hamburger. A lousy burger? She deserved better. She was attractive. She had a good body. She had turned down other boys. She couldn't go out publicly with someone else while she was seeing Paul in secret. If she did, she would have to do so behind Paul's back, and one stealth romance was enough.

As she reached the spot where she saw the other girl, Elinor stopped and looked around. What if it had been one of her sorority sisters? They may have ducked behind the hedge in order to leap out and scare her. She wasn't in the mood for such childish tricks. When all your dates are held in a closet, your nerves tend to get frayed.

Elinor leaned over the low hedge and peered into the murkiness; her right arm cocked to deliver a swift sock up the nose to any of her friends who might be foolish enough to spring out on her. There was no one. But there was a noise in the distance. It sounded like muffled footsteps. Whoever it was, they were running. She shrugged her shoulders. Some girl had been walking along the path then suddenly decided she had to be somewhere else in a hurry.

Elinor started to turn when she saw something just over the hedge. It was a notebook. She brought it under the street light and opened it. According to the name written on the inside cover, it belonged to some girl named Prudence Hoover. That name sounded familiar. Elinor thought a moment and then noticed below the name was the address of her sorority house. Oh, right, she thought, that was the new girl she had met a few days before; the odd one.

Elinor flipped through the notebook. There were less than two pages of notes in it. She almost threw it back to where she had found it. Then Elinor decided to lug it back to the sorority house. Even though the book was nearly empty, the girl might want it. She put the notebook under her arm and snorted. That new girl didn't have Elinor's problems, she couldn't. She recalled the day they met. Elinor had noticed it right away. The only photo Prudence had was one of her hugging some girl. There were no other photographs with it, no photos with boys. Most girls at Rho Delta had pictures of boyfriends.

Elinor didn't think too much of it at the moment until she found Prudence staring at her. When she asked her what she was looking at, Prudence said she was looking at Elinor's beauty, and then added that she liked beautiful girls.

Most girls didn't tell other girls they were beautiful, especially not girls they were meeting for the first time. That was a guy's line, a pick-up line. Girls didn't talk like that. She did recall a woman back in high school like that, a literature teacher who showed an inordinate interest in girls. There were rumors about her, but Elinor never paid too much attention to them one way or the other. She had never met another person like that, until now.

No, thought Elinor, as she returned to the house, that Hoover girl didn't have to worry about secret lovers, at least not secret boyfriends. She knocked on Prudence's door. There was no answer. Elinor glanced at her watch. It wasn't that late. Certainly, the girl wouldn't be in bed already.

"She's got a night class," said a voice.

Elinor turned. Ruby was coming up the hall from the bathroom. She was in her robe, drying her hair.

"Night class," repeated Elinor with a nod.

"World History," said Ruby, raising her eyebrows.

Elinor smirked. Nearly half the girls in the house had taken Bascomb's class, and Bertie Bascomb had enrolled almost half of that half in his private tutoring sessions.

"Yeah, well," said Elinor, "I don't think she'll enjoy him as much as most of the girls."

Ruby snickered. "Yeah, she seemed more interested in another person."

"Oh," said Elinor disinterestedly.

"Yes," said Ruby, "she seemed very interested in you."

"What?"

"I said, she's seemed very interested in you."

"Me?" said Elinor.

"Do you know any other Elinors living here?"

Just great, thought Elinor, that was just great. This new girl not only tells Elinor that she likes beautiful girls, and includes Elinor in that group, but now she's going around asking about her behind her back.

"What did she say?" asked Elinor and hoping Prudence's preferences hadn't been as clear to Ruby as they had been to her.

Ruby shrugged her shoulders. "Oh, I don't know, she just asked a lot of questions about you. We thought it was weird…"

"We?"

"Me and Myrna."

"Just the two of you?"

"Yeah, oh and then Yolanda…"

"So, what did she say about me?"

"Nothing, not really," confessed Ruby. "It was strange because she kept trying to steer the conversation around to you."

"And?"

"And nothing," said Ruby. "It was just odd because it was like she was fishing for information about you, like she was interested. It was really annoying. She's weird."

With that, Ruby put a towel over her head and walked to her room. Elinor stood watching her, and then just stared at Prudence's door. It was a good thing she wasn't there. The way Elinor felt at that moment, she'd serve Prudence Hoover a knuckle sandwich. It was bad enough that Prudence was asking questions about her behind her back, but asking Ruby made it worse. As far the girls knew Elinor didn't have a boyfriend. But she didn't want anyone to think she was weird. Elinor was normal. She had one steady boyfriend. Okay, so she had to meet with him in secret, but her boyfriend was a boy.

Elinor went into her room and threw Prudence's book on her desk. She didn't have time to worry about her stupid sorority sisters. Elinor had problems of her own. She glanced down at the name written in the book.

"Prudence Hoover," Elinor snorted to herself. "She doesn't have a boyfriend. She wouldn't want one, anyway."

Elinor stopped and stared at the wall. A thought began to crystallize in her mind.

"…And she can't go out in public on a date, at least not with the type of dates she would have, could she? No, she couldn't."

A broad smile overspread her face.

"So, she could go on a date with Paul and me. And if a certain person saw us, we could say that Prudence was Paul's date. I would be the extra wheel. I'd be the girl who couldn't get a date, the friend from across the hall. Oh, yes, that's perfect. She would be a decoy, a fake, a beard."

A brief pang of guilt clouded Elinor's reasoning at this point. It wasn't exactly nice to use an almost complete stranger like that, was it? But she wouldn't really be using Prudence. In fact, she would be doing Prudence a favor. This would be an opportunity for Prudence to get out in public and socialize. Given her inclinations, Prudence probably didn't get a lot of chances to go out socially. Yes, it would be a great favor to Prudence.

Elinor stopped again and looked towards the door. Would she tell Prudence what exactly she would be doing? She stared at the door as she thought over that one, before shaking her head. No, she didn't really need to know. It might only make her nervous if she knew. No, Elinor would just invite her along. It was after all the natural, friendly, sorority sisterly thing to do. Wasn't it? Yes, Elinor concluded, it was.

Elinor smiled, her conscious lulled back to sleep until one last objection stirred in her mind. What if Prudence wouldn't agree to go on a date with her and Paul? Her brow furrowed for a moment until the obvious solution presented itself. If Prudence wouldn't accept a nice, friendly, sisterly invitation, then Elinor would threaten to expose her little hobby.

Elinor Potoski walked out the door. First, she would call Paul to tell him the good news, and then she would find her new sorority sister and extend a friendly invitation.

– 10 –
How to Look at a Window
Without Looking Through It

A s Prudence Hoover struggled, she realized that her legs were free. Had her abductors only placed the bag over her head? And as she thrashed about on the cold concrete floor, Prudence noted that the sack was soft wool, with a fragrant hint of cedar. She'd have expected kidnappers to use coarse burlap. She also noticed a chilly breeze around her thighs.

Prudence reached up and discovered the sack was actually her own skirt that had flipped up over her head when she fell backward.

She stopped flailing, sat motionlessly, and thought. She was sprawled in an open doorway with her panties exposed for any passerby to see. Had anyone seen her? Raising her skirt slightly, Prudence listened. Aside from a gentle breeze rustling through the trees, all was quiet.

Prudence flipped her skirt down over her knees and sat up. She peered out the door. There was no one there. Then, behind her, she heard the scrape of shoe leather on concrete. Prudence pivoted on her rear and looked up. A man towered over her. He looked surly, with a surly nose, surly teeth, and one long surly eyebrow straddling two menacing eyes. Adding to the overall effect was the fact that he had a club in his hand, which he was now tapping rhythmically against his palm in a threatening manner.

"Vell, who do ve have here," he snarled with a malevolent grin. His accent only added to the chill running down Prudence's spine.

"Just me," squeaked Prudence.

In the background, she could hear the squeals and whistles of radio static. Probably a shortwave set, she surmised. They're probably radioing Moscow to tell them they'd captured the troublesome American girl. She had to do something. Recalling she had a weapon too, Prudence picked up her loafer and flung it with all her might at her attacker hitting him squarely on the forehead. It didn't help. Instead, the man now looked even meaner with an angry red heel print over his one angry eyebrow.

Then the man's expression melted from that of an angry villain to an admonished puppy. The squinting eyes that had a moment before seemed so threatening now grew wide, innocent, and hurt. The malevolent grin drooped into a heartbreaking pout. Indeed, his entire face and his body along with it, seemed to collapse into a smaller, less threatening version of its former self. The voice, which had sounded so scary now emitted a mewing whine.

"Ow! Cut it out," he bleated. "Vy you do dat?"

Prudence, her mouth open, poised for another scream, just left it hanging in amazement.

"Dat really hurt!" He complained as he staggered back against the wooden counter. The man massaged his forehead with his meaty hands as if to rearrange the bits of his face back to their proper places. "Dat hurt bad!"

"Badly," corrected Prudence.

"Man! Oh, man!" he continued. He was now stomping his feet in place as if doing so would alleviate his pain. Having done this, the man looked down at her shoe lying at his feet. The man picked up the shoe, examined for a moment as if he had never seen one at close range, and then looked at her with an odd expression. Thinking that she who lived by the shoe was about to be pummeled by the same, Prudence braced for the blow. Instead of winding up to hurl it, however, the man offered the shoe back to Prudence, but not before wiping a bit of wet grass from it on to his shirt.

"Here," he said, "you'd better put thees back on vere it can't do any more hurt to no one...like me. Man! Oh, man!" This last utterance accompanied another rubbing of his forehead.

Prudence put on her shoe and clambered off the floor. Upon standing, she was surprised to discover that the man was barely taller than she. This fact, along with his remarkable conversion, made Prudence wonder why she had felt threatened by him in the first place. She was about to scold him for scaring her when the radio static calmed down into some rather pleasant music.

"Paws," said a voice from behind the counter, "why did you switch the station on me? I told you not to monkey with the radio! What are you doing?" To her relief, this new voice sounded American.

Prudence turned and saw the top of a head behind the tall counter. Craning her neck, she saw a young man wearing the blue jacket and tie of a campus security guard. He was sitting behind a desk staring out the window. Why he would be staring out the window was a mystery since it was pitch dark outside and the window was only reflecting back the light of the room.

"Paws," he repeated and then turned to see why his companion hadn't answered. "Paws, I said what...oh, sorry."

With this apology, addressed to Prudence, the guard stood.

"I didn't hear anyone come in," he said.

Prudence just stared at him. Didn't hear anyone come in, she thought, an invading platoon of Marines would have been quieter.

"Paws," he said, turning to the first man, "why didn't you tell me I had a visitor?"

"I didn't know she vas visitor," said Paws. "The vay she came in I taught it vas some sort of security drill, or sumptin'."

"I fell in," explained Prudence. "I was putting on my shoe, and the door gave way."

At the mention of the shoe, Paws massaged his forehead.

"And that's probably why you were brandishing that club," said Prudence.

"Club?" said the security guard. "Look Paws, I don't really mind you stopping by when I'm on duty, even though it is kind of against the regulations...sort of, but you can't threaten visitors like that. Only I'm allowed to do that..."

"What?" said Prudence.

"I mean," said the guard, "if he thought it was a drill, he shouldn't have taken it upon himself to react. That's what they pay me for."

"Don't end your sentences in a preposition," said Prudence.

"Excuse me?"

"Sorry," she said, "I'm an English major."

"Dat outranks you," said Paws.

"Shut up," said the guard to his friend. "Don't you have someplace to go?"

"As a matter of fact, I do," said Paws. He lumbered towards the open door but paused to shake Prudence's hand with his own thick mitt. "It vas nice to meet you," he said, rubbing his temple, "I tink. See you back at the house, Rod." He closed the door on the way out, leaving Prudence alone with the guard. For a moment they stood there awkwardly. Prudence couldn't think of anything to say, but she didn't really want to go, not yet, not with Elinor Potoski on the prowl.

"Paws and I go way back," said the guard jerking his thumb towards the door.

"That's an unusual name..."

"Short for Pawelczak. His first name's Stanislav, or Stosh for short. He and his family moved into our neighborhood when he was about four. Never did completely shake his accent, though."

Prudence nodded.

"He's here on a sports scholarship," continued the guard after an awkward pause. "I suppose he's really just tagging along with me. If he weren't here, he'd be working in his father's boiler shop back home."

Prudence nodded again. With the subject of Stanislav Pawelczak, exhausted, the guard resumed gawking at Prudence. His expression reminded Prudence of a man looking at a freshly baked pie who couldn't quite decide if he was sufficiently hungry to have a slice. After a minute, he broke his fast.

"English major, eh?" said the guard, with a slight grin, as if English majors held some hidden source of amusement.

"Yes, I'm studying to be an English teacher."

"Nice to meet you," said the guard, "I'm an Engineering major. I'm only a campus guard in my spare time. It helps pay my way through school."

She agreed that was nice. He agreed too and then offered her a seat. She agreed that would be nice, as well, and sat down in one of the available chairs. He nodded, apparently in agreement, and observed her sitting there a moment. Noticing she was under observation, she nervously crossed her legs, uncrossed them, and then crossed them again on the other side. He crossed to the other side of the desk and then crossed back. He began to sit in the chair across from her, but at the last moment stood back up. After another few paces, he decided, at last, to sit on the edge of the desk. Then he grinned for a moment and then crossed his arms right over left. A second later he decided to switch to uncross it and then re-cross it, left over right. Finally, after several minutes of this mutual fidgeting festival, there came a moment of complete stillness in which she looked at him, and he looked at her.

Prudence was feeling more than a little self-conscious at the way the guard was eyeing her. She reasoned that if she sat perfectly still and returned his gaze with a disinterested look, he would soon tire of whatever it was that he was doing. It worked. The guard stopped looking at her face. Now he was scanning her whole body. After just a few seconds of this, Prudence realized she would have preferred him to just look at her face.

"I'm sorry," he finally said.

You should be, Prudence thought. She was itching all over her body from his attention but didn't dare to scratch anywhere.

"I mean," he added, "that I'm sorry I haven't asked you what I can do for you."

"Pardon?"

"You obviously came in here for a reason."

"I fell through your door."

"Yes, and I'm sorry for that, too," he said. "But you were here for a reason."

"What makes you say that? Maybe I was just passing, had a stone in my shoe, I leaned against your door to remove it, and..."

"You've got grass stains all over your socks, and there's another on your skirt, and there's a smudge of dirt, and scratches on your legs..."

"Well, perhaps…"

"And there's this…" He plucked a sprig of leaves from her hair then sniffed it. "Boxwood, I believe. We have a hedge of them in front of the house…back home."

"I thought you said you were majoring in engineering," she said, "not criminal justice."

"I am," he said, handing her the boxwood sprig.

"Thank you, but I don't want it!" she said, waving his hand away.

He smiled a funny little smile that was rather sweet. Then the guard shrugged, smelled the sprig again, and tucked it into his shirt pocket.

"I'm just trying to do my job, or at least my part-time job," he said. "Powers of observation are important in this job, even on a part-time basis."

"If you say so, Rodney."

The guard's smile fell from his lips as if he'd just been trumped in pinochle.

"How did you know my name?" He looked at his uniform jacket, almost expecting to find a name tag that hadn't been there a moment before.

"Simple," said Prudence. "Your friend called you 'Rod' when he left. So, either your name is 'Rodney,' or you're a pole."

"Rodney's not a Polish name."

"I didn't mean a Pole from Poland. I mean a rod, like a staff or a pole, … oh, never mind. I was trying to clever. I was just trying to show that I can be observant, too."

"Yes, I surmised as much. I suppose," he said with a smile. "you can learn a lot by observing. That's what I was doing when you came in."

"It looked like you were staring out the window into the darkness."

"What?"

"You were looking out the window."

"No, I wasn't."

"Yes, you were."

"No, I wasn't," he said. "I wasn't staring out the window. I was staring at the window." He nodded his head triumphantly.

Prudence saw little about which to boast unless perhaps she had found the only person in Upstate New York more pedantic than she.

"That's a fine distinction," she said.

"Yes," he said, "it is, isn't it?"

"It wasn't a compliment."

"Yes, I know," he added, "but I'll take it as one."

"What I meant was that it was splitting hairs," explained Prudence. "What difference does it make it you were looking out the window, or at the window? Windows are just glass. You can't look at them without looking out them."

"Just glass?" The guard recoiled in the same way that an artist would if told that Michelangelo's David was just a slab of stone with a few chips knocked away, or that the Mona Lisa was some cloth with a bit of paint smeared on it. "But that's where you're wrong," he said. "Windows are more than just glass, much more! To say that glass is all there is to a window is to say that the passengers are all there are to an automobile. True, the car is made for the passenger, but there are so many considerations: safety, style, utility, for example, that sets one car apart from another. If we lavish that much attention on a car, how much more should we pay attention to our windows? In the average American's lifetime, he might only ride in a handful of cars but think of all the windows he may encounter. It boggles the mind."

"It certainly does," said Prudence. She wondered if perhaps she weren't better off being chased by a communist co-ed, rather than being stuck in a shack with a boy with a window fetish. "I suppose I never realized. Sorry."

Her agreement and apology seemed to reign in the guard's passion for the subject momentarily.

"That's okay," he said, wiping his forehead with his handkerchief. "I guess I get a little worked up on the subject. You see, that's what I'm studying."

"Windows?"

"Fenestration," he said. He spoke slowly as if Prudence were five-years-old and slightly stupid. "I want to design windows. I'm going to design better windows, better windows for a better world."

"I suppose…" she had begun to say that someone has to do it, but she thought better of it. "…that's a very noble calling."

Upon this admission, a satisfied smile crossed his face. Prudence realized that you can't really tell what a person looks like until they start talking about what really interests them. It's then that the barriers come down, and the true self steps forth. She had to admit to herself that Rodney-the-Part-Time-Guard was cute despite his silly preoccupation with bits of wood and glass.

"Thank you for understanding," Rodney continued. "Most people don't concern themselves with their windows, but they really are a wonderful invention. Just think, they shield us from the cold, but then open to greet the gentle spring breeze. We watch for loved ones coming home out of them. We look through them in maternity wards to catch the first glimpse of a newborn baby. Lovers climb out of them to elope. Through them, we thrill to sunsets and amazing vistas. From the exciting to the mundane, windows are an integral part of our lives. But most people take them for granted. We never want a drink of water until the well runs dry."

"We never want a window until we're staring at a wall," she said. Prudence had never recalled staring at a wall wishing for a window but felt compelled to appear interested. Was she growing fond of this odd engineering student? Oh, he was marginally cute, she thought, even if he did have a strange obsession. No, she reasoned, her interest was purely professional, or semi-professional. He was a part-time guard, after all. Perhaps he could escort her safely back to her room. Yes, she told herself, that was the beginning and end of the attraction. Wasn't it?

– 11 –
The Knotting of the Toes

Rodney just stared at Prudence. She wondered if her comment about windows was too glib. As she wracked her brain for a more profound remark, a familiar song began on the radio.

"Oh," exclaimed Prudence, "It's *Whispering Grass!* I love this song!" In her excitement, she grabbed his arm. He stared down at her hand almost as intently as if it had been a window pane.

Prudence noticed that he was staring at his arm and that she was clutching it. "Sorry," she said, retrieving her hand, "I got carried away. You see, my father used to sing that song to me. Well, not often. He doesn't sing much. That's a good thing. He has a horrible singing voice, and he didn't sing it particularly well…"

"…and so, you like this song?"

"Oh, yes, he doesn't have a very good voice at all. In fact, he's been told not to sing in church…"

"By your mother?"

"By everyone. But he does sing deep bass nicely, well, relatively nicely, compared to his normal singing voice, which is just horrible. I remember when I was a little girl, one summer evening, he was sitting on the front porch, and this song came over the radio. It's the Ink Spots, you know. And he started singing along with the deep part…this part right here. And he swung me up on his knee and sang. It was lovely."

Prudence realized she was staring into space with a wistful grin on her face. Wistful grins were okay in private, but in front of almost total strangers, they made a person look insipid.

"Sorry, sorry," she said, trying to adopt a more serious expression.

"Don't be sorry."

"Oh, then you do understand," she almost grabbed his arm again but caught herself.

"No, not really," he said.

"Your father never bounced you on his knee?"

The guard looked down. "He couldn't."

Prudence gasped to herself. "I'm sorry. You mean you didn't have a father?"

"No, it's not that. My father didn't have a knee."

She laughed at what she thought was a joke.

"First World War," he said, "amputee. He had us quite late in life."

"Oh, what an idiot I am!"

"You didn't know," he said with a shrug. "It doesn't offend me. He's always been like that to me. In fact, when I was a little boy, I wondered why other fathers had two legs. I just thought it was the way fathers were, you know. Mothers had breasts…uh, I mean, mothers had certain bits, and fathers didn't have others. That's the way it's always been, so don't feel bad."

She looked into his eyes. They were so warm and kind, she thought that maybe he could be something more than just an escort back home; even if he did modify his verbs with adjectives instead of adverbs.

"Thank you," she said and lowered her eyes. She hoped she did so demurely. She had seen an actress lower her eyes demurely, maybe it was Donna Reed. Anyway, this actress had lowered her eyes demurely in front of the hero, who could have been Van Johnson, but she wasn't exactly sure. Prudence didn't know if she looked demure like Donna Reed. After several moments of silence in that pose, she started wondering if Donna Reed also felt idiotic while waiting for Van Johnson to appreciate her attempt at being demure. Another moment and she heard the sound of Rodney's shoes scuffling on the floor. She looked up and saw he was scanning the ground in front of her.

"What exactly are you looking for?" he asked.

"Pardon?"

"Did you lose something?" He asked.

"No, I…" She almost blurted out she was trying to be diffident but caught herself. "…I was just looking at…your floor."

Rodney the guard looked at the floor, then at Prudence, then at his beloved window, and then back at Prudence. He shrugged his shoulders as if to indicate that if he liked windows so much, there might be a girl who was just as interested in floors.

"I suppose it's a good floor," he said, "as floors go."

Prudence kept her head down so he wouldn't see her roll her eyes in exasperation. She wasn't sure who was a bigger dope: her for uttering such a silly excuse; or, him for believing it. Now she was stuck staring at the floor. Before she had been attempting to appear demure; now, she was trying to seem interested in linoleum. She debated which was more foolish, before concluding the most idiotic thing of all was trying to decide between the two.

She touched the side of her head only to find another sprig of boxwood. She plucked the sprig from her hair and dropped it on the floor. Reflexively, Rodney the guard took a step forward to retrieve it. Prudence saw his legs lurch forward, his feet get caught up in themselves, and his knees become twisted into the mix. As he began to fall towards her, Prudence reached out to steady him, and found that she was falling with him.

Rodney looked up, and in desperation, clutched at the nearest thing, which, as it happened, turned out to be Prudence. Rodney swung his arms around her, grabbing her and pressing her to himself. The two compressed bodies became as one. Prudence let out a tiny shriek which put her lips on a collision course with his. The pair fell back onto to the desk, their lips smashing together in a lock that Prudence was confident that most respectable couples didn't experience until at least their third date…and this wasn't even a date.

Despite her misgivings on the propriety of it all, a wild rush of emotions surged up through Prudence's lips and into her brain. Prudence thought of the movie she'd seen only a few weeks before. In it, a star kissed a starlet on a moonlit balcony, as they kissed fireworks exploded in the sky behind them. Now, Prudence realized she was no starlet, and this boy was no movie star. And in a film, the fireworks filled the entire sky, while ones she was now enjoying were confined to her body. At least now she understood the symbolism between those fireworks and human physiology.

After a moment, she felt her knees wobble, even though she wasn't putting any weight on them, and while Rodney now seemed to be trying to push her up, Prudence reached up and grabbed the handiest part of his head, which in this case happened to be his ears, and pulled herself closer. Now, her inner fireworks rushed further south, giving her the delicious feeling of her toes trying to tie themselves in knots.

"GGGTTTT," said Rodney, though his words made little sense with his mouth full of her lips.

"Hmmmm," she said.

"RRRRUUUCRRRZZZ?"

"Hmmmmm," she said, though it was more of a satisfied purr.

"What are you doing," he barked, though Prudence couldn't figure out how, as their lips were still fused together. Perhaps ventriloquism was a secondary interest after fenestration.

Prudence opened her eyes wide only to see his eyes opened even wider and filled with a look of distress.

"I said: what are you doing? Have you lost your mind?"

Prudence released Rodney and raised her head off his.

"How do you do that," she asked. "How do you talk without moving your lips?"

Rodney's face took on a pained expression. His lips, which a moment ago had been so scrumptiously supple, now were twisted into one word: "Rocher!"

"Rocher?" Prudence asked. What precisely a "Rocher" was soon evident, as another guard came into view standing next to the desk. This guard had a better fitting shirt with more stripes on his shoulder than Rodney.

"Have you lost your mind? Carrying on like this on duty? Turning a security facility into some sort of, of...passion pit?"

Prudence lifted herself off Rodney, while Rodney slid out from under her and stood up. He didn't snap to attention, as she might have supposed, but stood up straight, more in defiance than obedience.

"It wasn't what it seemed, Rocher," said Rodney. He gently took Prudence by the waist and guided her to one side to stand eye to eye with the other guard. Prudence was impressed by the fact that both young men were remarkably alike. They were both approximately the same height and the same build, and while Rocher's tailored shirt provided a fine showcase for his toned physique, Prudence supposed a similar form was hiding beneath the ill-fitting folds of Rodney's uniform. Even their hair was almost exactly the same shade of brown, though Rocher's seemed less unruly.

The most significant similarity lay in their eyes. Both shared a determined expression, locked over their firmly set jaws. Above all, they both held the same hostility in the icy stares they now exchanged at close range. The fierce duel of pupils was so intense Prudence took several steps back, lest she be hit in the ocular crossfire. It was apparent that Rodney and Rocher had a history that extended beyond the last few minutes. Finally, Rodney spoke.

"It was an accident," he said.

"Accident," Rocher snorted, "little accidents lead to bigger accidents."

Rodney's nostrils flared, and he cocked his arm back. Prudence buried her face in her hands, while still peeking between her fingers, but his fist froze just behind his right ear. The two men's eyes narrowed in unison, and their loathing looks intensified. After another moment, Rodney relaxed his arm.

"Not this time," he said in almost a growl. "Not now. Not yet."

His submission was filled with power and control, and Prudence was even more intrigued by the stand-off. To her surprise, Rocher didn't seem to count this as a victory, but rather, as Rodney had said, a mutually agreed upon postponement. She wondered how many times the resolution of this personal feud had been deferred.

The two young men exhaled, significantly reducing their apparent size, and Prudence sensed the long ticking bomb had been disarmed once more.

"You'd better go on rounds," said Rocher, "I'll take over here, and I'll speak to you when you get back."

"I'll speak to you, as well," said Rodney, not conceding the semantic high ground. He snapped on his blue peaked guard's cap and ushered Prudence towards the open door.

"I'll escort this young lady," he emphasized that last word, "safely back to her home."

Rocher opened his mouth to speak but was cut short.

"Just to her home," added Rodney. "I will report what you need to know when I return."

As he took her elbow in his hand to guide her, a feeling of security swept over Prudence. This, coupled with the intensity of their kiss, made Prudence wonder if she had found the love of her life; the man who would rescue her from a lonely lifetime educating other people's children of the dangers of dangling participles. This warm, safe aura lasted barely two seconds, long enough for Rocher to make his final retort. It had no doubt been aimed at Rodney, but it flew wide of its mark and punctured Prudence's heart instead.

"See that you do," said Rocher, in the form of an order, before adding, "Patrolman *Potoski*."

Prudence did a double take and gaped for a moment at Rodney's face. There were no multi-color eyes, but aside from that, she saw the resemblance to Elinor Potoski. Given their ages, they must be related; probably brother and sister. Potoski? The security blanket she had wrapped herself in was yanked away, replaced by a sheet of paranoia far worse that had first driven her to this brick hut of …of …disillusionment!

With a snap of her arm, she freed herself from Rodney Potoski's grip and ran. Prudence ran as fast and as far as her legs, and her surging adrenaline could carry her. She did not stop until she was at least a half mile beyond the campus, on small hill sheltered by a copse of birch trees. There, physically and mentally exhausted, Prudence collapsed under the trees and slumped forward to catch her breath and collect her thoughts. Before she could do much of either, her racing heart nearly came to a full stop as a hand grabbed her from behind and a dreaded voice said: "I've been looking for you."

– 12 –
Shoveling Off to Moscow

Prudence felt her blood run cold at the sound of the smooth contralto voice that only could belong to one person. Had she not used her last ounce of stamina fleeing the brother of the person now touching her, Prudence would have bolted from the copse of trees and run at least another half mile. Now all she could do, however, is emit a long, slow sigh, like a punctured beach ball.

"Are you all right?" Elinor asked. Her voice was so calm as to be disturbing, like an arch villain in a movie, reciting a pacifist philosophy while feeding white mice to her pet boa constrictor. Prudence felt like that small animal, as she awaited the pleasure of her tormentor.

"I'm fine!" said Prudence. She had tried to speak calmly. Instead, the words burst from her mouth like a steam whistle. She took a gulp of air and repeated her assertion. "I mean, I'm fine."

"You don't sound fine," said Elinor. "And you came tearing into here as if you were running for your life."

"Just, running…for exercise."

"Okaaay," said Elinor. She sounded doubtful. "I didn't mean to pry. I'm just concerned for you… as your sorority sister and neighbor, that is. If you say you're fine, I believe you. I hope that if you needed anything, you'd let me know…as a sorority sister and a neighbor. Okay?"

She punctuated this sincere sounding offer with a pat on Prudence's shoulder. The touch was gentle, but at the same time, felt tentative. For a split second, Prudence relaxed. Elinor's words sounded so comforting, her touch so soft, that Prudence almost…

No! Prudence sat up stiffly. Elinor Potoski was trying to lull her into a false sense of security. Wouldn't that be how she would recruit Prudence into her communist cell…with kindness and understanding? The radical slogans and violence would come later. As for now, well, you can catch more comrades with gentle words and soft pats on the shoulder than you can by chucking Molotov cocktails at them.

Prudence suppressed the urge to blurt out all she knew and to hurl a pallet of accusations at her captor. Biting her lip, she just sat there, quivering.

"You're shaking," said Elinor.

"So?"

"Well, at least turn around, so I don't have to keep talking to the back of your head!"

Prudence turned around on the soft carpet of fallen birch leaves. There in the light of the mid-September moon sat Elinor looking every bit as serene as her voice had sounded with one exception: the long club lying across her lap.

"What's that?" asked Prudence, afraid of the answer.

"What? This?" she gently ran her fingers along the knobby piece of wood. "It's my walking stick."

"What's it for?"

A grin spread across Elinor's face, and her eyes glistened in the moonlight. "Um....walking?"

"Walking?"

"Walking," repeated Elinor. "I know that seems terribly pedestrian. Perhaps I should have made up something more exciting, such as it's my jousting stick that I bring with me into the woods on the night of the full moon to battle belligerent Druids. But, it's just a stick that I like to carry with me when I go walking. I like to walk, don't you?"

"No," said Prudence. She was not in a conversational mood. She was still parsing Elinor's every word looking for subversive meanings.

"No," agreed Elinor, "that's right. You like to run, don't you?"

"Run? Not particularly."

"Then why were you running out here?"

Prudence sat there, trying to recall her own excuse. After a moment, it came back to her. "Uh, for exercise. That is, I don't usually run, but I was outside, and it was a nice evening, and I thought: I don't get enough exercise. Perhaps I'll take up running. Just like that, on the spur of the moment. Yes, that's right. It just seemed like a good idea at the time. And so, I just started running, until I got here, and then I decided I didn't like it. But it was just one of those crazy impulses, you know, on the spur of the moment."

"That would explain why you're running in a skirt and those loafers," said Elinor. "That's really not the ideal equipment for a good run. You might want to tie your hair back, as well, what's this?"

Elinor reached out and pulled a twig from Prudence's hair. She examined as best she could in the moonlight, and then raised it to her nostrils.

"Mmmm," she said, closing her eyes, "boxwood. I love the smell of boxwood. My parents have a boxwood hedge in front of the house."

"Yes, I know," said Prudence.

"You know?"

"I mean, I know it's a very popular shrub for a hedge. I, ha, I can't imagine how it got in my hair, just running, ha, ha."

Elinor scrutinized Prudence and then nodded her head as if she had reached a conclusion.

"What?"

"Nothing," said Elinor.

"What?"

"If you say you were out running for exercise, then that's what you were doing."

"I was!" protested Prudence. It was so challenging being an amateur liar.

"I believe you," though Prudence doubted if she did.

Prudence wracked her brain. What did Elinor think she was doing out in the woods. What could you do in the woods, dressed as she was in her best skirt and sweater set, and her new Bass Weejuns? Suddenly, it dawned on her.

"No! Oh, no! I know what you're thinking."

"You do?"

"Yes, and no," cried Prudence straightening her clothing. "I wasn't with a boy if that's what you think,"

"I didn't say anything."

"I wasn't with a boy," insisted Prudence. She didn't want anyone, even a communist, to think she was the type of girl who would roll around in the woods necking.

Elinor looked at her for a moment. "I see. I understand," she said before adding: "to each her own."

"Good," asserted Prudence, though she wasn't sure what was meant by that last comment. Why didn't Comrade Potoski just come out and tell her what she was going to do to her? Prudence decided to press the issue. Screwing up her courage, Prudence took a deep breath, sat up straight, and said it.

"Y-you," her voice quivered. "You said you were looking for me?"

"Yes," said Elinor.

Prudence swallowed. "What for? I mean, for what?" In her acute anxiety, she had ended a sentence with a preposition.

Elinor shrugged her shoulders and smiled disarmingly. "I don't know; because I wanted to see you. We still owe each other a nice friendly chat."

Prudence narrowed her eyes, which, in the moonlight, made it very difficult to see. A friendly chat sounded ominous.

"Go on..." said Prudence.

"You go on," said Elinor. "You live approximately four feet across the hall from me. Our first meeting was a bit rushed. You seem like a nice girl, and I just wanted to get acquainted."

"And?"

"And?"

"And, I don't know, maybe we'd go have a soda, or go shopping, or go get some shovels and dig a tunnel to China!"

"Or Moscow?"

"Where ever you want to go," said Elinor.

She gave Prudence a push that seemed playful, at least on the surface, but she may have just been sizing up Prudence's body mass for a future shove off a tall building.

"Do you always take people so literally?" Elinor asked. "Look, analyze this if you want, but I wanted to get to know you, so maybe we can be friends. I don't know about you, but I always thought it was good to know your neighbors, and you can't have too many friends."

"Or comrades…"

"If that's what you like to call them," shrugged Elinor. "I can tell, I'll have to watch my words with you."

"Oh, yes?"

"Yes, you seem to have some weird word fetish."

Prudence arched her back and sat up straight. "I'm going to be an *English* teacher. English: like Americans speak."

"I know, I speak it, too," said Elinor with a smile.

Prudence eyed Elinor. She wondered if this girl could really be a Soviet agent or even a rabble-rouser. Her smile was too genuine.

"I know it's presumptuous of me," said Elinor, "but could you do me a favor?"

Prudence's body stiffened. Here it was, at last, she thought, the pitch to join the movement of the international proletariat.

"Another one?" said Prudence.

"Another one?" repeated Elinor.

Don't play coy with me, thought Prudence. "The crate?"

"Crate?"

"Crate," echoed Prudence, "box, parcel, carton, or package, if you prefer. The one you gave me to hide?"

Elinor's face contorted in thought for a moment and then relaxed. "Oh, yes, that thing!" She gave Prudence another shove, though it was little more than a wave. "I'll have to take that back. Yes, I guess it's another favor. I'm sorry about that old box. I'd forgotten all about that old thing."

"You did?" Prudence.

"I know, it's irresponsible of me, but really it completely slipped my mind. I forgot all about it. After all, the dumb thing's not even mine."

In one simple sentence, the massive conspiracy surrounding Elinor Potoski came crashing down. When the metaphoric dust had settled, there was Elinor, still smiling at her, with the slight look of confusion.

"You must be terribly annoyed with me," said Elinor. "That was a big imposition on you. No wonder, you seemed bothered."

"Bothered?"

"When you came running up here," she said. "You seemed like I was the last person on earth that you wanted to run into."

Into whom you wanted to run, Prudence thought, rearranging the sentence into a more grammatically correct construction.

"So, the box doesn't belong to you?"

"No, it belongs to, well, let's say, a friend. Why?"

"No reason," said Prudence. "Don't they need it back? I mean, isn't there something in there that they need?"

Elinor shook her head, her shoulder length hair swaying about her neck. "I haven't the slightest idea. I don't even know what's in the stupid thing."

Prudence let out a burst of laughter. Elinor smiled, obviously pleased that someone was amused, but not getting the joke. Finally, she shrugged her shoulders.

"Do you know what's in it?" asked Elinor.

"No!" blurted Prudence, stopping in mid-chortle, and almost choking on the last laugh. "That is, no, I don't."

"Well, I'll get that out of your room as soon as we go home."

Prudence sighed in relief. Elinor wasn't a communist. She knew a communist but didn't even know she knew a communist. In that regard, Elinor was completely innocent, even more innocent than Prudence. Elinor knew a communist but didn't know that she knew one. Prudence knew that there was a communist somewhere, but she didn't know who it was. The barrier between them was now removed. They could be sorority sisters and friends. Her initial favorable impression of Elinor Potoski restored; Prudence reached out her arms to hug her. Elinor smiled weakly and gave a weak pat in return. But then, as Prudence started to squeeze, Elinor pushed her away gently, but firmly.

"That's okay," said Elinor. "I'm not really comfortable with that. I suppose it's okay for you, and all, but I'm just not... interested."

"Oh? Okay," said Prudence. "You know I don't normally hug a lot."

"Look, I'm not judging you," continued Elinor. "I'm fairly broadminded. I supported Adlai Stevenson."

Prudence nodded, though she had no idea what liking Stevenson or Eisenhower, or any politician had to do with feeling uncomfortable with hugging someone.

"No offense."

"Uh, no," said Prudence.

"But that aside," said Elinor, "I'd still like to ask you that favor."

"Anything!" said Prudence. "After all, you're my neighbor, my sister, my friend."

"Thank you. It's nothing really, quite easy, actually...especially for you."

"Oh?"

"Yes, I just need you to go out with my friend. Actually, I suppose he's my boyfriend."

"You want me to go out with your boyfriend?"

"Yes, well, not exactly," said Elinor, "I want you to go out with the two of us, only in public, that is. It's a bit complicated, but it would be a tremendous help to me."

"So, you want me to be your...chaperone?"

"Chaperone! Yes!" Elinor seemed delighted with Prudence's choice of words. "I would have used another word, but yours..."

"Fits better?"

"Much better!"

Prudence thought that an odd distinction, but the thought was driven from her mind as Elinor continued.

"Yes, chaperone, that works! And of course you wouldn't have to do anything, certainly nothing romantic, so you don't have to worry about... well, you know....violating your...preferences."

Prudence nodded, though she wasn't sure which preference those were. Still, they weren't going to be violated, whatever they were, so that was okay.

"You'd just be with us in public," said Elinor, "and if someone saw us, well, if someone sees us, well, it will all work out fine."

Prudence thought this was another strange choice of words. Still, she was relieved Elinor was a good American, and that overrode the parsing of her sentences. She had just pledged herself as a friend, neighbor, and sister. Now she was being asked to act as a chaperone. Could anything be more proper? It was almost old fashioned. Perhaps Elinor and her boyfriend couldn't trust themselves alone.

"Your boyfriend must be crazy about you," said Prudence.

Elinor gave her an odd look.

"I mean, that is, why not?" said Prudence fumbling for an explanation. "I mean, he must be crazy about you. You're a very attractive girl. Very attractive."

Elinor tightened her lips across her teeth and then relaxed into a smile.

"Yes, I suppose so," she said, "and I'm...flattered that you think I'm attractive, but that's that. Do you understand?"

"I...I suppose so," said Prudence, not understanding at all what was what.

"Good!" said Elinor. "Look, everyone has someone, and I have my boyfriend. You know how it is."

Prudence nodded. She did know how it was, or at least she thought she did. Prudence thought back to Rodney in the guard hut, their brief encounter, and their passionate kiss. Her toes curled up inside her loafers, and she felt a warmth swell inside her breast despite the chilled evening air. She didn't dare to mention it to Elinor, even though she was her only friend at the new school, and she was Rodney's sister, or at least Prudence was reasonably sure she was Rodney's sister. Maybe Rodney Potoski wasn't Elinor's brother. There must be plenty of Potoskis in upstate New York, perhaps they were cousins. Maybe they weren't even related. Now she wished she hadn't bolted from the guardhouse. What must Rodney think of her? Perhaps Elinor could put in a good word for her with Rodney, if, that is, she did know him. She could do that after she got to know Elinor better.

"Well," Elinor asked, interrupting Prudence's contemplations, "is it okay?"

"What? Oh, to be a chaperone for you and your boyfriend?" What possible harm could come of such a quaint request? "Sure, why not," said Prudence with a smile. "Why not?"

"Great," said Elinor. "That solves a lot of problems. Come on, it's getting chilly, let's get back to the house."

Prudence rose to her feet and extended a hand to Elinor who stood without assistance.

"Oh, and don't forget to remind me," said Elinor as they started home, "to ask him about picking up that box of his."

"Who?"

"My boyfriend, stupid," said Elinor with a laugh, "it's his box."

In the chill of the early autumn night, Prudence began stumbling in the dark over several "whys not."

– 13 –
The Gulag Wahpeton

W hy not?" Prudence was still brooding over those two words several days later; six little letters that haunted her as she lay sleepless on her bed.

Prudence's "why not" had ushered in even more problems. First was Elinor's short memory. While she had assured Prudence that she would get rid of the crate, Elinor quickly forgot about it. So it remained in Prudence's room. She didn't want to remind Elinor lest she discover what was in the box. It was bad enough that Prudence had found out. She didn't even know the boy. But if Elinor found out, she could get in trouble.

Next, was the matter of being a chaperone. How did one chaperone a communist? It was easy enough to chaperone Elinor. Elinor was now a nice girl, and generally nice girls had nice boyfriends. But a nice girl could be deceived and not know she had a diabolical boyfriend. Perhaps subconsciously Elinor sensed there was something un-American about him. Maybe that's why Elinor felt the need for a chaperone.

The more Prudence thought about it, the more confused she grew: about Elinor's choice of boyfriends; about how to escort a Soviet spy; about whether she should tell Elinor what was in the crate; about whether she should inform the authorities; about whether she should just pack her bag and get out of town. Of one thing, she was certain; in the future, she'd be very careful about using the phrase: "why not."

"Oh, Elinor," sighed Prudence as she eyed the box. "How could you have a boyfriend who was a communist?"

In Russia, people were happily dating communists all the time. She wondered if there was a college student somewhere outside of Minsk, who found that their Soviet sorority sister had a secret cachet of U.S. Constitutions or Hollywood movie magazines. If the Russian secret police found a stash of movie magazines would they haul the owner to Siberia? That wouldn't happen here in America, Prudence concluded.

America didn't have secret police. Though if America had a secret police force, how would she know it? After all, if Prudence knew about them, they couldn't be very secret. But, she reasoned, if America did have a secret police force, it would be the best and most clandestine of them all. Her brief swell of national pride dissolved into a wave of paranoia. Prudence rushed to the window and pulled down the shade.

Prudence turned off the light and sat on her bed. If there was an American secret police force, and if they found the crate, what would they do to her? In Russia, they sent people to Siberia. She knew Americans wouldn't send anyone to Siberia, but they'd have to put them somewhere. After all, everyone has to be someplace. If they wanted a cold place like Siberia, they couldn't beat Buffalo, New York in January. No, thought Prudence, that couldn't be. She's been to Buffalo, and there hadn't been any concentration camps. No, if America had a secret political prison, it would be somewhere remote, like Wahpeton, North Dakota. Well, perhaps not in downtown Wahpeton. That would be a little too obvious. Downtown Wahpeton: home to a grocery store, a hardware store, and the secret prison camp there behind the barbed wire fence.

Prudence realized that she had wandered into the realms of the ludicrous. She turned on the light and admitted that there probably wasn't a gulag in Wahpeton, North Dakota. Still, the crate would have to go. That's all there was to it.

With more than a little difficulty, Prudence slid the box out of her closet and hoisted it off of the floor. She pitched to one side under the crate's cumbersome weight and shifted the load on to her bed. Again, the top of the crate came loose. As if she were a modern-day Pandora, Prudence scrambled to put the top back in place, lest its contents somehow contaminate the campus. Looking around for a hammer and finding none, she settled for a pump with a sturdy two-inch heel, then Prudence banged the lid back into place.

Now, all there was to do was to go across the hall, fetch Elinor, and lug the crate back to her commie boyfriend.

Prudence was about to knock on Elinor's door when she thought better of the plan. It was one thing to give the box back to Elinor; it was another proposition to return it to the boyfriend. Surely, he would be suspicious if two girls came huffing and puffing across the campus with his box of propaganda. He would know that Prudence was on to him. She retreated behind her own door.

So, Prudence couldn't tell Elinor. Nor could she dump it back on Elinor without letting her know its contents. Prudence leaned against the crate and looked to the ceiling in desperation. Then the solution dawned on her. The sorority house had an attic, a big attic full of rafters and spiders and trunks. She had been shown the space when she first moved in. It was where everyone stored their empty luggage. There too, aside from all the current luggage were various crates, barrels, and cartons, long abandoned and unclaimed by previous residents. Prudence eyed the box on her bed. While it seemed huge in the middle of her coverlet, it would be invisible in a musty corner of the attic. She looked the box over on all sides. There were no names, no distinguishing marks on it that would connect it to anyone. If it was ever found, it couldn't be traced. It would look just like all the other abandoned property in the attic.

As she changed into her dungarees and laced up her tennis shoes, Prudence paused. What if Elinor came to claim it? What would she tell her? After a moment's pondering, Prudence concluded that Elinor had already forgotten the box once, she most likely would forget about it again, especially since it wasn't hers and she had no knowledge of its contents. Besides, it would be out of Prudence's room, and people tended not to notice things that weren't there. She would just have to rely on the probability that the crate would disappear to a remote corner of Elinor's mind as effectively as it would vanish into a far corner of the attic.

With minimal grunting and just a few squeaks of the floorboards to betray her Prudence managed to wrest the heavy crate out of her room, down the hall, and up to the attic. It was with great relief, and more than a little sweat, that she finally hoisted the box on to the rough wooden slats that made up the attic floor. Like a burglar in a pantomime, she tiptoed around, shifting trunks with broad movements and gingerly lifting suitcases to make way for the crate. It would be well hidden towards the back, halfway across the attic, behind an old china barrel, and cartons containing old college annuals and costumes from long-forgotten senior frolics. At one point, Prudence nearly stepped between the floor joists on to the lathe and plaster of the ceiling below. She steadied herself at the last minute by grabbing an overhead rafter.

Catching her breath, Prudence examined the unfinished floor, ending as it did halfway to the back of the house, and realized why everything was stored in a cluster around the attic entrance. Only half the attic had been finished. The rest of the area was rows of joists with nothing but a brittle layer of plaster between the floor below.

Retreating from the brink, Prudence arranged the crate on the last two planks of flooring, then meticulously organized the abandoned boxes of yesteryear. Then, working her way back to the staircase, she replaced the more current luggage to where she had found it. After surveying her work from the doorway, Prudence noted that the crate was well-hidden. She nodded with satisfaction, turned out the bare bulb that lit the space, and went back downstairs.

Moving stealthily down her hallway, Prudence realized that she would look suspicious should anyone see her tiptoeing around like that. She wasn't carrying anything incriminating, in fact, for the first time in many days she was in the clear. The crate was hidden, buried for decades at least. It couldn't cause any more trouble.

This last thought occurred to her as she approached Elinor's door. The contents of the crate couldn't hurt Elinor, that was true, but the owner of the crate could. Whether it was a desire to bring the whole mess to an end, or the irrationality that effects a tired mind at a late hour, Prudence couldn't tell, but for whatever reason, she turned the knob to Elinor's door, and finding it unlocked, slid into the darkened room.

– 14 –
The Creeping of the Midnight Sucker

Elinor Potoski was in that cusp between waking and sleep that belong to neither, when she heard her door open and a thin sliver of light cut across the darkness of her bedroom. In the pale light from the hallway, she could make out the profile of Prudence Hoover peering into the room. Elinor narrowed her eyes until she was squinting through her eyelashes, making it look as if Prudence had been swallowed by a giant Venus Fly Trap.

Elinor almost sat up and asked Prudence what she wanted. Since her visitor thought she was asleep, it was just as easy to lay still and find out the unfiltered truth. Prudence had seemed so square. If she sat up and asked her what she wanted, Prudence might give her some vapid excuse. On the other hand, if Elinor watched when Prudence thought she wasn't being watched, Elinor might learn something useful. With this strategy in mind, Elinor started breathing to approximate a deep slumber. She'd used the same trick as a little girl, though it never fooled anyone at home.

Either she'd become a better actress or Prudence was more easily fooled. After stopping for a moment in the doorway, her intruder stepped into the room and closed the door. Elinor didn't have much of value beyond her clothes, and while they weren't any more expensive than Prudence's wardrobe, they were more stylish. Still, she reasoned, Prudence couldn't very well steal her clothes, not while she was living across the hall.

Instead of rummaging through her dresser drawers or her closet, Prudence crept towards the bed. Elinor anticipated to be nudged awake, and she rehearsed in her mind how to play that. Instead, however, Prudence just crouched down beside the bed.

Rather than shake her, Prudence just seemed to be staring at Elinor. Though it was hard to see for sure, the girl looked concerned, almost troubled. Prudence alternatively shook her head and sighed. This went on for what seemed like ten minutes.

Perhaps Prudence figured out why she had been asked to accompany Elinor and her boyfriend on a date. She suppressed a smile as she thought of Prudence's use of the term "chaperone." It was so naïve; just like Prudence. Elinor had thought of other words to describe Prudence's role: "beard," "sucker," "tool," "patsy." No, Elinor decided, "chaperone" was perfect.

Just as Elinor was starting to feel just a little bit sorry for Prudence and her gullibility, the gullible girl did something that almost caused Elinor to forget she was supposed to be asleep. Prudence reached out and stroked Elinor's hair. At first, Elinor wanted to sit up, grab her by the throat, and ask what the hell she was up to. But Elinor caught herself, Prudence had different urges. That was why she was perfect to be the beard. Still, the touch, though soft and barely perceptible, caused Elinor to flinch slightly. She covered up her reaction with some murmuring.

"It's okay, it's okay," whispered Prudence. "It will be all right...I hope."

Elinor settled back into her imitation sleep, as Prudence continued to stroke her hair.

"That's it, sleep," continued Prudence, "at least you can sleep. You don't know, do you?"

Elinor suppressed a smirk. Oh, she knew, she knew too well, she thought.

"It's okay," said Prudence, "it'll be all right."

All right, thought Elinor, what was this girl was talking about now? She felt Prudence's hand lift and could hear Prudence creeping back towards the door.

Through squinted eyes, Elinor saw Prudence reach for the doorknob, before turning and looking back at the girl in the bed.

"It will be okay," said Prudence softly, "it will be fine...once we get rid of that boyfriend of yours."

– 15 –
Admissions of a Cake Shaver

With the crate stashed in the attic life almost returned to normal for Prudence. Her new friend wasn't a Russian agent, but she was unwittingly dating one. Elinor didn't know she had a boyfriend problem. Prudence would have a boyfriend problem if she had a boyfriend. She couldn't stop thinking about Rodney Potoski. It was just one kiss, one kiss that curled her toes. She lay awake at night; the mere recollection of their one kiss caused the balls of her feet to tingle with a delicious, maddening itch. That itch sent her weak imagination soaring into flights of fancy that culminated in a wedding ceremony, and a split-level house complete with two children…a boy first and then a girl. In the sanity of the morning light, Prudence realized that one kiss from a boy in a security hut was a flimsy foundation for split-level castles in the air.

Rodney probably didn't even think of her, or if he did, he thought she was some floozy who kissed strangers and then ran off into the night. Perhaps it would help that Prudence was going to act as a chaperone for Rodney's sister, that is if they were brother and sister.

Prudence's wandering and pondering that morning led her to the history building. She looked up at the epigram chiseled over the entrance: "Learning Something is the Portal to Knowing Something."

Prudence grimaced. She already knew too much, and what she had learned had been the doorway to her current dilemma. Then, she realized that was also the building where Associate Professor Bascomb had his office. His offer of guidance bubbled to the surface of her thoughts. She could use some of that now.

Scurrying up the steps, Prudence rearranged the problem in her mind. She couldn't admit that she was chaperoning a girl and a communist. If she did that she may have to name names. Instead, she would say she received a letter from a cousin at a similar college across the state, no, in another state. This cousin would have innocently fallen into a similar set of circumstances. Yes, that would work, she assured herself. Professor

Bascomb would have no idea that it was Prudence who was caught in the dangerous situation. She found the door to Bascomb's office, turned the knob, and proceeded to hit her nose against the door. It was stuck. Putting her full weight into the effort, Prudence rammed against the door and stumbled into the middle of the outer office.

"Ballet classes are somewhere else," said a woman's voice. "This is the history building."

Prudence spun around. There, sitting behind a desk was a small, neatly dressed woman. Her hair, which had traces of gray on the temples, was done up in a short permanent wave. Prudence tried to speak, but her mouth dropped open.

"And," said the woman with a slight smile, "it's not the ichthyology department, either."

"The what?" Prudence croaked.

"Fish, the study of fish. With your kisser hanging open like that you look like a large-mouthed bass."

"Oh, yes, of course," grinned Prudence. "How rude of me, I'm sorry."

"Skip it, honey. Getting the fish face is better than getting the fish eye."

"Yes, of course, yes, it is. How kind of you to say so." Prudence nervously fingered the buttons of her cardigan.

"So?" said the woman, "if it isn't dancing, and it isn't bass, what is it?"

"What is what?"

"So, what the…what do you want?" The woman snapped so sharply that Prudence pulled off her button. It clattered to the floor.

"Oh," gasped Prudence clambering after the button, "how clumsy of me."

"I'm sure you didn't come in here looking for an argument, so I won't give you one."

Prudence looked up at the woman who was eyeing her in a most disconcerting way.

"Look," continued the woman, "don't get your panties in a knot, honey. Sit down before you rip up all your clothes and I have to call the vice squad."

Prudence grabbed the button from under the chair in front of the desk and then slid into the seat.

"There, that wasn't so hard," she said. "Now, what's up?"

"Professor Bascomb?" mewed Prudence.

"Not guilty."

"Excuse me?"

"I'm not him."

"Yes, I, I know. I'm in one of the professor's history classes."

"I bet you are," she said with a wink. Prudence was even more confused, and wondered what kind of a secretary behaved in such a way, and if Bertram Bascomb knew about it. "Well, you can see he's not here unless he's a contortionist and is crammed into that filing cabinet.

But I'm sure you know how to get a hold of him." She leaned across the desk and whispered: "Just be careful, okay?"

This last admonition, punctuated with a cautionary nod, only increased Prudence's bewilderment.

"I'm, I'm sorry," she said, "but he told me I could find him here. I don't know of any other place, other than the classroom, of course, and my next class with him isn't until late tomorrow."

The woman sat up and adopted a more professional demeanor.

"Oh, so you really are one of his students."

"Yes, I am. I thought I said that."

"Yes," she smiled, "yes you did. And you're a student student."

"I suppose so," agreed Prudence, not exactly knowing the distinction between a "student" and a "student student."

"And you wanted to ask him something about your classwork."

"Yes, well, no, not exactly. It's of a more personal nature."

The woman's left eyebrow shot up. "Personal?"

"Yes," said Prudence, before correcting herself. "Oh, no, I don't mean it's personal with Professor Bascomb." She felt her cheeks glowing bright red. "I wouldn't dare imply anything improper with the Professor."

"No, no, of course, you wouldn't," agreed the woman.

"Or imply anything that would reflect negatively on his behavior."

"No, of course not," said the woman, this time with a slight upturn to the corners of her mouth, as if she had just recalled something amusing.

"I had a personal problem," said Prudence. "It's not really my personal problem. That is, it's a problem of a friend, but the friend doesn't know she has the problem. And I normally wouldn't bother a professor with this sort of thing, but you see I just transferred here from another school, and I don't really have anyone else I can talk to about it, except my one friend, and I don't want to talk to her about it, because it's her problem, only she doesn't know it's her problem. And Professor Bascomb told me that if I ever needed to talk to him about anything, he would listen. Oh but…" Prudence remembered that she had planned to make this all about some fictitious cousin, but now that veil had been lifted. "I mean, never mind."

The secretary bared her teeth in a sympathetic manner that bordered on a smile; either that or she was getting ready to bite someone.

"So, you got something that's bothering you, and you trust the Professor?"

"Oh, yes," said Prudence. "I mean he's very compassionate, in an entirely proper way, of course."

"Of course…entirely proper."

"And he's very wise. At least, he seems very wise, that is, I'm sure he's very wise."

"And good looking?" asked the secretary.

Prudence could once more feel the blood rushing to her cheeks. "I, I don't think that really matters, does it?"

"No," smiled the woman, "no, of course not, dear. Hmmmm."

They sat there for what became a protracted silence. After about a minute, Prudence began thinking about how long they had gone without speaking. She started wracking her brain for something to say, but after the odd responses she had already received from the secretary, Prudence was afraid to broach any new topics.

For her part, the secretary seemed content to study Prudence. She seemed to be looking at Prudence in a way she could only describe as "pondering." She looked like a woman examining a lamp in a shop. The woman appeared to be imagining Prudence in different settings. How would she look in this room, on that table? Would she fit the décor with a more flattering shade upon her head? Under this scrutiny, Prudence had nothing to do but sit there and be scrutinized. After a few minutes of this, she began to perspire. Prudence had been doing a lot of perspiring lately. She hadn't perspired at all at her previous college. She doubted that she had inadvertently transferred to a sweatier college. No, it was the stress of everything happening that had her glands all juiced up. And now, she was sitting here being examined like she was some piece of *objet d'art*. Finally, after several minutes of scrutiny, the woman spoke.

"What do you like, Dearie?"

It was such a personal question, from such an unexpected source, and after so prolonged a silence that for a moment, Prudence wondered if she had imagined it. For a second, she just looked at the secretary, and then leaned forward to confirm that she indeed had heard something. The woman repeated the question.

"I, uh," Prudence leaned back again in the chair and wondered what kind of information this woman was seeking with such an open-ended question. She decided to answer it in a manner appropriate to the academic setting.

"I, um, I'm an English major," she said.

"So, you study literature, and that sort of thing, eh," said the woman. "Going to be a writer?"

"A teacher," said Prudence.

The woman nodded in a vaguely approving manner. "Now," she continued, "what do you like? Unless that is, you like teaching kids."

"I don't actually know, actually," said Prudence.

"Actually actually, huh?" the woman nodded again.

"I mean, that I haven't actually taught anyone yet..."

"Actually."

"I suppose, that is, it's a good career...teaching grammar..."

"But it's not what you're crazy about, is it?" said the woman.

Prudence felt herself blush. "It's a fine...that is, it's a very noble..."

"MRS," said the woman cutting her off.

"Excuse me?"

"You're going for your MRS degree."

"MRS? Oh, you mean I'm here to get married," said Prudence. She squirmed in her seat and then pulled the hem of her skirt over her knees, though they were already covered. "I suppose if I met the right boy..."

"You'd give up your noble career aspirations of teaching runny-nosed kids and start making some of your own," said the woman. "Well, don't worry about it, kid. You're not the first co-ed to come to college to get a man, and I doubt you'll be the last. But that's not what I'm asking you, girl. I want to know what's burning below the surface?"

"Below?" Prudence looked at the floor then looked up.

The woman thumped her own slight bosom. "Here! Here! I mean what's driving you, girl?"

Prudence sat there bewildered for a moment. She half-considered saying the question was improper, and none of the secretary's business, but it was asked so forcefully she couldn't ignore it.

"Well," said Prudence trying to sound assertive but failing by half, "I do have my motivations. My parents raised me not to be a burden to others, that is, to make my own way in the world. I study hard. I get good grades. I'm considerate. I try to be kind..."

"Save that for your Miss America speech," said the woman. "What's really driving you? What do you really want?"

Prudence sat there as if her jaw was unhinged.

"Look," said the woman, "almost everybody wants something else, deep, deep inside. Oh, they say all the niceties in public, but deep down, living somewhere they can't even tell, there it is...a yearning, an ache for something, an itch they can't quite reach. When you're out in public, you keep your pleats nice and starched, prim, proper, but it's there. You keep a lid on it, and you take it out of your box when you're all alone, and it's peaceful and still and you play with it. Maybe while your pretty little head is resting on the pillow, after the lights are out, and just before you drop off to sleep, you visit it. You nudge it, you stroke it, and you whisper sweet little words of encouragement to it. 'Yes, my pet,' you say, 'someday we'll let you out,' and then you'll have it. You'll have everything you really want. Everybody, most everybody has that little thing inside that keeps them going, that helps you put up with all the everyday crapola that gets hefted at them every day. 'Someday, someday,' you say, and we all say it. Right, honey?"

Prudence didn't think her mouth could have opened any wider, but then she didn't think secretaries could be so bold with perfect strangers. She felt her jaw moving, trying to form some response. What was in the deep recesses of her soul? She had told the secretary, or rather the secretary guessed that Prudence's real motivation was to find a nice husband and get married. And she would like another kiss from Rodney Potoski, but she could barely admit that to herself. Apparently, those weren't deep or dark enough in the corners of Prudence's mind, or else the woman wouldn't have probed further. What was hiding inside of her? She hardly knew what to say in reply to such an odd question.

"I...I..." she groped for something, some word, some point of passion.

The secretary leaned forward, her tongue moistening her lower lip, like a thirsting soul anticipating a drop of cool water. She nodded encouragement for Prudence to continue.

"I..." Prudence reached deep, deep, inside. Suddenly, a long-forgotten childhood incident sprang to mind. For some odd reason, it was the only answer she could think of for the woman's pop quiz. "I...I like cake!"

Prudence exhaled as if some long resident demon had been exorcised.

"Cake!" said the woman.

Prudence bowed her head and nodded. It was her only crime of passion.

"When I was a little girl, I stole a piece of chocolate cake from under the cake dome. It was just a sliver, but it was so good and so tempting. My mother found the knife in the sink, but it was so thin a slice that she couldn't even tell it was missing."

The secretary slumped back in her seat as if the revelation had disappointed her, but then, she sat up again, and a sweet, sympathetic look crossed over her face.

"And I'm the first person you ever told," she said. "Is that so, dear?"

Prudence nodded her head without raising her eyes and drew a quivering intake of breath.

The woman gave Prudence a curious little smile.

"That's okay, Honey," said the secretary. "And if I can let you in on a little secret...I like cake, too!"

– 16 –
Here's Another Clue for You All, The Commie Is Paul

Usually, Prudence Hoover liked surprises. Christmas Eve was her favorite day of the year. It was a day of anticipation, a day ripe with possibilities. The wrapped gifts under the tree could contain almost anything. The next morning, the opened packages devolved into just a new scarf or a bottle of drugstore perfume. But before that, they were all potential, all wonderment, all magic.

Surprises weren't supposed to happen in late September. It wasn't the time for them; vacations were over; school years had begun. The weather was neither summer sizzle nor autumn crisp. It was indeed, a lukewarm time. Though she had no way of knowing as she sat in the visitor's parlor of her sorority house, tonight would be filled with surprises; none of them welcome.

She was sitting there alone, picking pills of lint from her best wool skirt when Elinor entered. She glanced at her wristwatch and then at Prudence.

"I'm early," said Prudence.

Elinor agreed.

"I'm always early for appointments," said Prudence.

"It's not an appointment," said Elinor.

Prudence nodded, and then added: "No, it's not, it's more than that."

"It is?"

"It's a responsibility," Prudence forced a smile on to her face. It was a very grave responsibility, but Elinor didn't know that. She didn't know she was dating some subversive.

"Oh," said Elinor and sat down next to Prudence.

They sat in silence for a moment. Prudence eyed Elinor's outfit which was nice, but more casual than her own.

"You look nice," Prudence said. Elinor looked at her for a moment. Maybe Elinor didn't believe her. Maybe Elinor felt that her outfit wasn't as nice as Prudence's. Was the chaperone allowed to look nicer than the girl actually on the date?

"I mean, you look very, very nice," Prudence added, "I...really like the way you look tonight."

"Uh, yeah...okay, thanks," she said and then for some reason scooted to the opposite end of the sofa.

Prudence suppressed a sigh and wished she knew more about chaperoning.

The sound of the mantel clock ticking pervaded their silence like a jackbooted sentry marching back and forth. Prudence looked down at her fingernails and then over at Elinor's. Elinor had painted hers. Prudence was relieved that she only had a clear coat of polish on hers. At least her fingers wouldn't outshine Elinor's. She glanced back at Elinor's fingernails. They were red. Red! Would that encourage Elinor's boyfriend politically? She glanced at her watch.

"Uh, your hands," said Prudence.

Elinor looked down at her hands and then back at Prudence. "My hands? What about them?"

"They're all wrong," said Prudence. "I don't mean your hands. You have nice hands, very lovely hands. I meant your fingernails."

"What's wrong with them?"

"Nothing, nothing," said Prudence. "Only I think a different color might look even nicer."

"A different..."

"Pink," said Prudence. "I have some pink polish upstairs. We could give you a quick coat. It wouldn't take a minute."

"I don't have time to redo my nails."

"I could do them for you," said Prudence scooting towards Elinor. "I'm ever so quick..."

"They'd have to dry..."

"I...I could blow on them for you," offered Prudence.

Elinor stood up and stepped away from the sofa. "No, really, they're fine. I don't...that is, they're fine. You don't have to blow on...that is, you don't need to do my nails. Besides, my boyfriend likes red."

"I'm not surprised," said Prudence.

"What?"

"I mean, red is a popular color...even in the United States." Prudence laughed nervously. Elinor raised one eyebrow and took another step away.

Great, thought Prudence, Elinor's giving me odd looks and must be thinking I've lost my mind. If only I could explain who this boyfriend really is and what he's up to.

Prudence sighed. Everything was going wrong. She hadn't been able to see Professor Bascomb for advice, and his odd secretary contributed nothing aside from some questions about cake.

Prudence glanced over at Elinor as she looked out of the window. In profile Prudence could see the resemblance between Elinor and her brother, Rodney; that is if they were brother and sister. She still hadn't been able to broach the subject with Elinor. Once Prudence helped Elinor out of the problem she didn't know she had, Elinor would be so grateful she would want to introduce Prudence to her brother; that is if Rodney was her brother.

Who was she kidding? Rodney Potoski only kissed her once and that by accident. And then she ran away. It had all been going well before that; before that other guard came in and said Rodney's last name. Perhaps, Prudence thought, perhaps she could go back and talk to that other guard. What had his name been? Something like…

"Rocher, Paul Rocher." Prudence, who had been looking down, heard a man's voice and saw a hand extended into her field of vision.

"Pardon?" said Prudence. She looked up, and her mouth dropped.

"Paul Rocher," repeated the man.

"Yes, that was the name," said Prudence. "I mean, yes, that's your name, isn't it? But what are you doing here?"

It was the security guard that she had met that night. But he wasn't wearing his uniform. Maybe he was working undercover. Maybe he was there to arrest Elinor's boyfriend for espionage or subversion.

"What do you think he's doing here?" said Elinor.

Prudence looked at Elinor. Then she looked up at Paul Rocher, his hand still extended. He smiled at her. Prudence smiled back and shook his hand.

"I'm your date," said Paul.

"My…"

"Or at least, you're going on our date…" he nodded toward Elinor.

"At last…" muttered Elinor.

"Oh," said Prudence, smiling. She understood now. Paul Rocher was Elinor's boyfriend. For a moment a wave of relief overspread Prudence. Elinor was dating the security guard, not the communist. Then a stronger, less naïve realization intruded on her mind. Paul Rocher, the security guard, and the communist were the same person. It made perfect sense. If Elinor's boyfriend were a subversive, then he would want to subvert; and where better to subvert a system than from inside of it? No wonder there had been such hostility between Rodney and Paul Rocher. Rodney must know about Rocher.

"Oh!" repeated Prudence, though this time, the word was pregnant with realization and dread.

"Is there something wrong," asked Paul.

"I doubt it. Whatever it is, I'm sure it doesn't matter," said Elinor grabbing her coat. "Come on, let's go."

She pulled on Paul's arm, and they headed for the doorway and then turned. Prudence was still sitting on the sofa, just gaping at them.

"Are you sure she's okay?" asked Paul.

"Sure, sure," said Elinor, "she's just…different. Come on Prudence!"

Prudence slowly rose to her feet.

"Hey, I remember you," said Paul, pointing at her. He laughed.

"Remember her?" said Elinor. "Do you two know each other?"

"Yes," said Paul.

"No!" snapped Prudence.

"Well, which is it," asked Elinor.

"I, uh, I don't think I know him," said Prudence.

"Well, I remember you," said Paul, "it was in the guard shack, you…" He broke into a hearty laugh. "Oh, that's rich, that's a good one…"

Elinor looked at Paul, then at Prudence, and then back at Paul. She punctuated the second glance with a punch on his arm.

"What's so funny?"

"That she's your beard…" he said.

"Beard?" said Prudence. "Is that another word for 'chaperone' used by you...security guards?'" She had almost said "communist."

"You didn't tell me you knew my boyfriend was a security guard," said Elinor.

Prudence almost replied that she had enough trouble not telling her that he was a traitor. Instead, she just stammered and shrugged her shoulders.

Paul leaned over and whispered something in Elinor's ear.

As a chaperone, Prudence almost pointed out that it was impolite to whisper, but then she didn't expect good manners from a revolutionary. Still, Prudence didn't want to know what he whispered. She already had more secrets than she could handle.

– 17 –
The Thespian Who Kissed
a Rutabaga

I waited all these years for this?" Elinor muttered.
For their first public date, Paul had brought her to The Torrid Orchid. Everyone on campus knew about the Orchid, or "The Ork," for short.

It wasn't really a public place. Technically, it was open to the public. You just couldn't prove it once you went past the purple metal door to the club, at least not with your eyes. The only thing clearly seen in the joint was a bare light bulb hanging over the cash register.

Slow jazz music played in the background, as cigarette smoke and the faint hint of sweat struggled for air supremacy.

Elinor glanced over at Paul. In the dim light, she could see his face, but couldn't see his expression. She felt a jab in her side, and for a second she thought she was being mugged.

"Is this where we're going," whispered Prudence in Elinor's ear, "I mean, is this where your date is?"

Elinor, despite her qualms over the atmosphere, didn't feel like making any excuses to Prudence. She agreed this was their destination.

"Oh," mewed Prudence. There was a short pause followed by another jab. "Do they have a ladies' room?"

In the faint light, Elinor couldn't tell whether or not this minimalist establishment had bathrooms. She was about to say she didn't know when a door opened to their left, allowing a shaft of light to pierce the darkness. A young woman emerged from a small room with tiled walls.

"There's the ladies' room," muttered Elinor with a jerk of her head.

She felt Prudence clutch her elbow. Reflexively she pulled herself free.

"Do you want to…" said Prudence.

"No," snapped Elinor. This place was enough of a passion pit without going to the ladies' room with someone of Prudence's persuasion.

"Are you sure," said Prudence. Her voice almost sounded as if it were pleading.

"Look, you're the chaperone for our date, bathrooms not included. We'll wait for you here."

Prudence nodded and slunk off through the door.

When they were alone, Elinor drove her fingernail into Paul's side.

"Thanks a lot," she said.

"For what?"

"Our first date in public and you bring me to the Black Hole of Calcutta!"

"Shh, not so loud," he said, though she had been whispering. "I just thought we'd ease into being seen, get used to the beard."

"You're a coward, but you're probably right."

"And from the look of your beard..." said Paul. He was suppressing a snicker.

"Yeah, well, beggars can't be choosers," she said. "Besides which, she's safe. I still don't know why you find her so amusing."

"That's because you didn't see who I saw her kissing."

"I don't want to hear what you do on your raids..." said Elinor imaging Paul breaking up some girl on girl necking in a secluded nook.

"Raids? I don't do raids. We don't have raids," said Paul. "No, I saw your beard..."

"I wish you'd stop calling her a beard, she thinks she's our chaperone..."

"Beard or chaperone," said Paul, "I caught her in the guard hut kissing your brother."

Elinor struggled to process that information. Finally, she answered: "Rodney?"

"Do you have another brother?"

"No."

"Well, then," he said, "based on that evidence, it must have been Rodney."

Elinor thought another moment. "It couldn't have been."

"No? Why not?"

"Because, well, because Prudence doesn't like that sort of thing."

"Kissing?"

"She might like kissing, all right," said Elinor, "but not kissing boys."

"What does she like kissing then, rutabagas?"

Elinor shot him a sarcastic expression which was probably lost in the dim lighting. "Girls," she finally said, "girls, Prudence likes kissing girls."

Paul thought for a moment. "Your brother's not a girl."

"No shit," said Elinor.

Paul stood pondering for another moment. "Well, that it explains it then."

"That explains what?"

"Why your beard, uh, chaperone, what's her name, Prudence, that's why she ran out of the building like she was fired out of a cannon."

"When?"

"When I walked in and found them kissing," said Paul with a laugh. "Yeah, that explains it. It was some kiss, too. It must run in the family. You Pollocks sure have something going there."

"Don't call me a Pollock, you Garlic Frog."

Paul laughed again and shook his head. "Leave it to old Roddy to plant one on a real thespian."

Elinor punched him. Not for Rodney, or Prudence, but for bringing her to this seedy joint.

"What?" asked Paul, still laughing. Apparently, she hadn't hit him hard enough.

"Shut up," said Elinor. "I don't want her to hear you. Besides, she's doing us a favor."

"Did you know about her...preferences?"

"Of course I did you jerk," she said. "I just told you, didn't I?"

"Oh, right, yeah, you did."

"That's why she perfect for the beard," said Elinor. "She looks all prim and normal, but she couldn't care less about you romantically. If Rodney should happen to see the three of us in public, I can say I'm the chaperone, and she's the date. After all, she does live across the hall from me."

"Yeah," agreed Paul, "and if your brother sees us together that'll be a good laugh on him."

"How do you figure that?"

"Because I'm going out with the girl who ran away from him," he explained. "I win, he loses. Perfect!"

"Oh, grow up, Paulie!" said Elinor. "Don't you think this has gone on long enough? Don't ruin everything with your feud. I've been waiting for a long time."

"I'm sorry, I tried to be as quick as possible," said Prudence, suddenly appearing at Elinor's side.

"What? Oh, no, not you, I didn't mean you, Prudence."

Paul reached out to take Elinor's hand. She pushed it away and stuck Prudence between the two of them, and then signaled as best she could that he needed to remember their roles. Extending his arm around both girls, Paul shepherded them towards the bare bulb and the cash register. A short man with a long cigarette dangling from his lower lip greeted them if you could call his grunt a greeting.

"Three, please," said Paul softly.

"Huh?"

"Three."

The man looked at Paul and then at Prudence, and finally at Elinor before returning to Paul.

"What are ya, kidding, Bub?"

"No," assured Paul. "There are three of us."

The man rubbed the side of his nose, apparently in consternation. "Well, that's a new one." Then he grabbed a flashlight from under the counter along with some small cards that seemed similar to menus and nodded for them to follow him. The man glanced back to make sure they were following him and muttered: "He could do worse."

Keeping his flashlight pointed down as a lamp unto their feet and precious little else, the mangy maître de led them past various tables where murmurs of close encounters could be heard but not quite seen. Elinor wondered how far back the room went. Was the apparent size of the room just an illusion enforced by the fact that they couldn't see anything? Or was it that their guide was winding them back and forth around the same tables. It was impossible to tell, the only landmarks being the yellow linoleum which they trod.

It was with no small relief when they stopped, and their guide muttered: "Here ya go."

He flashed his light on to a small booth against a wall, presumably the back wall of the room. The booth was semicircular in shape with a table shoved into it. As best as Elinor could tell the booth was covered in some shiny black material while the table was protected in a similar substance, only in red.

The man threw three of the cards of fare on the table. He threw them a limp gesture that was either a salute or a consignment to their fate and then left. As his flashlight retreated towards the distant star over the cash register, Elinor could see the reflection of eyes of nearby patrons, looking more like raccoons than customers.

It was only after he left that Elinor's eyes began adjusting to her surroundings. She could see a tiny light on the table courtesy of a small battery powered lamp. Squinting through the surrounding darkness, she began to notice similar lights on the tables around them. "I felt more public back in the boiler room," said Elinor.

"Pardon?" said Prudence.

"Nothing."

"Well, let's sit down," said Paul. Though it was impossible to tell how many patrons were around them, the atmosphere compelled them to speak in whispers.

Prudence sat down on the end of the booth, and Elinor slid around next to her to occupy the middle position. Paul just stood there.

"What," asked Elinor, "aren't you going to sit down?"

"I think I should be in the middle," he said, "don't you think so?"

Elinor thought a moment and agreed. While she doubted that anyone could see them in the darkness of The Torrid Orchid, having Paul between them would support their cover story.

"You're right," said Elinor sliding out of the booth. As she did so, she felt Prudence's hand clutching hers.

"Don't leave me," said Prudence with desperation in her voice.

"I'll be right over there," assured Elinor, jerking her hand free. Paul slid into the middle spot of the booth, and then Elinor sat down.

That was another good reason for having Paul in the middle, thought Elinor. Prudence was a nice enough girl, but Elinor didn't want Prudence taking advantage of the low lighting and groping her under the table.

"There, that's better," said Elinor settling into her seat. "Girl, Boy, Girl." Though to herself, she thought it was more like: "Girl, Boy, Kiki."

– 18 –
Too Much Dark, Then Too Much Light, Then Too Much Black

"Girl, Boy, Girl?"

Prudence squinted through the darkness of the seedy club at Elinor and Paul Rocher. It was more like: "Girl, Communist, Girl."

Prudence tried to smile despite the situation, but it felt as if her mouth were contorted into a grotesque grimace. Prudence looked around but could see nothing saving for the faint pinpoints of lights at other tables. The club's atmosphere was stifling. She felt like a firefighter in the middle of a burning building without an oxygen tank. Actually, a fire was a good analogy, since all around Prudence imagined smoldering bodies, many trying to combust spontaneously.

As she squirmed in the booth, her bare forearms peeled away from the leatherette upholstery with a tawdry sucking sound. Other soft sucking sounds emanated from the surrounding booths, though not courtesy of the leatherette. Even worse, she was there sitting next to a subversive. Paul Rocher seemed nice. He looked clean cut. He didn't have even a hint of an accent, but that made him all the more dangerous. She wondered if he had a switchblade at the ready if she dared to expose his real agenda.

Prudence picked up the menu card and immediately wished she hadn't. It was even stickier than the upholstery. In the light of the table's ten-watt red bulb, she could barely make out the selections offered: beer and cheese sandwiches (untoasted). The sparseness of the menu didn't seem to matter to anyone else in the place.

Glancing over at Elinor and Paul, Prudence saw they were kissing. She looked away for a moment. As their chaperone, she could ignore a brief kiss. After a modest interval, she looked back and saw that the kiss not only continued but seemed to be accelerating. Inexperienced as she was in the field of chaperoning, Prudence still thought she needed to get the couple's attention and encourage a more wholesome climate.

"Ahem," said Prudence, clearing her throat and waiting for them to look in her direction. They continued snogging. She repeated the maneuver with the same lack of response.

"This is a very interesting place," she finally said in a voice loud enough not to be ignored.

"SHUT UP!" demanded a voice from somewhere in the darkness. The command was accompanied by several sibilant noises encouraging silence.

"Sorry," said Prudence in a softer voice, though she wasn't sure to whom she was apologizing.

Rocher leaned over and muttered in her ear. "I'd keep it down if I were you; if you know what I mean."

Prudence nodded, though she wasn't sure what he meant. It could have been a threat.

His words were accompanied by a nudge. It wasn't a sharp nudge. It might have been made by his index finger, though it could have been the butt end of a gun. Prudence thought of that crate. Perhaps he knew she had it. Maybe he had other big wooden crates, empty ones, just the right size for the body of a girl who didn't know when to keep her mouth shut.

Prudence sat there, the only sound coming from the osculating of nearby couples. Beads of sweat started forming on Prudence's person as she contemplated her next move. Her next move? Well, for starters, it would help to be a little further away from Paul Rocher.

"Um, excuse me," said Prudence meekly, "but think I want to sit next to Elinor."

"What did she say?" Elinor asked Paul.

Prudence repeated her request a little more assertively. Her assertiveness resulted in a hail of shushes from the surrounding patrons.

"Keep it down," warned Paul. He sounded irritated.

"I want to sit next to Elinor," mewed Prudence, "over there, next to her, on the other side…"

"What difference…" began Rocher.

"Shh," said Elinor to Paul, "she's that way, you know." Elinor leaned across to Prudence. "It's okay; he won't do anything unless he has to."

Rather than calm Prudence's nerves that made matters worse. What would Rocher not do unless he had to? And how did Elinor know the desperate lengths to which her boyfriend would go? Elinor didn't know he was a communist, did she? Maybe she did. Maybe she was being coerced into silence. The uneasiness pervading Prudence's mind grew. It was as if the walls of the club, which she couldn't even see, were closing in on her. She had to escape somehow. Prudence chose the only course of action she could think of: she shouted.

"LEAVE ME ALONE. I DON'T KNOW ANYTHING!" She screamed.

"I WISH YOU KNEW HOW TO SHUT UP, YA LOUDMOUTH BITCH!" One voice bellowed from the darkness. Other, less polite epithets, quickly followed.

"Sorry, sorry," squeaked Prudence, and she tried to scoot as far away as possible from Rocher. Her skirt bunched up beneath her causing her leg to catch on the tacky covering of the booth. The resulting sound approximated that of flatulence and elicited more rude remarks from nearby guests. Prudence just slid down further in the booth and almost wished for a fatal wound from Rocher if for no other reason to bring her life to a merciful end.

Then, just as she was trying to decide between death by embarrassment or by revolutionary, a glimmer of hope sudden shone from beneath the club's lone 60-watt light bulb. There, standing beside the proprietor of The Torrid Orchid was Rodney Potoski.

Prudence hadn't seen him in person since the night she met him, though she had cherished the memory of him each time she recalled their kiss. Now, here he was in her hour of need. Had he known she was in danger? That was unlikely. He had no idea how she felt about him. As far as Rodney knew, Prudence was a girl who fell backward into his guard shack, fell frontwards into his lips, and then ran out again like a frightened rabbit. He couldn't know that she was there. But he was there, and she was greatly relieved.

Maybe, she thought, he was there on a date. Her heart sunk, not only that he would have a date with another girl, but that he would bring a girl to this passion pit.

As she watched, it became clear that Rodney was alone. He wasn't even looking around, like a boy waiting for his date. Instead, Rodney was trying to talk with the club's proprietor, but that man seemed uninterested.

Prudence glanced over at Elinor and Rocher. They were whispering in each other's ears and occasionally in each other's mouths. She looked back to the front of the club. Rodney was still there. Now she noticed something in his hands that looked like a chart. He was trying to explain something to the manager who was still not interested.

A thought occurred to Prudence that made sense of it all. Elinor was dating a communist, Paul Rocher. As part of his nefarious scheme, Rocher had wrangled a high-ranking position in the campus security force. Rodney was also on the force, reporting to Paul Rocher. While Rodney had nothing but animosity for Rocher, his sister was dating him. It was clear. Rodney and Elinor Potoski were government agents working the "Rocher case." Elinor softened him up on the one side while Rodney kept up the pressure on the other. Now, Rodney was here backing up Elinor. Perhaps this was the night of the big arrest.

But, thought Prudence, why did she have to be there? As far as anyone knew, Prudence was oblivious to Rocher's schemes. Wait, yes, she had stumbled into both their lives and...Prudence wracked her brain...of course! She was there as a witness.

Rodney was still up front with his chart. He was pointing out into the darkness, no doubt indicating to the owner how the building was surrounded by government agents. For some reason, the club's proprietor still appeared bored with it all. Probably raids on The Torrid Orchid were routine.

Now that she knew his true identity, Rodney took on even greater stature. He wasn't just a nice boy who was a good accidental kisser, now he was a government agent, one of the really good guys. She thought of his cover story and suppressed a giggle. Window designer, what was the word he had used? Oh, yes, "fenestrator!" He had seemed so passionate about windows that it was now obviously a put-on. How could anyone be so enthusiastic about windows?

While she was admiring Rodney in action up at the front of the club, Prudence heard a gasp. She turned to see Elinor, no longer gazing at Rocher, but also looking toward the cash register.

"Paul!" Elinor mumbled as best she could, her mouth full of his lips. "PAUL!" She repeated, now having completely unlocked lips with him.

"What?" snapped Rocher. Elinor nodded towards the front of the club. "Oh," he said indifferently.

"Is that all you can say?" said Elinor.

Rocher rolled his eyes. "Look," he said, "he can't see us, can he? He's standing in the light, and we're sitting in the dark." He turned to Prudence. "Hey, you...Penelope..."

"Prudence," corrected Elinor.

"Okay, Prudence," he said, "How long's he been there?"

"Huh?"

"Him, the guy standing there, under the light, how long's he been there?"

"I, uh," Prudence, "I guess a minute or two..."

Rocher turned back to Elinor. "See, nothing to worry about. Besides, he can't see us. He's standing under that light. He can't see us as long as nobody..."

Prudence guessed that Rocher's next words would have been something about someone turning on the lights. But before Rocher could complete his sentence, someone did turn on the lights, and that someone was Rodney Potoski. With a casual flick of his finger on a nearby light switch, the interior of the Torrid Orchid Club was flooded with illumination, destroying the scant mystique the darkness lent it.

The couples packed into The Orchid shielded their eyes and shouted for an immediate return of their cloak of darkness. If they had been cockroaches, they all would have scurried into the nearest holes. Prudence looked around and saw several people she recognized from around campus, including several instructors enjoying tête-à-têtes with their students. Aside from this breach of propriety, she was most astonished to find how small the club was, and how many bodies were stuffed inside it like chestnuts in her mother's Christmas turkey. Unlike those chestnuts, however, the club's patrons began to holler in protest.

Rodney seemed oblivious to it all, as Prudence expected a cool, controlled government agent would be. But instead of blowing a whistle to calling in a phalanx of agents, Rodney took advantage of the light to unroll a large piece of paper and started making broad gestures toward the far wall. Prudence was confused. The owner of the club wasn't a bit confused. He was extremely annoyed as the introduction of light transformed his establishment from a dusky rendezvous to a smelly room with dirty walls. He switched the lights back off. The crowd settled down, but only momentarily, since Rodney flipped them back on again.

The tumult rose again, though Rodney could be heard shouting over them, to the owner: "If you had some windows on that wall and that wall it would really brighten the place up..."

"That's the last thing anyone wants..." the owner shouted back as he struggled to turn the lights off, only now Rodney was blocking his attempts in order to show off his designs.

"...And the people outside could see in...."

"Nobody in here wants anyone looking in. Hell," shouted the owner, "they don't even want to be seen by the people they're with!"

"...a few well-placed, well-designed pieces of plate glass would increase the..."

Prudence wondered if perhaps Rodney wasn't carrying his cover story too far. Then she wondered if maybe it wasn't a cover story after all, and Rodney wasn't a clever G-man, but rather a goofy window fanatic. Up at the front of the club, Rodney froze in mid-sentence as he stopped looking at the far wall and suddenly recognized the people sitting in front of it. It was a look akin to realizing that the forest was comprised of trees.

Prudence looked at Rodney, whose mouth now hung open. His focus was not on her, but to her left. She turned and saw Rocher, whose mouth was also agape. Then Rocher grabbed Prudence's shoulders with both hands, smashed his lips into hers, nearly smothering her with his body. Prudence's eyes widened, though all she could see were his eyes – one closed, the other squinting off towards the front of the club. Her ears were filled with the noise of a swelling riot.

After several seconds of struggling, Rocher loosened his grip on Prudence, allowing her to lurch back up to a seated position just in time to see Rodney Potoski's eyes, looking at her from across the room. At first, they appeared large, as if in disbelief, but they quickly narrowed into a piercing squint. Rodney lowered his head and started across the room, much like a charging ram she'd once seen in a nature film. That animal had made his move in anticipation of butting heads with a rival. The analogy was confirmed in Prudence's mind as Rocher sprang to his feet, upending the table, and giving him unobstructed access to the field of battle. She flinched, fearing a horrific collision, though at the last moment both boys stopped dead in their tracks, their eyes only inches apart.

Despite the rapidly deteriorating situation and the melee surrounding them in the club, Rodney Potoski and Paul Rocher stood there eyeing each other as if each imagined himself to be the next to last man on earth with plans of becoming the last one. Never before had Prudence seen such intensity in two pairs of eyes, both burning with antipathy for the other.

"We never did settle this, Rocher," said Rodney, his voice little more than a growl.

"Potoski, I was always ready, you just never had the stomach for it."

"Rocher, you've got to answer for the leg."

"That was over ten years ago, are you still…"

"Thirteen years, and four months," said Rodney.

"Ha, well, I guess it is still eating you alive, Roddy. If I knew that you were the type to hold on to things like that, I would have put you out of your misery back then."

"Why didn't you? You always talked big, Rocher, but I've never seen you try and land the first punch."

"Me? Talk about not taking the first punch. We're here now. Why don't you get it started?"

Despite the inability of Rodney and Paul over the past decade to settle their disagreement, the other patrons of the club had little problem in allowing their frustrations to erupt into violence. The introduction of lights into The Torrid Orchid had revealed who was there, who shouldn't have been, who was there with whom they shouldn't have been, and who had been unfaithful to whom. This last group included a majority of those present. Verbal arguments gushed and fists flew. Men who had just minutes before been making love to their dates were now making war on each other with the same intensity. The women, who had previously been using their lips to vacuum their dates' faces, were now engaged in pulling hair and delivering kicks to the shins of their rivals. It was astonishing, reflected Prudence, how a handful of 60-watt light bulbs could provoke such a fierce effect. It was equally puzzling how such deep-seated, seething hatred as resided in Rodney and Rocher could remain in check while violence reigned all around them.

"Well," said Rocher, posturing as if he were going to move forward, but actually inching backward, "are you going to take a poke at me, or not?"

"You're my superior on guard duty."

"We're not on guard duty now," said Rocher.

"You'd love for me to take the first shot. You've been waiting for it since St. Simeon's."

Evidently, Prudence thought, this feud had been going on since the pair were schoolboys and had something to do with someone's leg. She looked down at the underpinnings of both but could see nothing wrong with either of them. Still, neither seemed willing to strike the first blow. Instead, they just stood there, like mirror images of each other, hunched forward, ready to strike if only the other would make the first move. They could have almost been bookends, though Rocher was slightly taller and wirier, Rodney seemed to possess greater brute strength. Rocher was the more handsome of the two, though, to Prudence, Rodney was more attractive.

They might have stood there like a set of pugilistic bookends, had not Rodney made a move. It wasn't anything as overt as a leading left or a right cross, but rather a glance over towards his sister, Elinor, standing on the other side of Paul, though not nearly as close to Rocher as Prudence was. Rodney's eyes took in his sister, standing there, and his brow furrowed as if he suspected that things were not quite as they seemed. He looked back at Elinor, who now feigned innocence as if she were waiting for a bus. He then looked back briefly at Rocher and then at Prudence.

"Yeah," said Rocher, grabbing Prudence's arm, "she's with me."

This revelation seemed even more surprising to Rodney than it did to Prudence. First Rocher's kiss, and now this blatant lie; Prudence looked at him, and then at Elinor for an explanation. Elinor's eyes met hers, and then she shrugged her shoulders as if she didn't understand what had come over her boyfriend either.

Prudence looked back at Rodney. His eyes had narrowed on her. His gaze degenerated from disappointment to realization, to anger, and finally to hatred. Prudence felt her eyes well up with tears. Prudence opened up her mouth and squeaked: "chaperone."

Rodney looked back at Rocher, who simply nodded towards Elinor as if to indicate that Elinor was the chaperone. Then to back up his assertion, with his eyes still locked on Rodney's, Rocher swung Prudence around and gave her another passionate kiss. Prudence first struggled, but then screwed her eyes shut as she succumbed to the power of Rocher's passion. She only dared to open her eyes after she felt the air rush back into her mouth as Rocher pushed her away, while he still glowered at Rodney. She looked over at Rodney, who now seemed even more enraged. Prudence tried to protest, but everything was happening too quickly. All she could do was offer half-formed thoughts and stammers against Rocher's outrageous behavior.

Despite his previous reluctance to act, Rodney cocked his arm to deliver the first punch at Paul Rocher. Rocher tensed to receive the blow, and return in kind.

"Wait!" cried Prudence. She didn't understand half of what was going on, especially why Elinor was just standing there while her boyfriend and brother were poised to murder each other. But Prudence was determined to offer a few calming words and disarm the situation. "Wait," she raised her hands, glanced back at Elinor, then back to the combatants. "I think I can explain…"

Before she could utter another word, Prudence Hoover felt a sharp blow to the back of her head, and her whole world went black.

– 19 –
The Annual
Saint Patrick's Day Massacre

E linor gazed on Prudence and shook her head. Prudence was still out cold from being whacked in the back of the head at The Torrid Orchid.

It was very sad; so sad that Elinor almost wished that she hadn't done it; almost, but not quite. Elinor hadn't a choice. Prudence, the naïve dope, was about to explain to her brother that Elinor was Paul's date and that Prudence was just the chaperone. That would have been intolerable, at least for Elinor. And Elinor couldn't tolerate situations that were intolerable for her. Prudence would have understood.

"Prudence," Elinor imagined saying, "You might mean well, but it really will make an awful mess for me. So, just let me knock you cold with this chair. I'll try my best not to hit you any harder than I have to. I'm sure you don't really mind."

But she didn't have time to explain all that to Prudence. And if she had had the time, there was no guarantee that Prudence would agree. No, the cleanest course of action was that good, solid whack on the back of Prudence's coconut. That diffused the standoff between Rodney and Paul or at least postponed it for the moment. The shock of seeing her knock a sorority sister cold certainly changed the conversation. Elinor pretended that she was as surprised as any of them, even more so.

"Oops, it slipped," she recalled saying. Then, in the surrounding chaos, Elinor had asked Paul to pick up Prudence so they could take her home. They got out just as the cops were coming to quell the riot. They were home free.

Elinor even put Prudence in her own bed so she could watch over her. It was the least she could do. No, she reasoned, it was really darn nice of her. After all, Prudence had practically begged to get clobbered.

Elinor turned and looked at the box containing a dozen long stem red roses and shook her head. They had been there when they got back, addressed to Prudence. Elinor had found the card and was about to open it when Prudence had moaned. Elinor quickly put the card back. Probably from some old girlfriend of Prudence's, thought Elinor, probably that girl in the picture on Prudence's dresser. Elinor didn't care. She had her own problems without having to listen to the details of Prudence's love life.

Elinor felt slightly guilty. She would get a vase and some water. It was the least she could do. Then, Elinor decided it was actually a very nice thing to do.

She was just returning to the room with the vase when she heard a faint voice from the bed.

"Roses, how pretty," said Prudence, "Elinor should put those in water."

"Elinor is putting them in water," said Elinor. She forced a smile and then began arranging the roses one by one in the vase. "How are you feeling?"

"My head..." Prudence began lifting herself off the pillow, before moaning and sinking down again.

"Don't worry, we saved most of the larger pieces of it," said Elinor as she cut the ends off the stems one by one, and placed them in the vase. "Mind you there was a lot of blood, and all those stitches..."

"What?"

"Sorry, I'm only kidding. I guess this isn't the best time for jokes. You're fine. No blood, no stitches, just a little first aid, and a quick return back to the house."

"How long..."

"You've been out less than an hour."

"Who..."

"Paul carried you back here."

"Not your brother?"

"My brother? Rodney? No, he wouldn't touch you. He wouldn't have risked it."

"Why would..."

Elinor put the last rose in the vase, balled up the tissue paper, and faced Prudence.

"Look," she said, casting her eyes downward, "I've got to fill you in on some things. I'm not exactly sure where to begin..."

"Why wouldn't your brother carry me home?"

"Why would he?" said Elinor. "Besides, he wouldn't touch you because if he did, he'd finally have to fight Paul."

"Finally? I had the impression they fought constantly. Back at the club, weren't they fighting then?"

"They may have looked like they were about to fight, but they've been looking like that since they were kids. They could have posed for a hundred statues by now, all like this..." She put up her fists like a bare-knuckle boxer.

"But why..."

"Look, Paul Rocher and my brother first met on the playground at St. Simeon's Parochial School. Ours was a one-hundred percent Irish parish, well, almost. Paul and Rodney were the only non-Irish kids in their class. They were also both the tallest boys in their grade, and they were both the toughest kid in their class."

"But they couldn't both be the toughest kid in the class," reasoned Prudence.

Elinor smiled. "Yes, they realized that, too, even back in the first grade; and, despite appearances, they're not complete dopes. They beat up every other kid in the school, but they never fought each other."

"Honor among bullies?"

"Honor? Don't give them so much credit," said Elinor. "It was more like fear."

"I don't understand."

"If they fought each other, one of them would have won..."

"So?"

"And the other would have lost," said Elinor. "And they wouldn't have only lost a fight; they would have lost their claim to being the toughest kid in the school."

"So, it's better to be co-bully than the second-place thug?"

Elinor shrugged. "Something like that. It was their own version of the Cold War before there was a Cold War. They both look like they're ready to fight, but neither would dare to start it. I suppose somewhere in their male minds it's preferable to leave the question in doubt than to settle it, especially if it settles in favor of the other one."

"And so that's why they hate each other," concluded Prudence.

"No, that's not it at all," said Elinor.

"But..."

"Actually, at first, when they both realized their combined status as the toughest kid in the school, they'd cooperate."

"To maintain the status quo, I suppose," nodded Prudence.

An involuntary laugh exploded from Elinor's mouth. "No, not exactly, I wouldn't say they used their powers for good. Oh, they didn't terrorize the other kids, either...except on St. Patrick's Day."

"Why then?"

"Being the only two boys in their class who weren't Irish, they used to set themselves up in the center of the schoolyard, each March 17th. They'd stand back to back, fifteen minutes before the opening bell, and challenge the other kids."

"Challenge them? How?"

"They'd stand like this," Elinor assumed the fighter's stance again and began weaving her fists in front of her. "And they'd say things like: 'C'mon, you Micks, come and get your St. Patrick's shamrock...'"

"That's terrible..."

"Oh, that's the least of it. They'd taunt the other kids with various illusions of their grandmothers' unnatural relationships with leprechauns and explicit uses their mothers had for potatoes. Naturally, the Irish boys wouldn't stand for it, and they didn't have to stand for it."

"No?"

"No, as soon as they rushed those two they'd find themselves on the ground, usually with a fat lip or a bloody nose. It would go on, with neither Rodney nor Paul suffering a scratch until someone called Father O'Malley. He'd come out, wringing his hands, and crying: 'Boys, boys, don't go beating up the poor Irish lads on St. Paddy's Day.'"

"Didn't they get punished?"

"Sure they did, but for those two idiots, it was a badge of honor. Neither showed any remorse, or any reaction whatsoever, for that matter."

"So, why do they hate each other?"

"Rodney hated Paul before Paul hated him back."

"I don't care, who hated who first," said Prudence. "I just want to know why!"

Elinor sat still for a moment trying to pretend that she hadn't heard the question; hoping to make Prudence believe she hadn't asked it. Instead, Prudence just kept looking at her, waiting. Elinor really didn't want to get into it, not with Prudence, not with anyone. There was only one person who knew the whole truth, and he knew better than to bring it up. Still, Prudence gave her the innocent stare. Well, thought Elinor, she didn't have to tell her everything.

"It's because our father was a hero," said Elinor drawing a deep breath, "in the First World War."

"World War I?"

"Yes, my father is quite a bit older than my mother. Anyway, he lost his leg in the war," said Elinor. Her eyes grew moist. She dabbed at them with a handkerchief. "I don't know why I'm getting so misty about it. I certainly wasn't that way when I was growing up. I thought everybody's father had a wooden leg. Mommies had two legs. Daddies one, or at least the good ones, only had one. When I reached the age when I realized that children grow up to be adults, I really thought that Rodney's leg was going to fall off some day, and then he'd be a father, too."

Elinor laughed. "Okay, so I was a dumb kid. My father has a wooden leg. In fact, he has two wooden legs, one good one, and one spare. Back then, he would keep the one he wasn't using hanging on the back of the closet door in his bedroom. It wasn't anything impressive. It was just a piece of wood, but you know how children are. Collecting things like bottle caps, rocks, bits of string, dead worms...it's remarkable what fascinates children. In any event, to make a long story short, one day, Rodney came home and found a group of the neighborhood kids standing in my parent's bedroom, looking at my father's wooden leg. They had paid a nickel each to look at it."

"Was Paul Rocher there?"

"Paul was holding the handful of nickels." Elinor looked out the window. "I never saw my brother so angry, before or since. He was paralyzed with anger, just like he was made of stone. I can still see him, standing there. He was probably ten, maybe eleven, standing there with his fists clenched so tightly that his arms were white up to his elbow."

"And Paul?"

"He just stared him down for what seemed like an hour, but it couldn't have been more than a minute."

"And he had no shame, no remorse?"

"Paul? No, not a speck of it," said Elinor quietly.

"Wow," said Prudence, "that must be why they hate each other."

"Yep," said Elinor curtly.

Prudence thought a moment. "And that's why you and Paul didn't want to be seen in public, at least not alone in public. You didn't want your brother to see his sister out with his biggest enemy."

Elinor sighed. Prudence was boring Elinor with her own history.

"Yeah, got it in one," said Elinor hoping Prudence was finished. She wasn't.

"And so, I wasn't really a chaperone," she continued slowly putting together the information as a young child will construct a simple jigsaw puzzle.

"Nope," said Elinor trying to be patient.

"I was...what was the term your boyfriend used?"

"Beard."

"Yes, that's it, a beard," said Prudence. "I was a beard. And that's like a decoy, right?"

"Right again," said Elinor staring at her fingernails. After another prolonged silence, she looked up. Prudence seemed deep in thought about something. Elinor wanted to shake her. She wanted to tell her that was the end of the story. Rodney and Paul didn't like each other. Paul was dating her. They had used Prudence to run interference for them. It hadn't quite worked. And that was everything.

Instead, Prudence was biting her lower lip as if something else was rattling around her brain.

"What?" snapped Elinor.

"Oh, nothing," said Prudence, "well, I mean, it's not exactly nothing. I just, oh, this is so difficult."

"Well, just spit it out," said Elinor.

"It's not so easy," she said. "It's pretty personal. I don't know how to..."

Oh, great, Elinor thought, Prudence is trying to tell her that she likes girls; like it was some big secret. She didn't have the time nor the inclination to listen to all this. She had her own problems.

"Wait," said Elinor, "you don't have to go on..."

"But I think I do," said Prudence.

"No, you don't," said Elinor.

"But there something you don't know…"

"No," said Elinor. "I know…"

"You know? How do you know?"

"I don't know how; I just know."

Prudence sat there for a moment in puzzlement. "But…"

"Look, I know," said Elinor, "I know."

"I don't think you know," said Prudence warily.

This was getting even more tedious, thought Elinor. "Listen, Prudence, I know your…well, your romantic bent."

"My…"

"Your inclination, your…oh, hell, who you like. I know."

"You do? How do you know?" asked Prudence.

Elinor rolled her eyes. "I'm not blind, and I'm not stupid."

Prudence looked down at the blankets. "I didn't think it was so obvious."

"Well, it was," said Elinor. She wanted out of this conversation. "I mean, it wasn't obvious to everyone. I guess I just was better at picking up on the signals."

Prudence thought a moment and then nodded her head. "Yes, I suppose you would be."

Elinor almost asked what that was supposed to mean, but she caught herself. It wasn't the time to be confrontational. Besides, there was only one chair handy, and she wasn't about to break another chair over this girl, especially not with Prudence looking right at her.

"Well, that settles that," said Elinor, hoping that the topic that was barely touched upon would never even be approached again.

"There's just one thing," said Prudence.

Elinor put her hands on her hips in frustration. It was worse than dealing with a persistent toddler.

"What?" snapped Elinor.

"Who sent the roses?"

"I don't know," she said, "There's a card, but I haven't opened it."

"Aren't you curious?"

"I wouldn't dream of reading the card."

"Why not? Don't you want to know who sent you those lovely roses?"

Elinor laughed. "Me? They're not my roses."

Prudence glanced around the room, searching for another possible recipient.

"You," said Elinor pointing at her, "they're your flowers. They were here when we got back. Paul carried you. I carried the roses."

"I wonder who sent them," said Prudence smiling. She sat up in bed, stopping to wince in pain and touch the back of her head.

"Why wonder?" said Elinor. "Just open the card."

"There's a card?"

Elinor plucked a small envelope from amidst the roses and handed it to Prudence. Prudence opened the envelope and extracted the handwritten note. She read it with considerable enthusiasm until she reached the end when her expression dropped. Prudence then examined the outside of the envelope before rereading the note, this time with studied deliberation. It was as if she were expecting a different message the second time, though, from her crestfallen expression, the note had remained the same.

"Everything okay?" asked Elinor, not really caring either way.

"What?" Prudence looked up as if she were surprised to see Elinor there. "Oh, no, I mean, yes, that is, I suppose. It's just not what I was expecting."

She handed the note to Elinor. After reading it, Elinor bit her lip and gave it back to the girl in her bed.

"How...interesting."

– 20 –
The Incomplete Man Meets the Overly Generous Bodice

Prudence Hoover found herself in another booth. Once more, the lights were low. In the background, music was playing. It was sensual but far removed from the tawdry sounds of the Torrid Orchid. The music was an encouragement to romance, not the starting signal for an intramural sex brawl. It was live music; played by musicians in dinner jackets, save for a singer in an elegant gown. None of the patrons were necking, and she could see them all quite clearly for, while the lights were low, they were in chandeliers, and not just a solitary bulb suspended over the cash register. There wasn't even a cash register in sight. Gentlemen and ladies conversed urbanely, while they sipped concoctions from conical cocktail glasses. There wasn't a bottle of beer in the place, not even behind the long, curved, leather tufted bar. Prudence was sipping champagne for the first time in her life. The oysters she was eating were far cry from the fried clams she enjoyed at Howard Johnson's.

Again, as a month earlier, Prudence was sharing the booth with a man and another woman. This time the man wasn't pretending that Prudence was his date; she really was his date. He was interested in her. She was repeatedly told so. He was careful to compliment her on her hair, her dress, and her accessories. Attention flustered Prudence. She tried to smile demurely. She couldn't help but wonder at his taste, however. He obviously was better dressed than she was, as was the other woman, as was just about everyone else in the place including the wait staff. Prudence, after all, was just a college student and her ensemble, such as it was, was borrowed from various sorority sisters. He thought she was elegant, or at least he said so. Still, his eyes scanned the room even as his words were aimed at her. Even more unsettling, was the fact that the other woman in their booth, more often than not, precipitated his remarks.

"Isn't that a stunning dress," said the other woman, nodding towards Prudence.

"Um? Oh, yes, the dress," he would agree, looking back at his date. "Yes, I noticed it immediately, so esthetically *entre nous*."

Prudence cast her eyes toward the linen tablecloth. She felt herself blush. She had no idea what it was about her gown, or more accurately Elinor Potoski's gown, that was *entre nous*. She had even less of an idea what *entre nous* meant, but in the context, it must be worthy of a blush.

"It compliments your *décolletage*," he added.

Prudence knew that was a refined way of mentioning her cleavage. The gown was the first strapless dress she had ever worn, and she wasn't entirely comfortable with the arrangement. Complicating matters was that Elinor was a size ten, while Prudence was an eight. And even though they had pinned up the extra material in the back, Prudence, being a full bust size smaller than her sorority sister, felt as if she was juggling two servings of Jell-O inside the bodice. More than once, she felt compelled to draw her elbows to her side and subtly push the satin gown up her thin frame. She felt like she was doing a poor imitation of Jimmy Cagney.

"I think Prudence is perfectly charming, perfectly charming," said the woman, who repeated the compliment to convince one of them, which one Prudence wasn't sure.

Prudence smiled, and tried to deliver an appropriate retort, but only managed to mutter: "Thank you, uh…so are you."

The woman smiled, but then she always smiled at Prudence. Prudence had first encountered that smile back in Bertram Bascomb's office. She had thought it was an odd smile, especially on the face of a secretary. Since then she had learned that the secretary wasn't a secretary, but Bascomb's sister and the smile became even more unsettling. It wasn't malicious, nor was it critical, but something was hiding behind her teeth that Prudence couldn't identify. Whenever Prudence thought about the smile, which was whenever it was flashed at her, which was whenever they were together, which was frequently, she wondered what this woman saw in her that pleased her so. That was it: it was a satisfied smile; as if she had been searching for something, and now had found it in Prudence. It was the sort of smile Prudence had once received from her mother after successfully completing her piece at a piano recital. It evinced a pride in ownership. Prudence had no idea how she could be so satisfying to an almost perfect stranger.

"Isn't Prudence charming, Bertie?"

"Yes, she is," said Bascomb, looking beyond the both of them, his focus halfway across the room. "I've told her so, Jeannie, repeatedly."

"Perhaps she'd like to dance," said Bascomb's sister. "Would you like to dance, dear?"

Prudence almost asked with whom. She bobbed her head in a non-committal fashion.

"Yes, that's a good idea," said Bascomb, rising from the table and offering his hand to Prudence. She took it and slid out of the booth and in doing so almost slid out of her dress. She glanced back at the booth to make sure none of the pins keeping her together had been left behind.

Bertram Bascomb looked marvelous in a white dinner jacket, even more marvelous than he looked in his classroom tweeds. And when he stood erect, with his arm around Prudence, and beyond the earshot of his sister, she could almost feel herself abandoning herself to his strong arms.

"I'm sorry about Jeannie," he said as he began to guide her around the floor, "she means very well, but sometimes she can come on a bit too strident."

"She obviously cares about you very much. Sorry..." Prudence added as she stepped on his foot. "I'm not a very good dancer. I had dance classes when I was a girl."

"Oh?" said Bascomb in a tone that neither endorsed nor condemned her terpsichorean education.

"Mostly ballet. The teacher, Mrs. Magruder, tried to teach us ballroom dancing, but we didn't have any boys. I was tall for my age back then, so I was one of the girls who had to do the boy's part. As a result...sorry...I'm not a very good dancer."

Bascomb smiled. "I notice you do try to lead."

"Sorry."

"There's no need to apologize continually."

"Sorry."

"You're fine the way you are," said Bascomb. "In fact, you're perfect."

"Sorry... I mean, I am?"

"Yes, you are."

"Do you really think so?"

"I do. And I'm not the only one who appreciates your distinct qualities."

Bascomb leaned down and kissed her on the nose, and then winced as she once more trod upon his foot.

"Sorry... I mean: distinct qualities? No one ever told me I had distinct qualities."

"I can assure you, Prudence, my pet, that of all the women I've ever known, none other has the rare combination of personality, talents, and oh, what shall I call it: fresh innocence? Yes, that will do, you have a clean, pure quality: the absence of guile, the banishment of cynicism. You trust the world, and more you invite the world to trust you."

"I do?" Prudence couldn't imagine anything she did that invited anyone to anything. If she had to, she would have guessed she invited the world to ignore her. "Do I really?"

"Yes, you do," Bascomb assured her with an appreciative smile and squeeze of her hand. "You have something no other woman I've ever met has."

"Really, Professor Bascomb, I never thought..."

"Prudence, you really must stop calling me Professor Bascomb. It's quite difficult to romance a girl, ah, uh, a woman, when she refers to you so formally. It's Bertram, or better still, Bertie."

"Romance?" She'd been going out with Bertram Bascomb for three weeks, ever since he sent her those roses. Still, Prudence hadn't realized it was a romance. Most of that time she had been trying to sort out the feelings in her head; not just her emotions concerning Rodney Potoski, but the lump on the back of her skull received at The Torrid Orchid. The bump went away, but she still thought about Rodney. Romance with Professor Bascomb? That was a different situation altogether.

"You seem surprised," said Bascomb. "Didn't you see this as a romance?"

"I just thought we were going out," said Prudence. "Romance is a bit more serious than going out, isn't it?"

Bascomb laughed. "There, that's what I'm talking about. Most girls, excuse me, I mean most women, would be actively engaged in the pursuit: the sport of courtship. They would thrust and parry – metaphorically speaking – as if it were all part of some larger contest. You, on the other hand, dear Prudence, merely saw it as going out…innocently going out. That's why you're so refreshingly different. You have no ulterior motive; you lay no trap for me."

"Why would I?"

"Most women would."

Prudence shrugged her shoulders, as much as to hoist her gown, as to express puzzlement. Bertram Bascomb twirled her around, and she narrowly avoided kicking him in the ankle. On the turn, Prudence noticed his sister, sitting back in the booth, watching them with rapt attention. Maybe Prudence didn't see their relationship as a game, but Jeannie was following their movements around the dance floor as if they were prizefighters in a ring, and she had bet on the outcome. That was one reason, Prudence thought, that she didn't consider their relationship a romance: she and Bascomb had never really been alone. Every time they had gone out, Jeannie was there, at least part of the time. Prudence didn't know much about romance, but she never thought it was a tag-team event.

"Your sister seems to like me," said Prudence, as they spun away to the other side of the floor.

"Jeannie? She adores you. In fact, I think she appreciates you even more than I."

"She does?"

"Well, not now perhaps," said Bascomb squeezing her hand, but neglecting to look into her eyes. She couldn't help but notice he seemed to be scanning an imaginary horizon as if he were anticipating the arrival of a bus. "It was Jeannie who first pointed out your multitude of charms and qualities."

"That's sort of strange," said Prudence thinking aloud, and then catching herself. "I mean, that's unusual, isn't it?"

Bascomb chuckled. "No, you're right. It's strange. At least it would be in a conventional brother-sister relationship. We don't have a conventional relationship, however, and for that, I'm thankful. She was seventeen years old when our parents died. I was only three at the time. She took upon herself the responsibility for my upbringing, my education; she guided me in my life choices, in short, Jeannie has devoted her life to my success. She's very ambitious on my behalf."

"And I thought she was your secretary, what a dope I am."

"On the contrary," he said, "you were very perceptive. Jeannie is in many respects my amanuensis, that is, my secretary, though not in the mundane tasks of organizing my daily schedule, but rather in administrating my life schedule."

"She must be very proud of you, now that you're an associate professor."

Bascomb smiled and kissed her forehead. "Sweet little Prudence, Jeannie merely sees this as the beginning. Many men would be content to settle into the comfortable ivy-covered existence of an academician, and it does hold its allure, but her, that is our sights are set higher."

Prudence wondered where those sights were set but didn't feel she had the right to ask, at least not without his sister present.

"Yes, Jeannie has mapped out a good course," he said wistfully. "She's devoted her life to me, and her devotion has allowed me to dedicate my life to other pursuits confident that my sister is taking care of the picayune details."

The orchestra reached the end of their song, and after a polite smattering of applause, they began a slow number. Bertram pulled her closer to himself and continued to dance. In compliment to the tune, the lights dimmed, but still nowhere near the level of the Ork.

Bertram Bascomb sighed into her ear, and she sighed back, though he still seemed preoccupied. Maybe he was thinking about his future, the one his sister had all mapped out. He might as just as well have been sighing out of impatience. Whatever the inspiration for his sigh, Prudence didn't feel that it was her. Hers was the ear that just happened to be beside his mouth when he exhaled.

Prudence, on the other hand, knew why she had sighed, and it wasn't for the future, but rather the past. She sighed for the moment she kissed Rodney Potoski. The thought of it caused her toes to scrunch up anew, causing her to kick Bertram's ankle yet again.

"Sorry," she murmured. She had said it so often that Bertram no longer replied. He often seemed to be thinking of other things when they were together. Prudence ascribed it to him being such a deep thinker.

His lack of a response steered Prudence's train of thoughts back to Rodney. As suave as Bertram was, she'd rather be with the part-time security guard who wanted nothing more than to gaze at windows. She couldn't imagine Rodney in a dinner jacket, which was just fine since she doubted he would take a girl anywhere that compelled her to be naked from her eyebrows to the tops of her breasts. She sighed again, wishing that Rodney could see the tops of her breasts rather than displaying them for a handsome associate professor, his very involved sister, and the room full of cultured strangers.

Who was she kidding? She'd never have another opportunity to trip onto Rodney's lips again. All Prudence had to do was recall the loathing in Rodney's eyes when she was kissed by Paul Rocher. She had tried to explain. But getting knocked senseless had made that difficult. Now, it was too late.

As the band continued, Prudence was aware that Bertram was whispering something in her ear. His soft voice was so unobtrusive, as to go unnoticed by her.

"...so supple, so gentle, so soft," he was saying. Prudence wondered what he was talking about. Could he be speaking of her? It was possible in the context, but as no one had ever used such language on her. Maybe he was commenting on her gown or his favorite brand of toilet tissue. Prudence almost asked for clarification but decided to let him continue and pick up the context as he spoke.

"I'm not a complete man."

Prudence wondered what that meant. Bascomb hadn't been in the military. Perhaps he had been in an accident with farm equipment. In any event, she was afraid to ask what parts he was missing.

"Oh, I seem to have a clear vision for my life," Bascomb continued, "but as vivid a picture as it is, it's a lonely, solitary canvas that I inhabit."

"But," Prudence interjected, "you have your sister."

"She's going back home," he explained. "She's only been visiting. She's married, you know."

That was a surprise. In the weeks that Prudence had been in the company of Bertram and Jeannie, there had never been any mention of the fact that she had a husband.

"I didn't realize," said Prudence.

"That's not important. My sister is a wonderful help to me, a trusted advisor, a meticulous planner, but she can't make me whole."

"Oh?" Prudence didn't know what else to say.

"A sister can only do so much. A man needs a helpmate. I need a helpmate."

"Oh?" Again Prudence wasn't exactly sure what Bertram was saying.

"My dear Prudence," he said, clutching her closer. "Will you be that helpmate?"

"What?"

"My helpmate, will you be it?"

The music had stopped. The other couples applauded. The orchestra leader announced a short intermission. While the gentlemen and ladies made their ways back to their tables, Prudence just stood there. Her arms dropped numbly to her side, like two large stalks of bologna. She stared at Bertram Bascomb. He was half smiling as he searched her face for her reply. While outwardly she may have appeared comatose, inwardly Prudence's mind was racing.

Helpmate, she thought. That was a wife, wasn't it? Did he just ask me to marry him? No, that couldn't be. He wasn't looking for a wife, was he? He was asking for another sister, a secretary, an organizer for his lofty plans, whatever those are. That wasn't a wife. He hadn't said anything about children, or homemaking, or baking pies, or laying shelf paper. In fact, in the past three weeks, neither Bertram nor his sister had asked any sort of domestic questions that would lead her to believe they were shopping for a wife. But what had he called her before? Supple? Gentle? Soft? Those weren't secretarial skills, were they? It wasn't at all clear to Prudence what he wanted.

He stood there, expectantly staring into her face. She wondered what to say. It wouldn't be very polite of her, if he were indeed proposing marriage, to ask for clarification. On the other hand, if he wanted to hire a secretary, it would be embarrassing to confuse a job offer with a marriage proposal. So she continued to stand there like a low-sodium version of Lot's wife.

"Well?" Jeannie joined them in the middle of the dance floor. "Well, what did she say?"

"She hasn't said anything," replied Bertram.

Jeannie slapped him on the arm. "What did you say to her? Did you bollocks this up? You know I can't keep running back East like this! I've got my own home to look after."

"I didn't say anything," he said, "at least nothing amiss. I extolled her virtues, expressed my need, and said she would be a perfect helpmate."

Jeannie rolled her eyes. "How can you be so smart and so stupid in the same day? I've told you to talk plainer. She's a good, ordinary, simple girl. You use that sort of language out on the stump, and they won't know whether you're asking for their votes or giving them an essay exam. You confused her, you dumbbell!"

With that, Jeannie shoved her brother to the side and there, in the middle of the dance floor, she grabbed Prudence by the arms and looked her in the eyes.

"Look, honey," she said, "this brain-dead brother of mine sometimes is a little hard to understand, but he really is a good egg, deep down. He's got too much polish on top, but underneath all that wax he's a regular enough Joe. What he was trying to ask was: will you marry him?"

Prudence blinked, she felt her throat constrict, as she croaked: "Marry him?"

Jeannie looked back at her brother in disgust. "You've made a real pig's dinner out of this, Mr. Softy!" Then she turned her kinder nature back to Prudence. "Yes, honey, he wants to marry you. He really does. We both really do. So, why don't you marry him, so I can go back home? He really needs you. He needs a good little woman by his side; a good and pretty little wife to give him a strong base, good roots." She was waving her fist as if she were clutching a handful of topsoil.

Suddenly, Prudence felt as if the whole room, as expansive as it was, was closing in on her. The rush of events; a marriage proposal from a man that she wasn't sure was a proposal; a marriage proposal from a woman that was definite, the music; the dancing; the champagne; the oysters; the gown, they all came flooding in on her so quickly that Prudence felt her head swimming. She didn't know whether to sit down on the dance floor and cry or make a dash for the exit. Then, what her mind couldn't resolve, her stomach decided for her. The unfamiliar combination of oysters and alcohol, which had been fomenting in her belly began to assert themselves. While Bertram and his sister debated the efficacy of his proposal, Prudence felt cold beads of sweat pop out on her forehead, followed by a rumbling rising up her throat.

"Jeannie," said Bertram, "I don't need you to argue my cause. I'm quite capable of proposing marriage."

"Donkey balls!" snorted his sister, "She didn't even know what you were talking about. If you can't seal the deal with one little girl, how are you going to convince big groups of people?"

"Driving a bulldozer – metaphorically speaking – isn't the way to do either!"

"At least she'd know what you meant," said Jeannie, as she turned back to Prudence. "Did you know what my genius brother was talking about?"

"I think…" said Prudence softly.

"Yes?"

"I think… I'm going to throw up," said Prudence. Then looking at her professor, she amended the statement. "No, I know I'm going to throw up."

With one hand she hiked up the hem of her gown, while with the other, she pulled up her sagging bodice, and made a wobbly dash for the ladies' room.

– 21 –
Confessions of a Homochromatic Dimwit

E ngaged?"
Elinor Potoski stood in the doorway in her flannel robe. There in the hallway was Prudence in her chenille robe and slippers. Elinor was tired. It was late. She could have misheard her. "Did you say 'engaged?'"

"Yes." Prudence handed her the evening gown. "Thank you for the loan of the dress," she said before adding, "I don't think I got any, um… stuff on it."

"What kind of stuff?" said Elinor, searching the folds of the gown.

"I was sort of, well, I was sick," admitted Prudence. "But I was very careful. If there is any…problem, well, I'll have it cleaned. In fact, let me have it back. I'll have it cleaned either way."

Elinor pulled back the gown and yanked Prudence into her room, and shut the door behind them.

"Who cares about some stupid dress," said Elinor pulling up a chair beside Prudence. "I want to know what's going on."

"Please don't end your sentences in a preposition," muttered Prudence. "Besides which, there's nothing to tell."

"You come in here, hand me back a gown, apologize for the vomit, casually mention you're engaged, and you think that's the end of the story. That must have been some shindig you went to!"

"Preposition," murmured Prudence.

"Never mind the grammar lesson! I'll beat the story out of you with that pillow if I have to. What happened?"

Prudence shrugged and pulled her robe closer about her. "We went to some fancy restaurant. They had an orchestra, they had champagne and oysters…"

Elinor whistled and shook her hand limply at the wrist.

"And then Bascomb asked you to marry him?"

"Sort of…"

"So, you're not really engaged?"

"No, I'm that. His sister settled it…"

"His sister closed the deal?"

Prudence nodded, "Yes, in the ladies' room."

Elinor shot her a skeptical look.

"What did she say?"

Prudence bit the inside her lip and looked up towards the ceiling as if her lavatory conversation were transcribed above Elinor's bed.

"She told me that Professor Bascomb, that is, Bertram, needed me."

All of the girls knew about Bascomb's reputation, all except one, apparently. At least a third of their sorority had firsthand knowledge.

"He said he needed you?" repeated Elinor. "How?"

"His sister told me that her brother, Professor Bascomb, that is Bertram, was a great man, or at least he was going to be a great man. She told me she'd seen the glimmer of greatness in him ever since their parents had died and she'd been raising him. She recognized Bertram's potential, and like an ember, she fanned it, fed it with kindling, and protected it from being extinguished. She kept his flame alive."

"She should have trimmed his wick," muttered Elinor.

"No, he's a fire, not a lamp. That's a different metaphor."

"Sorry, go on."

"Where was I?"

"Bertie's an ember shining out in the darkness of ignorance. Let me guess: she sent him to school so he could be a college professor and shed his light on our primordial minds."

"Not exactly," continued Prudence. "She sacrificed to send him to the best schools…"

"And he wound up here anyway."

"He's only teaching here now," said Prudence. "He graduated from Yale."

"And now she's here to get him a wife, to tie up the package nice and neat."

"Nicely and neatly," corrected Prudence. "Adverbs modify verbs, not adjectives. And, no, that's not it. Of course, she wants to see her brother married and settled down, but that's only the next step."

"The next step to what?"

Prudence looked around. "Promise you won't tell?"

Elinor crossed her heart.

"She told me Bertram is going to be president."

"Of the college?"

"Of the United States."

Elinor snorted.

"I'm not making that up," said Prudence. "That's what his sister told me. He was going to be president. Oh, not right away, but someday. She'd been planning it since he was a boy. First, he was going to get into an Ivy League school. Next, he would become a professor at a prestigious university…"

"He's an associate professor at a state college..."

"She said that was a momentary setback. That sort of thing was to be expected, she said."

"Oh, sure," said Elinor.

"He'll get there, she said, and while he was working his way up the academic ladder, he'd be working in the community. You may have noticed how active he is around the campus."

"Oh, yes, I've noticed his activity...around the campus...some places more than others." Elinor thought of the numerous times she'd seen Bascomb skulking around the sorority house and wondered why Prudence hadn't heard about his "civic involvement."

"He really does care about people," said Prudence. "When we're out together, I've noticed him looking around at other people. He really loves people."

"...Some more than others."

"Hmm?"

"Nothing."

"Eventually, he's going to apply his brains and his dedication to the community and run for public office."

"And become president of the United States?"

Prudence smiled weakly. "Well, that's what his sister thinks."

"And what does the good Professor think?"

Prudence's wan smile dissolved into a bemused grimace. "I suppose he thinks the same thing, or at least, he doesn't disagree with Jeannie, at least I've never heard him object."

"Well," said Elinor, "It's hard to object when you're so busy dedicating yourself to the community." Elinor hated to be so sarcastic to such a trusting little dope, but it wasn't her job to educate Prudence Hoover. After all, she wasn't even an associate professor.

"So, that's about it," said Prudence with a sheepish shrug.

"And what about you?" Elinor asked against her better judgment.

"Me?"

"Yes, you, Miss Hoover, while you are still Miss Hoover, do you have any objections to being the wife of a professor, and ultimately First Lady?"

"Well, it's not my plan," Prudence responded after a prolonged pause. She shrugged. "I mean, it's so silly, isn't it? I mean, the plans people have for other people, it's silly. Who knows what Bertram will wind up being? I'm sure a lot of sisters and parents, and friends have lofty aspirations for the people close to them. They think their loved one is the best, the brightest, the one perfectly suited to become...whatever. That doesn't mean it's going to happen, does it? It's silly, isn't it?"

Elinor looked at her for a moment and for the first time felt sorry for Prudence. She gritted her teeth and almost didn't say what was on her mind, but seeing the look in Prudence's eyes, she felt she had to.

"And you're really afraid that it would all happen," said Elinor. "Aren't you?"

"Me? Afraid?" Prudence tried to laugh, but the sound stuck in her throat. Then she swallowed hard. "Actually, I'm… I'm terrified. I mean, Jeanie, his sister, she's a very strong woman. I think she'd move heaven and Earth to get what she wanted for Professor Bascomb, I mean, Bertram."

Prudence looked down at her fingers, knotted in her lap, and continued. "But, well, it doesn't matter what she wants, after all, does it? She won't be liv… living with us. She doesn't even live around here. She's from out West. She'll be going home after the wedding. So that will be that. And besides, Bertram asked me." Prudence sighed. "He did ask me. Only I didn't understand, not at first. Then I suppose it all got to me: the champagne, the oysters, the music, the proposal. That's when I thought I was going to be sick, and I ran into the ladies' room."

"And were you sick?"

"A little," said Prudence. She reached for the gown. "I'm not sure what that is. Why don't I have it cleaned anyway…"

"I'll burn the damn thing!" shouted Elinor, throwing the gown into the corner where it died in a rustle of organdy. "So, you got the guided tour of Bertram's future in the ladies' room."

"Yes, she explained everything there."

Elinor stared at her, annoyed that she had been dragged into the middle of this mess. For her part, Prudence just sat there pathetically like a bag of emotionally spent kumquats.

Finally, Elinor spoke, cautiously at first.

"Okay, I don't want to offend you. You're a sorority sister, and you live right across the hall…"

"…and you're my friend."

"Huh? Oh, yeah, sure, friend. So, I don't want it to seem like I'm butting into your private life.

"I don't mind," said Prudence eagerly as if Elinor was the last straw of hope floating by.

"Having said that," Elinor looked down at the floor and paused. "Having said all that, this latest bit of news seems a bit… out of character for you?"

"You mean getting engaged so suddenly? I suppose getting engaged is always sudden. One minute you aren't the next minute you are. I suppose it's a lot like death, or being pregnant."

Elinor's jaw went slack. "You're not pregnant, are you?"

Prudence smirked. "That's not only ridiculous, it's also impossible!"

"You mean, you haven't…" she cleared her throat. "…with him."

"Not with anyone," clarified Prudence.

"That's rare," Elinor muttered thinking of Bascomb's reputation. She looked up to see Prudence's confused expression. "Oh, I don't mean it's rare that a girl your age is a virgin. That's not a reflection on you; it's more… well, never mind."

"Why is it out of character that I should get engaged?"

Elinor smiled knowingly. "Well, maybe 'character' isn't the right word. I guess it's more out of your… nature."

Prudence looked at her quizzically.

Elinor shot her an exasperated look in return. She was getting tired of this game. "C'mon, you don't have to pretend. After all, I suppose it's a convenient match for both of you. But I'd have to be a moron not to have figured it out. I had my suspicions the first time I met you."

"Okay," said Prudence impassively.

Elinor sighed. "I know… what you like…"

"The first time we met?" asked Prudence.

"Yes," said Elinor.

Prudence thought for a moment. "Shelf paper?"

"What?"

"The first time we met," said Prudence. "I was lining my shelves. I really like shelf paper."

Elinor rolled her eyes. "No, not shelf paper."

Prudence plunged back into thought. "Well, I sort of confessed to Bertram's sister, that I liked cake. You didn't mean cake, did you?"

Elinor slapped her own forehead, but only to prevent her from slapping Prudence's.

"I think you know what I'm talking about," said Elinor glowering at her.

"You don't think that boys realized it, do you?"

"No, not really, Paul didn't."

Prudence paused for a moment, picking at her cuticles. "And, um, do you think, well, that your brother noticed?"

Elinor knit her brows. "Rodney? Why would you care what he noticed?"

"Because…because I… care about Rodney… very much."

Elinor's mouth opened to reply, and then shut again. Then it opened. Then shut, and then opened once more to speak. "You care about him… how?"

Prudence looked up at Elinor. Tears were beginning to well up in her eyes. "How else would a girl care about a boy that she liked… a lot?"

Elinor sat back in the chair and drew a deep breath. "Wait a minute, hold on …okay, do you remember the first day I met you?"

Prudence blushed and nodded her head. "Yes," she admitted softly, "and I'm sorry."

"You're sorry? What for?"

"For what," whispered Prudence, "prepositions…"

"What for," insisted Elinor.

"Oh, well, the first time we met, I'm sorry that I stared at you like that," said Prudence. "It was very rude."

"Rude? It was downright weird."

"Was it?"

"It was from where I was standing," said Elinor. "You were looking at me all weird, and then you told me I was beautiful and that you liked beautiful girls. Remember?"

"Did I? If you say so."

Elinor cocked her arm back, but after a moment only slapped at the air instead of her preferred target. "You suppose! Why would you say something like that?"

"Well," said Prudence, "I had to say something. It was a very awkward moment. I'd never seen anything like..." she trailed off into a mumble.

"Like what? Like what?"

Prudence hung her head and muttered: "Your eyes."

Elinor burst out laughing.

"Are you all right?" asked Prudence cautiously.

"All right? I'm marvelous," chuckled Elinor, "you told me I was beautiful because of my eyes?"

"Well, no, I mean, yes, I guess. It's just that I'd never seen eyes like those, and I didn't want to be rude or embarrass you by staring at them. I didn't want to draw attention to them."

"They're just my eyes! It's no big deal."

"But I didn't know what to say."

"So, you tell me you like beautiful girls?"

Prudence shrugged her shoulders. "I didn't know..."

"I've got heterochromia iridis."

"Oh, how horrible! That's terrible! I'm so sorry, so very sorry!"

"You dope! It means I have two different colored irises. I was born this way. You didn't have to be embarrassed. You didn't have to look away. You certainly didn't have to tell me I was beautiful. It would have been better if you said I looked like a freak!"

"I didn't want to draw attention to your affliction."

"It's not an affliction, you homochromatic dimwit," said Elinor. "It's just my eye color. I was born this way. In fact, that's why my father gave me my extra middle name: Iris."

"And it doesn't hurt?"

"Does your eye color hurt you?"

"Of course not."

Elinor Iris Ann Potoski threw up her hands to punctuate the obvious.

Prudence looked at her for a moment and then smiled sheepishly. "I guess that was a little dopey, wasn't it?"

It was extremely dopey, but Elinor just nodded. She had made several miscalculations of her own based on Prudence's mistake. Well, those things happen, she thought, and then she looked at Prudence. She looked so pathetic sitting there. Still, she was engaged to a man, who by all outward appearances was the best catch on campus. So, what if

Prudence didn't know that she was the last girl to catch him. Prudence would be okay, Elinor told herself. Heaven took care of such trusting numbskulls. And if Prudence didn't understand now that she was marrying such an unmitigated hound, she probably never would, the poor sap.

Poor sap? Elinor stopped in mid-thought. She had her own problems without worrying about the dope across the hall. Besides, because of what happened at The Torrid Orchid she and Paul had to go underground again. No, she shouldn't feel any sympathy for Prudence. Okay, maybe she could feel sympathy for her, but she shouldn't feel at all responsible. Should she?

"Oh, damn," muttered Elinor.

Prudence looked up. "Pardon?"

"Never mind," said Elinor. Prudence smiled and nodded. The poor little dope. She'd probably go through life smiling and nodding for people who would use her, people like Bascomb and his scheming sister. Of course, Elinor had used her, a little bit, but that was different she told herself. Elinor had only asked her to be a beard on a date. That wasn't so bad, was it? Certainly, it wasn't as bad as being the beard in your own marriage. The thought occurred to Elinor. Had making Prudence the beard ruined her chances with Rodney and pushed her into this sham marriage to Bascomb?

She studied Prudence for a moment. Elinor could see Prudence with her brother. He was a bit of sap. And Prudence was a something of a drip, as well. But Rodney and Prudence would at least be a benignly drippy couple, and quite happy in their mutual dopiness.

Elinor took a deep breath, in some ways already regretting what she was about to say, but...

"Can you answer me one question?"

"It's not about eyes, is it?" Prudence asked warily.

"No."

"Sure, if I can," she said with a smile.

"Do you like my brother?"

The smile dropped from her face, and she looked around the room as if she were searching for a previously unseen exit.

"Your... your brother?"

"Yes, my brother, Rodney, Rodney Potoski, do you like him?"

Prudence tried to look away, but Elinor grabbed her by the shoulders and stared into her eyes. They grew moist, and Prudence took a deep intake of breath.

"Yes, I do..." Her eyes filled with tears, and they began to run down her cheeks.

Elinor let go of her shoulders and stood up. "As much as that, huh," she said to herself. She had to ask. Well, so what? She knew. That didn't mean...

Another question entered her head, and Elinor almost punched herself, but instead, she heard herself asking it anyway.

"And do you love Bascomb?"

Prudence buried her face in her hands and started sobbing.

Great, thought Elinor, just great.

She handed Prudence a tissue. Prudence daubed her eyes and forced a smile on her face.

"I'm sorry, sorry about that," said Prudence. "That wasn't, I mean, well, that was silly of me? I...I respect Professor...that is, Bertram...B-Bertie very much. And he thinks the world of me. And I admire him, and his goals, and I think it's a wonderful opportunity to help him and help others."

Oh, great, thought Elinor. Up until that little speech, she could have just let it alone. She could have let the little dope marry the hound. Okay, she would say something else. Against her better judgment, she would.

"You know," she said, "if you don't love him, you don't have to marry him."

"Oh, no," she said, "I have to marry him."

Elinor was about to ask why, but Prudence started talking about when she was a little girl, and the way she was raised, and how she was taught one must always keep the promises they made. She mentioned that the Hoovers had all lived by their word for generations. Elinor knew she couldn't argue against generations and generations of Hoovers, all of whom it seemed would go diving headlong off a steep cliff if they had promised to do so.

Despite it being her own room, Elinor just threw up her hands and started for the door.

"Wait," she said as Elinor stood in the doorway, "you're...you're not angry with me, are you?"

Elinor stopped and looked at her and smirked. This girl was obviously hard-wired to make everyone happy. She would marry a two-timing rat rather than break a promise.

"No," said Elinor as she exited, "I guess I'm mad at myself."

– 22 –
A Jug of Violets,
a Chunk of Spanakopita, and Thou

As cryptic as Elinor's parting remark was, Prudence had very little time to think about it. For the next month, she had very little time to think about anything of her own choosing. Her life was beyond her control. All her waking moments were guided by Bertram's sister as she corralled Prudence through wedding preparations.

She rarely saw Elinor. Elinor seemed just as busy in some pursuit of her own. Only once did their paths cross on purpose. Elinor came to Prudence, late one night after Prudence was already in bed. Elinor asked if she was still going through with the wedding to Bascomb. Her tone revealed that she knew Prudence didn't love him any more than she had during their previous discussion of the matter. Prudence restated that her code of honor made it impossible to break a promise, no matter how inconvenient. She started reciting Hoover family adages on being reliable.

As before, Elinor excused herself, muttering something about cleaning up her own mess by herself. After Elinor left, Prudence wondered if there wasn't a way to break the Code of the Hoovers. It was happening so quickly, like being rushed on to a train without knowing its destination. She did want to be married, she told herself, and Professor Bascomb – she still had a hard time thinking of him as "Bertie" – was very handsome and smart. Most girls would have given anything to be in her situation. She thought about Rodney. As far as she knew, no one wanted to marry Rodney. Rodney wasn't as handsome. He might be as smart as Bertram, maybe even smarter, at least if the subject was windows.

The other girls at the sorority reacted oddly to the news of the wedding. At first, they seemed annoyed by it. After a few days, however, they treated Prudence sweetly, almost patronizingly, as if she were just a little girl playing bride. Prudence attributed this reaction to jealousy and ignored it as best she could.

Prudence fantasized about breaking off the engagement if only she could figure out how. The most direct approach wasn't an option. She'd never been able to reject someone without at least two good excuses to back her up. Consequently, she had gone to many dull parties and performed countless imposing favors all because she had not been quick enough with enough excuses.

Most girls could have easily said: "I've decided I'm not going to marry you after all."

"Why not?"

"Because I said so;" or, "Because my morning egg was too runny;" or, simply: "I don't have to explain myself to you or anyone…that's why!"

Prudence sighed as she pondered the backbone of girls who could toss out excuses as easily as pulling tissues from a box of Kleenex. Unfortunately, when she reached into the same box, she always found it empty. It would take at least seven really strong, logical reasons to get out of this marriage: three for Bertram and at least four more for his sister.

Prudence imagined mock arguments with the Bascombs.

"I…I can't marry Professor Basc… that is, Bertram."

"Why not?"

"Well, I love someone else."

"Who?"

"Another boy…"

"I didn't think it was a duck!" (that retort came from Jeannie).

"No, he's just a boy, a very nice boy."

"Does he love you?"

"No, at least I don't think he does."

From here, the fictitious debate devolved into Prudence being called silly and cajoled into giving up her devotion to someone who couldn't give her the time of day in return. No matter how she played the alternatives in her mind, Prudence lost the argument and was forced to admit, even in her own fantasies that she had no other choice than to become Mrs. Bertram Bascomb.

Bertram's sister wouldn't allow any other outcome. She even informed Prudence's parents of the wedding and smoothed over their initial shock. It was Jeannie who assured the Hoovers that their little girl was well taken care of. It was Jeannie who attested to the fact that their future son-in-law had a prestigious profession with even greater prospects just over the horizon. It was Jeannie who practically guaranteed that their precious, but awkward daughter was now set comfortably for life financially as well as socially. And, it was Jeannie who provided detailed reports on the upcoming nuptials.

Though Prudence rarely saw Elinor, Rodney began popping up at the oddest times and in the most unusual places while she was making wedding preparations.

The first came when she was helping Jeannie pick out wedding invitations at the local stationery store. It should have been that Jeannie was helping her, but somehow it worked out the other way around. The stationer had just placed an oversized book of samples on the table when Prudence looked out of the shop's window. There, she saw Rodney under the awning of the butcher shop across the street.

"This one's darling," said Jeannie, waving a fussy design filled with way too many violets being attacked by overly cute robins. "Isn't it?"

In her distracted state, Prudence reacted with uncharacteristic honesty. "Oh, no it's terrible…"

"What?" squinted Jeannie.

"I, uh, mean, it's terrible…terribly…sad, that's it, the violets…"

"Sad? What's sad about violets?"

Prudence looked up again. Rodney was staring at the stationary shop, looking right in the window, directly at Prudence.

"I said, what about the violets?"

Prudence looked down at Jeannie's scowling face, and then back across the street at Rodney.

"Spit it out," said Jeannie, "what's your beef with violets?"

Prudence glanced down at her, then back to Rodney, and for the first time in her life, she fabricated a total lie.

"Uh, my father, that is my grandfather, yes, my grandfather," she began haltingly, "he hated violets. That is, he lost his…his leg…be…because of violets."

"What?"

"Yes, a, uh, violet truck, that is, a truck carrying violets ran over him, and he lost his leg because of it, so violets are very upsetting to my family."

Jeannie stared at her. Prudence could almost see a profanity forming along her lower lip, but instead, she just flipped the page of the catalog. "Okay, no violets…"

Prudence looked out the window; Rodney was gone, but she continued to look where he had been.

"Jonquils all right?"

"Pardon?"

"I said," snapped Jeannie, "are jonquils all right? Or did your Great Aunt Tilly get pushed over a cliff by a jonquil salesman?"

Prudence looked down at the sample book. Jeannie was pointing at a hideous invitation that made the one with the violets look elegant. Jonquils surrounded by fat little kittens lolling on their backs. She'd never seen cats on a wedding invitation before and hoped she never would again. Having vetoed the previous choice, and fresh out of new lies, Prudence swallowed hard and agreed that cats and jonquils were a perfect choice.

While Jeanine completed the order, Prudence stared at the spot where Rodney had stood. His look lingered in her mind. It wasn't the same as the last time he had stared at her. Gone was the glower of anger. She could only guess what constituted this new expression. Prudence was still turning these questions over in her mind when she found herself being prodded again by Jeannie.

"Oh, yes," said Prudence, thinking an opinion was needed from her, "yes, kittens and flowers are fine…"

"What? That's all settled," said Jeannie, grabbing her by the wrist and dragging her out the door like an over-sized rag doll, "They'll be ready next week. Come on." Jeannie looked back over her shoulder at the shopkeeper as they exited. "Girls in love! Live in their own little dream world, they do! She couldn't wipe her nose without me!"

But it wasn't Prudence's nose that needed wiping. That night she was wiping tears from her eyes, thinking about Rodney. Two days later, the issues were forced to the surface again. This time it happened at Papageorgiou's, a local bakery, where Jeannie dragged her in search of a wedding cake.

"Ah, you must be the girl getting married," greeted Mrs. Papageorgiou, a pleasantly stout woman, "come in, come in…"

She led them to a table towards the rear of the room and beckoned them to sit. Once seated, Mrs. Papageorgiou looked around as if they had misplaced something.

"The groom," she asked in her lyrical Greek accent, "he's no come?"

"He's…" Prudence began to answer before being verbally run over by Jeannie.

"He'll be here," said Jeannie glancing at her wristwatch more for effect than to ascertain the time, "I'm his sister. We can go ahead. He just has to show up at the altar, and don't worry about that. What sort of cakes do you have? We want a big one. White, it's got to be white. Right? White?"

Jeannie looked at Prudence as if she was being asked to verify her virginity in every aspect of the wedding, including the cake. Prudence's mouth hung open halfway, and she gave a feeble nod.

"That's right, a white cake with lots of tiers," said Jeannie. "Can you do lots of tiers?"

"As many as you like," assured Mrs. Papageorgiou before turning her head and calling: "Aristedes!"

A man, presumably Mr. Papageorgio, emerged from the kitchen.

"Yes, Christina, my dear," the man said, or at least Prudence thought that's what he said. She wouldn't have testified to it in court because his accent was as thick as the large black mustache that overhung his mouth.

"Some pastry, and some…coffee or tea?" The first half of the sentence was a command to Mrs. Papageorgiou's husband, the rest of it a question to her customers, which Jeannie answered for both of them in favor of tea.

"I want you to sample some of my Aristedes' artistry," she said, beaming with pride. "He is a magician with the phyllo!"

Prudence exchanged a puzzled look with Jeannie.

"Phyllo dough," said Mrs. Papageorgiou, "it's a Greek pastry dough, very thin, paper thin, and…" She completed her description by rolling her eyes back into her head, crossing her arms over her breasts and giving herself a rapturous squeeze.

"Huh, must be better than…" Jeannie glanced at Prudence and censored herself, "…marriage."

"It's very nice," assured Mrs. Papageorgiou. They didn't have to wait very long for confirmation, as Mr. Papageorgiou returned through the swinging door, carrying a tray of samples. With a flourish he waved the tray across the table, bringing it to rest in front of them. Then he and his wife unloaded an array of items that all seemed quite foreign.

"Isn't all this…interesting," said Prudence.

"I'd say it's all Greek to me," said Jeannie squinting at the pastries, "but that's obvious, isn't it?"

Mr. and Mrs. Papageorgiou exchanged confused looks before the female side of the partnership replied. "Yes, Greek, it's all Greek."

Jeannie picked up an item carefully. "What's this?"

"Ah, is spanakopita," said Aristides proudly.

"Spana-what?" said Jeannie. "Looks like it's stuffed with spinach."

"Yes, yes," said Mrs. Papageorgiou, "is spinach pie."

"It's very nice," said Prudence nibbling a sample.

"Is excellent," said Mr. Papageorgiou as he picked up another pastry and practically shoved it into Jeannie's mouth. "Try, try…"

"Whatcha…" Jeannie's question was cut short by the introduction of the pastry into her face.

"Baklava!" announced Mr. Papageorgiou. "I make best Baklava in whole town!" His wife nodded.

Prudence guessed he made the only baklava in the town, as well.

"Yeah, good stuff," said Jeannie wiping her mouth and taking a swig of tea. "But we don't want a spinach wedding cake or one shaped like a triangle."

"She means it's all very nice, very, very nice," said Prudence, "but don't you think we should ask Professor… that is, Bertram what he'd like? He said he was going to meet us here."

Jeannie sneered. "He's just the groom. He'll cut what I give him to cut. He doesn't care about cake!" Then she eyed Prudence slyly. "Not like you, eh, honey?"

Prudence blushed, thinking of her confession about the stolen piece of cake. She looked away, feeling her cheeks redden, but what she saw as she turned made her face glow an even brighter shade of scarlet. There, in the front of the shop was Rodney. Mrs. Papageorgiou also looked towards the front of the shop.

"Oh, here he is," said Tina Papageorgiou, "here's your young man! "

Prudence nearly swallowed her tongue. How could this Greek woman know she was in love with Rodney? Before she could say anything, Jeannie had turned around and got an eyeful of Rodney.

"What? Him?" spat Jeannie. "A wiry, drippy-nosed kid like that? That's not my brother!"

Mr. Papageorgiou excused himself and approached Rodney, who was studying the display cases. Rodney looked up as Mr. Papageorgiou greeted him and saw Prudence. Their eyes met awkwardly, though neither looked away. Mrs. Papageorgiou and Jeannie kept talking, while Mr. Papageorgiou spoke to Rodney. Finally, Rodney broke his gaze and began speaking with the baker, though Prudence couldn't make out what was being said. Throughout their exchange, Rodney only offered Mr. Papageorgiou brief looks, reserving most of his attention for Prudence. Finally, Rodney muttered something, and then walked out, stealing glances at Prudence as he went.

"Crazy boy," said Mr. Papageorgiou as he returned to the table. He was shaking his head, causing the fringe of curls around his balding noggin to bounce playfully about his ears. "He crazy boy! Want to put in glass!"

"He wants to put what in glass," asked Tina Papageorgiou, "milk?"

"No," replied her husband and spreading his palms flat as if he were outlining the top of a display case, "he want to put in new counter. Glass counter, he wants to put in."

"But we got counters."

Mr. Papageorgiou rolled his eyes. "That's what I say to him, crazy boy! I say, 'looking, I got glass, see? I got glass. Inside glass I got cake, I got cookies. You want baklava? I sell you. You want amigdelota? I sell you. You want taste?' No, he no wants to buy, he no wants taste. He wants to give me new glass. He says he get call to make new glass. You call this boy to come bother me! Why?"

"Me," said his wife, "Now, you're crazy!"

"Well, somebody..."

"Excuse me, but what about my cake," said Jeannie. "Rebuild your shop some other time. I gotta get this one," - her thumb was jerked towards Prudence – "to a dress fitting."

"I no gonna rebuild my shop," protested Mr. Papageorgiou pushing back his chest with all ten fingers splayed. "He's crazy boy."

"Look, I want to know if you can do me a cake. A round cake, with four tiers. That's all I want. I'd do it myself, but all my pans are back home. All I want is a nice round cake. Go out and buy a few boxes of Betty Crocker..."

"Betty Crocker!" The culinary artist behind the sizable bushy mustache recoiled at the intimation that a box mix should ever pollute his kitchen.

"If you want to go up-scale and spring for Duncan Hines, that's fine, too," said Jeannie with a flick of her wrist.

Papageorgiou glared at Jeannie though she took little notice of his reaction. After ten seconds of his devastating gaze, Jeannie remained as unyielding as a week-old lump of milopita. Mr. Papageorgiou turned to Prudence, though with a much-softened expression. He smiled at her sympathetically. That look was short-lived, however, as he turned back to Jeannie. Mr. Papageorgiou's salt and pepper eyebrows seemed to swell, like the storm clouds building in a thunderhead. His brow lowered, his mustache rose to meet them, and if it were possible would have met in the middle, covering his eyes in the dark undergrowth. Tina Papageorgiou must have known what was coming. She gathered up her notebook, and slid out of range.

"Out," said Mr. Papageorgiou.

Jeannie nonchalantly cocked her ear towards him. "What?"

He raised his arm and threw his plump but insistent finger toward the door.

"OUT! You! You...Out! With your cake from boxes...OUT!"

Jeannie looked at him with an expression of amusement, as if this were just a scene from a Greek comedy.

"Perhaps we'd better..." said Prudence, rising slowly.

"Lady, maybe you'd like a cake from some other..." said Tina before being drowned out by her husband's bellowing.

Mr. Papageorgiou pulled his thinning hair from its thickest fringes around his ears as he bellowed. Jeannie strolled to the door. There she turned and paused to study the shop before announcing: "Come, Dear, we can do better."

Prudence followed her out, the shouting of the Greek baker fading as they walked down the street. She found it difficult to keep up with Jeannie. She was too busy looking for any sign of Rodney Potoski.

– 23 –
In a White House without Curtains

If she only had someone to whom she could pour out her heart. Prudence's first choice would have been Elinor, but Elinor was not to be found.

She thought of calling her parents, but they were so enamored of the thought of her becoming the wife of a professor they would probably excuse her anxieties as pre-nuptial jitters.

Jeannie was always around of late, but the last person to whom she would bare her soul.

That left only Bertram. Questioning him was almost as bad as questioning her father. In some ways, she felt that he was like another father in her life. Bertram was much younger than Mr. Hoover, but in other ways, he was older. Perhaps older wasn't the word. He was more scholarly than her father. There was an air about him, an aura, something not quite of this world, or at least of her world. Still, if she was going to be his helpmate, she had to speak now or forever hold her peace.

In a rare bit of luck, Prudence found herself alone with Bertram one afternoon. Jeannie was shopping for a dress for herself for the wedding. Prudence offered to accompany her but nearly had her head taken off at the suggestion.

"Whatdya think; that I can't buy a dress for myself?" Jeannie had snapped. Prudence just stood there; her mouth agape since she apparently hadn't been trusted to complete the simplest tasks for herself since the engagement. Only after her future sister-in-law had stomped out of Bertram's house did Prudence realize that her best, and perhaps last opportunity had arrived. She had to voice her doubts now.

Her intended had just given her a glancing peck on the cheek when Prudence cleared her throat as a precursor to more significant utterances. When he failed to recognize the significance of her throat clearing and started for the kitchen, she repeated the noise, louder, but still with a nervous quiver at its end. Then he stopped and turned.

"Would you like a drink of water," Bertram asked.

"No," she said. It came out high-pitched. Prudence swallowed hard and aimed for a lower register. "No, no thank you, Bertram, that is, Bertie. I would like to talk, though."

"About what?" he asked.

"Oh, uh, nothing in particular," she nonchalantly swung her hips.

"Do you want to dance?" He asked, looking at her swaying.

"Uh, no," she stopped. "I just thought it would be nice to sit down and have a little chat. We don't talk much, that is, we don't talk much alone, by ourselves."

He raised his hands in surrender and sat on the sofa. He adopted the kind, wise, almost avuncular smile that he usually gave her. Had he not given her that look ninety percent of the time, Prudence would have thought it was patronizing. She sat down next to him, and he put his arm around her.

"Okay," he said, "what did you want to talk about?

"Oh, nothing, that is, nothing specific, like I said, we don't get much time alone."

He nodded, and his smile grew as if he had figured out what was on her mind.

"Yes," he said, "Jeannie can be a little overpowering. Well, more than a little. She's more like a Sherman Tank when she gets a goal in her sights. I guess she's been running over your toes, huh?"

"No…" Prudence was being honest. His sister hadn't run over her toes. It was more like she had run up her back, rotated her turret on her head, fired several rounds of shells, and then set the parking brake.

"Well," Bertram continued, "don't worry about my sister. I know she has strong ideas about the way things should be. Still, I don't know what I'd do without her. I doubt if I'd have had the drive to get where I am today without her…guidance. And you wouldn't be here, either. After all, it was Jeannie who pointed out all your…unique qualities. Not that I wouldn't have seen them myself, but, well, it would have taken longer, perhaps. But soon we'll get all these wedding plans over, and Jeannie will go back home, and then it will be back to normal, eh?"

Prudence looked at him. He seemed content with his notion of normal, but she had no idea what that was.

"Normal?" she asked. "What's normal?"

"Normal married life. Just you and I."

"Normal married life," she repeated.

"Yes, you know, me and you, in a new home."

"A new home?"

"Of course," said Bertram as if it were long settled. "We won't live here, will we?"

"We won't?" She hadn't thought about it, not in the frenzy of Jeannie's preparations.

He laughed as one would at a naïve child.

"No, of course not. You wouldn't want to live here, would you? This is a nice little place for a musty bachelor, but not for a rising young couple."

"No, and I guess we couldn't live at my place, either, could we?"

"At the sorority house?" His eye seemed to twitch and then relax. "No, of course not. It's a nice place to visit, that is, it's a nice home for a few years if you're in a sorority, but no, I don't imagine many married couples live in sorority houses, do they?"

They both laughed in a spasm of forced jocularity.

"No, we'll get a nicer house," said Bertram. "I've already had someone looking for us."

Prudence almost asked who, but then decided she didn't want to know, especially if it was his sister.

"That will be nice," said Prudence, imagining a cute cottage, "a nice little nest."

"Or not so little. I have to think of my... our rising position. I'll have to do quite a bit of entertaining, you know."

"Oh, yes," she nodded her head, trying to hide her disappointment and then brightened. "Still, big or small, the size doesn't matter, does it? I mean, it'll just mean more curtains to make, more closets, more shelves, more shelf paper..."

Her catalog was interrupted by another patronizing chuckle. "Oh, Prudence, Prudence, how sweet you are!"

"I am?"

"We'll have all that taken care of.."

"I can make the curtains, and put up the shelf paper, make the beds..."

"Curtains? Making beds? You'll be too busy with important things; things like arranging receptions and serving on committees and panels. Those are what a professor's wife does."

"But, I can make the curtains. It's those little touches that make a home a home."

"They're only curtains," he said.

She recoiled inwardly at the suggestion that curtains were insignificant. Her mother made every curtain in their house, and Prudence had always assumed that she would do the same someday with her home. Homemade curtains were a given, as integral a part of marriage as wedding rings, children, and home cooking. But Bertram wouldn't know that; he was an orphan raised by his sister, and he was a man. She patted his hand and thought about how she would explain such a basic fact of human existence.

"Bertram, Bertie, dear." For the first time, Prudence felt wiser than him, at least in one small area, "you don't understand. Curtains are very important. Curtains, homemade curtains, are, well, they're a very important part of a home. They, they are one of the ways a wife shows love."

"Look, don't worry about the curtains," he said cutting her short, "there's one way a wife can show her love, and they don't have anything to do with windows, okay?"

Windows? He would have to mention windows. Windows meant Rodney Potoski. She imagined Rodney wouldn't be so dismissive of curtains. Curtains were meant for windows, and windows were meant for Rodney, and she, well, apparently she wasn't meant for Rodney. Prudence sat there trying to imagine the life of a wife of a college professor, then a politician, then a President of the United States. She glanced at Bertram, who was now stuffing his pipe as if he were all alone, waiting for a train. Perhaps it wasn't a train he was waiting for, but his future; a future that had curtains, and shelf paper, and fresh-baked cookies, but all ready-made from a store. He was used to ready-made things. He had a ready-made life, hadn't he? And that made her his ready-made wife.

Prudence sighed. How could she bring up her doubts and her fears when he didn't even understand curtains? Curtains, after all, covered the windows to her soul or at least the windows to comprehending her. She sighed again, and he lit his pipe as if she were just another accouterment of his furnished life.

She wondered as they sat there in silence, who hung the curtains in the White House.

– 24 –
The Vaunting of
the Vol-au-Vent

The wedding preparations continued, as did the Rodney encounters. A few days after the bakery, Prudence was at a caterer with Jeannie, or rather she had been taken there by Jeannie. Bertram's sister was a human tugboat, towing the nuptials into the harbor of matrimony. At least Prudence was beginning to feel, like a large object capable of self-propulsion being maneuvered by a much smaller, but more determined force. As she was being guided through menus and samples of tiny crustless sandwiches, Prudence looked up. There again was Rodney looking in the window.

While Jeannie and the caterer debated the merits of cocktail wienies for appetizers versus stuffed artichokes, Prudence strained to watch Rodney while not appearing to do so. Rodney must have had the same plan, though he seemed to be better at it than she was. He was following her every move without betraying a direct glance. Their eyes seemed to stare around each other without actually meeting head-on as if their gazes were of two opposite magnetic polarities. Finally, Rodney locked on her eyes with a focus that was steely and determined. After several moments Prudence forced herself to look away.

"What's this," snapped Jeannie, "it looks like a little pie or something. Hey, you, girl…Prudence…get a load of this!"

Prudence looked at the tray.

"It a vol-au-vent," said the caterer.

"Never heard of it," said Jeannie as she picked one of them up and snorted with the delicacy of a basset hound. "What's in it? Smells fishy."

"It is filled with a tuna salad mixture, though it can be filled with a variety of items: mushrooms, vegetables, or… "

"And whatd'ya call it, vole cement?"

"Vol-au-vent," sniffed the caterer. "It's a very genteel canape, it's a puff pastry, they're hollow. Then you cut off the top and…"

"Puff pastry!" Jeannie squinted. "You're not working with that Greek a few blocks over, are you? He tried pushing a spinach wedding cake off on us, didn't he?" Jeannie jabbed Prudence in her ribs. "Don't you have cheese and crackers?"

"It's not Greek. It's French, actually. It means 'windblown...'"

"Windblown? I'll say it's windblown. Looks like one good sneeze would blow away the whole tray. Figures the Frenchies would come up with it. All they can do is cook, and then only for sissies. That's why we have to keep kicking the Germans out of their country. Windblown! Ha! I'll tell the world! That's all we need, a pastry to give all the guests a dose of the Parisian wind! It doesn't look like it would stick to your ribs, eh?" This comment was punctuated with another jab to Prudence's side. "No, we want something that'll hold 'em, you know, something with some real heft to it, but not too expensive."

"I'll see if the Oscar Mayer truck has arrived," said the caterer before turning on his heels and walking towards the kitchen.

"He even walks like a frog," muttered Jeannie.

Prudence glanced at the retreating caterer. When she looked back at the window, Rodney was gone.

Later, after she had defeated the hapless caterer, Jeannie broached a surprising subject with Prudence as they left the shop.

"Did you see that kid?" she asked.

Prudence looked down, thinking she was referring to a small child.

"The one looking in the window," said Jeannie. Prudence realized she was referring to Rodney. Not knowing where the question was leading, she kept quiet as Jennie continued. "After we came in, the one gawking in the window when that glorified short-order cook was trying to sell me those billabongs."

"You mean the vol-au-vent," said Prudence, hoping to deflect her original question. "I thought they were very nice."

"They were crap, and not even American crap, they were French crap. But I'm not asking you about them. There was this kid looking in the window. Not a little kid, a big kid, you know a college student. He was gawking in the window."

"Per-perhaps he was looking for a caterer..."

"He wasn't looking, he was gawking," asserted Jeannie. "I know gawking when I see it, and that kid was a gawker. I know because I've seen him gawking before. Gawker!"

"You-you've seen him before?"

"He was the chimp that came into that Greek's place, Mr. Pop-a-pimple-head..."

"Mr. Papageorgiou..."

"He said he was interested in their display case," snorted Jeannie.

"Well, perhaps he was..."

"He was interested in gawking. I've seen his type before."

"Y-you have?" Prudence braced herself, certain that Jeannie had made the connection between Rodney and herself.

"His type," said Jeannie with a sneer, "they lurk around, gawking through windows, trying to catch a peek at women. The dirty little gawker!"

"Maybe," Prudence's voice tightened a half octave, "maybe he just likes windows."

Jeannie stopped and looked at her for a minute. "Likes windows," she said incredulously. "That's weird. That's worse than lurking. That's even worse than gawking. No, he's a little pervert. I've seen enough of them in my day. He's a little pervert, alright, but I'm not accusing him of being a full-fledged sexual psychopath. Likes windows, ha, that's a good one. Where'd you get that psychosis, in your abnormal psychology class?"

Prudence was about to point out that she never took abnormal psychology, but Jeannie continued.

"I've been bothered by his type before."

Prudence did a double-take. "You?"

"Plenty of times," said Jeannie. "They just think this body's a free show, sexual playground, a meat market..."

Prudence scanned Jeannie's thin frame and was forced to the conclusion that if Jeannie were in a meat market, she would only be as a scrawny hen past her prime.

"You'll see," Jeannie assured her, "you'll see when you get a little older and fill out some."

Prudence forced herself to keep her jaw from hanging slackly. There were pre-mature babies more filled out than Jeannie.

"Well, let's change the subject," said Jeannie climbing into Bertram's Oldsmobile, "this is a happy time. Don't let some filthy gawker who can't keep his eyes off me spoil your big day. But," she continued as she slammed the car into gear, "if I see that little pervert around me again, I'll trim his wick, but good!"

Prudence looked around hoping that Rodney and his wick were not in sight.

"Never mind," said Jeannie, "I got bigger fish to fry to have this shindig come off."

"Oh, yes, the flowers, the hall..."

Jeannie blew a raspberry. "Took care of those!"

"But..."

"Don't worry, I know what I'm doing, you'll like it."

"I hope..."

"So, all you need to do is show up and look pretty," said Jeannie. "Oh, yeah, and there's the dress fitting."

"Are you sure you need me there," said Prudence, trying to sound sarcastic.

"Yeah," replied Jeannie, missing her intent, "they don't have a dummy your size."

– 25 –
The Double-Hung Conspiracy

How blind, Elinor wondered, could a person be? If the person was Prudence, she could be blind as a bat with a severe astigmatism who had mislaid its glasses. Either Prudence was the most gullible girl on Earth, or she was willfully ignoring every sign shoved in her face.

Once Elinor learned that Prudence liked boys in general, and Rodney specifically, Elinor had been setting them up. Neither knew why they both kept running into each other. Given their dopey natures, the best strategy would be just to throw them together and let nature take its course. Unfortunately, neither Prudence nor Rodney had anything natural about them.

Once Elinor knew Prudence's schedule of wedding preparations, it was easy to get Rodney to show up in the general area. She made anonymous calls to him regarding windows of local shops hoping that he would come and stare at the windows, and then see past the glass to the girl inside. Her best call was the one where she adopted a Greek accent and pretended to be the wife of the owner of the Greek bakery telling Rodney they wanted their display cases redesigned.

Each time Elinor watched from a distance. Each time Rodney had shown up, apparently saw Prudence but never did anything about it. She wasn't sure what she hoped he would do, but at the very least Elinor expected him to talk to the girl.

Now the wedding was getting closer, and Elinor was running out of options. Rodney was not going to act without additional motivation. Nor would Prudence call off her sham marriage without an irrefutable reason to do so. So, that left it to Elinor.

She would work on her brother. Rodney had always been an honorable sort of sap. Certainly, he was more honorable than his younger sister. Rodney wouldn't have charged the neighborhood kids for a peek at their father's spare wooden leg. And, when caught, Rodney wouldn't have allowed someone else to take the blame. Elinor felt bad about that; not enough to tell Rodney the truth, but still kind of bad. Besides, Paul probably liked playing the stoic hero.

No, Rodney wouldn't have done those things. Nor would Rodney forge a love note to someone and sign another girl's name.

"My dearest Rodney," she began on a sheet of Prudence's personal stationery that she'd stolen for the occasion.

Elinor placed the end of the pen in her mouth and thought. What would motivate a lunkhead to action? He had dated other girls in the past, of course. Rodney had even gone steady a few times. But now that he was in college, her brother seemed focused on one overriding passion. Yes, that was it. She would write a letter in Prudence's name confessing a similar passion for windows. She touched the pen to the paper to begin, but then jerked it away.

That was too obvious, she thought. Such an open declaration could be uncovered as a bald-faced lie. If she succeeded in getting Rodney to sweep Prudence off her feet and away from Bascomb it would only take a few minutes of conversation to reveal that Prudence had no enthusiasm for windows. No, this letter would have to be cleverer, cleverer by half, to incite Rodney, save Prudence, and most importantly, keep Elinor's hand in it well-hidden.

"Dearest Rodney," she began anew, "I long to throw open wide the window of my heart to you, but another has forced down the sash and closed the shutters on me, blocking your sunshine from me. How I wish I could gaze into your eyes. Doing so would relieve the pain of my existence. I cherish still that one passionate embrace we shared."

A devious smile crossed Elinor's lips. She had carefully penned the words "gaze," "pain," and "still," so they might be read as "glaze," "pane," and "sill." Reading them quickly, those terms would pluck passionately at Rodney's dopey subconscious. That just left Prudence. It would take more than silly words to convince her. Prudence would need hard proof. Elinor looked up and grinned. She knew just how to get that evidence. That and another little strategy might just do it.

– 26 –
The Late, Great
Packing Crate

Nothing else had gone according to her dreams, but at least the dress was pretty. It was just a simple A-line skirt, a bodice embroidered with lace and pearl appliqués, topped off with a full veil. It was as classic and traditional as when she imagined when she was a little girl.

As she stood in the dress, admiring it in the bridal salon's triple mirror, Prudence could almost see herself walking up the shimmering aisle, in the iridescent chapel of her childhood fantasies. As she squinted, she could see, the young man she had always imagined standing at the altar, awaiting her. Not surprisingly, the groom was more a boy, younger and more Rodney-ish than mature and Bertram-like. She twisted her eyes more tightly as if that would make her dream a reality. It was almost succeeding until a cloud of cigarette smoke blew into her face. The vision fell apart as Prudence was caught in an involuntary coughing spasm.

"What's the matter," croaked Jeannie, a Lucky Strike bouncing upon her bottom lip, "you're not getting sick, are you?"

Prudence tried to answer through the hacking, but could only manage to shake her head, while trying to fan the acrid fumes away from her fairytale gown.

Jeannie removed the cigarette from her mouth. Prudence hoped she was going to tamp the butt out in a nearby ashtray. Instead, Jeannie merely flicked her ash to the carpet, stuck the cigarette back between her lips, and took a deep drag. She looked at Prudence and winked.

"Be happy, go Lucky," she smiled, repeating her brand's slogan.

Prudence smiled weakly through watery eyes and tried to avoid getting ashes on her gown. A moment later, all thoughts of nicotine and lace were driven from her mind by the tinkle of the shop bell, the trod of reinforced-toed shoes, and a familiar voice, speaking in official tones.

"Police," said the voice.

Prudence turned to see Paul Rocher.

"Somebody reported a robbery," he said.

"You," said Prudence.

"Who called the law?" said Jeannie taking another drag on her Lucky.

"I'm the proprietor," said the woman fitting Prudence's gown.

"Ma'am," asked Paul, "did you call the police?"

"No," said the owner removing a pin from her mouth and returning it to the pincushion strapped to her wrist.

"You're not the police," said Prudence. She almost blurted out that he was a communist, but caught herself. "You… you're campus security."

Paul Rocher flashed the badge pinned to his jacket. It was heavier than the campus badge.

"I'm working part-time for the town," he explained.

"Great, a junior G-Man," snorted Jeannie under her breath. She flicked an ash in Paul's direction. "Amateur dick."

"I didn't call the police," said the owner, scanning her small shop to see if anything was out of place. "These are the only two ladies that have been in here all day."

"Well, someone phoned. This is serious business, calling in a false report."

Jeannie just rolled her eyes, while Rocher and the dress shop owner debated who have could have made the call. As they argued back and forth, Prudence from her perch atop the platform could see over the café curtains in the shop window, and out across the street. There she saw Rodney, leaning against a phone booth.

"He probably called from that very booth," muttered Prudence to herself. It was bad enough tailing her, but Rodney was now dragging the police into his campaign of harassment.

"Paul, I mean, Officer," said Prudence, "I think this is a false alarm."

Officer Rocher didn't hear Prudence's assessment of the situation, he had already hefted his oversized Walkie-Talkie to his ear, "Mobile to base: it appears to be a false alarm," he said into the contraption.

"I think…" Prudence almost drew Rocher's attention to his boyhood rival, who was still loitering across the street. She caught herself, not wanting to land Rodney in trouble with the police. It didn't matter, however, since Paul was listening to the squawks and whistles from his radio.

"What? Where?" Paul was almost shouting, his free finger plugging up his free ear. "Schenectady? That's over seventy miles away? Oh! Sorority! Which one? Rho Delta Delta!"

"Rho Delta?" exclaimed Prudence, finally loud enough to attract Rocher's attention. "That's my sorority."

"I'm on my way," said Rocher, "over and out!"

"That's my sorority!" repeated Prudence.

"Oh, shit," muttered Jeannie, for no apparent reason, but with enough motivation to grind out her cigarette on the carpet.

"Hey," said the owner, looking at the burn hole in the rug.

"Rho Delta, that's where I live," said Prudence grabbing Paul by the arm.

"I gotta go! Big trouble!" said Rocher.

He rushed for the exit, dragging Prudence, wedding gown and all, off the platform and out the door with him.

"Hey," repeated the shop owner, "wait."

"Keep your crinoline out of your crack," said Jeannie, rushing after Prudence. "She'll be back."

"She had better," cautioned the owner. "Some of those seams are only lightly basted."

"Will you let go of me," said Rocher, pulling the half-stitched bride down the street, "I'm on duty."

"Not until you tell me what's happening at my house," said Prudence.

"It's official business," said Paul, trying to wrench his arm free. "Leggo!"

"What's official? I'm not letting go until you tell me!"

"It's a ra...assault."

"Assault? Ra? RRRaa? Rape? Someone's being raped?"

"Allegedly," said Paul.

The fact that Rocher was a part-time cop now overrode that he was a full-time subversive. She hoped his sense of duty would now override his political philosophy.

"Allegedly or not, hurry up," shouted Prudence, who had sprinted ahead of Rocher. She hiked up her voluminous skirt. Prudence had already lost her train, and one lightly tacked lace sleeve. Out of the corner of her eye, as she glanced back at Rocher, she could see Jeannie picking up the pieces of the gown. Beyond Jeannie, bringing up the rear, Rodney Potoski was chasing them all, yelling something about an elopement.

Prudence glanced back at Rodney, but only for a moment. Her focus was ahead, to the Sorority. Even in a wedding dress, Prudence was ahead of Officer Rocher as they ran out of town and onto the street filled with sorority and fraternity houses. She picked up speed as she went, glad that she had chosen to wear flat shoes under her gown. Prudence heard panting behind her and realized she had towed Rocher for the last half-block.

"If you were a real red-blooded American, you'd keep up," she called to him. "Don't they make you do physical fitness?"

His reply was delivered in gasps and wheezes.

When they reached the sorority house, Prudence started up the steps on to the porch but was jerked backward. Paul Rocher had become a dead weight now, coming to a full stop on the lawn.

"Come on, Paul, I mean, Officer," urged Prudence.

Paul panted as he hunched over, his hands on his knees. "Just...just...a minute..."

"Hurry!"

Paul sucked down a deep breath of air.

"Yeah, okay..." he said. "Where...where'd you learn to run like that?"

Prudence didn't know and told him as much.

Having regained enough of his wind, Officer Rocher straightened his cap and tie and started up the steps of the Rho Delta House behind Prudence. He only made it to the second step when he was grabbed from behind.

"No, you don't," growled a voice.

Prudence wheeled around to see Rodney face to face with Rocher, as they'd been innumerable times since the second grade. Though Prudence had only witnessed the faceoff twice before, this time, she sensed a difference, at least in Rodney. There seemed to be a fresh determination in his brown eyes. Even his arms looked ready for action: loaded, coiled, fully cocked, or whatever metaphor one applied to fist fights.

Paul's bearing was also different, but in complete opposite to Rodney's. Whereas Rodney was in earnest, Paul was looking at his longtime rival as a discarded remnant from his childhood.

"Roddy, beat it," said Paul. "I'm on a call." He turned to go, only to be grabbed by the shoulder, and whipped back around again.

"I know what 'call' you're on," said Rodney.

"Not now..."

"Now," said Rodney. "I should have settled this back at St. Simeon's."

"Look," said Paul, raising his voice, "I don't have time to stand here talking..."

"For once, you're right," said Rodney. In the place of a discussion, Rodney Potoski shot out his right fist, cold-cocking the jaw of Paul Rocher, and finally settling who was the toughest kid at St. Simeon's.

Prudence let out a gasp as she witnessed Officer Rocher fly backward on the lawn, out cold; a bemused expression frozen on his face testifying to his genuine surprise.

"What did you do that for?"

"You're not eloping with that skunk," said Rodney.

"You knocked him out!"

Rodney looked down with a new found admiration for his knuckles. He looked up with a boyish wonderment postponed for over a decade.

"Yeah, I did, didn't I?"

Prudence realized Rodney had said: "Eloping."

"You're not eloping with him," affirmed Rodney.

"But..."

"Look, I've seen you making wedding plans. I saw you with the caterer and the baker and..."

"But I'm not eloping..."

"No, you didn't want to," said Rodney. "It was obvious you wanted a nice decent wedding. You were making all the good, decent preparations because you're a nice girl. Unfortunately, you couldn't have that kind of marriage, not with that snake." He pointed to the recumbent part-time policeman on the lawn.

"Him?" Rodney thought Paul Rocher was the groom.

"Yes, him," said Rodney. "I know it's a shock. You didn't see it, but he's a pure rat. Why else would he do what he just did?"

"What he did?"

"He took one look at you, looking so beautiful, so virginal – pardon my language – and he had to have you that minute. The slug had to satisfy his selfish desires. The nickel-grabbing lowlife! This swine had to gobble your purity. So, this hedgehog grabbed you and tried to run off with you. I saw him. I saw him drag you out the door of that dress shop."

Prudence almost explained that he hadn't been dragging her out of the door, but she'd been holding on to him. If not for their head start, Rodney would have seen that after the first half-block, Prudence was pulling Paul. She almost explained that, but she stopped herself. Rodney knew nothing about Bertram Bascomb.

"What about her," asked Prudence, seeing Jeannie in the distance hustling up the street.

"Who? You mean the wedding planner?"

"Wedding planner? Who told you she was a wedding planner?"

"She is the wedding planner, isn't she?"

Prudence thought a moment. Jeannie certainly was the person planning the wedding, so technically, that made her the wedding planner. She just nodded her head.

"See, I knew," said Rodney. "And too bad for her, but her plans aren't coming off. You're marrying me!"

"I am? Why would I marry you?"

"Because I don't want you marrying this, this… buzzard!"

"And?"

"And maybe I'm a little in love with you," said Rodney defiantly. "Maybe I was from that time I kissed you. But I didn't think there was any rush, not at least until I saw you out with this weasel at that nightclub."

"Your sister was there, too."

"Yeah, well, I'm not marrying her. And I'm certainly not marrying this chimp. That only leaves you!"

Prudence's chest swelled with pride. Rodney was even cuter than when she had first seen him in his little guard uniform, even cuter than when he was trying to sell windows to a disinterested nightclub owner. He was so stupidly wrong, so valiantly wrong, that he was downright handsome in his self-confident miscalculations, and she loved him all the more for it.

Prudence's wave of joy was dashed against a shoal of reality as Jeannie caught up to them on to the lawn. She looked at Jeannie and then up at the house and remembered what had caused her to run out of the dressmaker's in the first place – one of her sorority sisters was being assaulted in the house behind her.

"Who decked Dick Tracy?" asked Jeannie as she stopped next to Prudence.

"I did," said Rodney, "and I've been waiting thirteen years to do it, and I'd wait another thirteen to take another poke at that hyena!"

"Thirteen years? You're not superstitious, are you Tarzan?"

"Who assaulted this officer?" asked another voice.

"I told you…" Rodney turned around. Standing there was an older policeman. From the look of him, Prudence knew he was a full-time, genuine cop.

"There's been an assault," said Prudence.

The cop looked down at Rocher, who was now snoring. He scratched the side of his head beneath his peaked cap. "I'd say so," said the cop.

"Not him," said Prudence.

The cop looked at her incredulously. "Yeah, well, I saw Officer Rocher an hour ago, and he didn't look so tired he'd take a nap on the grass, and he also didn't have that knot on his chin, either." The cop looked at the three individuals standing there, and then fixed his gaze on Rodney.

"Perhaps you want to tell me what you know about this, son."

Rodney opened his mouth to speak, but instead of an explanation, a crash and shrill scream pierced the air.

The cop looked at Rodney for a second, then the sound of a window sash flying open with a clatter and a bang redirected his attention to the second floor of the sorority house. There was a young girl's head poking out of the window. She let out a second scream, even louder than the first.

Prudence recognized Ruby, who lived at the end of the hall. She had always thought Ruby was one of the prettier girls in the sorority, with a stunning face and a lovely figure. At the moment, however, Ruby's face was contorted in terror. Her figure, at least the upper half of it, could be seen as nature had bestowed it hanging out of the window. Their allure was diminished by Ruby's next scream.

"He's dead! He's dead! He's dead!"

Prudence, Rodney, and the policeman rushed into the house to learn the identity of the dead man.

"Oh, shit," muttered Jeannie, who was trudged after them, with apparently a good guess at the answer.

Prudence was the first up the stairs to Ruby's room. There she found Elinor standing by the open door, blocking Prudence's way. She embraced Prudence.

"I'm sorry," said Elinor, "I'm sorry you had to find out…this way."

Prudence looked into Elinor's eyes, and though they were still mismatched in hue, they were both moist with sympathy. She looked over Elinor's shoulder. There was Ruby who had covered herself with a robe. She was standing, crying, beside her bed, or what was left of her bed. The bed frame was in splinters, demolished from above by a large wooden crate. A glance upward revealed that the crate had fallen through the ceiling and burst open on impact. On the remnants of the bed was the body of a naked man, his face obscured under the wreckage, which included reams of magazines, leaflets, and flyers, most in Russian.

Prudence buried her face in Elinor's shoulder.

Prudence's first thought was that she had killed this man. She put the crate in the attic, and it had somehow fallen through the floor.

"Poor Ruby," she whispered.

"Ruby?" repeated Elinor.

"It's my fault," said Prudence. She lifted her head. Now the Policeman and Rodney were in the room. She began to repeat her confession, more vocally, when she felt Elinor's fingers over her mouth.

"Shhh, not now," said Elinor, "trust me."

Jeannie had entered the room with a look of resignation and disgust that Prudence didn't understand, at least not until Rodney and the Policeman removed the crate to reveal the face of Associate Professor and would-be future President of the United States Bertram Bascomb.

"Dickhead," muttered Jeannie, before adding more vocally to the corpse, "You couldn't keep your pants on, could you? Well, that won't be a problem anymore now, will it?"

She looked up and examined the hole in the ceiling, and snorted. "A hole in the roof, an old packing crate; I always thought you'd buy it from a jealous husband!"

Jeannie looked at Prudence and shook her head. Her glance spoke volumes. Prudence buried her face in Elinor's shoulder.

"Another b-beard?" she whispered.

Elinor stroked Prudence's hair and nodded. "I tried to figure out some way to tell you. I'm sorry, I'm so, so sorry."

Prudence felt Elinor loosen her hold and then clutch her more tightly. She found herself crying, as a thousand thoughts raced through her head. How could she have been so stupid? What about her wedding dress, could she take it back now that the alternations had begun? Is that why he didn't like shelf paper? All the time he'd been looking around when he was with her, had Bertram only been looking for his next conquest? Had the wedding invitations already gone out? What would she tell her mother? How long would she have to go to prison for death by crate? Who was going to be president in twenty or thirty years now that Bertram was dead? Had Ruby called the police to report her own rape? If she had, she would have had to go downstairs to the phone in the parlor. And if Ruby had, then why would she have gone back for him to complete the job? Would she still have to take orders from Jeannie? What would the wedding cake have tasted like? How did that box come through the floor at that minute?

That last question was a good one to start with. Apparently, Elinor was home at the time. Maybe she heard something.

"Where were you when... when it happened?" Prudence asked in Elinor's ear.

"I was with you," replied a voice deeper than Elinor's.

Prudence opened her eyes to realize she'd been cradled in Rodney's arms. She turned her head. There, down the hall, Elinor was talking to the cop who was nodding and jotting down the details on his notepad.

"What's she doing?" Prudence asked, pulling towards Elinor and the policeman.

"She's just telling them what she knew," he said, holding her back. Though she wanted to join the confession, she felt comfort in Rodney's strong arms – keeping her in check, but with a tenderness that was comforting.

"I, I want to talk, too," she said.

"Why? You were outside with me. You just need to calm down. You're all upset by seeing all this. Especially after seeing what I did to your fiancée."

"You did?" Prudence looked back at the bed. By now, an ambulance had arrived, and they were covering the body. Jeannie was still hovering around, almost daring her brother to rise from the dead so she could kill him. "You did that?"

"You saw me deck him," said Rodney. He added "the Rat," but now, having finally confronted his rival, it was with much less intensity.

Prudence thought for a moment. "Oh, Paul."

Rodney pulled her chin towards his. That felt right, too.

"Tell me the truth," he said, "you really wouldn't have married Rocher, would you?"

"No," Prudence admitted with complete honesty, "never."

Rodney began to squeeze her again but pulled up short when another scream came from the bedroom.

"Commie bastards! F**kin' Commie bastards!"

They turned to look in the doorway. There stood Jeannie, clutching two fistfuls of the contents of the crate that had crushed her brother. "I want the cops! I want the FBI! Get me J. Edgar Hoover! This is a conspiracy! A communist plot to assassinate a president of the United States! I want justice! I want revenge!"

Jeannie ranted so that when the coroner arrived, he gave her a sedative. The small woman continued to rave, but now like a wind-up toy whose spring was running down. Finally, she collapsed into the arms of one of the attendants.

"Anybody know who this woman is?" The doctor asked.

"She's his sister," said Prudence. Her arms were being tightly held by Rodney, so she had to nod at the corpse.

"Miss Bascomb..." the coroner began to write in his notes.

"She's married," Prudence corrected. "Her name's Jeannie...I think that's short for Eugenia... Eugenia Bupp. She's visiting from Idaho."

The coroner thanked Prudence and asked if she were all right.

"We're fine," said Rodney, guiding her back down the hall. "We'll be fine."

- 27 -
The Faded Album
and the Fresh Shelf Paper

A nd they were fine, just as Rodney Potoski said they would be, within the peaks and valleys of an average middle-class American life.

Prudence Potoski looked down at the photograph of her sister-in-law as the orange rays of the rising sun fell on it. Another night spent awake. Oh, well, she told herself, she would have a nap later and be right as rain.

She placed the yearbook on the shelf. There, next to it, was her wedding album. She ran her palm across its yellowed leatherette cover with the date embossed in gold stamping, half of which had fallen out. Prudence flipped to the group shot of the bridal party. There was Rodney, looking so handsome, his eyes shining as brightly as the windows he would soon be designing. Next to him was Prudence, herself, with much more of a figure than three pregnancies had left her with. She was wearing a dress similar to the one that she had nearly taken up the aisle with Bertram Bascomb.

The wedding entourage was comprised of friends from her hometown and a few friends of Rodney's. Stosh Pawelczak was his best man. Conspicuously absent was Elinor. She had disappeared soon after the accident. Bascomb's death had been officially termed an accident. There had been a lot of crying girls at that funeral, all of whom sat well behind Prudence in her spot in the first pew. She shed no tears. Those girls had more reasons to miss him than she had. The day of the funeral was the last time Prudence would see Elinor for many years.

Earlier that morning, they bumped into each other in the hallway, both dressed in their best clothes. Prudence assumed Elinor was dressed for the service. When she returned from the funeral, Prudence found a note, written in Elinor's hand, slid under her door.

It was agonizingly brief: "Hope I've cleaned up the mess that I made. I have to leave. You and that brother of mine take good care of each other. Elinor."

Prudence ran across the hall. Elinor's room was empty. Rodney knew less than Prudence. Paul Rocher knew even less than that, at least concerning Elinor's departure.

To his credit, Rocher came to see Prudence. He apologized for using her. He seemed sincere.

"It's no excuse," he said, "but I guess she, that is we, didn't think about you in the whole scheme of things. We just didn't want Rodney to know about us. You see, he's still pretty sore about when were we kids..."

"Yes, I know," said Prudence. "Elinor told me all about that. The grade school, and the wooden leg..."

"She told you about the leg?"

"Yes, why?"

He shook his head. "I didn't think she would tell anyone about that. I certainly never have mentioned it."

Prudence's eyes narrowed. Of course, you wouldn't mention it, she thought. Imagine being so low as to take advantage of a man's disability, one incurred in the service to his country, and to sell it for a nickel a peek. They were silent for several moments.

"I wanted to marry her, you know," he said softly. "I asked her several times."

"No, I didn't know that," said Prudence.

"Funny," he continued but displaying no humor, "funny how you plan things out. I wanted to marry her ever since we were kids. That's just how I thought things would work out. I was going to graduate, work for the Bureau, marry Elinor..."

"The Bureau?" Asked Prudence. The first bureau that sprung to mind, aside from the one in her room, was the weather bureau.

"The FBI, the Federal Bureau of Investigation."

"Oh..." Her mind ran back through the history of the fatal crate: from it sitting atop of Bertram Bascomb's crushed body, to her hiding it in the attic, back to her discovery of its contents. It was filled with just the sort of items you want if you were trying to recruit... or study communists.

"You can still join the FBI," said Prudence hopefully.

"Oh, yeah, I meant, well, you know, I just won't be doing all that with her with me."

"Oh."

An awkward silence followed, broken by Rocher. "Well, I guess I'd better be going," he said, rising to his feet. "I just wanted to stop by and say I'm sorry, and, well, wish you luck, and all that."

"Yes, thank you," said Prudence, "it was very kind of you." As she stood, she emitted a slight groan and touched the back of her head.

"Are you okay?" asked Paul.

"It's nothing," she said, "I still get a little ache sometimes, there in the back of my head, from when I was knocked cold in that nightclub. It's getting better…"

Paul shook his head as he walked to the door. "I told her afterward she shouldn't have done that."

"Who?"

"Elinor," he said, "She was so afraid of us being found out. I didn't know she had it in her, I mean, to clout one of her friends in the head with a chair, especially someone who was doing her a favor. But, then she told you all about that."

Prudence just stared into space for a moment, trying to grasp Elinor's dishonesty, the treachery of the girl who she thought was her friend, the girl who would be her sister-in-law. Before she could reply, her thoughts were interrupted by Paul's turning to leave.

"She said she'd set it all right," he said, "at least she settled things for you and Rodney. Well, good luck."

Rocher walked out of the sorority house, into the night, and had been gone a full minute before Prudence softly replied: "Yes, it's all settled. Thank you."

Prudence never did share with Rodney those details of their courtship, preferring the old adage: least said, soonest mended. She had always meant to say something, someday, when the time was right. But the time never was quite right, and then there wasn't any more time. Still, she consoled herself; it had been a happy marriage.

She closed the album, glanced again at the newspaper photo of Lorraine Innis. No, they may look alike, she concluded, but that was where the similarity ended. Lorraine Innis would never do anything wrong.

The morning sun streamed in the window, shining on Prudence's now gray hair. It promised to be a beautiful spring day.

A good day, Prudence thought, to change the shelf-paper. Then she closed her eyes and fell asleep.

– 28 –
Sliding Down a
Nineteenth Century Barrister

The nightly regimen of moisturizers that would have been inappropriate for Chesney Potts' monthly call to his mother, now were slathered over Lorraine Innis' face and neck. Valerie Fierro called them "vital." Being a methodical individual, Lorraine adopted the advice and made it her routine.

With all her obligations met, Lorraine sat in the easy chair next to her bed, closed her eyes, threw back her head, and sighed. Faces and locales flashed through her mind. Images of Peter Liverot, Valerie, Patsy Einfalt, Purvis Twankey, spirits of the present, fought for position with ghosts of the past. Martina Fergus was there, along with Verity Goodhue, and of course Aunt Elinor. The visitors from the past didn't belong to her. They were Chesney Potts' property. She could only guess what they all would think of her.

She thought of Chesney and her face contorted. She was Chesney, or at least, she had been, or had he been her? It was so hard to say, the lines between them had become blurred like a charcoal sketch left out in the rain. If only she could speak to some of them, especially all the women Chesney had lost. But they were all gone now: Verity, Martina... and of course, Elinor. Elinor, more than any of the others, was on her mind since speaking with Mrs. Potoski. Was Lorraine just a replacement for all of them?

How could she have been so wrong? How had such a straight path grown so twisted? A myriad of feelings swirled inside her head as if her mind was a blender mixing her life and that of Chesney Potts, but the ingredients weren't compatible.

159

"No," said Lorraine opening her eyes. "This won't work. You're chasing yourself in circles. You always come back to the same point you started from...how could you have gotten it all so wrong?"

Lorraine wrenched her eyes shut as if that would stop the swirl of emotions running through her head. Suddenly, as if she had found the switch, she sat up. "You know the answer. You thought of it before, when you were driving: Jaggers! Jaggers had it right. Where is Jaggers?"

Lorraine retrieved the worn suitcase she had left downstairs. The case was covered in a stiff, heavily-lacquered fabric. Beneath the metal reinforced corners, the material was frayed to give a small glimpse of wood underneath. It had belonged to Aunt Elinor. She'd had it since college. It had accompanied her on her wanderings. It was covered with stickers from her travels. She had taken it around the world with her, finally bequeathing it to Chesney when she embarked on her final journey.

Lorraine brought the case up to the bedroom, and set it reverently on the bed. Opening the jewelry case on her dresser, Lorraine removed a small key and unlocked the two latches. There was still a wonderful musty smell to the faded purple satin lining of the case, smells not only from its elegant, slow decay, but vestiges of every far-flung locale it had visited over the past fifty-plus years. It had carried that exotic miasma from the first time Chesney had seen it as a boy. Now it was the repository for the worthless items that were priceless to him, a personal treasure chest in a dilapidated frame.

"You held a present for me the first time I saw you," sighed Lorraine, running her fingers over the rim of the case, "but the real present..."

Lorraine stopped herself. This wasn't a leisurely stroll through the past, but a journey of purpose. "Jaggers," she reminded herself.

Most of Chesney Potts' keepsakes were books. Each had its own story to tell beyond the words they contained. Most recalled a person in his life. Towards the bottom was the most precious of all: a book bound in brown leather. Lorraine held the book to her nose and inhaled deeply. A smile crossed her lips, akin to the type manifested by connoisseurs of fine wines or choice cigars. This, to her, was luxury. She sat down in the easy chair and examined the book's spine: "*Great Expectations* – Dickens," was embossed in gold. On the inside, she smiled at the handwritten dedication, as she twirled her shoulder-length hair between her fingers. She caught herself, untangled her fingers, and used them to flip approximately three-quarters of the way through the book. Finding the passage she sought was simple, as that was as far as she had gotten through the book. There, on the top of page 320, she found the advice given by Mr. Jaggers, the attorney:

> "*Take nothing on looks; take everything on evidence.*
> *There is no better rule.*"

Lorraine closed the book and squeezed it to her chest.

"Nothing on looks," she whispered. "Evidence, hard facts: that would have saved a lot of trouble."

She exhaled with a shudder. She had been so preoccupied debating justice vs. revenge that she had ignored the wise advice of the fictitious Victorian lawyer. But hadn't she had the evidence on Liverot? She thought about it for a moment and then admitted that she had not. She had the assurance of Valerie, but this was only hearsay, only second-hand testimony. Mr. Jaggers wouldn't have accepted that. Valerie hadn't intentionally led her astray. Why would she? She was Lorraine's closest relation and Chesney Potts' closest friend. No, Valerie had been wrong about Liverot's guilt in Martina's death, but it was an honest mistake about a dishonest person. It wasn't Valerie's fault, but Lorraine's.

She looked down at the various articles in the old suitcase and shook her head. Each represented a relationship, and more often than not, each relationship had its own miscalculation, misunderstanding, or mistake. How, Lorraine wondered, could such deformed results be the fruit of such good intentions? Had Chesney ever gotten anything right? To answer that, she'd have to dig deeper. Back to that other year where everything went wrong.

– 29 –
Fritz Dust Memories

"Help! HELP! HELP ME!"

Chesney Potts was a soft boy. His arms were barely suitable for keeping his shoulders and wrists the proper distance from each other. At the age of 12, Chesney didn't use his arms for much more than his two favorite activities: reading, and eating. At a time when most boys his age were building up their muscles in anticipation for the physical challenges of teenage and adulthood, Chesney was content to allow his muscles to degenerate into Crisco shortening, subservient to his head and his belly, with no ambitions of their own.

Now, however, as he dangled from the limb of an oak tree, he wished that he had beefier biceps. Perhaps if he had used his arms to carry heavier books, or if they had delivered more protein and fewer carbohydrates to his mouth, Chesney would have the strength now needed.

It was an unusual situation. Chesney rarely ventured up trees. He preferred reading about them, or better yet, to have them ground into pulp to makes books. Now, however, he was dangling from one. That was bad enough, but underneath him was the most feared animal in the neighborhood: a massive dog named Fritz. His mind flashed back...

◆

"Uh, oh...Fritz dust."

"Fritz dust?"

"Fritz dust," Chesney's older brother Stosh had explained one day.

"What's Fritz dust?"

"That's Fritz dust," said Stosh, pointing to a glob on his younger brother's shirtsleeve.

Chesney fingered the gooey substance. He looked back at Stosh.

"Yeah," said Stosh with an authoritative nod, "that's it all right. Fritz dust. You know Fritz?"

It was a rhetorical question. Everyone knew Fritz. Fritz was the biggest, most ferocious dog in the world. No one was exactly sure what manner of canine and demon interbred to spawn Fritz. There was evidence of Wolfhound, Mastiff, Great Dane, Rottweiler, and Bengal Tiger in the animal. Still, worrying about Fritz's bloodline as he gnashed his teeth just inches from your toes was like wondering about the purity of the plutonium 239 in the nuclear device exploding over your head at ground zero. Most kids in Earswick, Long Island, were more worried about the possibility of Fritz being unleashed than of the Russian's launching a first strike. Chesney doubted the efficacy of the monthly nuclear drills in school. Fritz drills would have been a more practical part of civil defense training.

Everyone knew Fritz. Stosh especially. Being the biggest, strongest, oldest boy around, Stosh had the most Fritz experience. He had been the first one chased by Fritz after the dog appeared one day (via alien intervention, Stosh contended). He was the first one to have a healthy swatch of corduroy taken from his trouser seat by Fritz's fangs; and, he was the only one brave enough to taunt the animal daily through the ten-foot tall chain link fence that surrounded Fritz's yard. Stosh was the only person in Earswick to experience any of these things, which is why he was the acknowledged expert on all things Fritz. So, when Stosh explained the properties of Fritz dust, Chesney, and all others in earshot, listened.

"That's Fritz dust," continued Stosh with the authority of an Oxford don. "It falls from the sky. No one knows just how, but it does. And if it lands on you…watch out!"

The other kids around Chesney retreated one pace, while Chesney leaned as far away as he could from his own shoulder.

"You see, that marks you. Fritz smells Fritz dust. It drives him wild, even wilder than he usually is. He craves the stuff. Whatever it lands on, he comes after. Not right away," said Stosh, "He waits until dark. And then he comes out once a week when old man McConnegy lets him loose to quench his bloodlust; otherwise, Fritz would go even crazier. He eats all the stuff the Fritz dust has landed on."

The children stood with their mouths agape, until an older girl, Denise Clott, interrupted.

"Stosh Potoski," she charged, "you're full of beans!"

Stosh leaned back and nodded.

"Oh? Am I? Remember Mr. Larson's old Buick? The car that disappeared, and no one ever saw again?" Stosh paused for effect. "Fritz dust fell on that last month. What do you think happened to that?"

An audible gasp rose from the crowd.

"Are you trying to tell me," challenged Denise, "that a dog ate a Buick?"

"What do you think he did," sneered Stosh, "drove it away?"

The children all laughed, unifying behind Stosh's version of events. It was ridiculous to imagine Fritz driving a car. A dog eating a Buick was much more plausible. Years later, Chesney would discover that Mr. Larson had smashed up the car in a drunken wreck that was not talked about in polite neighborhood conversation. He would also realize that Old Man McConnegy was at the time only thirty-six years old. But the clear reasoning of adulthood is beyond the comprehension of a kid with a glob Fritz dust on his sleeve.

"W-what do I do about…it?" asked Chesney, his mouth dry, his voice barely a whisper.

"There's nothing you can do," Stosh shook his head, "aside from burning it."

"Can't I just wipe it off?"

Stosh snorted. "Sure you can wipe it off. But then anything it gets wiped on just spreads it out. Larson only would have lost a fender, but he started wiping it! And you saw Mr. Larson the next day with that bandage around his head, didn't you? No, either you burn it, or Fritz eats it."

Chesney swallowed hard at his limited options. He could either be burned now or eaten sometime in the next week. "So…I h-have to burn it?"

"Not the whole shirt, Cheesy," he said. "Don't be a dope all the time! All we have to do is cut out the part with the Fritz dust and then burn that. Gimme that magnifying glass." Stosh whipped out his Boy Scout knife, and one of his minions handed him a magnifying glass. "Now stand still, I don't want to cut you…too bad."

"Too badly," murmured Chesney. He was loathe to correct Stosh's grammar at such a delicate moment, but couldn't help himself.

Stosh cut a jagged patch from his brother's shirt and proceeded to incinerate in with the magnifying glass.

Later that day, after Chesney had been scolded and punished for ruining a practically new hand-me-down shirt, Stosh privately assured him the action had saved his life.

This and other less pertinent episodes of his brief life flashed through Chesney's mind while fifteen feet below Fritz was rehearsing the growls, snarls, and gnashes that were the basis of his reputation.

"HELP!" Chesney cried once more.

"Just swing your feet a little to the left."

"What? Where?"

"Your feet, and to the left! Calm down!"

"Fritz is right under me," whined Chesney, "right under me, Clo."

"And that other branch is even closer. Stop worrying about the dog, and look at what's right there. Honestly!"

Indeed, a foot to the left of his feet was another branch. It was an easy maneuver, even for an avowed sedentarian. Once he had both feet firmly planted on the tree limb, he nudged his hands along the upper branch to a position of safety. It was only then that he turned to see the face of the person who had been talking him out of danger.

"See, I was right here all the time," she said.

"I saw my life pass in front of my eyes," said Chesney, "it was scary, Clo."

"Really? I've always found that sort of thing fascinating."

"A person disappearing down the gullet of a killer dog is fascinating?"

"No, the whole life before your eyes bit, it's paranormal," said Clo. "I mean if you had fallen, and Fritz had mauled you..."

Chesney looked at his best friend, Clodagh, but her focus was someplace else, almost rapturous as she continued.

"...and if you'd have died," she placed a reassuring hand on his arm, "only for a minute, I'd have jumped down and pulled out your lifeless body, and then gotten you resuscitated..."

"Thank you, very much," said Chesney.

"...but in the meantime," she continued, "you probably would have had an out-of-body experience."

"A what?"

"Out-of-body; your soul would float up, and you'd be looking down on your chewed-up carcass."

Chesney looked down and then up, and then down again. "If I'd be looking at the thing that killed me in the first place, why would I go back up just to look down again?"

Clo laughed then reached out and punched him on the forearm. She hit pretty good for a girl. He tried not to wince at how well.

"You dumbbell," she said, "that's not what I mean. You'd be out of your body..."

"Out of my mind is more like it..."

"No, your mind, your soul, your spirit, whatever you want to call it, it would be free, and you could go anywhere you wanted to, just by thinking it, and like a flash, you'd be there. Not just on Earth, but heaven, outer space, anywhere."

"I could go anywhere? And I'd want to float above a stupid dog and a fat kid's carcass?"

"Well, you probably wouldn't realize what had happened right away, so you'd stick around for a bit until they either buried you or revived you. They'd revive you, I'd make certain of that, Ches. But in the meantime, you could go anywhere just by thinking about it!"

Chesney sighed. "Right now, I'd just like to get out of this tree." He wondered why he'd let her talk him into retrieving a cluster of acorns from that branch. With her leading the way, the pair shinnied down the tree trunk, just on the other side of the fence from the growling dog.

"There, safe and sound and good as new," said Clodagh, as the pair retreated up the block and sat beneath a tree.

"I didn't even get the acorns," said Chesney.

"Don't worry about it."

"But did you say you wanted them for that herbal stuff you're doing?"

"Yeah," she said, reaching into her pocket, "I got some, here."

"Then why did you have me..."

"Just a little adventure," she smiled.

It couldn't be easy for her to be cheery. It's bad enough to be a girl saddled with the name "Clodagh," but it was especially challenging when your last name happened to be "Clott."

"This outer body thing," said Chesney, "is it like being invisible?"

"Well..." Clodagh rubbed her hands through her thick brown hair, "not exactly. I mean, no one could see you, but you couldn't go around playing tricks on people, or anything. You'd be like a spirit."

"Could I haunt Stosh?"

Clo rolled her eyes. "You're just being silly now. You read too many ghost stories."

"Well, still," said Chesney with a grimace, "I bet I could find out a lot."

"Like what?"

"Oh, like who plays all those practical jokes in our house."

"Duh! There's only four of you. If it's not your parents, then it's you or your brother, and you'd know if you did it to yourself."

"I meant, I'd see who short-sheeted my bed, and who put onion gum in my sandwiches."

"Yeah, it's probably your mother."

"I know it's Stosh."

"So why would you need to be invisible?"

"So I could catch him at it," he said, "to prove it."

Clodagh shook her head. "Why? So you could turn him into the FBI? 'Please, FBI, my brother is short-sheeting my bed, and I've got the evidence right here from an out-of-body experience!' What a waste of invisibility. You should have my problems. You've got one big brother. I've got three older sisters."

"But they're girls..."

"Which is much worse," she said. "You can see right through Stosh."

"Metaphorically speaking," said Chesney, displaying a word he'd learned the week before.

"Well, I didn't mean metaphysically," said Clodagh, flexing her own vocabulary. "You know when Stosh does something. It's obvious. He's a big, dumb, boy. He's like an elephant leaving his footprints in wet cement at the scene of the crime. There's nothing subtle about Stosh. My sisters, on the other hand, are all sweet, at least in front of my parents. They stick the dagger in with one hand, while they use the other hand to straighten their halos."

Chesney nodded. Clodagh's three older sisters were pretty rough on her, teasing her, especially for her eyes, which were almond-shaped, a trait of some gene in her Irish ancestry that her sisters avoided. They taunted her as the illegitimate daughter of some wayfaring Chinaman who had sold his daughter to Mr. and Mrs. Clott for a bowl of rice. Even if she had occidental eyes, Clodagh's sisters had her hairline to fall back upon. Clodagh was the owner of a well-defined widow's peak. When her siblings were tired of poking fun at her eyes, they drew comparisons between her hair and Count Dracula's or Eddie Munster's. As he looked at her eyes and her hair, Chesney had to agree that life was no picnic for the youngest in any family.

"No, you need to fight Stosh on his own terms," Clodagh continued, "like I do with the unholy trio."

"Like how?"

A satisfied smile overtook her lips. "Last week Rhoda lost her new sweater, she probably left it on the bus."

"So?"

"So, she tried to blame it on me, because the day before I'd said how much I liked it, and she didn't want to get blamed for being careless. Anyway, it didn't really work since her name was on the tag and the bus driver called up the next day. Still, I didn't appreciate that, so I got back at her."

"What'd you do?"

She held up her index finger, and moved it back and forth, pantomiming a knife in the act of cutting. "I sliced…halfway through her bra straps."

Chesney gulped. No one around his house mentioned ladies' underwear, except Stosh, and then only in lewd ways.

"Yep, not enough that she noticed it, but enough to weaken them. You cut them underneath, right at the top of the shoulder." Clodagh drew a schematic of the operation in the air with her fingers. "She was doing jumping jacks at cheerleading practice when they gave out and…BOMBS AWAY!"

Chesney felt the blood rush to his face, and he cleared his throat to hide his embarrassment.

"I only wish I'd been there! See, that's what you need to do to Stosh," said Clo.

"Uh, Stosh, he doesn't wear a…those things."

"Duh! I mean you need to get him back the way he gets you. Fill his jock with BenGay, or something. Still, I must admit the bra trick was perfect because she can't get back at me…" Clodagh looked down at her own chest, "not yet, not quite."

Chesney felt his face glow a deeper shade of crimson.

"That's what you need to do," said Clodagh, "give it back to him like he's giving it to you, only better, bigger, and harder."

"But he'll get mad," said Chesney.

"So what?"

"Well, he's bigger, a lot bigger than me."

"You worry too much," she said. "If you keep letting Stosh do whatever he wants to you, do you know what he'll do to you?"

Chesney shook his head.

"Whatever he wants! He's a bully. If you let him keep pushing you around, he'll do it your whole life. You've got to stop him. Bullies only pick on people who let themselves be picked on."

"Preposition," muttered Chesney.

"Shut up," said Clodagh. "Once he sees you have a backbone, he'll go pick on someone else. You know I'm right!"

Chesney did know she was right, but he also knew Stosh was almost as twice as big as he was and more than three times as strong. He felt his insides knot up as he struggled with the truth of Clo's advice versus the painful awareness that he was a weakling. He wracked his mind for a change of topic.

"Um…my…my aunt is coming to visit," he blurted out.

"Oh?" said Clo, who had gone back to examining her chest for nascent signs of things to come. "Is she nice, or does she like Stosh?"

"No, she's nice," assured Chesney, "I mean, I guess she's nice. I've never met her. Not in person."

"Really? Not in person?" Clodagh stopped looking down her shirt and looked up at her friend. "Does she do out-of-body visitations?"

"No, I don't think so. Aunt Elinor writes me lots of letters."

"Oh," Clo's expression dropped. "Well, that's nice, too."

"And she sends me presents."

"Good presents, or galoshes? I got an aunt that sends galoshes. The other one sends writing paper."

"No, my Aunt El sends me books, records, and puzzles, stuff like that."

"Oh right, those. What does she send Stosh?"

Chesney stared into the air. He'd never really thought about it. "She doesn't really send him anything, that is, I can't think of anything she's ever sent him."

"Maybe she'd like to help you give Stosh a jock full of Mexican jumping beans," said Clo. A wicked look narrowed her eyes even further, making her look like a leprechaun about to perpetrate mischief on a lumbering human.

"Why would she do that?"

"Because she likes you? Honestly, Ches, someone's got to stand up for you. I can use all the help I can get!"

– 30 –

In the Town Where I Was Born
Lived a Lad Who Flicked His Peas

Thoughts of Fritz dust and near-death encounters faded in the face of a fresh menace: a lump of his mother's mashed potatoes and one of her underdone chicken legs. One day Chesney would learn that not all chicken was baked to an unseasoned blandness and accompanied by a dollop of petrified starch.

The perfect complement to this culinary purgatory came courtesy of a green pea that was flicked off his right ear. Though he hadn't seen the pea coming, Chesney knew it came from Stosh. As with most of Stosh's taunts, the pea flicking was executed so deftly that it went unnoticed by his parents. Their only comment came from his mother when she chided Chesney for "whimpering at the table," after he gave an involuntary cry when he was hit.

"But..." Chesney started, hoping to explain.

"Don't interrupt your father when he's going to talk," said Mrs. Potoski anticipating Mr. Potoski's nightly review of the day's events.

As he plowed a drift of potato to the side, Chesney pedantically parsed his mother's admonition. He could only interrupt his father when he was talking. If he weren't talking, it wouldn't be an interruption.

His father began his latest report on the deficiencies of the Long Island Railroad. Chesney glanced at Stosh. He had a smug look on his face. Yet again, he had gotten away with one of his attacks.

Stosh's expression must have been just like the one Hitler wore at Munich after having made off with half of Czechoslovakia. They had studied the origins of the Second World War that day in history class. Chesney saw parallels between his brother and the Fuhrer. Still, he had to admit to himself, he was more a Neville Chamberlain than a Winston Churchill. Chesney was definitely following a policy of appeasement. He wondered as he removed the residue of the pea if Chamberlain ever had to pick bits of vegetables from his ear hole.

Chesney's historical musings were interrupted by a sudden change in the conversation. Most nights, his father provided monologues on topics from the latest trends in casement windows to the daily special at his favorite lunch counter. The reaction to these discourses ranged from his mother's bland replies to Stosh's sycophantic responses. Being the youngest, Chesney kept his head down and his mouth shut. This evening, however, there was a scarcity of window news, and Mr. Potoski had skipped lunch, so he solicited news from the other correspondents at the table.

"I got news, Dad," said Stosh.

Years of fatherhood had developed selective deafness in Mr. Potoski. He sat in silence until Stosh continued.

"There's going to be a junior golf tournament. They're going to hold it up at the golf club."

Chesney rolled his eyes. Where else, he thought, would they be holding a stupid golf tournament, but at a stupid golf club?

Mr. Potoski looked up, a flicker of recognition in his eyes. "A golf tournament, eh?"

Stosh beamed. "Yes, for teenagers around my age."

"Well, you'll want to enter that."

"Enter it? I'm going to win it," assured Stosh. He began to prattle on about his skill as a golfer, but even that topic of mutual interest failed to hold Mr. Potoski's attention. His lack of a response soon caused Stosh's soliloquy on golf to gradually peter out in mid-sentence.

Thirty seconds of silence filled the room.

"And you...Chesney?" His father always seemed to pause before saying his name. It was as if the pause was for an unspoken adjective that expressed his true opinion of his younger son.

"Me?"

"You're the only one named....Chesney."

"Oh, no, there's nothing new," he fidgeted in his chair. "Well, we have a history test tomorrow."

"Study hard."

"I did."

"Good."

That lone syllable was less an endorsement of Chesney's efforts than an expectation of performance. Chesney earned good grades, especially in history, and English. His good grades had become unremarkable and were rarely mentioned. Apart from innovations in window design, Mr. Potoski was a great advocate of the status quo. Once a person's benchmarks were established, they merely had to be maintained. As such, Mrs. Potoski was regarded as a meticulous housekeeper and horrible cook; Stosh was an able athlete, and a total suck up; and, Chesney was a good student and a physical marshmallow. Though Mr. Potoski never said so, Chesney suspected his father thought more highly of Stosh's abilities.

Another silence followed as Mr. Potoski picked at his meal. He craned his neck towards the counter, most likely looking for dessert, when Mrs. Potoski announced a news flash of her own.

"We had a letter," she began, pausing to clear her throat, "from your sister."

"Oh, yes?" said Mr. Potoski. In twelve years, Chesney had learned that his father's vocalizing an "oh, yes," meant that he wasn't particularly happy about something, but was withholding full displeasure awaiting further details.

"Yes," said Mrs. Potoski, clearing her throat once more. She had had even more years to study her husband's moods and signals. "Yes, she's going to be coming to visit. She didn't exactly say when...but she is coming..."

"Very nice," said Mr. Potoski, which meant that it wasn't nice at all. Even a stranger to the Potoski table would have realized this, if not from the edge to his voice, then from the way he jabbed at a lump of potato as if it were a vital organ of someone he found annoying. "Is it too much to ask a person to supply a little more warning, a little bit of advanced notice? We're not running a hotel here for vagabond spinsters."

"Yeah," added Stosh, quick to ally himself with his father whether or not he understood the nuances of the discussion, "it's not even a motel." His comment went ignored.

"I know," said Mrs. Potoski, who hated confrontation, "but it's not too much trouble..."

"That's not the point. It's just common courtesy. She never did have a mind for planning anything. I'm surprised she even bothered to write. She's always gone through life like that. Remember how she walked away from college? Halfway through and she just up and left. I suppose that's to be expected from a flighty...uh...will o' the wisp..."

"Yeah, a willow whip," agreed Stosh.

"It's really not a problem," said Mrs. Potoski, beginning to clear the dishes, "we haven't seen her for years, and she is your only sister..."

"That's not...Chesney, help your mother clear the table...the point."

Chesney got up to help.

"She was just like that when we were children," continued Mr. Potoski. It must be getting good, Chesney thought as he placed the dishes in the sink, because his father had switched to more hushed tones, even though he was still audible to everyone in the room. "Always looking out for herself first. You know whose influence that was?"

Mrs. Potoski shrugged her shoulders.

"Yours, Dad!" piped in Stosh, not understanding his father's sarcasm.

"No one is talking to you," said his father. "It's you-know...."

"You mean the name we don't mention," said Mrs. Potoski through the corner of her mouth.

Mr. Potoski agreed with a grunt and a sharp nod. "Well, he got his, didn't he? She cut and run on him too when the going got tough. And where's he now?"

"He's a Secret Service agent," she said.

"A spy? Like *The Man from Uncle*? Cool!" said Stosh. Aside from a pair of dirty looks, one from each of his parents, his comment was ignored.

"Secret Service? How do you know…"

"It was in the alumni newsletter years ago."

"Oh," said Mr. Potoski. He furrowed his brow as if his notes for the conversation were scribbled inside his frontal lobe. After a moment, he picked up the thread. "Taking off for who knows where…"

"Washington, he works in Washington."

"Not him, I mean Elinor."

"Oh, sorry, Dear."

"Gallivanting around the world, never letting her family know if she's dead or alive…"

"Well, she must be alive," reasoned Mrs. Potoski, "or how else could she write." Chesney was thinking the same thing.

"She never writes to me," said Mr. Potoski.

"Me neither, Dad," agreed Stosh.

"Well, she writes to Chesney."

Chesney froze. He could feel his father's glare on the back of his neck.

Like most boys, Chesney Potoski was eager to win his father's approval. Unlike Stosh, however, Chesney hadn't the instinct for ingratiation that serves toadies, crawlers, and career politicians so well. Consequently, Chesney had as much chance of spontaneously pleasing his father as a pig farmer had of catering a Passover Seder. The harder he tried, the more ham-fisted the results. He was sure that his father loved him; at least he was pretty sure that he didn't hate him, but it just seemed that he liked Stosh more. Stosh was good at the things that interested Mr. Potoski. Stosh was pretty good at science and golf. Chesney was better at reading and writing, which, as he was oft reminded, were inherited from his mother's side of the family. Even their names marked the clear divide. "Stosh" was the name of one of his father's boyhood friends. "Stosh" went with "Potoski" as sauerkraut went with kielbasa. "Chesney" was the name of some old favorite uncle of his mother's. Chesney had felt some connection with his Potoski side through his correspondence with Aunt Elinor. But now, he discovered that this too was a stumbling block between him and his father.

Chesney tried to think of a rationale for writing to Aunt El, as she signed herself. The easiest would have been the truth. She wrote to him, and he wrote back; but in the mind of a twelve-year-old, the truth is often the least obvious justification when trying to please an adult. He stood pretending to arrange the dishes in the sink while expecting his father to demand an explanation, or deliver a punishment. Out of the corner of his eye, Chesney could see Stosh's face brighten in anticipation of pulling further ahead in the unspoken sibling sweepstakes. Instead, his father's expression relaxed somewhat.

"Well, then, she can sleep in Chesney's room," was all he said with a shrug. After another moment, the crisis passed, and the topic was changed to the state of the tires on the family station wagon.

Chesney would have been more than willing to give up his bed for his Aunt Elinor. But forfeiting his room meant moving in with Stosh. Stosh flashed him a menacing smile which spread into a wicked grin. His eyes narrowed, and he nodded his head slowly at Chesney, like a hungry man realizing that the bacon sizzling on the stove was frying for him and him alone.

"Can't I stay over at Clo's," asked Chesney, picking up a dishtowel.

"No," said Mrs. Potoski, without even raising her head, "Clodagh is… well, she's becoming…"

"She's getting her tits," muttered Stosh, audible only to Chesney.

"You're both too old for sleepovers," interjected Mr. Potoski, who was now ensconced behind the evening paper.

Stosh's grin spread. "We'll have a good time, Cheesy," he said, punctuating his remarks with a slashing motion across his throat, adding under his breath: "hope she stays a good long time."

"What was that, Stosh?" asked his mother.

"I said, we'll have a real good time."

Mrs. Potoski looked up from the sink and smiled that naïve, blissful smile that mothers display, oblivious to the fact that her firstborn was planning to devour another of her young. Still, there was nothing Chesney could do about it within the composition of the family.

Mrs. Potoski doted on Stosh.

Because he was secure in his mother's devotion, Stosh was repulsed by her attention, and constantly sought his father's approval.

Mr. Potoski found his validation at work and on the golf course. The fact that he continued subjecting himself to the daily tortures of the Long Island Railroad proved his devotion to them all. He loved his wife; he grimaced at Stosh's clumsy attempts to follow in his footsteps; and, was genuinely mystified by Chesney's interests.

Chesney, being the junior member of the group, tried to fit in with the others, and not get in the way. This meant taking what Stosh dished out; not confusing his father with his own self-expression; and, suffering his mother's simplistic outlook. Deep down, he longed for acceptance and approval. His correspondence with Aunt El represented a glimmer of hope that some blood relation understood him. It also refuted the story Stosh often told him. Like Clodagh's sisters, Stosh had an adoption legend. According to Stosh, Chesney had been entrusted to the Potoski family by a roving band of congenital idiots who couldn't afford yet another imbecilic mouth to feed. While he doubted this, at times, he almost wished he was adopted, if only for the comfort of not having emerged from the same gene pool as Stosh.

Chesney hid his face in the dishtowel. As much as he looked forward to finally meeting his aunt face to face, he couldn't help hoping that her visit would be a short one, at least during the nights.

– 31 –
The Attack of the Analogous Hemorrhoids

T his is getting to be like an attack of hemorrhoids."
The thin walls of Potoski's tract house made Chesney privy to many late-night adult conversations.

"Are your hemorrhoids acting up again," Chesney could hear his mother sigh in the adjacent bedroom. Mr. Potoski was a good provider, a loving husband, a dutiful father, but not a particularly good patient.

"No, my hemorrhoids aren't acting up," said his father. "I said it's like an attack of hemorrhoids."

"Oh."

Several moments passed. Chesney glanced at the clock. It was a quarter after eleven.

"Aren't you going to ask me?" his father's voice broke the silence.

"Ask you what?"

"Ask me what is like an attack of hemorrhoids."

There followed a pause of several beats. His parents' timing often made Chesney wonder if they'd ever done a double act in vaudeville.

"All right, what is like an attack of hemorrhoids…Dear." By the way his mother said that "Dear," it was apparent she was patronizing him but didn't enjoy doing so at this time of night.

"My sister."

"Elinor?"

"It's the only sister I have."

Another sigh came through the wall.

"How is she like an attack of hemorrhoids?"

"Because," said his father with his punchline, "you know they're coming, but you don't exactly know when, and when they get here it's a pain in the ass!"

Being only twelve, Chesney knew little of hemorrhoids, except as one of Stosh's favorite terms for him. "Scum-Wad," "Douche Bag," "Snot-Face," and "Toe-Jam," completed the top five. Now, here was his Aunt

175

El, his pen pal, being branded with the same name. Perhaps, he thought, it was an inalienable right of older brothers to refer younger siblings as "hemorrhoids."

"You don't know when hemorrhoids are coming," said his mother pedantically.

"I know I don't," said his father. "That's my point. It's just like my sister's visit."

"But Elinor wrote to us saying she was coming."

"Yes, but she didn't tell us when."

"But the analogy doesn't work. Your hemorrhoids don't send you notification that they're going to flare up."

"Yes, but I know that they'll be back," said his father annoyed that his simile was being contested. "That is the point!"

"I'll get you some mineral oil."

"What for?"

"If your hemorrhoids are acting up, mineral oil will help soften your stool. And it's 'for what.' Don't end your sentence with a preposition."

"I don't need my stool softened. My hemorrhoids aren't acting up!"

"You said you could tell when they were."

"Well, I know they'll act up sometime in the future. That's not what I'm talking about…"

"You press too hard."

"What?"

"In the bathroom. You press too hard."

"How would you know how hard I press?"

"A wife knows these things," said his mother intimating that she was omniscient about anything that took place within their home. "Besides, I can hear you. You press too hard. I hear you grunting. You're not delivering a baby, you know."

Chesney was perplexed by this last comment and made a mental note to ask Clodagh Clott about the connection between the birthing process and his father's bathroom habits.

"Look this isn't about…it's not about anything but my sister coming to visit."

"What of it?"

"We don't know when she's coming," said Mr. Potoski, "that's the point. It's been more than three weeks since she wrote that she was coming and she's not here yet."

From years of having a front row seat for their act, Chesney imagined that his mother had just shrugged her shoulders.

"Well, it's upsetting the whole house," Mr. Potoski continued.

"It's not upsetting me," said Mrs. Potoski. "When she shows up, I'll change the sheets in Chesney's room, and he'll sleep in the sleeping bag in Stosh's room."

Chesney's whole body shuddered at that reminder.

"It's just rude. You'll see. Traveling all over the world, chasing after mystics and gurus like some sort of hippie. She'll just upset everything."

"That's silly."

"You never lived with her."

"I lived across the hall from her."

There was a brief silence: "Oh, yeah. Still, it's not the same, not exactly."

"You never shared a room with her either. So, I've lived as close to her as you have."

His father grunted.

"I know Elinor can be difficult," said his mother, "and I know she's a very selfish, self-centered person. But you can't pick your family…"

Chesney looked in the direction of Stosh's room.

"…so there's no use getting upset about it. You just deal with it as best you can. This too shall pass."

"Like hemorrhoids…"

"Yes, dear, like hemorrhoids. Good night."

"….Night," came his father's reply. From the way he said goodnight, Chesney imagined that his father thought he had won the debate. He was also sure that his mother didn't think so but would let him rest in that illusion.

Chesney heard the bedside lamps in his parent's room click off, placing the entire Potoski house into darkness. As he lay on his back, staring at the ceiling, he wondered what his mother meant when she said his aunt was selfish and self-centered. His only contact with Aunt El had been by her letters, and those were cheery, often funny, but with very little mention of herself. She sent him little presents, even when it wasn't a holiday, and none of these drew attention to herself. He didn't even have a picture of her, he didn't know if she was short, tall, thin, or fat. He tried to form a mental picture of her, and while doing so, fell asleep.

– 32 –
Great Fulfillment of
Great Expectations

The long-anticipated visitation came when it was least suspected. It wasn't exactly like a thief in the night, but rather like a door-to-door salesman on a Tuesday afternoon. Mr. Potoski was at work, designing better windows for a better tomorrow. Mrs. Potoski was out at some appointment. Stosh was probably up to no good, as he usually was on any given afternoon between the final bell at school and the first call for dinner.

Chesney was home alone. Popeye was on. Not the inferior color cartoons. Chesney rarely bothered with those. His tastes had matured. He preferred the black and white cartoons from the 1930s. He felt, watching them, that he wasn't just watching a crude sailor eat spinach and beat up his shipmates, but rather that it was like being on an archeological dig, delving into the habits and mores of an earlier time. Still, while he found them entertaining, Chesney couldn't help but wonder how Popeye could repeatedly be rejected by Olive, have to fight to win her back, and then do it all over again after an intervening commercial for breakfast cereal. He sensed there was a more profound allegorical insight there, like something from an ancient Greek tragedy. To Chesney, the cycle of rejection and redemption, failure and atonement, reflected the whole of the human condition – all encapsulated in seven-minute dramas featuring a one-eyed sailor with poor language skills. Perhaps it was an animated Rosetta stone that held a clue to his never-ending struggles for survival against Stosh. Or maybe, he thought, it was just a cartoon. Still, the absence of anyone else in the house meant that Chesney was all alone with his thoughts, the 22-inch RCA television set, and a fistful of cookies. This was as near a state of Nirvana as a twelve-year-old could attain in Earswick.

In was in the middle of this philosophical musing and toward the end of the Hydrox cookies that both activities were interrupted by a knock on the front door. Pausing only to lower the volume and shove the last cookie in his mouth, Chesney scampered to the front door. He casually opened the door, expecting to see nothing more exciting than a neighbor lady who wanted his mother. It was a lady, but none he'd ever seen in the neighborhood.

She stood about five and a half feet tall, which was still several inches taller than Chesney, and looked to be about his mother's age, but thinner without being skinny. Her dress was colorful, almost psychedelic paisley, and was trendy without being flashy. She wore purple sandals on her feet and large, clunky bracelets on her wrist.

Her hair was "just there," not long, not short, coming to her shoulders, covering her forehead in bangs, but no more. The face was as pleasant as a face can be with a nose striving for attention in its midst. If noses may have their own sensibilities, then Chesney's nose felt a kindred spirit with this nose, which while not exactly large, was definitely assertive. He started to reach for his own beak but stopped himself feeling it wasn't quite polite to grab one's nose in front of strangers. The only thing more compelling than the woman's nose was her eyes. They were bright, even sparkling, and of two different colors, both of which were warm and friendly. This study took all of three seconds. An additional second was all it took for Chesney to identify the stranger.

"Aunt El," he exclaimed, grabbing her in a hug that coincided with the embrace she was already sending his direction. His excitement was momentarily checked as he pushed the woman away and looked up at her. "You are my Aunt Elinor, aren't you?"

"Yes, Chesney, I'm your Aunt Elinor," she said, hugging him even more tightly. "You are my Chesney, aren't you?" She didn't wait for an answer before smothering him afresh.

When he had been allowed to come up for air, Chesney felt he needed to explain himself. "I thought it was you," he said. "That is, we were expecting you, but I…I didn't know who, I mean, I didn't know what you looked like. I mean, I've only seen old pictures. Not that you're old. It's just the pictures that are old, you were young then. I don't mean that you're old now, of course, you're older. Everyone is older than they were a little while ago. What I'm trying to say is…"

"…that you don't have a recent photograph of me," she said, with an affectionate smile.

Chesney exhaled and nodded.

"You've got your father's features, and you talk like your mother." This observation was offered with such grace that all Chesney could do was thank her for it.

"No one is home," he apologized.

"You're home, and you're somebody," she said. She smiled again as if to convey that was enough.

Chesney nodded sheepishly, "I mean, no one else is home," and pulled her off the front stoop and into the house, rushing back out to fetch her case, an impressive, battered affair covered with travel stickers. He led her into the living room and placed the suitcase at her feet.

"I've had that since college," she said, noticing how he stared at the old case.

"You went there with Mom and Dad."

"That's right," she said, her smile clouded, but only for a brief moment, "for a time. I didn't graduate. But let me look at you. You look just like the pictures you sent me. Your letters are very special to me."

Chesney felt his face redden and fumbled for a reply that was more profound than just: "yours too." Aunt El seemed to brush away the need for any words with a wave of her hand, which ended with a point toward her suitcase.

"I've brought you something."

Chesney smiled, but then remembered his training for these situations. "You didn't need to bring me anything, Aunt Elinor."

Her blue eye seemed to twinkle a bit more brightly, as she pulled him down next to her on the sofa. "Now," she began in conspiratorial tones, "that was just the right thing to say. Very polite. Your mother?"

Chesney nodded his head, a bit stunned that she seemed to be reading his mind.

"Good. Mothers are always telling their children to say things like that. Your grandmother was always making me say things like that, and that's good. You should always listen to your parents. Now, we're alone, aren't we?"

Chesney looked both ways, confirming what Aunt Elinor must have known since she didn't turn her head at all.

"Good," she continued, "so, now I can give you what I've brought you without any more disclaimers." She reached down and hoisted her bag atop the replica early-American coffee table. "I didn't wrap it, you don't mind, do you? No, of course not. Who needs wrapping paper? It's still a surprise whether it's wrapped in fancy paper or sitting in my suitcase."

With that, she pushed back the two buttons on the case causing the brass clasps to fly up with a smart "snap." Lifting the top of the case, Chesney peered into the suitcase but saw nothing but some women's clothing and a couple of jars.

"Here it is," said Elinor, reaching under the pile and pulling out a pale blue satiny looking piece of fabric. "Oh, don't worry," she laughed, in reaction to his expression dropping. "I'm not giving you a nightgown. I just wrapped it up in this to protect it." With that, she reached between the folds of the garment and paused, the way a magician will before pulling a rabbit out of a hat. "Ready?"

Chesney nodded.

With a dramatic flourish, Aunt El pulled out a brown, rectangular object and dropped it on her nephew's lap.

"There! All the way from England!"

It was a book.

Chesney sat staring at it, and then cautiously ran his fingertips along its edge. It was leather, real leather, like his baseball glove, only better. His glove was cheap leather with red stitching and the signature "Luis Aparicio" stamped on the pocket. The baseball glove was orangy brown with plenty of stains. It was a hand-me-down from Stosh. This book wasn't new either, but unlike the glove, it couldn't be considered a hand-me-down, at least not from anyone like his older brother. The book's leather was a dark brown, like a fancy chocolate bar, only more luxurious. It had fancy swirls and curlicues in gold stamped into it, and rigid bumps along the spine. Chesney slowly turned the volume on its edge. There also in gold were the letters: "*Great Expectations*. Dickens."

"Do you like it?"

Her voice sounded far off; his senses were so engrossed in the magnificence of the book. It was the best present he had ever received: all birthdays and Christmases included.

"I only thought," she continued, "that you'd like it, based on all the other little things I've sent you. You like books and English things, don't you?"

Chesney did like all the things Aunt El had sent to him over the years. She had a knack for sending him things new and different, yet that somehow fit his personality; things he found he loved before he'd even heard of them. She sent him odd comics and magazines that weren't sold in America, records by English artists he'd never heard of, books of word puzzles that made him think without seeming at all "educational." It was almost as if his Aunt Elinor were a long-distance tutor, a correspondence course in how to be himself but even more so. Her gifts were never inappropriate to his age level, but rather always seemed the next step in his development. And the best thing was that he never had to ask for any of them. How could he ask? He never knew what cryptograms or anagrams were before she sent him a book of them. Every kid on the block had Beatles records, but thanks to Aunt Elinor he was the only one who had albums by Flanagan and Allen, Arthur Askey, and his favorite: Hugh Goode. The other kids didn't even know who those performers were. Of course, none of his classmates or friends appreciated any of these things, and they made him seem a little weird whenever he dared to mention them. Chesney agreed they may have made him weird if he thought about it much, but more importantly, they made him: him. And now, he was holding a leather-bound book, a real piece of literature, or so he had heard. It was the most adult gift he'd ever received, maybe the first adult gift he'd ever received. And she wondered if he liked it?

"It's not new," she apologized, "I have a friend, Mr. Postlewaite who has a little shop in Marylebone, that's an area in London. He gets in a lot of old gewgaws. Anyway, it came into the shop, and I thought you might like it, but if you don't…"

Chesney clutched the book to his chest and looked up at his Aunt, his eyes moist.

"It's...it's..." he struggled for the proper words. Apparently, they were written all over his face, for a smile spread across her lips.

"You're welcome," she said and hugged him tightly.

That moment Chesney felt if the world came to an end, he would die without regret. He had found someone who understood him perfectly and liked him for who he was. His parents loved him, Clodagh liked him a lot and was rarely judgmental in her acceptance of him, but here was someone who "got" him.

They sat there for at least half-a-minute, hugging. Chesney's nose buried in her hair, the smell of her shampoo was fresh and different, probably English, he thought, and her hair was soft, not like his mother's. She used enough hairspray to embalm a Pomeranian. How, he wondered, as he nestled there, could his father ever not want his sister around? How could his mother think she was selfish? They just didn't understand her the way he did. Perhaps, they felt the same way about him. Was he a bother to them? Was he demanding or self-centered? After turning this supposition over in his mind, Chesney concluded that it didn't really matter, not at the moment at least. At that moment, for all intents and purposes, they were the only two people in the world.

Their world became over-populated by fifty percent as Chesney heard a noise a few feet away. It sounded like someone suppressing a snicker. He twisted his eyes tighter as if doing so would shut out any interlopers to his private paradise. Apparently, Aunt Elinor heard the sound, too, and relaxed her arms from around him. Her next words confirmed his worst suspicions.

"Hello, Stosh, I'm your Aunt Elinor. You are Stosh, aren't you? If not, excuse me while I call the cops."

"Call them anyway," Chesney muttered. He opened his eyes. There, sitting in the chair opposite the sofa was his older brother. Stosh rose and shook hands with his aunt, who chided him for so formal a greeting, and hugged him. She added observations on his height, and his altered appearance from the last photograph she had. As he stood there, looking over her shoulder, his eyes met Chesney's with a sort of silent taunting that only a bully like Stosh, could deliver. The expression, including fluttering eyelashes and pursed lips, cast aspersions on Chesney's masculinity, while also including the promise for a good thumping redeemable at some future date. That was no less than he had come to expect from his brother. What made it worse, however, was a subtle twitch of his eyes that transformed the mocking Stosh into the predatory Stosh; a much more dangerous creature. The mocking Stosh was cruel, but the predatory Stosh was all that and more. Predatory Stosh hunted and tracked his prey, whereas the standard incarnation of Stosh enjoyed a good tease, but wouldn't go to very much trouble to execute it. Predatory Stosh was Stosh stripped of his laziness, it was a Stosh inspired to greater depths, and that was frightening to small, timid creatures…like his brother. The evidence of Predatory Stosh's arrival came as his eyes darted from Chesney's face down to his lap. Chesney looked down… at his new book.

Chesney tried to hide the book behind his back, but it was too late. Stosh was now free of his aunt's embrace, but still looking at Chesney. Their eyes met again, and Stosh's gaze was no longer one of benign ridicule, but instead, it had narrowed into a cold, hungry antipathy. It was a look that he'd seen in nature documentaries, shining from the eyes of jackals, hyenas, and other scavenging beasts. Stosh had as little interest in a leather-bound edition of Dickens as would the hyena, but the fact that another creature valued it made the book enviable. Chesney felt the hairs on the back of his neck prickle and his skin chill. The feeling would have continued had not Aunt Elinor turned their attention to her suitcase. No doubt, Chesney thought, there would be a gift for Stosh that would divert the focus from his own present. Instead of pulling another gift from the canvas-covered case, however, she snapped close its latches and handed to Stosh.

"Stosh, dear," she said as if she actually believed that there was something beloved about him, "you're such a strong lad, oh, I mean young man – I'm afraid a lot of British phrases have started creeping into my conversation – you're such a strong young man…"

A foolish grin spread over Stosh's face as he nodded in agreement.

"…I'm sure you'd love to take my bag…well, wherever it is you take the luggage of visitors."

His face dropped as he realized the compliment had only qualified him for a chore.

"Cheesey's room," he muttered, as he took the suitcase and started up the stairs.

Aunt Elinor watched him go, and as soon as he was out of earshot, she grimaced.

"Cheesey?" she asked, nodding towards Chesney, who gave a sad, silent assent. "It's not always easy having an older brother," she said, stroking the side of his head.

"Did you bring him anything," asked Chesney, hoping for something that would appease Stosh's jealousy.

"No," she said as if the question were odd. "Why?"

"You brought me something." She just looked at him. "It isn't fair," added Chesney.

"If you mean by 'fair' that you both received something, then no, it isn't fair. To strictly follow that rule, I'd have brought Stosh the same book, and I doubt he would have found that 'fair' either. You'll find, Chesney, that very little is fair," she said. "I don't strive for fair, but I hope what I do is just."

"Just?" said Chesney. The concept of justice versus fairness was foreign to him. He did know that simply because something was just didn't mean it would prevent Stosh's fist from soon finding its way up his brother's nose.

Aunt El sat beside him and put her arm around his shoulder.

"Do you know why I brought you that book?"

He shrugged.

"Although we've only just met in person," she said softly, "you have been my favorite relative for a very long time. That's not fair, but if we're going by that superficial measuring rod, I'd have no favorite relative. By the same token, you wouldn't have any best friends, or a favorite subject in school, or favorite books, or favorite food. We're all individuals, and we all have persons and things that we prefer over other persons and things. In that respect, it isn't fair that I gave you a present and didn't give one to your brother. It is just, however. I don't owe Stosh anything. I don't owe you anything, either, Chesney. The difference is that had I brought Stosh a present, he may have been happier to see me then if I didn't bring him a present; while you'd be just as glad to see me with or without a present, though you obviously like that book."

"But ..." He stopped.

"Why did I bring you that book?" she continued. "It's because you are my favorite. Because when I'm in London or anywhere on my travels and something catches my eye, my thoughts naturally go to you, and I wonder: 'how would Chesney like that?' And that didn't just happen by accident. It's a relationship that grew because of who you are, and who I am, and who we are together. We're aunt and nephew, but we're friends, too, because we have shared interests, and because you're very considerate to a lady you never laid eyes upon until today. Did you know I used to write to Stosh and send him things?"

"You did?"

"Yes, it was a long time ago when he was younger than you are now."

"Why did you stop?"

"I didn't, not right away," she said with a casual toss of her head. "Actually, Stosh stopped first. He rarely wrote to me, and when he did, I could tell it was probably your mother making him do it, mostly to say thank you for something or other I'd sent, and those often came months after the fact. He never extended himself, never put himself out, and that's fine, that was his choice. You, on the other hand, you sent me letters, and not just letters, you sent me something else."

Chesney couldn't remember much else than some letters, some pictures, and few drawings, certainly nothing of value. He looked blankly into her eyes.

"You sent me yourself," she said with a smile. "You may not think that seems like much, but as the wise Li Gao, says: 'the greatest gift one person can bestow upon another is himself.' When I get your letters, I get a little bit of Chesney in each letter, and all those pieces add up to a whole person, and that person is my favorite relative, and one of my very favorite people in entire the world. So, it may not be 'fair' that I send you things and bring you presents, but it is right and proper. Life is not making sure everyone gets the same size piece of pie. And you'll find that there are people out there who will like Stosh more than they like you, and they'll treat him as if he's special, and to them, he will be. And that's alright, too. Do you understand?"

Chesney nodded his head, and his Aunt kissed him on the cheek.

"You're very sweet," she said.

He enjoyed the compliment for a brief moment and then caught himself. "Not so loud, Aunt Elinor," he said under his breath and motioning to forces outside the living room, "do you want to get me killed?"

Aunt El straightened up, put a safe distance between her and her nephew and winked her eye, the blue one, at him. "Right, gotcha. By the way," she said, pulling a small bundle of papers from her handbag, "speaking of getting killed, are you going into the spy business?"

"Spy business?"

"I only ask because in your last letter you gave me a code name," she looked down at the paper and read: "'Dear Nature Lion,' and you signed it 'Yes, I Shock No Pet.' So either you think I'm a ferocious beast and fancy yourself benign to dogs and cats, or there's another explanation."

"It was that last book you sent me," said Chesney, "the anagrams?"

"And Nature Lion is…"

"'Aunt Elinor,' all scrambled up. I've been practicing on names."

"Very clever," she said, beaming at him. "That's very good. My friend, Mr. Postlewaite, the man with the shop, told me there was a lot of truth in anagrams. I thought it was just his sales pitch, but who am I to question it if I'm one of nature's lions!"

"Yes, and it's better than 'Toenail Urn,'" said Chesney. "That was the first one I came up with from 'Aunt Elinor.'"

"Yes, much better," she agreed. "Perhaps you should try something with my full name: Elinor Iris Ann Potoski, and don't forget, your grandparents used the alternate spelling of 'Elinor.'"

"That's a lot more letters to work with," he said, "that'll be tricky."

"Good! It's good to have a challenge. Better to have a nephew with a challenge than to be a… toenail urn."

He laughed, and she smiled.

"Now, tell me what else you've been up to aside from rearranging the English language. What are you learning in school?"

Before Chesney could answer, the front door opened and shut so rapidly that he wondered how there was time for anyone to enter in the interval. Then his mother flew into the room as if her coat were on fire.

"Chesney, is your father home, yet," she said, looking everywhere at once but not stopping to focus on any one thing. "No," she answered herself. "No, how could he be here, he doesn't have the car. I dropped him off at the station this morning myself, didn't I? Well, it will have to wait until he gets home. I can't tell him if he's not here, can I? No, of course, I can't, Chesney, can I? Did you do your homework? Did you have any? Is Stosh home yet, I hope he's…I hope he's…"

Mrs. Potoski repeated herself several more times as she stood there, her handbag dangling from her arm, swaying in harmony to the perpetual motion she'd been displaying since entering the room. Now, however, instead of her head darting about without any fixed focus, she was staring at the woman on the sofa beside her son.

"Hello, Pru," said Aunt Elinor standing, "it's wonderful to see you. I'm sorry I didn't call, but my plans were rather up in the air until the last minute."

His mother's mouth moved up and down for a moment as if she were waiting for someone to pop a wad of bubble gum into it. Finally, she cleared her mind enough to say: "Now? Oh, no, this isn't good…what…of course, that doesn't matter right now, but…"

"I can go to a hotel."

The suggestion stung his mother like a slap in the face. She shuddered, and concentration came back to her eyes. She looked at her sister-in-law, then at her son, and then back to her sister-in-law, and smiled. In was a wan smile, but genuine nonetheless.

"Hotel? Don't be silly, it's all arranged. You'll be in Chesney's room, we just need to change the linens, and you'll be all set. Nothing could be easier…"

"Are you alright, Pru?"

"Me? Yes, yes, I'm fine, I was just a little pre-occupied, that's all. Actually, it's been a bit of a shock…not you…I just found…well, we'll talk later, after I had a chance to talk to Roddy, that's your brother…"

"Yes, I know he is," said Elinor.

"Of course, you do," said Mrs. Potoski, who gave a playful slap to her own head.

Chesney stood there, taking it all in. He'd never seen his mother act so oddly. It was as if someone had just played a trick on her and caught her completely off-guard. He knew the feeling, spending so many years as the victim of Stosh's practical jokes. Aside from this, it was also strange to hear her referred to as "Pru," and his father as "Roddy."

"Mom…"

"Oh, Chesney," said Mrs. Potoski, "I've got to change the sheets on your bed, and make dinner, will you help Mommy and pick up your father?"

"But Mom, I can't drive…"

Aunt Elinor put her arm around his mother's shoulder. "Why doesn't Chesney change the sheets, and I'll make dinner, and you can go pick up Rodney?" Her suggestion, delivered in soothing tones, was quickly adopted.

"Yes, yes," she agreed with several nods of her head, "that's a good idea. Chesney can make the bed, and…"

"And I can make dinner. Just point me to the kitchen…"

"We keep it over there," said Prudence, pointing across the living room. "Oh, it was only going to be hot dogs…"

"That will be fine. I can work with frankfurters."

"And beans…"

"Even greater epicurean heights will be scaled," said Aunt Elinor.

Chesney made a mental note to use that line in the school cafeteria the next time they had beans.

"Now, are you sure you're okay to drive?"

"Hmm? Oh, yes. I'm better… now."

Aunt Elinor gave her another hug and said, "It will all be fine. As Li Gao says: some of life's greatest blessings are wrapped as surprise packages, aren't they?"

She held her sister-in-law at arm's length. Mrs. Potoski smiled and nodded.

"Yes, you're right, not the first time is it?" she said.

"Nor will it be the last," said Elinor, "broadly speaking, I mean, not necessarily…" They both smiled at each other, leaving Chesney to wonder what had happened that had happened before, may happen again, and was making his mother nutty in the head.

"Okay, yes," Prudence took a deep breath, "I'm fine." She looked at Chesney. "I'm going to get your father. Use the blue sheets in the linen closet."

"And I'll use the pink hot dogs in the fridge?" added Elinor.

She nodded again in agreement and started for the door, then stopped and began looking around frantically.

"They're in your hand," said Elinor. Prudence looked down at the keys and nodded once more.

She was almost out of the room when she turned abruptly.

"No," said Aunt Elinor, "I won't tell."

Mrs. Potoski smiled and exited; relieved at something.

"Won't tell what?" asked Chesney.

"That would be telling," said Aunt Elinor as she turned toward the kitchen.

– 33 –
For a Handful of Nickels

The world seemed much more normal after dinner. After Chesney changed the sheets on his bed for Aunt Elinor, he joined her in the kitchen. He was amazed to learn there were more ways to prepare food other than the ones employed by his mother and primordial man. Aunt Elinor was baking the hot dogs into some sort of pie. It was, she explained, a variation on something called: "toad in the hole."

If he hadn't known better, Chesney would have thought Stosh had a hand in it. He was always threatening to force feed his younger brother a nauseating selection of reptiles and amphibians. "Don't look so worried," said Aunt El. "It's just a name. It's an English dish, usually made with sausages, but we'll muddle through with the hot dogs."

Given his father's opinion of his sister, Chesney held his breath when he heard the family car pull into the garage. He stood out of the way when his father entered. From the neck down, his father looked like he usually did when coming home after a long day's work in the city, and two rounds on the Long Island Railroad. His suit was rumpled, his tie loosened, his white shirt wilted, and his feet almost visibly throbbing inside his wingtip shoes. Above this, however, was a beaming expression, the type usually reserved for vacations, and golf courses. His father, Chesney concluded, must have made peace with all the hemorrhoids in his life.

He had his arm around his wife and was almost guiding her through the door, around the kitchen table, and across the floor as if she were the window designer's lifetime achievement award. Then, the woman whom he considered the bane of his existence just days before was greeted with a hug, a peck on the cheek, and was even dubbed "Sis." Mr. Potoski then flushed Chesney out of the corner to muss his hair, pat his back, and told him: "you're getting to be such a big fella…and just in time."

Even the toad in the hole did nothing to dampen Mr. Potoski's odd mood. The conversation was pleasant but vague. The only clouds on his father's countenance came when his sister made some reference to the past. His mother, wishing to preserve the atmosphere, quickly changed the subject. After two such attempts, Aunt Elinor confined her comments to her nephews' schooling, the wallpaper, and even the state of the yews growing outside the kitchen window. She even listened while Stosh bragged about his plan to "murder" the competition in the upcoming junior golf tournament.

The bliss evaporated as Chesney's bedtime approached. He crept into Stosh's room to find a sleeping bag unfurled beside his brother's bed. He slipped into his pajamas to save himself the embarrassment of changing in front of Stosh. His brother was never without a denigrating observation on any part of the human anatomy on anyone aside from himself.

Chesney sat down on the sleeping bag just as Stosh entered.

"Oh, Cheesy," he sneered, "it's you. I thought we had mice."

"Rat," muttered Chesney.

"Thanks for changing before I got here. That weird grub is sitting heavy on my gut and seeing your naked butt would be libel to make me puke. What'd she call that? Frog down the toilet?"

"It was toad in the hole, it's English," said Chesney.

"Yeah, so is King Arthur's dick, but I wouldn't put that in my mouth either."

Chesney let that witticism go unanswered. He laid down when something caught his eye under the bed. It was a glass of water. He looked up at Stosh, who quickly looked away. He was gazing the blank wall with the intensity of an art critic studying a masterpiece at the Louvre.

Chesney nodded. He had little doubt that the glass of water was placed there for the purpose of giving his hand for a late-night dip after he had fallen asleep. It was a stunt Stosh had often performed at Boy Scout camp, and it never ceased to delight him in the execution or the recounting.

"You should have seen it," Stosh would boast to his cronies, "I dipped his hand in... you gotta do it carefully, or the guy will wake up... and the water's gotta be body temperature... then, you wait a minute, and the guy gets this big, dopey, happy kinda smile across his face... all in his sleep... and then..." at this point Stosh would break into fits of knee-slapping laughter, "...and then he...PEES HISSELF!"

Chesney shuddered at the prospect of wetting the sleeping bag, especially with Aunt Elinor in the house.

"Where are you going?" asked Stosh, as Chesney rose from his makeshift bed.

"I, uh, I've got to go...to the bathroom," said Chesney.

"To the bathroom?" Stosh sounded disappointed.

"Uh, yes, I want a drink of water," said Chesney, "I'm thirsty – very, very thirsty."

Stosh smiled. "Yeah, that's a good idea. Go get a drink of water. Get lots of drinks of water. It's the best thing for you if you're thirsty, Ches, ol' pal."

Chesney crept from Stosh's room and closed the door behind him. Instead of going to the bathroom, however, he listened at the top of the stairs. Below, he could hear his father, his mother, and Aunt Elinor talking, but he couldn't make out their words. He tiptoed down the hall to his room, slipped inside and shut the door behind him. Chesney crossed to his old pine toy box, raised the lid stenciled with a silhouette of a stagecoach, and peered inside. Rummaging around through the accumulated treasures of his short life, he stopped when he came upon a Mickey Mouse hand puppet. The black paint was chipping off its rubber head, and the cloth body had grown threadbare, but it would serve at least half of his purpose. Next, Chesney opened the door to his closet, which was next to the door to the hallway. There was his baseball mitt. With Mickey doing sentry duty on his right and with the glove on his left hand, his fingers would be protected from any nocturnal swims. If Stosh tried to remove them, Chesney would wake up and catch Stosh in the act. Now, all he had to do was sneak the puppet and the glove back into the room without being noticed. He had put Mickey down the front of his pajama bottoms and was maneuvering the bulkier mitt into place in the rear when his bedroom door swung open, hitting the closet door, and shutting Chesney inside.

His first thought was Stosh had figured out he was up to something and had come to deliver a preemptive pummeling. Chesney held his breath and then relaxed as he realized from the gentle humming that it was his Aunt. He started to reach for the knob when he heard the sound of a zipper and froze. Was that the zipper to her dress? He felt his face turn red, and he swallowed hard. He didn't want to see her in her underwear. He didn't like to see anyone in their underwear, especially people he knew and most of all ladies, and ladies he liked. Chesney pushed behind the clothes hanging there, hoping they would conceal him if she opened the closet door. This strategy was foiled when, in the dark, he bumped into a baseball bat. It fell with a dull thud against the door. He held his breath; certain that in a moment, he would be discovered and lose his most-favored-relative status. Instead, he heard another thud. The second thud came from outside the closet.

"Just a minute," he heard his Aunt call. He heard her re-zip her zipper, and then open the bedroom door.

"You decent?" It was his father.

Chesney's heart rose up to his throat. Now he would not only be embarrassed in front of his Aunt; his father would catch him. They would probably think he was trying to watch Aunt El undress. He would be accused of the sorts of things that Stosh would do. He could hear the blood pulsing through his temple, and thought that it must be audible for at least half a block. When he heard the conversation continuing beyond the door in normal tones, however, he realized that for the moment at least, he was safe.

"...just wanted to make sure you were all settled in," he heard his father continue.

"Yes, thank you," said Aunt Elinor. "You and Pru have a lovely home, Roddy."

His father snorted a little laugh. "Not many people call me that much anymore."

"You don't mind?"

"I guess not ...Ellie." His tone had a sharper edge.

She chuckled, either not catching or choosing to ignore his inflection. "There's another blast from the past."

"Yeah...the past." His tone darkened even more.

After an awkward pause that was palpable even inside the closet, both brother and sister began to speak at once, then stopped as abruptly as they had started, leading to a longer, more uncomfortable silence.

"I...I want to explain, Rodney," said Elinor, "about, about a lot of different things."

"Oh, yes," said his father employing his favorite open-ended phrase.

"Yes," she said softly.

"You don't owe me any explanation," he said in a way that indicated that he thought she did owe him one, and with interest.

"Well, that's nice of you to say that, but..." she began but was cut short.

"No, what's past is past..."

"Apparently not, by the sound of it..."

"Oh, I'm fine," he said.

Chesney could hear the floorboards squeak as his father paced. "You said it yourself. We've got a good house. I've got a good career...one that I enjoy..."

"That's wonderful, Roddy..."

"So, I don't look back. There's nothing for my family or me in the past. We look ahead. The marketing boys have a phrase for it..."

"Marketing boys?" She asked.

"Yes, you know, the guys at work who sell the windows I design. Mind you, they think they've got the tough job, sitting around all day till their pencils get blunt, to think up a slogan. It's us fenestrators who put in the real work; designing window systems with a high insulating value, or ones with a built-in screen, or other improvements that are secret. Still, they seem to think they've got the hard job..."

"Um," she said, "what was their phrase?"

There was a brief silence as Mr. Potoski shunted his train of thought back onto the main line of the conversation. "Phrase? Oh, right, for our new double-hung, high R-value, aluminum clad window, the A-700, they came up with the phrase 'Look Through to the Future!'"

"Very clever," said Elinor, though she was quick to add, "of course, not as clever as the window it advertises."

"Look through to the future," he repeated. "That's what I do at the office, and what we do in this house. The past is gone."

"But it still happened."

"And you can't change it," he said.

"True," she said, "but you can rectify mistakes, mend damaged... relationships."

There was another brief silence. This time, however, the anxiety level was so tangible that Chesney expected to see it seeping under the door like some fetid mist.

"So, that settles that," said his father, though nothing had been settled except his faith in the A-700 window system. "I mainly came in here to know what your plans were."

"My plans?"

"Uh, yes, like, uh, how long you're planning to stay?"

Chesney heard his aunt take a deep breath. The exhale seemed tinged with emotion.

"I can leave right now if you like," she said, her voice quivering.

"Okay, wait, no, I didn't mean it like that," he said.

"That's all right," she said, "I don't deserve any consideration. I know what you must think of me. That's obvious. Apparently, any warm greeting you gave me was spillover from the good news about the baby."

Baby? Chesney thought. What baby? He now felt he was in the dark both literally and figuratively.

"That was a surprise," said his father, "a pleasant, very pleasant surprise. You know, I almost flew home from the train station when she told me. We weren't planning it. It was a surprise, just like last time."

Like last time? The last time they had a baby around, it was him. Had he been a surprise? Chesney wondered if his mother had been nervous and his father delighted when first they had learned he was on the way.

"Yes, I'm very, very happy for you both," said Elinor, "and even a little envious."

"Hmm, oh, yes..."

Chesney could imagine his father was now staring at the floor and rubbing his nose with his forefinger, as was his habit when at a loss for words.

"I never got married," she said.

"Well, you know..." his father seemed to be searching for something to say. "You know, you could have married...you know...him!"

"You mean Paul?"

"You know I mean him." He waited for a further response, and when none was forthcoming, continued. "You could have married him if you didn't go running off on him and, uh...everyone."

This was unfamiliar to Chesney.

"I suppose you mean I ran off on you."

"You ran off on everyone, him, me, Pru...the folks."

"I wrote to the folks."

"Yeah that you were running off to the Himalayas..."

"Tibet."

Tibet? Chesney thought. He'd never known anyone who had gone to anywhere as exotic as Tibet.

"Tibet, Himalayas, same thing," said Mr. Potoski trying to keep his voice down. "You left me and everyone else to clean up after you. That whole business at the sorority house..."

"Why do you think I left?" She said. Chesney could hear tears in her voice. "Did you ever kill someone?"

Chesney's eyes widened. Aunt Elinor had killed somebody? The lady who sent him books and puzzles and funny records killed someone?

"Oh, I knew at the time that it was an accident," she said, "but still, that's a horrible thing to carry around inside of you. I had to get away..."

"To Tibet? Doesn't your brain work at lower altitudes?"

"When you do something so horrible, you to want run as far as possible, you want to jump off the world," she said very quietly.

"So you were going to jump off a mountain? It doesn't work that way. There's this thing called gravity. The boys in marketing are going to start advertising it next week."

"There's no need for sarcasm, Roddy. It's a spiritual thing," she said, now barely audible. "You wouldn't understand. Li Gao put it this way..."

"I wouldn't understand? I've seen *Lost Horizon*, too. What were you expecting Ronald Coleman to explain it all to you or give you absolution? No, it was easier to run off to Tibet, or Timbuktu, or East Jabip, and sit at the feet of Kung Pao..."

"Li Gao, he's a very wise..."

"Yeah, well, you can pile up Oriental philosophers from here to the moon, but it's still easier than staying to clean up the mess you made, and to finish the life you'd started here. Throwing away three years of college..."

"I didn't leave anything unfinished, at least not anything I wanted to finish. And as for cleaning up, I explained everything to the police. As for finishing the life I'd started here, I really didn't think it was worth finishing here. You're very lucky, Rodney. You always knew what you wanted to be and who you were. I don't think you realize it, but that's a great gift. It makes the rest of your life much simpler, and I hope much happier."

There was another long silence. Finally, his father spoke.

"I guess things did work out pretty good for me, Sis. I only wished you'd been around for it."

"I was there for the part I was needed," she said. "It may have been an accident that Bascomb was killed, but it wasn't an accident that I was up in the attic that day. I just couldn't let Pru go through with that. I felt responsible."

Chesney thought he heard his father say: "I know."

"And I was the one who made all those anonymous calls to you."

"I know. I figured it all out later. I had a lot of time to think about it."

"You never told her?"

He must have shaken his head, for a moment later, Chesney heard his Aunt say: "good."

"I took care of it," he said quietly, but with a determination to his voice. "I stayed and took care of it."

"And I took care of it, too," she shot back, "and after I took care of what I needed to take care of I left, so I could take care of myself. So that settles that, and the past is in the past, just as you want it."

"Just one thing I'm not sure of," said Mr. Potoski. "At the sorority house... you called the police?"

"Yes, of course," she said.

"After the accident?"

"Before," she said.

"But if it was an accident, how did you know there was going to be an accident?"

"I didn't know there was going to be an accident. I didn't call to report the accident. I called to report an intruder in the house. I was hoping that you'd all show up. I was just hoping that Pru would see Bascomb for what he was, and you'd settle things with Paul once and for all."

"Oh, I settled him!"

"Yes, I know," she sighed.

"Settled it once and for all."

"I hope you called St. Simeon's."

"What for?

"So they'd finally know who was the toughest kid in the school."

"Yeah, well, it all worked out."

There was another silence, broken by a sharp intake of breath by Aunt Elinor.

"Well, it worked out for us, Pru and I, um, I heard Rocher, that is Paul, did okay for himself, too."

"Yes, he's quite high up in law enforcement, he has a lovely wife and... family, too. But that's in the past. W-we can't live in the past, can we? Can't let the boys in marketing down, can we?"

"Sis, I wanted to ask, you something else..."

"Yes?"

"About Dad's trunk," he said, "you know his war chest."

"What about it?"

"What's in it?"

"Nothing really," she said, "nothing to speak of..."

"It's just that, well, you know, Dad..."

194

There was an uncomfortable silence broken by Aunt Elinor's voice. It sounded strained.

"About Dad," she began.

"...the trunk..."

"No, not the trunk," she said, "I want to tell you something else about him, something that happened a long time ago when we were kids."

"Oh, yes," said his father in his non-committal way.

"Yes, do you remember the time you caught all the kids up in Dad's room?"

"I remember..." His father said slow cadence, which usually indicated he was trying to control himself, "I remember that snake Rocher holding all those nickels."

"Well, yes, he was holding the nickels, but they weren't his nickels."

"Huh?"

"They were mine, at least, the idea was mine."

"You? Your own father?"

Chesney was completely mystified now. He had no idea what his grandfather, a room full of kids, and a handful of nickels had to do with anything a million years later.

"It was my idea..."

"Then why..."

"He was holding it for me. He took the money from my hands when he heard you come in. He didn't want you to hate me, though I guess you should have. You should have punched me right there and then rather than have that silly feud for all those years."

"But..." Mr. Potoski's voice sounded strangely detached. "I mean, then he didn't..."

"No," said Aunt Elinor, "he didn't. He was covering up for me because he liked me. And he kept covering up for me. He wanted to marry me. I guess I liked him too, in fact, I loved him, but I guess not enough to tell the truth. It's funny what you can ultimately lose by trying to hold on to a handful of nickels."

"Yeah, I guess...it's just that I thought, maybe, with everything, I thought the old man would have wanted me to have his trunk."

"I-I'm very tired, Roddy," she said. "We can talk more about the trunk in the morning, okay?"

Mr. Potoski agreed, said goodnight, and left the room closing the door behind him. Chesney waited for a moment, and reached for the doorknob, but stopped when he heard soft crying. He wanted to step out of the closet and comfort his aunt, but not knowing exactly how to comfort a crying adult, he waited. When he finally did emerge from hiding, Chesney saw his Aunt, still clothed, lying on the bed asleep with the light on. He crept out of the room and back to Stosh's room. Thankfully Stosh was asleep as well. He started to put on the puppet and the baseball glove but decided to drink the water in the glass instead.

Then, as the last person awake in the house, he stared at the ceiling, trying to sort out all the confusing revelations he had overheard that night.

– 34 –
The Sandals Slip Away

The next morning she was gone. On his way downstairs, Chesney found the door to his room open, the bed made, and no signs of his Aunt or her luggage.

Entering the kitchen, he asked his mother what had happened. She said that Aunt Elinor had left early that morning. She had misjudged her travel time and had to leave abruptly. All this was explained in a brief note, which his mother tucked into her pocket before taking her husband to the station to catch the morning train.

As he sat down to his bowl of Cheerios, Chesney wondered if the appointment was with the FBI, or with the monks in Tibet. He turned over in his mind the conversation of the previous night. Perhaps she was running from the police. Maybe they had changed their mind about the person she had killed. Perhaps the body was in that old trunk that his father had asked about. Chesney was jarred from his reverie by a sharp flick to the back of his ear.

"Hey, Cheesy," muttered Stosh, still half-asleep, but with his obnoxiousness already at mid-day form, "where'd you get to last night?"

"Nowhere…"

"Yeah, too bad," he snickered to himself as he scratched his crotch with one hand while pouring a glass of orange juice with the other. "I waited up for you. We coulda had lots of fun." Chesney looked up. Stosh smiled a twisted smile. Then he pantomimed dipping his hands in an imaginary glass.

"You're getting wise, snot rag," he continued, offering Chesney a glimmer of hope that perhaps the reign of practical jokes was coming to an end. That notion enjoyed a very brief life. "Of course, you're not as smart as me, not by a long shot, eh, Cheesy?" Then he added ominously: "And you never will be."

Things were back to normal. The brief respite was over, hardly before it had begun. It was almost like a dream, he thought. It was the dream that he was someone's favorite; that someone loved him, not just because they had to, but because they wanted to; because they appreciated him. He would still have her letters, he told himself in consolation. Otherwise, life in Earswick would go on as usual.

A sopping wet wad of paper towel slapped Chesney on the back of his neck to confirm this thought.

– 35 –
Farewell, My Fatty Clown

At least he still had the reading spot. It was just a tree house, a relic of Stosh's arboreal days, and one of his few positive contributions, albeit unintentional, to Chesney's world. It featured a floor, eight-feet square, and half walls all the way around. The broad leaves of the maple tree served as most of the roof, though a piece of canvas from an old tent provided additional shelter. Stosh never referred to it as a reading spot or even a tree house. To Stosh it was a fort, but he had since outgrown it. During Stosh's reign, reading was all but forbidden in the fort aside from the occasional comic book or dirty magazine.

"I must study politics and war that my sons may have liberty to study mathematics and philosophy," said John Adams. While Chesney wasn't very good at math, Adams would have understood and approved of the evolution of Stosh's fort into his younger brother's outdoor library, its only patrons: Chesney and Clodagh Clott.

On a warm May afternoon, they were both there in their sanctuary from the world below. Chesney always allowed Clo to ascend first; not just to be gallant, but so she wouldn't see his puny muscles straining to lift himself to the top. As she clambered up the crude ladder, Chesney noticed her rear end. He had of course seen it before. Clodagh had been around as long as he could remember, and in all that time, she always had a rear end. Only now it was taking on different proportions and in a strangely compelling way. In his mind, he heard Stosh's lewd comment about Clodagh "getting her tits." Somehow those changes were related to the ones taking place in her southern hemisphere. He closed his eyes as if doing so would shut out Stosh's encroachment on his thoughts, but it only made him miss the next rung on the ladder and fall to the ground with a thud.

"Are you okay?"

Chesney opened his eyes and rubbed his own posterior, which unlike hers was under-padded for the purposes of falling off ladders. He looked up to see Clodagh, on the platform above, leaning over, looking down at him and allowing him a peek up her shirt. He closed his eyes and then shook his head as if to mask his thoughts with a feigned injury.

"Hit your head?" Clodagh asked.

He looked off to the side, not trusting himself to look upward at her and her developing body. He wondered if these developments continued would he someday start thinking of Clodagh as more than a friend. It could happen, he thought, and for some reason the idea was enticing.

"I said," repeated Clodagh, "did you hit your head?"

"Yeah, no, I landed on my...butt, but I'm okay,"

Clodagh laughed. "Well, get your but butt up here."

She disappeared above the edge of the tree house, and Chesney climbed up without any further distractions. Once over the top, he was relieved to find Clodagh looking more like his old friend, rather than the creature emerging from her prepubescent cocoon. She was there in shorts and a shirt propped against the far wall of the tree house, her legs crossed, and her nose inside a paperback book.

"Herbs and Natural Cures," said Chesney reading aloud the cover of her book.

"Yeah," she said, without looking up.

"Interesting?" It probably was to her, since she had been reading similar books for years. Natural cures, herbs, the paranormal, the workings of the mind, alternative medicine: if it was different, Clodagh was probably interested in it.

"It's okay," she said without looking up, indicating it was much more than just "okay."

"I got a letter yesterday," he said, pulling an envelope out of his pocket.

"Oh?" she said, still without looking up.

"It's in code..."

"Oh?" This time he had her full attention. Coded messages bordered on the fringes of the unknown world that interested Clodagh. "Who from?"

"From whom..." he said.

"Shut up," she said.

"It's from my Aunt Elinor," he said, handing her the envelope.

She studied the envelope for a moment and then pushed it back at him.

"The return address says: 'Nature Lion.'"

"That's her code name," explained Chesney, "or at least that's the anagram of her name. She wrote that so that no one else would know it was from her."

"Either that or she's trying to be funny."

Chesney looked at the envelope. He hadn't thought of that possibility. "She isn't generally like that. She probably didn't want anyone else to know she sent it."

"Why would she do that?"

"Because I'm her favorite."

"Favorite what?"

"Favorite relative."

Clodagh grimaced. "Sorry, I don't get that. When you have three older sisters, there are no such things as favorite relatives."

"Her other anagram is 'toenail urn,' but we like 'nature lion' better."

"Did you ever do it to me, you know that anagram thing?"

Chesney blushed.

"Well, did you," she repeated.

"Yes," he said quietly.

"Well, what's my name all scrambled up and then put back together?"

"Well, there are several," he said, looking away.

"And?" He didn't answer. "You'd better tell me. If you don't, there are some very nasty poisonous plants in this book; any of which will give you a honking great rash when I push you into them."

He unconsciously scratched at his arm, recalling a case of poison oak from the previous summer. Not wishing to risk the wrath of his only friend, he muttered the anagram of "Clodagh Clott."

"What?!"

"Gold Cloth Cat," he repeated.

"Gold Cloth Cat?"

"That's one of the anagrams of Clodagh Clott," he said. "You wanted to know."

"Gold Cloth Cat?" she twisted her expression in disgust, making it look like her face was going down a drain. "That's the best you could do?"

He got defensive. "Yes, as a matter of fact, it was the best I could do! It's better than Cold Hag!"

"Cold Hag?"

"That's an anagram for Clodagh," he said.

"Yes, A Gold Cloth Cat is better than a Cold Hag."

"You're not mad at me?"

She gave him a crooked smile. "Nah! You didn't name me. And it's better than what I almost got named."

"What's that?"

"You promise not to tell?"

"I swear."

Clodagh grimaced and said: "Myfanwy."

"Ma what?"

She repeated the name, along with the spelling.

"Myfanwy?" he said, trying it out for himself. "Myfanwy Clott."

"It's Welsh," she said.

"My fatty clown..." said Chesney after a moment's thought.

"What?"

"That's the anagram for Myfanwy Clott."

Her almond eyes narrowed.

"If you ever say Myfanwy or Fatty Clown to me again, I'll pound you."

Chesney flinched. "I wouldn't do that."

"Well, see that you don't." She looked at him a moment. The anger slid from her face, replaced by an expression he couldn't identify.

"Sorry," said Chesney, though he wasn't sure for what he was apologizing.

"Oh, it's not your fault."

"No," he agreed. "I didn't name you."

She stared at him and then looked away. "I guess I'm not even mad at my parents. At least not for that." She cast her eyes down at the rough floor. After several moments she stole a look back up at him as if they were in a play and he had missed his cue.

"What?" asked Chesney.

"I swear, Chesney Potoski," she said, throwing the paperback book at him. "Can't you tell when someone has something to say?"

"Yes. They usually say: 'I've got something to say.'"

"Well, I've got something to say. Can't you pick up a hint?"

He looked around as if the missing words were hanging in the air.

"You have no intuitive powers at all, do you?" she said.

Chesney shrugged.

"I said," repeated Clodagh, "that I wasn't mad at my parents, at least not for naming me what they named me."

He looked at her for a moment. "So you are mad at them for something else?"

Clodagh stared at him for ten seconds and then took a deep breath.

"We're moving."

After such a vague introduction, the directness of the announcement struck him like a wet paper towel on the back of his neck; like a mushy pea flicked in his ear; in fact, it equaled the cumulative effect of every attack Stosh had ever inflicted upon him.

"Move..." he whispered.

"...ing!"

"Why?"

"Because my Dad's being transferred," she said. "I know it stinks." She raised her shoulders around her ears and then let them fall again.

"Stinks?" Chesney said. Stinks didn't begin to describe it. "It's...terrible! You're, you're... my friend."

"You're my friend, too," she said. "How do you think I feel? I've got to go half-way across the country. I don't know anybody half-way across the country. At least you know everyone here."

Chesney nodded. He did know everyone here. The best of them left him alone. He thought of Stosh, who he wished would leave him alone. He might like a place where nobody knew him.

"You don't think about a psychologist being transferred," she continued, "but when you're shrink working for the Air Force, I guess it can happen."

Chesney nodded again. He never knew what to call Clodagh's father. He could have called him Major Clott; but he was also a psychologist, thus making Dr. Clott correct, too. He was such a nice man that he probably would have even answered to "Mr. Clott."

"Everyone else is okay with it," she said, in a way that indicated she was not. "Well, Caprice was upset at first. She thought she was going to have to miss that stupid golf tournament."

"Stupid golf tournament," he repeated. Neither of them would have been surprised if signs started appearing around town publicizing "The Annual Stupid Golf Tournament." He thought for a moment. "So you're not leaving until after that?"

"We're not leaving until the end of August," she said. "Though at times I wish I was already gone…not, not because I won't miss you, just because…I hate to say goodbye. Long goodbyes are just like ripping off a Band-Aid. The longer you draw it out, the more it hurts. I say, just yank them off quick."

"Quickly," he said automatically.

She glowered at him. "I feel bad…badly enough, without having to sock you, Chesney. I'm going to miss that…"

"Socking me?"

"You correcting me, you dope!"

He apologized, and they sat in silent reflection until Clodagh sighed.

"Yes, August," she said, "I wish it were tomorrow. Yank it off quickly…"

"Sometimes, if the Band-Aid's been on a while, my mother puts some rubbing alcohol on it first, you know, to loosen it up."

"I doubt I can put rubbing alcohol on moving, so that's not a very helpful suggestion."

He lowered his head. "No, I guess not; not for moving."

They fell quiet again, this time for several minutes. The maple leaves around them whispered in the warm spring breeze. Finally, Clodagh plucked a leaf from the nearest branch. She pretended to study it for a moment, then, without looking up, she broke the silence.

"You okay?"

Chesney could feel a gurgle in his throat as he took a deep breath. Better, he thought, to be crying down in your throat than out of your eyes.

"I just figured…I figured you'd be around. I mean, I thought you'd be there. I get scared of the future, of growing up, of going to high school, and all that. And when I'm afraid, I get through it by thinking that at least you'll be there, that I have at least one friend who I can count on, one friend who doesn't think I'm weird. And then I tell myself, I'll be okay, I'll get through it…because you'll be there, too."

He took a deep breath which caught in his throat with several short spasms.

Clodagh looked at him.

"I don't know whether to console you," she said, "or push you out of this tree."

When he just stared back at her, unable to form a reply, she continued.

"Look, I don't want to move, but that's life," she began. "I'm going to miss you, but I'm not going to stop living, and you won't either. And as far as the future, well, you've just got to deal with it. I mean it, Ches, what were you going to do after high school...take me to college with you?"

He fumbled for an answer, afraid to say what he had thought deep down in the hidden recesses of his mind. Yes, he thought maybe they would go to the same college. Why not? Why did things have to change? Why did the Air Force need psychologists? None of these thoughts formed into words. Instead, he stumbled through a series of sentence fragments accompanied by similarly incomplete hand gestures.

"You've just got to believe in yourself," she said. "You're a smart kid or at least smarter than most of the other kids walking around. You just lack self-confidence."

He opened his mouth to speak but wasn't exactly sure what to say, which proved her point. It also reinforced something else he had been told recently. He stuck his letter into his back pocket.

"What's the worst thing that could happen? Ask yourself that. What's the worst thing that could happen, today, for example?"

Chesney thought a moment. "I could die? The tree could fall down, and I could die."

"Yeah, well," said Clodagh, "that's a bit extreme, isn't it? It's not very likely. But, okay, if you died you wouldn't have to worry about me moving away, or going to school, and high school, and all that stuff. But let's step away from your grave for a minute, okay? Now, supposing you get out of this tree, and given the normal flow of your life as we now know it, what's the worst thing that could happen today. What are you most worried about?"

One constant sprung to mind.

"I suppose the worst thing that could happen, the worst normal thing, is that I'd go home and Stosh would do something to me."

"Hit you?"

He shook his head. "He doesn't hit me, at least not often or very hard. It's more psychological. Practical jokes, threats, nasty tricks, that's the sort of stuff Stosh does."

Clodagh nodded in agreement. "Too bad he's smarter than you."

"What? He's barely passing in school. He doesn't have a clue on history, he can't write a complete sentence, he's never read anything deeper than a comic book, and it's been years since he did that..."

"So what's he got that you don't have?"

"He's bigger than I am!"

"But you said he doesn't hit you."

Chesney blinked. Her logic was sound.

"So if he doesn't hit you, and you're smarter than he is," Clodagh argued, "why does he get away with it? It's because he's got self-confidence, at least when it comes to you. He's been playing you so long that he's got you right where he wants you. You're his dupe, his patsy, his stooge, his…"

"I get the idea, thank you."

"And so you go around defeated. You're always on the defensive with everyone else because rattling around in your head is the idea that there might be more Stoshes out there, waiting to pounce!"

He blanched at the thought of more than one Stosh in the world. "Do you think so?"

"Sure," she said, "I was reading something about it in one of my Dad's books. It's the whole sibling rivalry thing. Stosh had it pretty good until you showed up. Then you're born, and he's goes from getting all the attention to having to split it with you. So, he does all he can to make you look bad, and himself look good. It's like you're both in a race, at least as far as he figures it…"

"…and he's got a five-year head start!" It was as if a light went off in a corner of his mind that had been in the shadows.

"Right," she said, "so what are you going to do about it?"

The light flickered out again. "Do about it?"

"Sure," she said, "if you stand up to Stosh…"

"Whoa, whoa," he said, waving her off, "this started about you moving away, and now you have me taking on Stosh."

"Of course," she said.

"Of course?" He jumped to his feet and started pacing around the tree house. "No, no, I mean, yeah, I understand what you said, and why I'm the way I am. And it makes sense, and all, but that's no reason to go after the big lunatic. I mean, yeah, Stosh has been playing cat and mouse with me before I can remember. My mother still tells stories about the defective nipples in the baby bottles, the ones that had the openings that were mysteriously clogged up. And my face nearly imploded I sucked on them so hard. She still doesn't get it, but I figured that one out years ago. They have a picture of me like this…" Chesney sucked in his cheeks and bulged out his eyes. "Every time she shows the photo album to someone, she tells the story like it's some big, funny mystery. But I see Stosh when she tells it. And I look at him, and he looks at me, I know he glued that nipple closed. And he knows I know. And it's been like that ever since. I'm getting better. You learn to live with the constant terror."

"But don't you see," said Clodagh grabbing his shoulders. "Don't you get it? You're on defense. He's a bully. All it will take to stop him is one good shot!" She punctuated this with a right hook to the air that nearly caught Chesney on the chin.

He thought for a moment. "No, that's not right. I'll do something to him, and then he'll just come back with something worse on me."

"But, Chesney..."

"No, I appreciate what you've said, and I agree with most of it. But I think that knowing the problem will help me deal with it better. And I'll be able to learn how to deal with other people now that I see that not everyone is Stosh. Really, I'll be okay, honest."

Chesney tried to smile bravely but could feel the anxiety welling up in his eyes.

"Really, it will all be okay," he repeated. "What did you say? What's the worst that could happen, right?"

But, he thought, the worst was already happening. His best friend was leaving his life. What could top that?

– 36 –
If There's Anything That You Want, Then It's Anything I Can Glue

Despite it being within the realm of possibility, the maple tree did not fall down with Chesney in it. And despite Clodagh's wishes, time did not leap forward like a yanked off Band-Aid.

Instead, Chesney went home, as usual, had a reliably bad dinner courtesy of his mother, and retreated to his room in one piece. There, safe and secure, he was able to concentrate on his new worry. With Clodagh gone, what would he do? How would he get through junior high, or high school, or college, or life? Who would talk to him? There was no affinity between him and anyone else. As he lay on his bed in the gathering dusk, he thought of his only other acquaintances: one a boy, the other a girl.

The boy, Jimmy Oosterhouse, lived down the street. Jimmy didn't think Chesney was odd; probably because he was even stranger than Chesney. Jimmy was fascinated by insects. He could often be seen on his belly with his nose close to a freshly dug flower bed, studying the micro-civilization contained within. He also loved pickles almost to the point of having a cucumber fetish. While other kids would scrape together their loose change for candy, Jimmy would collect his nickels for jars of dill pickles. He was branded "Jimmy Outhouse," not only because of his last name but because his lying around in dirt made him look like he'd fallen into one. Still, Jimmy was popular thanks to his natural athletic ability. He readily joined in neighborhood games when not distracted by insects or pickles.

The girl, Peggy Legotti, lived one block over. She was the kind of girl that mothers liked more than their own kids. She was safe and non-threatening to adults. To boys, at least to Chesney, she was dangerous. In some ways, she was more dangerous than even Stosh because she liked Chesney; a lot; an awful lot. Peggy was even worse off in the name category than Clodagh Clott. Her first name, coupled with an easily bastardized last name (and there were plenty of little bastards around to do so), meant that from an early age she had been taunted with "Piggy Leg," "Pig Leg," and, most frequently, "Peg Leg." These taunts, coupled with her mother's delicious Italian cooking, made Margaret Legotti the chubby female counterpart of Chesney.

Chesney sighed. The only two people who would want to hang around with him reminded him of his own worst qualities. Perhaps he would enter a monastery. Or, not wanting to shave his head, he'd cloister himself in his books. That was it; he would preserve his sanity between the pages of books. Currently, he was hiding in the greatest literary treasure of his young life.

Chesney had stashed his leather-bound copy of *Great Expectations* in the safest place he knew: a battered old Erector Set box. It was safe because it had once belonged to Stosh. Anything Stosh handed down to his younger brother was either broken or no longer of any use to him. In this way, Chesney obtained picture books with ripped pages, games with more than fifty percent of their pieces lost, and toys that no longer performed as designed. Chesney had no memory of a time when any of these items had been complete. He imagined how they must have appeared, shiny and bright on some distant Christmas morning. He was like an archeologist piecing together the life of a long-dead civilization by examining a few shards of pottery. Whereas an archeologist might surmise this group had been hunter-gathers, or that tribe had tilled the soil, Chesney didn't need to speculate. He knew Stosh had been a destructive little maniac who grew into a larger version of the same.

By the time it had been tossed in Chesney's direction, the Erector set was little more than a few metal girders, most of them twisted, some bolts and even fewer nuts. The motor, proudly illustrated on the inside lid powering a small Ferris wheel, had long been burnt out. The battered red tin box, however, was still functional as a container in which to keep his most precious treasures, those things which he didn't want anyone, least of all his brother, to see. He kept the box in plain view, neither hidden nor too prominent, just there.

With his door closed, Chesney removed the box from the shelf, beneath a hand-me-down box of Chinese Checkers with most of the marbles gone, and above a Bingo game with few numbers to call its own. The box contained the artifacts of his twelve-year-old life: his membership card to the Cub Scouts, Pack 124; his well-worn Public Library card; several ribbons of honorable mention from various school fairs; a few buttons from local political campaigns; a postcard from Disneyland; another from the 1964 New York World's Fair; and, assorted other items that gave testimony to a life of esoteric interests.

Also, in the box was a bundle of letters secured with a rubber band: his correspondence with his Aunt Elinor. He reached into the pocket of his dungarees and pulled out his latest letter. He started to place it under the rubber band with the others when he paused and extracted the letter for one more read before entering it into the archives. He raised the paper to his nose and inhaled. It smelled nice, not too girly, just nice.

"Dear No Pets," she began in her distinctive handwriting, *"I hope you don't mind me using our private anagrams in this letter, though, of course, I didn't use yours on the envelope as I wanted you to receive this without causing the Post Office too much confusion (ha, ha). Our special names are a lot of fun, and just a bit mysterious to others, which makes them even more fun.*

It was wonderful to finally see you face to face, though regrettably, my visit had to be cut short as I had pressing business to attend to. Still, I was glad to see what a fine young man you are turning out to be. It was nice to see your mother and father again, after so many years. I know they love you very much and that's a very good quality to have in parents. I'm glad we had a chance to talk about things, and I especially was glad to tell you that you are my favorite. It's not always easy to be the youngest in a family. I know, because even though I now must seem like a grown-up person to you, at one time, I was the youngest in the family. It's not always easy having an older brother, either. But remember, being an older brother can be difficult, too, especially when your parents' love and attention is suddenly divided."

Chesney paused at this sentence. He wondered if this was a reference, not only to Stosh being an older brother but himself, as well. Even though it had been two weeks since that day Aunt El had visited, his parents still hadn't announced that a baby was on the way, though Chesney was reasonably certain this was the case. In the ensuing fortnight, his parents had done more than their share of whispering and talking in half-sentences.

"We'll have to paint the room for....you know."

"I hope it's a...well, it doesn't really matter, does it? But still..."

In addition, his mother seemed especially cheery in the afternoons and evenings. In the mornings, she was often nowhere to be seen. On those days his father helped get them off to school. That was okay, as his father, rather than packing them a lunch, slipped both he and Stosh a few bucks and told them to buy lunch at school. Having overheard the details of his mother's condition second-hand, through the closet door, Chesney felt the information was not for sharing, not even with Clodagh. It was private until it was formally announced, he figured, though he did wonder what was taking so long. Stosh, usually a good source for rumors, didn't seem to know anything about it. His mind was preoccupied with the Stupid Golf Tournament, and his usual bodily functions.

Chesney returned to the letter.

"It can be difficult, but try to get along with your family, all of them, and try to be understanding of them. I hope to see you all again soon and will try to wrap up my business early so I can drop in again before I return to England. Perhaps

someday you can visit me, and I can show you all the sights. That would be great fun. I'm so happy you enjoyed the book. I had little doubt you would, but still, it's nice to know when something goes right, especially when it's for someone so dear. Love, your Aunt, Toenail Urn."

He folded the letter, placed it back in the envelope, and slid it on top of the others. Lying back on his bed, he thought about Aunt El's comment about getting along with his family. He knew she meant Stosh. He glanced around his room and felt satisfied, especially when his eyes fell upon his leather-bound edition of *Great Expectations*. He would try to give Stosh the benefit of the doubt. The thought struck Chesney that he was becoming more mature. He stroked his chin, half-expecting it to have sprung a sage crop of whiskers in the last few minutes. Yes, he was growing up, and soon he would be a big brother. He would be a better one than Stosh had been. Poor, Stosh, he must still be trying to deal with his feelings from when Chesney was born. He shook his head. What a rut to be in, poor fellow.

This psychological pondering made him think of Clodagh. Clodagh had it wrong, didn't she? Thinking he had to begin paying Stosh back for all his past bullying. That would only lead to retaliation from Stosh. Stosh couldn't keep up his reign of terror forever, Chesney reasoned. He was getting older, too. He must be picking up some maturity. And even if he didn't rise to the maturity level of his younger brother, Stosh would leave home eventually, perhaps for college.

Stosh in college? He tried to think of any schools that gave away Bully Scholarships or offered majors in knuckle-dragging. Chesney caught himself. Such thoughts weren't worthy of his burgeoning maturity. No, Stosh would go to school to study... he wracked his brain for several seconds, and then completed the thought... to study... something. In any event, one way or another, Stosh would put away his childish tricks, and move away from home. With that prospect in view, Chesney put away his letters and picked up his copy of *Great Expectations*.

He ran his hand over the hand-tooled leather, his fingertips pressing down into the grain to further luxuriate in the experience. He glanced, for comparison, to some of the paperback books on the nearby shelf, and shook his head. Books had become so commonplace over time, and that was a good thing for the world, he supposed. But this book, this volume, this tome, recalled a day when books were precious and so revered that their makers took almost as much care binding and finishing them as their authors had taken in writing them. Books were golden, he thought, as he fingered the gilt edges of the paper. His mind raced back to what his Aunt had told him, what some Chinese guy had said, about the greatest gift you could give someone was yourself. That fellow must have been right, Chesney thought, as he studied the book before him. For here, in his hands, was a piece of Charles Dickens; his mind and his feelings put down on paper and preserved so that one hundred years later he could share a part of himself with a kid from Long Island.

He lingered over these thoughts before opening the book. Dickens was a bit rougher going than *The Weekly Reader*, or *Charlie and the Chocolate Factory*. He kept a dictionary handy to help him with the unfamiliar and antiquated words in the book. Still, it was worth it. He was enjoying the story immensely and identified with the hero, the boy Pip who had been plucked from rural poverty and given the promise of a future fortune by a mysterious benefactor. He was roughly two-thirds through the book, as he pulled back the satin ribbon bookmark that was attached to the spine and found the page where he had left off.

Yes, he nodded to himself, Chapter Thirty-Nine, he had ended there, closing with the words: *"This is the end of the second stage of Pip's expectations."*

He turned the page and began the next chapter with the hero being visited by a mysterious person. Chesney nodded to himself and hoped this was the person who would reveal the mystery of the fortune. He had read the first two pages of the chapter and began to turn the page, but in doing so, a very odd thing happened. He shut the book.

His thumb must have caught all the pages rather than just the next page. He opened the book again to the page he had been on. He glanced to the bottom, Page 313, then with more deliberate care, fingered the upper corner of the page and proceeded to turn it. Again, he shut the whole book. Now suspecting something was amiss beyond his clumsiness, he once more returned to Page 313. He examined the top of the page. He ran his thumb and index finger over it, to catch the next page, but it did not yield, at least not individually. It was as if the rest of the book had unionized, formed a collective of pages, and had henceforth unanimously decided to act as one. For a brief moment, he wondered what had happened. Perhaps humidity or age had somehow fused them together. With great effort and exceeding care, Chesney was able to separate the upper corner, a mere eighth of an inch of the next page when he came to a conclusion. The page had been glued together. Page 313, the back of which was of course 314, had been glued to pages 315 and 316. Those, in turn, had been cemented to 317 and 318, which in turn had been forever bonded to 319 and 320, and so on, to the end of the book - whatever that was since he could no longer see the final page.

Chesney's eyes narrowed. In his new maturity, he tried to reject his first suspicion, to find another cause, but his reasoning would have none of it. He knew better and too well. No, this was deliberate, willful violence on a scale so personal that only one name sprung to mind as its source: Stosh.

For a dozen years, 100 percent of his life, Chesney had suffered at the hands of his brother. Until now he had been unwilling to respond; cowed by the fear of retribution if he dared to retaliate. Now, however, a line had been crossed. It was no longer whoopee cushions and dribble glasses, short-sheeted beds or sabotaged sandwiches. Now it went beyond Chesney, the easy victim, the soft target. Now Stosh had done violence to him, to his Aunt Elinor, and to Charles Dickens.

He clenched his fist and brought it down on the back of the book. He was ready to strike back.

– 37 –
Vengeance for Amateurs

W ell, all I can say is: that it's about time."
Chesney Potoski sat quietly. Inwardly, however, he seethed, simmering just below a furious boil.

"How you managed to take it all those years, I can't say. All I can say is: that it's about time. That's all I can say."

For being all you can say, Chesney thought as he looked at Clodagh Clott, you certainly are saying it over and over. Still, he kept his remarks to himself. He wouldn't waste the vitriol he was steeping for Stosh. It was all for Stosh, and it would be repayment for the past twelve years.

He looked at Clodagh, as they sat in the tree house, her long bare legs crossed at the ankles, her mouth moving, her hands examining the ruined copy of *Great Expectations*. He wanted to scream, to vent his pent-up anger. But he kept quiet, waiting for Clo to finish saying what she had to say, though she kept assuring him again and again that all she had to say had been said. Finally, she stopped. He raised his head. She looked at him quizzically, as if her rambling had been but a sentence or two.

"Well?" She said.

"I'm going to get him," said Chesney in a voice older than his years. "I'm going to get the bastard."

"Yes?"

"Oh, yes. Yes, I'm going to get him." Chesney's jaw tightened, and his hands clenched so that they trembled. "I'm going to get him. I swear it. I'm going to get him."

"Okay," said Clodagh. "How?"

The retributive force that had been pulsing through the sinews of his puny muscles suddenly departed, like an evil spirit from an exorcized soul. His shoulders slumped forward, and he mewed in a voice much younger than his actual years: "I haven't the slightest idea."

Clodagh shook her head. "Amateur. You have no idea. You've never even played the game, and now you want to take your first swing in the big leagues. Face it: you don't have a clue about what to do or how to do it. You don't even know where to begin. Am I right?"

Chesney nodded impotently.

"Right," she said. She handed him the book. "Funny, the things that set people off. Everyone has something different. I suppose it goes down to what you value. For some people, it would be money, or prestige, for you... a book, just a book..."

"It's not just a book," said Chesney, clutching the volume to his chest as if he were the guardian of the last printed word on earth.

"Calm down," she said. "I didn't mean just a book; of course it wasn't just a book to you. But everyone's different. You could have welded shut every book in the Library of Congress, and your brother wouldn't have cared. And that's the point."

"What's the point?"

"That's how you get back at Stosh: revenge with a cherry on top."

Chesney looked at her quizzically.

"Look, Ches," she said, "do you remember when I told you at how I got back at Rhoda when she accused me of losing her sweater?"

Chesney nodded, though he didn't see what good that did for him getting back at Stosh. "Bombs away," he said.

"Exactly, and why was that effective?"

He shrugged.

She tapped the side of her head.

"Psychology," she said. "It fits up here, with the way she thinks. You've got to know your enemy so you can think like them; so you can get them where they live... up here."

"Up there?"

"Everyone lives in their own head," Clodagh assured him. "They don't go anywhere without their brain. You've got to get them through the old cerebellum. Climb up in their heads, look around, find out what's important and then kick 'em hard in that spot. When I wanted to get Rhoda, I could have spiked her orange juice or stuck a rubber snake in her bed. That may have satisfying to me, but it really wouldn't have struck at her where she lived...in her head. I had to ask myself: what is her greatest pleasure, and what's her greatest fear?"

Chesney shook his head.

"Rhoda is really big on her body. She wasn't given a great mind, not like Denise, but she's got a good figure. She spends twice as much time in front of the mirror as all the rest of us combined."

"She does?"

Clodagh rolled her eyes. "At least! And she thinks she's got the greatest boobs in the world. I mean, she thinks she invented knockers. You should see her in her room in front of the mirror when she thinks nobody else is watching..."

Chesney could feel his face redden.

"Well, maybe you shouldn't see her," she said, noticing his embarrassment, "but she's just all this... and that..." At this point, Clodagh sat up straight, put her hands beneath her own nascent breasts, and twisted into various silly poses imitating Rhoda. "It's idiotic."

"Uh, yeah," agreed Chesney looking away.

"So that told me what her greatest pleasure is. She's super proud of her body, especially her chest."

"Okay."

"And she's really into cheerleading."

"Okay."

"So, all I had to do is to bring all that together and make her look stupid at the thing that she's most proud of. You know: embarrass her with the thing she usually takes a lot of pride in."

"Wow! How long did it take you to figure all that out?"

"About two seconds," she said. "It isn't difficult. You're just not used to thinking that way. Most people walk around with billboards on their body, advertising their big weaknesses and their greatest fears."

Chesney looked at the book in his lap.

"It's really amazing," said Clo glancing at the book, "that Stosh took so long to really hit you where your head was at. I mean, all those years and he never really got you where it hurt, did he?"

Chesney shook his head. "He could have short-sheeted my bed every night until I was an old man and it would have been better than..." He nodded at his violated Dickens.

"So," she said with a devious grin, "what are you going to do to Stosh?"

Chesney rose to his feet and looked over the edge of the tree house. Through the boughs of the maple tree, he could see their neighborhood basking peacefully in the sunshine. He turned to Clodagh, nodded his head, and said: "Something."

"Good...what?"

He opened his mouth, waited several seconds, and then closed it again.

"Look, Ches," she said, "it obvious you're going to need my help in this..."

"Yes, please!"

"...you've never been sneaky, have you?" He shook his head. "No, I didn't think so. First, remember what I said. You've got to keep two things in mind. What does he like? And what's his greatest fear? So, let's start there. What does Stosh like?"

Chesney paced the floor of the tree house for several minutes.

"Well, Stosh likes to pull practical jokes."

Clodagh's brow formed a ledge over her almond-shaped eyes and hummed. "Umm, yes, yes, that's important. In fact, it's very fitting, especially from a psychological point of view."

"Is it?" Chesney's face brightened.

"Oh, yes, it's got a nice sense of irony..."

"Poetic justice…"

"Yes, that too," Clo agreed. "But of course, you'll be playing a practical joke on him, in the truest sense of the term. So, that's sort of obvious, isn't it? What you need is something that he really likes."

"Torture. He likes torture. And he likes to torture me."

"Yessss, okay…" It was apparent from her reaction that she didn't think he was quite grasping the basic concept.

"Oh, I don't know," Chesney slumped down, "I can't do this. I can't think like Stosh. I don't even know why I'm trying. It's just stupid… stupid…"

His eyes widened, a "eureka" grin spread across his face.

"Stupid," he repeated, nodding at Clodagh as if it should be evident to her as well. "Stupid!"

"Stupid?" she asked.

"Stupid, don't' you see? It's so obvious," he said, "the stupid golf tournament!"

"The stupid golf tournament!"

"Stosh, really wants to win that stupid thing," said Chesney. "So, all I have to do is figure a way to make him lose, right?"

"Well, that would be fun to watch all by itself," Clo agreed, "but he's got to realize you did it to him."

"What am I supposed to do, run out and steal the ball when he's trying to hit it? He'd kill me. He'd kill me, then take out another ball hit that, and then turn around and kill me again."

"No, we sabotage him in such a way that he almost knows for certain that you did it, but he can't prove it." Clodagh rubbed her hands together with glee. "The stupid golf tournament, eh?"

"That's all he's been talking about for weeks."

"Well, then," she said, "that takes care of what he's passionate about. Now, what is Stosh afraid of?"

The gleeful anticipation of revenge drained from Chesney's face. It was as if a parole had been dangled in front of a prisoner, only to be informed the guards had lost the key to his cell.

"Afraid?" He said. "Stosh isn't afraid of anything."

– 38 –
Beyond the Glued Nipple and Under the Railroad Bridge

Stosh Potoski was fearless. Chesney didn't know if this was because his brother was genuinely courageous or that he was a cold stone idiot.

Stosh was always the kid out in front of the pack, especially if the activity was dangerous. He'd personally witnessed Stosh jump off the roof of their house to prove a point. It had been a dumb point, but he had still done it! Stosh had also once ridden his bike off the end of a dock, trying to duplicate a stunt he'd seen in an animated cartoon. That the original had been accomplished by a two-dimensional drawing had little bearing on his reasoning. It had been done by someone else, so why shouldn't he try it? Accidentally setting his pants on fire, running through screen doors, blowing up all sorts of things with cherry bombs, all these attested to the blind, ignorant courage of Stosh.

Chesney was so occupied with his own phobias he had never noticed what Stosh's fear might be. Previously he had tried to figure out what someone liked so he could surprise them with a present on their birthday or at Christmas. To figure out what terrified someone so he could use it against them was not nice. It was nasty, it was cruel. It was positively... Stosh-like.

He sat on the edge of the vacant lot where the neighborhood kids played war; Stosh, of course, leading them all. War games: that made Chesney think of his grandfather, his father's father, Aunt El's father. His grandfather Potoski served in World War I and was a genuine hero. He had won a medal and lost a leg. Chesney had only recalled meeting him once. He was very old and pretty scary to a child of four. Chesney didn't remember the medal, but he never forgot the wooden leg. Stosh, then nine, had dared him to stick a fork into the leg, but Chesney had been afraid. He still wasn't quite sure exactly what he'd been more afraid of: poking the wrong leg, putting a hole in his grandfather's trouser leg, or getting yelled at by the ancient man. Or perhaps it was just his nature to shrivel up in the face of a challenge.

Chesney sighed. Just about everyone in his family had courage, but him: Stosh, his grandfather, his father. Even his Aunt Elinor had the courage to kill someone and then escaped to Tibet. Chesney rose, dusted the dirt off the seat of his dungarees, and ambled along hoping to find a place in the neighborhood that did not remind him of his shortcomings.

He wandered past the tall pine tree in a neighbor's yard. It was the best climbing tree on the block. Chesney craned his neck upwards only to be reminded that he had never reached as high as most of the other kids. He'd always make a good start, ascending to at least six feet off the ground. That was the point when problems of perspective encroached upon his imagination. For every foot climbed beyond six feet, the distance from the ground seemed to be an additional three feet. It didn't help when the other kids urged him not to look down. Looking up only made him dizzy. By the height of ten feet, he made up some excuse, such a hearing his mother calling him, or having to go to the bathroom, and even then, his descent was painstakingly cautious.

Every spot he visited in the neighborhood, the wooded lot with scary undergrowth, the street where they played their asphalt version of baseball, even the local news shop where the kids would go to buy candy and comic books, brought fresh reminders of Chesney's own fears and his brother's lack of the same. Defeated, he dragged himself home late in the afternoon only to find another reminder of his weakness greeting him: his mother was sticking a frozen "TV" dinner in the oven.

"There you are," said Mrs. Potoski. "I was just about to call for you."

The smell of her perfume cut through even the overpowering pungency of yesterday's tuna casserole, and the miasma of innumerable overcooked meatloaves. His mother was wearing a nice dress, a new one that seemed baggier than those she usually wore, and high heeled shoes. That evidence, coupled with the Swanson Chicken Dinner in the oven meant his parents were going out for the evening.

"Your father and I are going over to the Oosterhouse's to have dinner and play bridge," she informed him. "But don't worry, I got you your favorite for dinner."

Chesney nodded, though it wasn't his favorite. He had liked the industrially-produced entrée of two scrawny chicken legs, pasty potatoes, and rubber peas the first time he had had them, but that was six years ago. Even the novelty of eating off a compartmentalized piece of aluminum had faded. That first time could have been a possum stew garnished with a bed of weeds, and he would have thought it unique enough to gain his approval. Six years ago, Chesney agreed that he liked it...just once. That was all that his mother ever needed or ever solicited. That single vote went down forever, indelibly etched in her mind, forever dooming him to a sentence of frozen chicken dinners when his parents went out on a Saturday night. As they lived in a sociable neighborhood, this meant that Chesney ingested between forty-five and fifty frozen chicken dinners annually.

Stosh was assertive enough to reject this suburban staple, and now that he was older, he eschewed the wonders of reheated meals for a burger down at one of Earwick's two fast food joints.

It wasn't only that Chesney had to choke down another frozen dinner while Stosh feasted on juicy hamburgers that underscored his feelings of inferiority. What made him feel even more of a failure, and by contrast made Stosh seem that much more invincible was what always followed a frozen dinner: Denise Clott.

Denise Clott, the oldest of the four Clott sisters, had been Chesney's babysitter for years. That they thought he needed a sitter at the age of twelve was irksome. Chesney didn't really mind Denise Clott. Their evenings together were not unlike those of an elderly married couple who had learned to enjoy each other's company alone together. Like Clodagh, Denise was bookish, though while Clo's interests ran more towards the eclectic, Denise's pursuits were practical. She was already a sophomore in college, working toward a law degree. Denise had plotted out her course with the precision of a railroad upon which she was the engine.

Chesney was half-way through his frozen dinner when Denise arrived with an armload of textbooks, as usual. While she exchanged pleasantries with his parents, Chesney picked at his meal, which was overdone according to his mother's custom. He was probing the middle of what had begun existence as mashed potatoes when his father interrupted.

"…And you'll be good for Denise, won't you?"

He nodded in compliance, though they both knew that the warning was unnecessary. It was just the obligatory speech parents had to deliver regardless of the individual child. A boy like Chesney wouldn't have been bad even if he had been given a generous government grant to start a riot, while Stosh couldn't have stayed out of trouble if he had to put up a cash bond. It was like warning a lamb not to eat the neighborhood lions.

"And keep your eyes open…"

Chesney's eyes narrowed. He'd never heard that admonition before.

"…watch how Denise, uh, how she watches you. You never know, you might have to…I mean, you might want to do some babysitting yourself, someday, uh, soon. Okay, Sport?"

Chesney pondered the cryptic advice while attempting to chew some dark pellets that had once been peas. There was no mystery about the vegetable, though his father's remarks were open to interpretation. Either it was a hint that Chesney needed to find a job, or that a job was barreling toward him in the guise of a new brother or sister. He glanced over at his mother. Her baggy new outfit could very well be a maternity dress.

Was his father indicating that he would be allowed to watch the baby? This notion was revolutionary. In the Potoski household rarely did older brothers watch their younger siblings, and that was fine with both Stosh and Chesney. Chesney wouldn't want to be left alone with Stosh in charge, nor would Stosh want the chore.

Chesney thought the idea of him becoming a babysitter was odd since he was still being babysat. It was strange that today he was being safeguarded by Denise Clott, and in another few months, he would be expected to safeguard an infant. Shouldn't there be an interim period where he would prove himself responsible by watching himself?

"My, aren't we pensive tonight?"

Chesney, still absorbed in thought, looked up to find he was sitting on the sofa with a book in his lap, though he hadn't recalled sitting down and the book wasn't opened.

"Huh?"

"Pensive," said Denise Clott, "it means…"

"Thoughtful, I know what it means," said Chesney.

Denise smiled like a satisfied schoolmarm. She closed her textbook. "So? Is there anything you want to talk about?"

He looked at her for a moment, weighing in his mind whether he should broach the subject of younger siblings. He hadn't even told Clodagh. It would be a violation of their friendship to tell her older sister the news first. He was still thinking when Denise advanced the conversation.

"Is something bothering you?"

Was something bothering him? Only one thing and that had been going on as long as he could remember. How could anyone live in the same house with a madman and not be bothered? He often wondered why nobody else in Earswick was uncomfortable sharing the town with Stosh.

"Well," she said, opening her book again, and looking down, "I just want you to know that everyone gets afraid now and then."

The room was silent save for the ticking of the mantel clock, as Chesney digested that last statement. Where, he wondered, had that come from? Yes, he thought, everyone does get afraid now and then, but why bring it up now?

He stared at her for a moment. "Uh, okay…" he said.

Denise flashed a closed-mouth smile as if the gesture were part of her checklist on how to be a supportive person.

"It's okay," she said, "I don't want to betray a confidence, but… Clodagh told me all about it."

He looked at Denise blankly. After a moment, she tilted her head forward and made a nodding gesture, as if she were nudging an imaginary clothespin with her nose. He took this to be an encouragement to unburden his soul, though what specific item his soul needed release from, he had no idea.

"Clodagh?"

"Yes, Clodagh, my sister," she said, though that was evident. He doubted there was another Clodagh in Earswick. "Clodagh told me you were afraid."

He looked at the imitation oil painting on the wall as if a clue to what she was talking about was hidden in the boat George Washington was commanding across the Delaware. Why? He asked himself, would Clodagh tell her older sister that he was having a problem with fear?

"Don't worry," she continued, "I won't tell anyone...if you want to talk about it, everyone's afraid of something. Do you want to know what I'm afraid of?"

He squinted at her. This was getting weirder by the minute. What *she* was afraid of? That was something he was afraid of: learning the secret fears of his babysitter. Instead of saying no, however, he nodded, "yes."

Denise took a deep breath.

"I'm afraid," she said as if she were sneaking up on it, "I am afraid of... going under railroad bridges."

Railroad bridges, he thought. He was living under the same roof as a person who glued shut the nipples on baby bottles, and she thought railroad bridges were scary?

"...especially when there's a train going over them." She exhaled and looked up, then flashed another brief smile. "There! A burden shared is a burden halved, isn't it?"

He nodded and wondered if she would be half as afraid of a short train going over a railroad bridge.

"So," said Denise, a little more relaxed, which meant she was still as rigid as a plank, "that's better. Would you like to talk?"

Again, he stared at her. He wished he could excuse himself, run out, and call Clodagh to see what she was up to. There must be some logical motive behind it, but he couldn't figure out what. If anything, he reasoned, Clodagh should have talked to Denise about Stosh's fears. That would have made much more sense.

Chesney sat there for a moment as that last thought echoed through his mind, bouncing off the side of his brain until it grew into a clear message: Clodagh was being sneaky on his behalf. In her search for Stosh's weakness, Clodagh was using her older sister, the one "kid" in the neighborhood older than Stosh. He almost slapped his forehead for it being so obvious, now that he saw it. Clodagh couldn't have asked Denise outright, nor could Chesney. They were both older siblings, and so she wouldn't volunteer any information against one of their own. On top of that, Denise was responsible and mature, and no doubt would have balked at assisting in any scheme of revenge, even one whose lofty purpose was to avenge a 19th Century author. Good old Clodagh, she had set up her own sister.

"You can trust me, Chesney," she said.

"I can?"

"Certainly, you can tell Denny."

"Who?"

"Denny," she said gesturing to herself. "That's me. That's my nickname. Only not many people use it except my very closest friends."

He nodded, though he had never heard anyone call her "Denny."

"Go ahead," she continued, "you can tell Denny." Denise Clott, by trying to appear warm and sympathetic, only came across even more robotic. Still, she seemed willing to talk. Maybe this would work.

He tried to wipe the look of confusion off his face and replace it with one that displayed this supposed deep fear that had been hounding him. He had no idea what Clodagh had told her sister, so he had to keep talking in vague generalities.

"So, so Clodagh told you?" His voice cracked, more from the outset of puberty than from emotion, but still, it was a nice touch.

Denise smiled. He had never seen her this caring. Even so, she still behaved like a female version of Spock from *Star Trek*.

"Did she tell you all about it?" Chesney asked.

"Well, most of it."

"And you're not..." he groped for the right phrase, "shocked?"

"It's nothing to be shocked about. If you're afraid of it, it's very real."

That hadn't helped at all. He just looked at her and tried to appear worried. Fortunately, she picked up the dangling thread of the conversation.

"A lot of boys are afraid of that, I imagine."

Oh, great, he thought, it was a boy thing, and she was a girl. What had Clodagh gotten him into? "They are?" was all he could ask in reply.

"I'm sure of it," she said laboring to be compassionate, though she soon reverted to her usual pedantic form, "that is, I suppose so, of course, it's only a guess since I'm not a boy. But I imagine if I were a boy this fear wouldn't fall out of the realm of possibility. By that, I mean, it's not really strange to have that fear, but of course, I'm no doctor..."

Her rambling wound to a stop under its own weight. Denise must have realized that instead of being empathetic, her attempts at reassurance came out like a legal disclaimer at the end of a car commercial. She took a moment to compose herself, flashed a brief grin, and then said as if it were the first thing she had said that evening: "I understand."

Again, not having any clue to the cause of his mystery phobia, Chesney merely said: "You do? Well, that's a relief."

Denise nodded. "There's a lot of pressures on a boy growing up...that is, I would imagine there are..."

"Yes! There are."

There was a moment of silence as Denise tried to show him that she cared, but didn't really know how to, and Chesney had no idea what she was caring about. He broke the silence. "So, are you sure Clodagh told you everything?"

"Yes, she did," said Denise. "She told me all about your fear."

"Of…" Had he been a lawyer, he would have been accused of leading the witness.

"Of how you're afraid you won't… well, that you won't live up to expectations…"

He felt himself blush deep red at this point. For a boy approaching puberty that was loaded with embarrassing possibilities. Denise must have noticed his red face as she quickly amended her last statement.

"… That you'll be a disappointment."

He almost asked "to whom," but that would give away the fact that he still didn't know his own anxiety. Instead, he just nodded and tried to look sorrowful. It must have had some effect since she continued.

"It's difficult to live up to the reputation of an older sibling."

It took every ounce of strength for him not to fall off the sofa in a fit of laughter. Live up to the reputation of an older sibling? Live up to Stosh's reputation? Since he entered school, he'd been doing his damnedest to live it down. Fortunately, the stifling of his true feelings must have been mistaken for the repression of sobs, rather than guffaws, since she patted him on the shoulder.

"There, there," Denise said, trying to soothe, but sounding more like voice synthesized speech. "I know from experience how these sibling dynamics work. In my case, it's from the other end, me being the oldest, but it's just as hard to be the oldest and set a good example as it is to be younger and try to follow it."

Again, Chesney repressed the urge to laugh in her face, choosing instead to bury his face in his hands. He began to see the trail Clodagh had laid out.

"Oh, right, I mean, yes, that's right," he said, "Stosh has set such an example that I'm afraid…very, very afraid that I won't be able to follow in his footsteps." He took a gulp of air. "And the bar has been set so high," he continued. "It's so difficult being the kid brother, especially when you have such a…perfect older brother." Perfect nincompoop, he thought.

"Well, I know it's a challenge for the younger brothers and, in my case, sisters, to follow in the footsteps of their older siblings. But you must remember, Chesney, that we're not perfect either."

"No?" Chesney tried to feign genuine surprise.

"Not at all," she said. "For example, being a few years older than your brother, I've seen him from a different perspective. No doubt you've always looked up to him, literally and figurative, and so you tend to idolize him."

Chesney bit his lip.

"But your brother is just a boy, a flawed individual. Believe me, I've seen Stosh do his share of foolish things. They might not seem that way to you, admiring him as you do, but take my word for it, in some ways he's fairly typical."

Typical pea-brained bully, Chesney thought.

"But, Stosh is so much stronger than I, so much taller..."

She waved her hand, dismissively. "It seems that way because he's older than you. You haven't fully developed yet into the person you'll be."

"But," Chesney paused as he prepared to play the trump card, "I'm so... timid, and Stosh is so brave. He's not afraid of anything."

He waited for a moment as her lips began to part and then stopped.

"That's true," she said after a short silence. "Your brother is very brave."

Very brave? That was Chesney's greatest fear...that Stosh had no fear. He let out a deep sigh.

"Of course," she added, "when he was younger."

His brow raised, he looked up. "Yes?"

"Well, it's sort of silly, actually," she said.

"Yes?"

"I wouldn't want to lower his reputation in your eyes."

Lower his reputation? To drop Stosh's reputation any lower Denise would have to rent a backhoe and dig a ten-foot pit in the backyard.

"Oh, no," he assured her, trying not to appear too anxious, "I mean, my opinion of my brother could never change..."

"And this would give you a more realistic view," she said, weighing in her mind whether or not to continue.

"Yes, it would," he agreed. "And that way I wouldn't be so worried about..." he swallowed hard, "...living up to an unobtainable standard."

She agreed and began to speak in a much lower, more confidential tone of voice. "When Stosh was little, this is years ago, mind you..."

Chesney nodded.

"...I personally witnessed your brother afraid, actually, now that I think about it, I saw him display real fear twice."

Two times? This was even better, Chesney thought. He leaned closer so as not to miss a single word.

– 39 –
Air-Conditioned Penguin
Slinging Out His Patrons

It wasn't fair, thought Clodagh Clott as she pedaled her powder blue Schwinn Starlet bicycle down the street. Denise had enjoyed the luxury of growing up in the same town, and Caprice and Rhoda had almost had the same advantage. She was the only one who was being uprooted just as things were getting good for her in Earswick. She was on the cusp of adolescence, a critical time in the maturation process of a young girl, or at least that's what her father's psychology books told her. This opinion was seconded by Clodagh's budding hormones. Puberty was awkward enough, but all its challenges would be magnified amidst a group of strange kids, in a strange school, in the middle of a strange town.

Though it was still early June, summer had forced its hand early, bringing sticky days, sultry nights, and a persistent humidity that threatened to frizz even the straightest heads of hair. Clodagh, Chesney and their fellow inmates had to swelter in the brick and mortar sweatbox of Birchwood School, with nothing for relief but crude fans made from construction paper. Along with the others, Clodagh had spent the better part of the last five days peeling various parts of her arms and legs from almost every piece of furniture at home and at school. With two weeks of school remaining and no relief in the offing, the sixth grade had to endure having their bare arms adhere to the desktops while their teachers advised them to "think cool thoughts," and "you won't feel so hot if you don't think about it." Both statements were transparently false.

A sardonic smirk played across her lips at the notion of thinking oneself cool, while her index finger unconsciously dug at the band of the new bra forced on her by her mother. What sort of a sadist, she wondered, would introduce their youngest child to an extra layer of clothing, and that tight, restrictive spandex, in a heat wave? Other girls in her class saw the garment as a status symbol. None of them had three older sisters who had long dispelled the novelty of the bra. She didn't really need one yet, well, maybe she did, she reasoned, but certainly, it could wait until the fall, couldn't it? Besides, what sort of idiotic invention was a training bra, anyway? It made no sense to her. Either you needed one, or you didn't, and she didn't, at least not on a day when the temperature and the relative humidity met at 95. A training bra, how embarrassing, how ludicrous! Why it made as much sense as, as, training dentures would for people who still had their own teeth or training glasses for people with 20/20 vision. She pushed her own glasses back up to the bridge of her nose, though they'd only slide down again within a few minutes with the perspiration rolling down her face. Her protests fell on deaf ears, at least where her mother was concerned. And she wouldn't complain to her sisters since they would just pat her on her head and offer sarcastic remarks about the "Little Chinese girl smuggling two little bags of rice." Clodagh's only other court of appeal, her father, was out of the question given the subject. A gap in the traffic allowed Clodagh to pedal onward towards one of the few islands of blissful relief in the steaming bowl of porridge that Earswick had become: the town's new public library.

The new library had central air conditioning. The head librarian, a rotund, bespectacled man named Mr. Repaupo, but known behind his back to all the kids as "The Penguin," insisted on it. The air conditioning was not, it turned out, for the benefit of the tax-paying patrons, but for the sake of preserving Repaupo's precious books in a state of optimum humidity. Fortunately, the Penguin was generous enough to allow all card-carrying library members to frequent his slice of artic happiness during regular operating hours.

It was to this oasis, that Clodagh Clott now pedaled, as much as to return some books as to enjoy some relief from the heat. Locking her bike to the rack in front of the building, she noticed the bike with the speckled banana seat. It was Chesney's. The sporty seat didn't really fit Chesney's image, it was hand-me-down from his older brother. Poor Ches, she thought, doesn't even stick up for himself in the choice of his own bicycle seat.

Entering the library, Clodagh felt the immediate plunge in temperature. The contrast between the sultry outside and the chilly inside caused goose pimples to sprout on her legs and arms. She dropped off the books she was returning then walked to the literature section, expecting to find Chesney. He wasn't there. She thought for a moment. History? Yes, he sometimes took out history books, she reminded herself and proceeded to that section, but he wasn't there either. This was a greater mystery than those shelved in the entire whodunit section which, incidentally, he wasn't in either. Clodagh began a search of every section. A great disciple of Dewey and his Decimals, the librarian, had arranged the new library according to that system. Starting at the front desk, Clodagh walked through the 100's, her own usual haunt with its psychology and paranormal volumes, past the 200's, the 300's. Social sciences? He wasn't there. Neither was Chesney cloistered in among the 400's with its books on foreign languages, nor the 500's with its books on science. Technology, medicine, engineering, home economics... by the end of the 600's she still hadn't found Chesney.

She continued her search: back to the 800's – literature, 900 – history, which only left the 700 section – the Arts. Chesney was no Philistine; still, she didn't expect to find her friend pouring over pages on classic sculpture or baroque chamber music, and she was correct. He wasn't there.

Finally, Clodagh found him seated on a small step stool, studying a book on the last subject she would have expected him to be interested in. There, amidst a shelf full of 796's, Chesney Potoski was mesmerized by a book… on golf!

It was the most unlikely subject she could imagine; even more unlikely than if he'd been reading *100 Ways to Cook Broccoli*, *Advanced Calculus for Kids*, or *Great Older Brothers I Admire*.

After standing over him for a good 30 seconds with no sign of him stirring, Clodagh cleared her throat. Rather than look up, he merely swung his legs to the left, as if he had been blocking the aisle.

"Ches?" she finally said in a stern whisper out of respect for the sanctity of the library.

He finally looked up; his focus so intense that it took a moment for him to recognize her before relaxing into a smile. "Oh, hello, Clo. Hey, look what I found. Isn't this great?"

She shook her head.

"Oh, Chesney! Golf?" She said mournfully.

A week ago, she had told him that he would have to stand on his own and that he'd have to learn to survive without her support. She wasn't even gone yet, and she found him going over to the enemy. But there was something in her that took comfort in his helplessness. She wasn't sure if it was because she was being uprooted from the only home she had known or was there something else? But it was Chesney who needed her more than she needed him, wasn't it? Perhaps, she thought, the person who was needed, needed to be needed as much as the person who needed them. She looked down at him, slumped on the stool, his shoulders hunched forwards, his soft body piled there like a lump of wet paste, and she was confused. Clodagh didn't know if she wanted to hug him or punch his face in, but she did know that she didn't want to leave him. She especially didn't want to leave him if he was going to devolve into some drastically different boy than the one with whom she had grown comfortable with. It was like finding that the bedroom she was leaving was going to be painted some hideous color after she'd gone. Golf? Golf! He had more character than to degenerate into some half-assed version of a jock. That settled it. In one sharp motion, she shoved him off the stool and on to the carpeted floor.

He just sat there for a moment with a stunned look on his face.

"I'm sorry, Ches," she whispered, "let me help you up."

"What was that for?" he said, climbing back on to the stool.

"I…I suppose I got a little angry," she said. "I mean, I saw your bike outside, and I looked all over the library for you, and I couldn't find you, and you're here in the last place I looked."

"Everything's always in the last place you look," he said.

"What?"

"If you're looking for something it will always be in the last place you look because you stop looking after you've found it."

She pushed her glasses back up her nose. Here she was upset about, well, a lot of things, and he's going all pedantic on her.

"Shut up! What I meant is this is the last place I would expect to find you. If you're going to end up being some athletic, muscle-headed, peabrain, then I'm not so sure I'm going to miss you!"

"Athletic peabrain?" He looked down at the volume in his hand, and a look of understanding spread across his face. "Oh, I get it," he said. "This?"

He held up the cover of *Winning Golf Techniques and Strategies.*

"This," he continued, "is the answer to my problem."

"Golf? Well, that's great," she hoped her words were dripping with sarcasm. "If you can't beat them, join them, I suppose."

"I can't beat them unless I join them. Remember, Stosh and messing up his tournament? But there was the missing piece. Your sister gave me the rest of it, the other night when she was baby, uh, sitting."

"Denise? My sister Denise?" Clodagh repeated. "The one who's going to be a lawyer and could live happily with nothing but her brain in a jar and public broadcasting? She told you to become a golfer?"

"Yeah, no, not exactly," he said. "Denise let me in on Stosh's weaknesses…"

"You're welcome," said Clodagh, pointing out that she had set the whole thing up.

"Thank you," Chesney added, "that was really clever of you. I almost didn't figure out what you were doing. Denise told me some things about Stosh I didn't know, but she also gave me the idea of how to get at them." At this point, he waved the book before her anew.

"But your brother loves golf. That's his greatest passion. We knew that. What's he afraid of?"

"Two things…"

"You youngsters will have to be quiet or leave the library," a staccato voice quacked. They looked up to see the squat form of the Penguin waddling down the aisle. His eyes blinked furiously behind his thick glasses, and his tongue wetted his thick lips as he spoke as if he were anticipating a raw fish being tossed in his direction. "This is not a social club. This is a library. People are reading. People are studying."

Chesney froze, as he did when confronted by authority, even by Repaupo who had less authority than the average cafeteria monitor. Clodagh looked at Chesney, then at the Penguin, and then back at Chesney. Would he ever stand up for himself? His timidity and the fact that he had been interrupted at a critical point of their conversation annoyed her even more. She could feel the blood rushing to her cheeks as she stood up to her full height, which equaled that of the librarian.

"Excuse me," she said, "but this is a private conversation."

Chesney's eyes grew large. "Clodagh," he whispered, "what are you doing?"

"Hush," she barked.

"Young lady, how dare you?" Mr. Repaupo's lower lip jutted out even further than usual, which was really quite a bit indeed. As he spoke, it flapped with each syllable uttered. "This is my library, and…"

"This is the public library," interrupted Clodagh, "and we are the public. And aside from some old lady ripping recipes out of *The Ladies Home Journal*, and some old man sleeping in the Architecture section, there's no one here to disturb, even if we were shouting at the top of our lungs! Which is not such a bad idea." At this, Clodagh threw back her head and let out a sound not heard in the building since the last civil defense drill. "EEEEEEEEEEEEEEEEEEEEK!"

Repaupo recoiled twice: first at the news that someone was tearing up his periodicals, and second at the sound of screaming amidst his stacks.

Clodagh didn't know what came over her, but whatever it was, it felt good to just let loose like that. In fact, it felt so good she repeated it in a higher register. "EEEEEE…"

Suddenly Chesney clamped his hand over her mouth. She would have bitten him to make him remove it, but she was proud that he had shown initiative, even if it was only reactive.

"Clo, please remember where you are…" Chesney said. "Sorry, Mr. Repaupo, I don't know what came over Miss Clott."

The Penguin leaned forward, his arms pressed to his side, validating his nickname. He looked at Clodagh.

"Clott, eh?"

"Penguin, eh?" replied Clodagh, though the insult was unintelligible through Chesney's hand.

Then the librarian peered at Chesney through his thick glasses.

"Potoski, isn't it?" He should know Chesney. Chesney had visited the library at least twice a week for the last ten years.

"Yes, sir," he said to Repaupo.

"Well…" the librarian looked them up and down. His expression softened, but then his eyes squashed in around his nose in a sneer. "… you'll have to leave."

"But, I…" Chesney waved the book on golf. Mr. Repaupo snatched it from his hand.

"And I'll take this!" The Penguin turned on one foot and began shuffling down the aisle, the book under his arm.

"But I want to borrow it," said Chesney, following with Clodagh in tow, his hand still clamped over her face. She could have easily pried herself free. Clodagh knew she was stronger than him, but there was something about this contact that was oddly pleasurable. She decided to let it continue until she could figure out why.

They rushed to the main desk, Repaupo, his chest puffed out like an Emperor Penguin, Chesney following close behind pleading for mercy. In the process of his appeal, Chesney was reciting his school grades for the last four years, his stellar record as an auxiliary hall monitor, his offer to read to the preschoolers, and the fact that his mother thought him a fine boy – all to no avail. Once behind the desk, Repaupo pulled a key from the retractable chain on his belt, unlocked a drawer in the counter, stuck the book inside, and relocked the drawer. Having finished this coup de grace, Repaupo struck a masterful pose suggesting he was a colossus of knowledge rather than just a fat little man with a bunch of books.

His eyes riveted on the drawer which held his desired prize, Chesney's arms drooped to his side freeing Clodagh's mouth. She opened her mouth to speak, but Repaupo raised his hand.

"Cease!" He said it in the loudest voice he'd ever used in his holy of holies.

"But, my book..." said Chesney.

"*My* book," said the Penguin, poking his own chest with his stubby little thumb. "You may borrow it in September. Your library privileges are suspended until then. Please vacate the library."

Chesney's jaw dropped. Banned from the library? His body slumped as if he'd been de-boned.

"Hey, you can't do that, it wasn't his fault..." said Clodagh.

"You!" Repaupo said thrusting a chubby index finger in Clodagh's direction, "you may not come back until...one year from today!"

Clodagh felt her face grow red all the way up to the tips of her ears. Her father being career military had instilled in her a respect for authority. She clenched her fists and literally shook as she wrestled between accepting the sentence of this sawed-off dictator, or throwing all restraint to the wind and letting him have it with every vile word she knew. Not surprisingly, her response fell somewhere in between, and like most compromises left no one satisfied.

"I won't..." she said, "be coming back...not in a year...not in ten-thousand years. I'm moving from this crummy town in two months!"

"Then you're banned for life!" announced the librarian.

"Yours or mine?" snapped Clodagh.

His only response was to show them to the door as authoritatively as a short, fat, middle-aged man could manage.

Chesney regained enough muscle to hold the door for Clodagh as they were swallowed up by the steamy haze of early June. As a parting shot, Clodagh rushed back into the library and shouted: "Gestapo!" Then grabbed Chesney's hand and pulled him around the back of the building where they sat beneath a shady locust tree.

"Whoo," said Clodagh, fanning herself by waving her cotton blouse from the neck, half from the excitement and half from the heat. "I never expected to tell off the Penguin."

Chesney sat there, staring at the ground.

"Wow, getting banned from the library for life," she continued, "That puffed up little Hitler." Clodagh looked at her friend. "I'm sorry, Ches," she said, reaching out to touch his shoulder, but not quite completing the gesture. "I know how much the library means to you."

"What'll I tell my Mom? She'll be pretty upset. She was going to be an English teacher before she married my Dad. To her, getting kicked out of the public library is as bad as being excommunicated from the church. My Dad won't like it either."

"I'm sorry," she said. "I could explain to them that it was my fault..."

"...Being kicked out of the library all summer is bad enough, but I really need that book."

"Maybe the school library will have the book," suggested Clodagh.

Chesney sighed. "Less than two weeks left in the school year. All the books have been returned, and no one can take out any more."

She studied his bowed head, still unclear how learning about golf fit into his plan. Odd, she thought, but in all the years that she'd known him, Clodagh never noticed how good-looking Chesney Potoski was...in a Pillsbury Doughboy sort of way. Maybe golf or some kind of physical activity would tone him up a bit, give some definition to his body. He looked like a half-completed sculpture, the rough shape was there, but the finer chiseling still had to be done. His face was good, too, bordering on cute. She caught herself. This was crazy. Chesney was her best friend, annoyingly pedantic, puffy, spineless, cowed, timid, and several other traits, all of them less than alluring. She had known him forever. She couldn't recall a time without Chesney. Falling in love with Chesney would be like falling in love with the curtains in her bedroom, or the drippy faucet of the bathroom sink. One didn't fall in love with ordinary, everyday fixtures. Besides, she told herself, she had never thought of him romantically, not even when they were pre-schoolers, and she pushed him into playing "house." Clodagh was always the mommy, but Chesney was never the daddy. Instead, he executed a range of character roles from the visiting uncle, to the local butcher, or grocer, or whatever service was required. Chesney as a husband, or a daddy? The notion had never crossed her mind, yet there he was sitting under the tree while he rattled on about something.

"I'll ride to Northreach," he said so assertively that it jarred Clodagh out of her reverie.

"Northreach? All the way on your bike? What for?"

He looked up at her quizzically. "To go to their library, I can read it there, if they have it. It's only eight miles."

Only Eight miles? It wasn't the distance she found remarkable, but that he had diminished it. She had never known Chesney to pedal more than two miles before, and then under duress. He was afraid to cross major roads, and now he was cavalierly suggesting a sixteen-mile round trip over busy highways.

"You can come if you like," he added.

If you like? Something was changing in this boy who just days ago had seemed set for a mousy, nervous life. She could come along if she liked? It wasn't that he had invited her, but that he was determined to go with her or without her. For the first time in their lives, he wasn't leaning on her like a crutch, or using her as a human shield against the stones from the world's slingshot.

"S-sure," she said, cautiously agreeing with this new Chesney, "I'd like to go with you if you want me along." Maybe he wouldn't want her along.

"Good," he said as if she were the most inconsequential part of the trip.

Stupid Chesney! Why did he have to start turning into a man after all these years? Oh, she knew that he couldn't have been a man at four or seven, and even at twelve he wasn't really a man yet. But he was displaying a potential that she had never even imagined existed before. And he was doing it now, just before she'd move a thousand miles away. Suddenly, after sharing a tree house with a nice, but soppy kid, Clodagh had the strange desire to share a life with him. Now that he was showing signs of becoming something better, she wouldn't be there to capitalize on it. She imagined some stuck-up girl would grab him when this new Chesney reached his full development. Some girl, who now either ignored him or even made fun of him, would see the burgeoning manhood in him after Clodagh was gone. She had nurtured him all these years, and some other girl would get the prize.

"It's not fair!" Clodagh said out loud with such force that she stunned herself, but not Chesney, who had been going on about some plan.

"No, of course, it's not fair," he agreed without missing a beat. "Life isn't fair," he said, "my Aunt told me that. We can't make things fair, but we should try to be just."

"Just?" Clodagh was confused, especially since she hadn't been listening to what he'd been saying.

"Yeah, you know, just, justice. I want Stosh to get back some of all the dirty tricks he's played on me my whole life."

"But why do you have to get books on golf?" she asked. "What are you going to do, give them to Stosh and then cement them shut the way he did to your book? He'd see that coming a mile off, and besides, you can't glue library books shut."

"Haven't you heard a word I've been saying?"

Clodagh was too embarrassed to admit she hadn't, especially since she'd been thinking about him instead. So, she played dumb and confessed to not being able to follow all the details of his intricate plan.

"Okay," he said patiently, "let me go through it again. Remember, it starts with finding out what Stosh really likes, and what he's terrified of, and then using the one to ruin the other. Right?"

She resisted the impulse to roll her eyes since that was her plan. Instead, she just nodded.

"Right," said Chesney, "we know he likes golf, and that he's playing in that stupid tournament. But we didn't know what his fears are…"

"Not until I set up Denise," Clodagh piped in. Playing dumb was one thing, but she deserved at least some credit.

"Yes, thank you again. Now, as I already mentioned, Stosh is afraid of two things: girls and dogs," said Chesney.

"Girls and dogs? I've seen him tease girls, and dogs, too, for that matter."

"You're the one who reads all the psychology books. According to Denise, Stosh had a bad experience with both of them. Your sister beat him up when he was about five."

"Denise? Beat up Stosh?" It was amazing, not because she doubted she could do it. Denise was several years older than Stosh and would have been more than a match physically when he was only five. But Denise wouldn't attack anyone, not physically at least. She'd bore them to the point where they'd hurl themselves off a cliff, but she'd never lift a finger in anger.

"Not Denise," he said, "Caprice."

"But she's younger than he is," Clodagh laughed. "If he were five, she would have been not quite four-years-old!" Still, it made sense. Caprice always was the tomboy of the sisters. It only took a moment to imagine Caprice, smaller by a third than Stosh, sitting atop him, both fists flailing, her dirty blonde hair in pigtails, bobbing up and down in rhythm.

"What were they fighting over?" she asked.

"Denise couldn't recall, but she said that Stosh wound up with a bloody nose. Stosh can't stand the sight of blood, especially his own. According to your sister, he went running home, crying for his mommy."

"That explains a lot," said Clodagh. "It explains why Stosh is such a bully and why my folks always encouraged Caprice in sports… she's got a lot of energy to burn off."

"And if your sister is in that stupid golf tournament, and Stosh is too," said Chesney, "he's probably deathly afraid of her giving him another public beating."

"What about the dogs?"

"Oh, yeah, that's good, too," he said. "Again, according to Denise, once Stosh had gotten beaten up by a little girl, he went further down the pecking order…"

"No doubt trying to boost his bruised ego," said Clodagh, and feeling very clinical in her assessment.

"That meant even smaller kids…"

"…including baby brothers…"

Chesney blushed and nodded. "Yes, little kids, cats, birds, bugs, and small dogs. There was one puppy in particular who wouldn't stand for it. I guess you could say he was the Caprice of canines. One day, about eight years ago, the kids in the neighborhood were playing with a puppy in one of the neighbor's yard. They were having a good time until Stosh showed up. Then, to show off to the kids, Stosh tied a tin can to this puppy's tail and started hitting it with a stick to make it run around. Even though he was just a little thing, Denise said something snapped inside the puppy, and it turned on Stosh. At first, Stosh thought it was funny, and started poking the animal in the face with the stick. That's when it started attacking Stosh. The puppy got in quite a few good bites until the owner heard the ruckus and came out to pull his dogs off of Stosh. Stosh had to get some stitches, and there was big stink with my parents accusing the man of having a wild dog, and the owner of the dog accusing my parents of not keeping Stosh on a leash. Anyway, the owner of the dog had to either keep his dog fenced in or it would be destroyed..."

Clodagh gasped and put her hand in front of her mouth. "Fritz..."

Chesney nodded.

"He's very brave," she noted, "when that dog is behind that big fence." All the times she had seen Stosh taunt Fritz through the chain link enclosure came rushing back to her memory.

Chesney rose to his feet. "That's why I need books on golf."

"You're going to play in the stupid golf tournament and beat him?"

"No, Caprice is going to beat him. I'm going to be his caddy. I'm going to become an expert on golf and convince Stosh that he can't win without me..."

"...and then when you've got him, he won't be able to win with you."

"Right," he said, "too, bad we can't work some dogs into the plan."

Clodagh stopped. "Dogs?" A thought crossed her mind. "I've got an idea about that."

"Great!" Chesney smiled, his face radiating a confidence that she'd never seen before. She had a sudden impulse to kiss him. Clodagh started to lean in his direction.

At that moment, Chesney swung his leg over his ridiculous banana-seated bicycle, and the confident young man was once more smothered beneath the layers of doughy little kid, and the impulse became eminently resistible.

She was confused by the mixed signals her body was sending her mind, and the countermanding orders her mind was sending back to her body. Clodagh looked at him, waiting to see which Chesney Potoski would appear next, but the nice but unappealing version just sat there staring at her.

"You said something about dogs?"

"Uh, yeah," she said, as she climbed on her bike, "I know something that will let every dog have his day, and then some."

– 40 –
The Complexion Crisis
of Li'l Chez

lans were progressing well, or so Chesney guessed. He had never been the mastermind of a scheme before. Fortunately, he had the help of Clodagh, even though she kept looking at him in the most curious way. It was Clodagh, for example, who reasoned he wouldn't have to pedal all day to another town's library. Instead, they could get one of her sisters to borrow the book. They couldn't ask Denise since she was too smart and might get suspicious. They couldn't ask Caprice since she was also in the Stupid Golf Tournament and might decide to read the book herself. That left Rhoda. It would work because Rhoda never went to the library. To her, "going to the library" was code for: "going to see boys."

Rhoda was reluctant to help, when first approached, thinking the favor was for Clodagh.

"It's not for me," explained Clodagh, pointing to her friend, "it's for Chesney."

Rhoda eyed him sideways. "I don't get it," she said, uttering one of her top three most repeated phrases (the other two were "I want that," and "Does this go with…").

Rhoda had a reputation for not "getting" a lot of things, especially those things involving thought. Whole generations of local teachers in subjects from grammar, to spelling, to arithmetic, to geography, to science had been treated to the phrase: "I don't get it." The words pranced from Rhoda's lips like an insipid gazelle. The four Clott sisters were bookends with Denise and Clodagh forming the beginning and end of the brains, while Caprice and Rhoda filled the middle with more than their share of physical attributes. Even between these two middle sisters, there was a demarcation leaving Rhoda with the greatest beauty and the least amount of sense.

"What don't you understand?" asked Chesney.

"I'll handle this," interrupted Clodagh, who had experience translating the difficult into the simple for her older sister. "What don't you get?"

"Why do I have to go to the library for him?" asked Rhoda, simultaneously twirling her tongue counter-clockwise inside the right side of her cheek, while twirling her hair clockwise with her index finger on the left side of her head.

Clodagh paused for a moment, a hesitation that even Rhoda noticed.

"Well?" She asked, tapping her foot. "C'mon, I've got things to do."

"Well..." Clodagh looked around, "...it's kind of personal..."

Chesney blushed, wondering what excuse Clodagh might give.

"It's okay," said Rhoda, "you can tell me. I've known Li'l Chez here his whole life."

Chesney winced. Rhoda was the only person who called him "Li'l Chez," and it always made him feel like a small cartoon animal.

Clodagh looked at Chesney, searching for an answer to her sister's simple question. Suddenly she smiled and pointed at his chin.

"He's got a pimple," said Clodagh.

"A pimple?" said Rhoda.

Chesney rubbed his chin, where indeed he felt the beginnings of a blemish.

"See?" said Clodagh. "He's very self-conscious about it."

"Eww," said Rhoda, as she began reaching for her own chin, but stopped. "Oh, that's a nasty one, Li'l Chez. That's going to be one humungous zit. It'll be positively oblique!"

He started reaching for it again.

"Don't touch it," advised Rhoda, "and whatever you do, don't pop it! It could scar you for life." She studied his face for a moment and then nodded, knowingly, as if she had a bright thought and was pleased by the novelty. "I get it."

"I knew you would," said Clodagh, encouraging her.

"There's probably some girl he likes at the library, right?"

Chesney began to object, but Clodagh jumped in.

"Probably..." said Clodagh in such a way that the "probably" would be interpreted as a "definitely."

"And he doesn't want to go into the library with a giant zit on his face. Does he?"

"Would you?" asked Clodagh rhetorically.

Rhoda blanched at the thought. "No chance! Yuck! Okay, sure, I'll help you out, Li'l Chez." She almost gave him a playful punch to the shoulder, but after another look at his pimple thought better of direct bodily contact with an acne leper. "Just let me know what you need at the library, and I'll take care of it for you. I know what it's like to be in love."

Chesney looked at Clodagh and then back at Rhoda. She knew what it was like to be in love? Rhoda Clott barely managed to be conscious.

"What book do you want me to get you?"

"Uh, it's called *Winning Golf Techniques and Strategies*," he handed her a scrap of notebook paper. "I wrote it out."

Rhoda took the paper and studied it for a moment, and then folded it up and put it in her pocket. "No problem," she said. "This afternoon, okay?" Chesney nodded. "I'll get one of my boyfriends to drive me over."

Chesney thanked her.

"Not a problem, Li'l Chez," she said, "I'm glad to help out. See?" This was directed towards her sister, "I don't hold a grudge." She reached up a gently touched her own shoulder while giving a sharp look to Clodagh, no doubt in reference to the "bombs away" affair. Then Rhoda reached out and fingered the same part of Clodagh's anatomy and offered her a very insincere smile. "I don't hold a grudge... but I do buy my time."

Chesney was sure Rhoda had meant to "bide" her time. He was anxious for Rhoda to get the book, so he didn't correct her. After she had left, however, he turned to Clodagh.

"You don't think she suspects what we're up to, do you?"

Clodagh rolled her eyes. "Rhoda? Not hardly! You saw how easily she bought that excuse about you having a pimple."

"What was that about 'buying' her time, then?"

"It's a sister thing," said Clodagh. "Have you got any money?"

"A little, I suppose, why?"

"Come on," she said, climbing on her bike, "We have to do some shopping."

– 41 –
Phil Acton's Profunny Anise Emporium

Aside from trips with his mother to the A&P, the only shopping Chesney Potoski did was at the local candy store for comic books and sodas. Now Clodagh was leading him into unexplored territory; to parts of town he'd only seen from the back seat of the family's station wagon. They went past the Gulf station, past the travel agency, past even the town's other grocery store. They rode all the way to the Chinese restaurant. There Clodagh stopped and waited for him to pull alongside him. Chesney looked up at the restaurant.

"Is this it?"

She looked at him oddly. "Why would we go shopping at a Chinese restaurant?"

He merely shrugged.

"This way," she said, making a turn up the side street. It was a street Chesney had never been down. There wasn't much down it aside from a few houses and a car repair garage. None of the homes was as nice or as new as those in their neighborhood. The trees lining the short street were older, too, overhanging the pavement with a shady canopy.

They pedaled towards the repair garage, though Chesney couldn't imagine what sort of shopping a girl would want to do there. It was only as they went past it, however, that he saw the other building, partially hidden by the garage. It was an older house with a large porch in front, and a dormer poking out of the roofline. It was sort of rundown, but at the same time covered in a fresh coat of bright orange paint and purple shutters. The color scheme was repeated on the sign hanging from the porch eaves. Aside from being so bright as to be nearly self-illuminating, the sign featured script so fanciful that it was hardly legible.

"Verb and Herb?" he asked, deciphering the lettering.

Clodagh climbed off her bike.

"'Erb," she corrected. "It's not a name, it's like, well, you know, growing things, plants."

Chesney shrugged. Apparently, the store had something to do with plants and grammar. They climbed the steps and Clodagh opened the door, to reveal a curtain of hanging beads. She pushed this aside and went inside. Chesney paused a moment as if he was on the threshold of a strange world. Beyond the beads, he found himself in a large room, oddly dark in a bright sort of way. The light sources, from both the tall windows and from the various light fixtures, were all filtered by different means. Some of the windows were covered with what appeared to be watered-down paints in an attempt to replicate stained glass, although the subjects portrayed were far different from anything Chesney had ever seen in church. Those windows not painted, were covered with pieces of plastic film cut into psychedelic patterns. The interior lights were also filtered, either through colored shades and fixtures or were fitted with colored light bulbs. The effect was challenging to the unprepared eye, or at least that was what Chesney surmised, having escorted two such eyes into the place.

He could make out a wooden counter running the length of the room, barring access to a staircase leading to the second floor. This counter was filled with all sorts of things, none of which were familiar to him. Little packets with names like "Bambu" and "Zig-Zag" were in boxes, but as to what they were used for he had no idea. Also mystifying were various implements on a shelf behind the counter that looked like something in a weird science lab. On the counter and the shelf was a collection of things, which for lack of a better guess, looked like pipes. He guessed they were pipes in that they had bowls and stems, but aside from that looked very different from the conventional brier pipe on which his father sometimes puffed.

Elsewhere around the store were more tables and racks containing books, little plastic bags, what looked like seed packets, and even some rudimentary gardening tools. Aside from the lighting, and the strange objects, the place almost could have been mistaken for the gardening section of Cregan's Hardware store. And while Cregan's featured the strong miasma of fertilizer, a sweet aroma overhung this store emanating from the incense burner sitting atop the old ornate cash register.

In addition to those other exotic features, Mr. Cregan didn't have *Lucy in the Sky with Diamonds* playing from a portable 8-track tape player.

Chesney knew the song but never thought he'd actually enter a room that brought the lyrics to life. It was almost like the shoebox dioramas he used to make back in elementary school to illustrate a scene from a book. He half expected to see a plasticine porter with a looking glass tie. Instead, there was a less colorful man, sitting on a stool in the corner, checking his stock of seeds against an inventory on a clipboard. The man was older, at least in his late twenties. He had long hair, longer than most people he knew, certainly longer than any man he knew. It was brown, and hung down below his shoulders, straight, and somewhat straggly at its furthest reaches. A full beard, not nearly as long, kept his face well-insulated. Completing his look were a thick pair of plastic-framed glasses. He wore well-worn jeans, a Day-Glo t-shirt, and a corduroy vest. The man was so engrossed in his work and the music that he didn't notice his visitors at first. He only looked up after Clodagh moved into his field of vision.

"Oh, hey," he said, looking up and offering Clodagh a benign, almost drowsy, smile. "Hey, here you are."

"Here I am," she said.

He studied her from head to toe, and only then nodded to confirm the fact. "All right! Yeah, everybody's gotta be somewhere, you know?" At this point, the man noticed Chesney standing a few steps behind and to the side of Clodagh. "That little dude's gotta be somewhere, too... proven by the fact that there he is."

"Oh, this is my friend Chesney," said Clodagh.

"Far out name...Chesney. *Chesney*." He said it slowly, and even more slowly the second time. Chesney never knew his name was far out, or even slightly groovy. The man was starting to say it a third time even more melodically when Chesney interrupted.

"Nobody ever said they liked my name before."

The man seemed genuinely surprised. "Really? Whoa. It's a very happening sort of name..."

"It's British."

"And that's very, very happening. Still, you know, like if a rose was called something else it would still be a rose like that dude said."

"Shakespeare," said Chesney.

The man nodded. "A well-read little dude," he said to Clodagh, "very cool. It's good to read. There's a lot to read, especially in books. Like the printed word has so much to say, you know what I mean? I mean, it's just there waiting to feast your eyeballs on."

Chesney resisted the impulse to rearrange his sentence so it wouldn't end in a preposition.

"That's an interesting thought," continued the man, "I mean, eyeballs feasting like they had little mouths right under their irises. And the mouths opened up and literally ate the words off the page. Literally eating literature, right?" He nodded to himself, pleased at the image he'd spun. "And then they digest all those words into, like, a knowledge paste and spit it into the brain, nourishing and expanding the mind. Can you dig it? You can learn a lot by letting your eyeballs feast. Huh?"

"I guess that's why part of the eye is called a pupil," said Chesney.

The man laughed. "Hey, that's funny. That's very funny...but it's also heavy, full of profound profundity, but funny too, you know?"

"It's profunny," said Chesney.

"Far out," he said with a straight face as if that were even more profound.

"Why are you talking like that," asked Clodagh, "and do you have my order?"

The man, shook his head as if to stir himself from some self-hypnotic state, and before their eyes, seemed to transform himself into an average shopkeeper, albeit one that still looked like a hippie.

"Sorry, sorry," he said with more gravity to his voice. "Just keeping in practice, you understand. Don't you?"

"Practice? Practice for what?" asked Chesney.

"For most of my customers," he said. "When you sell organic seeds, and herbs, macrobiotic corn chips, and other implements you got to keep up appearances. You've got to give the customer what they expect. That's what my old man, that is, my father always said."

Chesney nodded but wasn't sure he understood.

"Oh, but that was pretty funny," the man added, "you know, what you said. I was being sincere, though maybe a bit insincere in my delivery."

"Chesney," said Clodagh, "this is Mr. Acton." Chesney shook Acton's hand.

"Phil," he said, "call me Phil."

Chesney looked around the store before returning to Phil Acton. "I can see the Herbs, but where are the verbs?"

Acton smiled. "I'm the verb. It's my nickname, you know, Acton… action, action word… verb. Get it? It's what I've been called since junior high English class. My brother suffered a similar fate. He was always a bit strange, so after they started calling me 'Verb,' they started calling him 'Irregular Verb.'" Acton chuckled to himself at the wit of his classmates. "And it didn't end there. We have a sister, too. She's between us in age."

"Linking Verb?" said Chesney.

"You guessed it," said Phil Acton. "Pretty wild, huh?"

As Mr. Acton hadn't budged from his stool, Chesney would have called him "Intransient Verb," but he kept the thought to himself.

"And do they still call him that?" asked Clodagh. "Does he have a store somewhere called 'Irregular Verb's'?"

"Perhaps," said Chesney, "he sells manufacturers' rejects."

This, along with most of Chesney's observations, amused Mr. Acton as well.

"No, no," said Acton, "he's a musical manager. I don't mean that he sings while he manages, he manages musical performers. Nobody you've heard of."

"…of whom you've heard," said Chesney under his breath.

"Maybe someday he'll be a famous manager of a famous rock group," said Clodagh.

Acton shrugged. "He was managing a rock group, but they broke up, and he had to change his name."

"*They* broke up," asked Clodagh, "and he had to change *his* name?"

"Yeah, he's got the same philosophy as me, you know, go with the flow, live up to the customer's expectations. He didn't think Wilbur Acton was a good name for the manager of a rock and roll band, so he was Mick

Sparkler. But then they broke up. So now he's down in Nashville fronting for country and western acts with a new name."

"Mick Sparkler isn't a country name?" asked Chesney.

"No, now he's Parvo Slouch. Far out, huh?"

They both nodded for lack of a better response.

"But, you didn't come in here for my family history. You're here for your order," said Acton, laying down his clipboard and crossing to the counter. He pulled out a parcel that was the most ordinary item in the eclectic shop, but its effect on Clodagh was transcendent.

"This is it," she whispered, "slipping her hands under the box to determine its weight. "Yes, very solid. There's a lot in there."

"It's chock full," agreed Phi Acton.

Chesney stood there looking back and forth at the two of them, as they admired the carton. Finally, his curiosity compelled him to speak.

"I know it's none of my business…" began Chesney.

Clodagh looked up. "Oh, but it is."

"What?"

"This," she said, stroking the box, "is pure *pimpinella anisum*."

"And lots of it," Acton chimed in. "That's more than I'd sell in a year… two years!"

"What?"

Clodagh spoke to Chesney as if he were a slow child. "Anise seed, remember? Dogs?"

Chesney nodded. Clodagh had mentioned something about having something for dogs but hadn't provided any more details. He looked at the box again.

"And there's enough there for," Chesney paused, not know what exactly she planned to do with it, "…for whatever you're going to do?"

"It's very good for digestion," said Acton, though no one had asked him. "Good for colic, and also cuts down on flatulence."

Chesney looked at Clodagh. "Dog flatulence?"

"No," she said, "dogs love anise seed. It's sort of like catnip is for cats, only for dogs."

He gave her a blank stare.

"Your brother's afraid of dogs, right?" she said. He nodded. "So, I figured it would add to the atmosphere of the day if we had a few happy hounds around."

"Tripping pooches," smiled Acton, "far out, man!"

– 42 –
The Smuggling of
Poise and Beauty

If it was winter and he had been wearing a coat, it would have been easy to sneak something into the house. In this warm weather, he would have been hard-pressed to smuggle a stick of gum.

Second thoughts were common in Chesney's young mind. He rarely had a first thought without it being hotly pursued by an indecisive second thought. After weeks of plotting revenge on Stosh, Chesney was having doubts. The proof of his anxiety was tucked under his arm. If something so simple had gone wrong, how could his more intricate plan succeed? Perhaps Stosh wasn't such bad a guy after all…

Chesney turned the knob on the door that led from the garage into the family room and listened. With the door opened a half-inch, he paused: no sound. The coast was clear. From the family room, it was only seven steps up the stairs to the main level of the split-level house, through a door, a sharp right, up another seven steps then down the hall to his bedroom. Confident of at least his first move, he slid into the room as silently as a pudgy boy could slide.

"Well, looks like James Bond's home," he heard Stosh's voice say. "Where ya been 007?"

With his face to the door and clutching the book to his chest, Chesney froze for a moment, and then spun around, trying to keep the book out of view. He was surprised to find not only Stosh but his mother and father sitting there. On any given weeknight around a quarter to eight, Mr. Potoski would be upstairs, hanging over the edge of his bed, playing solitaire. Mrs. Potoski was likely to be in the living room, reading a romance novel. Stosh, well, there were hundreds of guesses as to what Stosh was up to at any time of the day or night, but "sitting quietly with his parents" wasn't one of them.

"Hello, Chesney," said his mother.

"What are you all doing here?" he asked.

"Anywhere else you'd like us to be?" said his father.

"No," he replied. He didn't begrudge his family sitting together in the family room, but he'd rather they had chosen another time to do so.

"We're just having a little talk with your brother," said Mrs. Potoski.

Chesney wondered what Stosh had done now, but his brother's relaxed posture indicated that it wasn't an interrogation. Chesney smiled nervously and agreed that was nice, while he tried to walk sideways towards the stairs with the book behind his back.

"Whatcha got behind your back, Chez?" said Stosh with mock interest. Being an inveterate sneak himself, Stosh knew Chesney was hiding something.

Chesney shrugged as if he always walked around sideways with his hand behind his back. He could have gotten away with it if only his mother had been there, or if it had just been Stosh he would have had a fifty chance of getting away with a head start, but as his father was there as well, it was a futile charade.

"Chesney," said Mr. Potoski, "what do you have behind your back?"

"A…book. Just a book."

"May I see it?"

Stupid Rhoda Clott, Chesney thought. Stupid, stupid, Rhoda! Fifteen minutes ago, she stood there, so proud of herself for going to the library on his behalf. She handed him the book, the book that was now hidden behind his back. He hadn't wanted it but never being one for confrontation, he accepted the book from her. He had wanted to yell at her. He had wanted to say it was all wrong and he didn't want the dumb thing. But Rhoda had stood there beaming at him, seeking confirmation that she had exceeded his expectations, that she had taken the initiative and turned an ordinary task into a triumph. Chesney looked to Clodagh, who was standing beside her sister. Clodagh just shook her head, rolled her eyes, and then silently urged him to take the book. He did so and then slumped home.

Now, he slowly pulled the book out from behind his back, hoping against hope that it wasn't the same book that it had been moments before. He'd even be happy if the book magically transmogrified into a small animal and bit him. That was more than he could hope for in this modern age. Chesney handed the book to his father, turning it front down, affording him a momentary reprieve. His father only turned the book over again and read the title.

"*The Teen Girl's Guide to Poise and Beauty?*"

It sounded even worse when his father read it, though his voice had the same bemused quality as Chesney's had a quarter of an hour earlier when he had first laid eyes on the volume.

◆

"*The Teen Girl's Guide to Poise and Beauty?*"

"They didn't have that other book," Rhoda Clott explained.

"The Teen Girl's Guide to Poise and Beauty?" Chesney repeated.

"What about the other book?" Clodagh asked.

"That guy, you know, the library guy,"

"The librarian?" said Clodagh.

"Yeah, him, he said it was out of calculation..."

"Circulation," said Clodagh.

"The Teen Girl's Guide to Poise and Beauty?" Chesney said again, though the repetition did nothing to improve the title.

"So, you took out this book for yourself," said Clodagh.

Rhoda looked at her sister as though the suggestion that she would want to borrow a book from a public library was somehow bizarre.

"I got it for Li'l Chez," she said.

"The Teen Girl's Guide to Poise and Beauty?" said Chesney.

"I knew you'd like it," said Rhoda, interpreting his repetitions as appreciation.

"Why, Rhoda?" said Clodagh.

Rhoda looked at her sister as if it were obvious. She sighed and said in a condescending voice: "Because, Clodagh, it's the best book I could find on blemishes!"

"Blemishes?" said Clodagh.

"Blemishes," said Rhoda. "You know, pimples, zits..." She pointed at Chesney's chin. "Li'l Chez just has to follow the skin cleansing regime in this book, and then he can go back to the library all by himself, holding his radiant complexion high!"

◆

Now, as his father examined the contents of the book, Chesney wished that he and his radiant complexion were six feet below ground level in a box. Mr. Potoski's complexion was anything but radiant, though Stosh was having a wonderful time peering over his father's shoulder at the chapter titles.

"*'Your Changing Body,'*" Stosh read aloud gleefully. "*'Grace and Beauty, Partners in Poise,' 'Make Up Tips That Will Attract the Nice Boys!'* Oh, brother, or should I say: 'Oh! Sister!'"

"Shut up!" said Chesney.

Mrs. Potoski didn't know who to scold first, Stosh for mentioning "ladies'" things out loud, or Chesney for telling his brother to shut up. She spluttered for a moment and then said: "That's enough, Stoshney!"

Stosh ignored his mother, while Chesney tried to take back the book. As both brothers grabbed for the book, Mr. Potoski's ire rose. He detested ruckuses, especially those taking place within ten feet of windows.

"That's enough! Horseplay often leads to tragedy!" barked Mr. Potoski employing one of his favorite aphorisms. "I said that's ENOUGH!"

Their father rarely raised his voice, which was why it was such an effective tool whenever he did so. In an instant, both boys froze. Stosh, being behind his father, had the advantage of being able to make faces at Chesney while Mr. Potoski continued.

"This isn't a roughhouse," he said. "If you want to wrestle, I'll finish off any comers, right now. Is that what you want?"

Even though the question was rhetorical, Chesney wasn't listening. His attention was on Stosh who was making mincing, effeminate faces at him from behind his father's back.

"I said: IS THAT WHAT YOU WANT?"

Both boys flinched.

"No, sir," came the pair of mewing responses.

"Chesney, we will discuss this in a moment, in private. Stosh, since you seem to enjoy making silly faces…"

"But I wasn't…" he began to protest.

"Don't do things behind my back," said Mr. Potoski, "especially when I can see you." He nodded at the framed picture opposite them. Stosh looked into the glass, saw his reflection there, and emitted a low groan.

"Since you think this is so funny," Mr. Potoski continued, "you can go empty the dishwasher."

"But that's a job for…" he began to protest.

"But he always breaks…" began Mrs. Potoski.

Mr. Potoski's arm shot up ending debate on the subject. Stosh trudged up the stairs like an inmate on his way to Devil's Island, pausing just long enough to mutter a promise of retribution in his brother's ear.

"And shut the door," added Mr. Potoski. Stosh shut the door with just enough force to make one wonder if it had been slammed in anger, but softly enough as to leave it open to debate.

Mr. Potoski motioned for Chesney to take a seat, and surprisingly, he offered him his own recliner. Chesney had sat in it dozens of times, hundreds, in fact, but rarely when anyone else was in the room. He was at the bottom of the family pecking order when it came to seat selection. He sat down as respectfully as he knew how.

Mrs. Potoski stayed seated on the sofa while Mr. Potoski stood over him. The library book was still in his hand. He looked at it while hefting it up and down. It was almost as if he was trying to determine how far he could throw it, or how hard he could whack someone with it. This musing was interrupted by a gentle clearing of his mother's throat.

"Rodney," she said, "shouldn't we tell him what we wanted to tell him before you say…whatever it is that you're going to say?"

"No," said Mr. Potoski, "first things first."

The pedantic thought occurred to Chesney that the explanation for the book was actually the second topic introduced and that the first topic, whatever it may be, was being pushed aside. He glanced at his mother, who, being his role model in pedantry, seemed to be having the same thought. Mr. Potoski held out *The Teen Girl's Guide to Poise and Beauty* and made a silent appeal that begged an explanation.

"It's not mine," said Chesney.

"There you see…" Mrs. Potoski eagerly agreed.

"I know it's not your book," said his father with calm deliberation, "it's a library book."

"I didn't borrow it."

"There you see…"

"Who did?"

"Mmm…Rhoda Clott."

"Clodagh's sister…" offered Mrs. Potoski.

"I'm well aware of the make up, uh," Mr. Potoski looked down at the book, "I mean, the composition of the Clott family." He turned his back, took a step, and then turned back around just like Chesney had seen Perry Mason do on television.

As his father got nearer the truth, Chesney wondered how long he could continue without lying. To the best of his knowledge, he had never lied to his parents. They double-teamed their investigations. His father did the cross-examination, then his mother would softly ask: "Are you telling the truth, Chesney…" before adding: "on your love for God?" That was the killer phrase, the clause he could never get around. But they had it all backward, he thought. Usually, in courtrooms, they made you swear an oath and then grilled you. For some reason, his mother did it in reverse, like most of the things she did, especially in the kitchen.

Mr. Potoski leveled his next question: "Did Rhoda Clott take out this book for you?"

Chesney's shoulders slumped. She had taken it out for him, it was utterly unasked for and unwanted, but she had. He wracked his brain, parsing his father's question, looking for a way to answer truthfully without appearing like some sort of sissy in his father's eyes. He was already battling uphill for his father's approval. The admission that he was using a girl to secure girl books would be a sin for which it would be impossible to atone. He would have to become a Marine or win an Olympic Gold Medal in boxing to even begin to recover from admitting he was the intended recipient of *The Teen Girl's Guide to Poise and Beauty*. The only thing worse would be admitting the whole truth: that they had sent Rhoda into the library to get him a book on golf so he could sabotage Stosh in the upcoming Stupid Tournament. The harder he thought, the more muddled his thinking grew, until he felt a hand on his forearm.

"Chesney," he looked up to see his mother. "Chesney, dear, answer your father. Did you want that book?"

A lifeline appeared. His mother had unintentionally changed the question.

"Well," said his father, inadvertently accepting the revision, "did you want this book?"

"NO!" he shouted. "I mean, no. I never wanted that book."

"Then why would that silly Clott girl take out this book and give it to you? I think I'll call Charley Clott and get to the bottom of this. Poor kid, getting embarrassed by some stupid teenaged girl's idea of a joke."

Call Major Clott? That might blow the cover off the whole scheme.

"No, please, don't call," he said.

His father stopped. "Why not?"

Again, his mother unwittingly came to his rescue. "Wait, Rodney, I think I understand."

Chesney looked sideways at his mother, wondering if she had some mystical insight into the deepest recesses of his mind. She smiled back at him sweetly, and stroked his hair.

"Don't you see," she said to her husband, "he's covering up for someone. Aren't you, Chesney?"

"Covering up?" Chesney thought a moment and nodded his head in agreement. Yes, he was covering up for someone. He wasn't sure who his mother had in mind, but he was covering up... for himself.

"I thought so," his mother smiled.

"What?" said Mr. Potoski.

"Chesney didn't want this book, did you, dear?"

Had he shaken his head any harder, it would have come loose from his neck.

"He already admitted as much," said Mr. Potoski. "So, who is the book for?"

"Whom, Dear," said his wife. "The book is for Clodagh."

"Clodagh?"

"Clodagh Clott, Chesney's little friend," she explained.

"I know who Clodagh is. Is this right, Chesney?"

Before he could reply, his mother continued. "Of course, it is. Clodagh is becoming a young lady."

"So? So why didn't she go take out the book for herself?"

Mrs. Potoski rolled her eyes as if to ask heaven how much longer she would have to endure the density of the male mind. "Because there are very... sensitive topics in the book. A nice girl like Clodagh has her modesty."

"So why didn't she ask her sister to take it out for her?"

This time the obvious was met with a wifely sigh. "Do you know how much teasing a big sister can give to a little sister?"

"How would I know what it's like to be a twelve-year-old girl?!"

"Exactly. It's very different for girls. Sisters can be very cruel at times. It's not like brothers, is it, Chesney?"

Had he not been concentrating on his mother's main line of reasoning, this last aside would have made Chesney fall out of his chair. He barely managed to nod his head in mute agreement.

"So," said Mr. Potoski trying to complete the thread of his wife's deductions, "so Clodagh, who is too embarrassed to take out a book on being a teenaged girl for herself, and is too embarrassed to ask her sister to take it out, has no hesitation in asking a boy to do it? But that boy is too embarrassed to do it himself, as well, so he asks an older girl to do it for him, so he can give it to another girl. Is that what you're trying to tell me?"

She looked at him as if he were a beloved, but slightly stupid, pet. "Something like that. You've never been a young girl, dear."

He looked at her as if she'd never been a sane adult, then shook his head and looked at Chesney.

"Are you going to give this to Clodagh?"

Finally, thought Chesney, a question he could answer.

"Yes, sir," he said. Of course, he could give it to Clodagh. That was easy enough.

His father looked at his mother in amazement. She looked back at him in triumph.

"Fine," he said, with bemusement, "give this to Clodagh and tell her... oh...good luck."

Chesney took the book and stashed it behind his back. Mr. Potoski turned to leave until his wife reminded him of their original reason for the impromptu meeting. She did this with a sharp clearing of her throat to get his attention, and then gently patted her belly.

"Oh, yes, right," said Mr. Potoski, back on subject. "Yes, Chesney, your mother and I wanted to discuss something with you."

From the way his mother was stroking her distended stomach and the way his father was watching her do so, Chesney guessed that he was finally being told what he had overheard several months before and what had been terribly apparent for at least three weeks. It was becoming increasingly difficult to ignore her belly. Not looking at something was much harder than looking at it, especially when it was something that was demanding more and more attention. In the last few days, Chesney had estimated that his mother's belly was about the size of a deflated football, or perhaps the quarter of a good-sized watermelon.

"You're going to be a big brother," said his father. Chesney smiled wanly, and then remembered that he should try to appear surprised.

"Just like Stosh," added his mother. That comparison was enough to plaster genuine astonishment on his face.

"How about that?" asked his father.

Chesney wasn't sure what he was being asked. If it was the prospect of following in Stosh's footsteps, then he was revolted. If it was that his mother was going to have a baby, he wondered what took them so long to tell him. If it was merely how he felt about being a big brother....

"That's...that's pretty neat," a genuine smile crossed his lips. Chesney hadn't considered that before. He would be a big brother, not like Stosh, but the way a big brother was supposed to be. He could be supportive, protective, and encouraging to the little...he stopped, what would it be? Perhaps it would be a boy. That would be okay. But maybe he'd have a baby sister. Maybe she would be like Clodagh, which would be ideal, now that Clodagh was moving away. If the baby were a girl, it might be like Clodagh, smart, and like to read, and then maybe she would grow up to be like Aunt Elinor. Yes, he nodded to himself, a girl would be very nice.

"So, you see," said Mrs. Potoski, "we'll be relying on you..."

"This means a lot of responsibility, you know. You're not a baby anymore," continued Mr. Potoski. "Your little brother or sister will be depending on you, and they'll look up to you."

Chesney nodded and smiled.

"Just like you look up to Stosh," added Mrs. Potoski.

He shuddered and felt his fingernails dig into his clenched fists. It would be different, Chesney thought. He resolved to be the best big brother he could be for the new arrival. And he also resolved anew to settle the score with Stosh. Not just for himself, or Dickens, but now for his new brother or sister. A sister, yes, he'd much rather have a sister; someone like his Aunt or even like Clodagh. He'd make sure that his little sister would grow up without having to fear anything named: "Stosh."

– 43 –
Pisting Amidst
the Forsythia

The next morning, before school, Chesney went to Clodagh's to return *The Teen Girl's Guide to Beauty and Poise*. Being a sultry morning that promised to be the introduction to yet another muggy day, her window was open. Crouching in the forsythia bush below the window he tried to catch her attention with his imitation of a mourning dove. After several fruitless coos, he realized that he had never known Clodagh to come to the window to converse with a bird. He stopped and listened. He could hear someone shuffling around her room, opening drawers. Since it was a split-level house, Clodagh's window was only a half-a-story off the ground. Chesney could just reach the bottom of the sill if he stood on his toes. He found a stick and reached up to scratch on her window screen.

"Hey," he whispered. "Hey…Psst!" Hearing no reply, repeated the call a bit louder. "PSSSST!"

"What?!" A voice shouted from inside the house. It belonged to Major Clott. "Who's calling me?"

"What?" replied Mrs. Clott.

"Who wants me?"

"Now?"

"Of course now," said Mr. Clott. "Someone was saying 'hey,' and pisting me. I was in the bathroom, dammit!"

Chesney cowered against the house. How would a military psychiatrist react if a dumb kid interrupted him in the bathroom? Perhaps he would think he was crazy or dangerous. Maybe he would have him committed to a military hospital for observation. He held his breath and could feel his heart pounding.

"What?" called Mrs. Clott.

"What?" he replied.

"You said someone was 'pissing' you!"

"Pisting," shouted the Major, annoyed that he had to explain to the people who were interrupting him how they had interrupted him. "You know, going…PSST!"

"Nobody was pissing you," Mrs. Clott shouted back.

"Not 'pissing,'…PISTING!"

"Nobody was doing that either!"

"What?"

"NOBODY! Go back to…whatever you were doing!"

"I WAS SHAVING!"

"FINE! Then go do that!"

Chesney exhaled, but only after he had heard several doors slam. It was a revelation that other people's parents could yell at each other, just like his own. He peered upward, half expecting the foam-faced Major Dr. Clott to lunge at him brandishing a razor. The coast was clear.

Chesney was just about to emerge from the bush when he was startled by a clear voice.

"Yes… what do you want?"

He grabbed his chest and fell backward into the forsythia. Chesney looked up to see Clodagh leaning out of the window. She had the oddest look on her face. She wasn't angry, though she wasn't exactly happy either, at least not any way he'd ever seen her happy in the past. It was almost a hungry expression, though at the same time, one that was satisfied. He couldn't think what she was hungry about, or what was giving her satisfaction. Maybe she hadn't had breakfast yet and was anticipating a stack of waffles. But he couldn't tell.

"Well," Clodagh repeated, "what is it?" Her words were sharp, though her tone was anything but severe.

"I, uh, wanted…"

She motioned him to keep his voice down and nodded towards the next window, which he presumed to belong to her parents.

Chesney nodded and rose to his feet.

"I got your book…" he said lifting up *The Teen Girl's Guide to Poise and Beauty*.

"I don't want it," she said coolly. "Do you think I need it?"

"Uh, no…"

"Then why would you bring it to me?"

He told her how his parents had caught him with the book and how they had presumed that it was for Clodagh's benefit and that he promised he would return it to her.

"But you know I don't want it," she said.

"But I couldn't lie to my parents," he said. "I barely got out of it without lying."

"How did you manage that?"

"They did all the lying themselves," said Chesney. "I just didn't correct them." He lifted the book up to her again.

"I don't want it. Take it back to the library."

"I'm banned from the library."

She rolled her eyes. "Use the night drop. You could do it on your way to school."

"Right, good idea; do you want to go with me?"

The strangest hint of a smile crossed Clodagh's lips, and she tilted her head in the oddest way.

"Do you want me to go with you?"

"Well, sure," he said. "I asked you, didn't I?" She tilted her head in the opposite direction, and another unusual look crossed her face.

"You got an earache or something?" he asked her.

Clodagh's recent spate of unfamiliar expressions was quickly replaced with one he'd seen before, and it wasn't pleasant.

"NO! I don't have an earache!"

"Shh," he cautioned her and pointed to the other window.

"Oh, shut up! And go by yourself!"

With that, she slammed the window shut, and Chesney scrambled back to the shelter of the forsythia bush. From inside, he could hear Dr. Clott asking in threatening tones who was telling whom to shut up, and Mrs. Clott asking who was supposed to go by themselves and to where. He couldn't quite tell, but there was also a sobbing sound, and wondering if indeed Clodagh didn't have an earache or something that was causing her goofy expressions. All Chesney could do was shake his head. He was used to not understanding girls, but he had never not understood Clodagh.

Chesney crept away to return the book via the night drop. He still hadn't lied to his parents and wasn't in danger of doing so, either. He imagined his father asking him that evening if he'd given the book back to Clodagh.

"Yes, I did," he said aloud, as if in practice, "but she asked me to return to the library for her, so I did." He nodded his head as he pedaled along, confident that it sounded truthful because it was the truth, and he wasn't in any danger of lying.

He pulled up by library night drop. It was a heavily fortified contraption. Chesney pulled down the metal handle, placed the book in the drawer, and then shut it. He listened as he heard the spring-activated trap open, and the book tumble down the chute swallowed up into the belly of Mr. Repaupo's domain. Even though his ears testified that the book was gone, Chesney couldn't help opening the drawer again to make sure. For a moment he stood there, staring down into steel bin. Holding the drawer open with his elbow, Chesney used his hands to make a rough measurement of its width. Then, he brought his hands down to his midsection. Just as he thought, he was much too round in the middle. If only he were skinnier, he could try sliding into the library via the night drop and get the book on golf. He was careful to think of it as "obtaining" the book, though he reasoned if he could sneak into the library after hours, it wouldn't really be stealing. He would return the book after he was done with it. He would just be going outside the normal borrowing channels.

Even if he were thinner, he reasoned, there wasn't a clear way into the library through the chute. There was that spring-loaded drawer that prevented anything larger than a stack of books to go beyond it. What was the same size as a big stack of books? Two cats, but even twice that number of cats wouldn't be of use, cats being so independent in nature. A medium size dog would fit down the chute he thought, as he pedaled towards school. But again, while a dog was a much more willing accomplice than a cat, he doubted any dog would be focused enough to sneak into the library, retrieve the right book, and then come back out again. It would take more intelligence and skill than that possessed by a domestic pet. A small chimpanzee could probably do it ...or a midget. Unfortunately, Earswick was bereft of both.

He stopped at a busy intersection. A clever toddler could probably negotiate the chute, and might even be able to find the right book. The only problem was that he didn't know any clever toddlers or even dimwitted toddlers for that matter. His youngest acquaintance was Clodagh, and while Clodagh was slim, she was much too tall. If only his baby sister, or baby brother, were already born, he was sure they would be intelligent enough by the age of two to do the job. He couldn't wait that long, however. No, Stosh had to be taken care of before the new baby arrived lest he or she become another victim of his practical jokes. No, unless he happened upon a willing monkey in the next day or so, that particular plan was not likely to succeed.

While he waited for the light to change, Chesney watched a pedestrian standing on the opposite corner. His face was hidden behind a bushy beard. He stared at the man for about thirty seconds. By the time the light changed, another light had illuminated his thoughts.

– 44 –
A Timely Roar from Nature's Lion

disguise?" Clodagh Clott asked as they walked towards the bike rack after school. "And a stranger told you to do it?" "No, he didn't tell me, but he gave me the idea. His beard was so thick I couldn't see his face. He could have been anyone behind that shrubbery. I'll get the book using a disguise."

Clodagh pushed her eyeglasses up her nose and cocked her head sideways.

"Simple, isn't it?" Asked Chesney.

"Oh, it's simple all right!" She shook her head as she entered the combination on her bike lock.

"What?"

"It's just that it's not very easy for a twelve-year-old to disguise himself as anything very different from a twelve-year-old kid. Think about it. You can't make yourself look older. A fake beard or a fake mustache wouldn't work because you're not tall enough. And not to get too personal, but if you were skinny, you could pad yourself out to look fat. But as you are now, there's not a whole lot you can do. Until you're a little taller, or older, or thinner, you're stuck being you."

He had to admit that Clodagh was right, though he resented her for being so. It was better to have a harebrained scheme than no scheme at all. He was about to agree grudgingly; when Clodagh continued.

"…Of course," she added, slowly, "there is one way."

"One way?"

"Margaret Legotti…"

Chesney's face dropped. "She wouldn't do it for me. Well, she probably would do it for me, but I wouldn't want her to."

"Doesn't she like you?"

"I think she may like me too much."

Another mysterious expression crossed Clodagh face.

"So," said Chesney, "I'd rather not owe Peg Leg a favor. I'd rather have her not like me."

"Keep calling her Peg Leg, and she'll soon get over liking you," said Clodagh.

"No," he shook his head, "It's better that we don't get anyone else involved in this. Your sister taught me that lesson. This is supposed to be a secret plan, and I'm afraid of letting too many more people in on it... especially Peg...Margaret."

"I wasn't suggesting that Margaret take out the book..."

"But..."

She held up her hand. "I wasn't going to send her to get the book. But your talk about disguises..."

"What would she be disguised as?"

"Margaret wouldn't be disguised as anybody. You could go to the library disguised as her."

"What?" Chesney nearly fell off the bike rack. "Are you crazy?"

"Not at all. She's your height. She's about your weight. She wears glasses. Her hair is a lot like a wig that my sister wore last year for Halloween. You could be her at the library, get your book, and then go on with your scheme."

Chesney tried to stand up taller, to no longer be the same height as "Peg Leg" Legotti. He attempted a more macho pose, to prove that it would be impossible for him to impersonate a girl. After ten-seconds of machismo, the task grew too burdensome, and he slumped back into his usual self.

None of this impressed Clodagh who continued rattling on about how he could accomplish borrowing Peg's identity for an hour or two. He merely sighed and wondered to what lengths a person had to go to avenge an author who had been dead for a hundred years. While he thought, Chesney realized that outwardly he was numbly nodding as Clodagh outlined the steps it would take to assume the identity of a dumpy, bespectacled, girl.

Chesney didn't utter another word all the way home, submitting to her scheming, as a lamb led to the slaughter. Even after he left her and staggering into his house, he found his head was still bobbing up and down.

"What am I doing?" he cried. "How could I?" He wracked his mind for another way, but the wellspring of his imagination had become a dustbowl filling his skull. He walked past his mother in the kitchen, who was busy perpetrating another tuna casserole. She said something to him, but he only nodded. She repeated herself, this time in a sharper tone, and he looked at the thick, Day-Glo slabs of cheese food she was placing atop the casserole, and nodded.

"What's the matter with you!" his mother barked. "I said there's a package for you."

Chesney looked down to the side of the counter, past the breadcrumbs, beyond the empty tins of tuna, and saw the brown parcel. Chesney picked it up and nodded. It was from Aunt El. How nice. He muttered thanks and started shuffling to his room.

Usually, a package from Aunt Elinor would cause him to hurry up the stairs with excitement. At the moment, however, he had little enthusiasm for another book of anagrams. He threw himself and the package on his bed and looked up at the plastic models suspended over his bed. He stared at the Spitfire that he had built, diving in to intercept a German Stuka, while a Gemini space capsule orbited just beyond the line of fire, though he really didn't see any of it. The more he gazed, the more it all vanished from view. In its place, as if projected on the ceiling, all he could see was himself entering the library in that mortifying disguise. He imagined it all going well, the book in his hand, then at the desk every person he had ever known was standing there, led by Stosh, who pulled off his Peg-Leg wig and then led the chorus of scorn and ridicule. He closed his eyes and rolled over on the bed, almost wishing the plastic planes above him had real ammunition. Better to die being strafed by a scale-model airplane than suffer a lifetime of full-sized embarrassment.

That was it. He wouldn't go through with it. He couldn't. He would have to live with Stosh. His sister or brother-to-be would have to do the same. He was quite willing to risk physical harm, but impersonate a girl? Never! Never in a million years!

Chesney sat up and sighed. His breath caught deep down his throat. He felt his eyes grow swollen with tears. Still, there was nothing else for it. He was defeated. Stosh would no doubt go on to win the golf tournament, which would embolden him to greater feats of terror. Chesney would just have to accept it. It was part of the natural order of the universe. That's just the way it was...

Playing Golf and Playing It Well.

Playing Golf and Playing It Well?

That's what it said: *Playing Golf and Playing It Well,* by E.J. Sweeney. The cover was worn blue cloth, but imprinted on the front was the line drawing of a man wearing short pants that came just below his knees (Chesney would later learn this style of trousers were called "plus fours.") He wore a sleeveless sweater and a rakish necktie which perfectly complimented his oversized cap. The man was balancing a golf club on this shoulder, his left foot raised slightly, while with his right hand shading his eyes, he scanned the flight of his ball soaring off into the distance. Apparently, this was an example of playing golf well, though whether the person portrayed was actually E.J. Sweeney was not clear.

Playing Golf and Play It Well?

Chesney took his eyes off the cover of the book and then realized it had come from the heavy paper now lying beside him on the bed; the parcel he had absent-mindedly torn open while lost in thought. He flipped open to the front of the book, half expecting to find a different title inside since there was no logical reason his Aunt would send him a book on playing golf...well or otherwise.

The front piece of the book confirmed that it was indeed the same tome: copyright 1926 by Mr. E.J. Sweeney. But why would she send him this? Already mired in defeat, it took Chesney a moment to realize that the solution to his dilemma was in his hands.

Golf. Golf! He needed a book on golf, and now he had one: via Parcel Post, and just in time. This meant he wouldn't have to break into the library, train a chimp, or endure the misguided help of Rhoda Clott. And to his greatest relief, he would not have to impersonate a girl.

He flipped through the yellowed pages scanning the chapter titles. "Achieving Balance Between Your Brassie and Spoon." "Mastering Your Mashie Irons," "The Pitching Niblick and You." He didn't understand the terminology but knew he must become conversant in this odd language if his plan was to succeed. Sticking out of the back of the book was a loose sheet of paper with familiar handwriting.

"Dearest Shock No Pets, just a little book I came across that made me think of you. No, I haven't gone barmy. I realize that your brother is the one who is interested in golf. But I saw it and thought of him, and that made me think of you, and your concern that it wasn't fair that I didn't think of him when encountering little niceties on my travels. So, there it is; if you can follow my logic, but then I'm sure you'll understand since we're both peanuts from the same shell. Or if you don't understand, you'll just smile and indulge a silly lady who loves you very much. In any event, you can give it to your brother, or not, or keep it yourself to admire its splendid binding, or have it made into a pile of confetti. Just know that whatever you do with it, it's sent with great affection... from your Aunt El...a.k.a.: Nature's Lion."

He turned over the wrapping again. The postmark was smudged, but the stamps were American. Maybe, he hoped, he would see her again before she returned to England or Tibet, or wherever she was off to next. That thought was entertained only as long as it took him to fold up the wrapping, place it in the wastebasket, sit back on his bed, and read:

"The origins of golf reach back to the Roman times, but one needn't be a modern-day Marcus Aurelius to achieve a mastery of the sport that will provide a lifetime of enjoyment..."

Chesney smiled and nodded. He would only need to master golf for a few weeks, several months at the most. But in that time, he hoped the sport would provide him with everlasting relief from his brother's torture, and enough sweet revenge to be savored for a lifetime.

– 45 –
Self-Inflicted Crimes of Youth

The spring fulfilled its earlier threats as Earswick slid into a summery soup. The Clott family had little time to notice as they prepared to move half a continent away. The Clott house - it really didn't feel like much of a home anymore - was in disarray. Packing crates littered every room. It was left to Mrs. Clott to try and bring order to the operation. Though he was career military, Mr. Dr. Major Clott was better at reorganizing the insides of minds, not their outside effects. The four Clott daughters helped their mother in their usual degrees, ranging from too much to not at all. Denise, the oldest and most systematic could have orchestrated the entire move single-handedly but was busy with her studies. Caprice was preoccupied with the upcoming golf tournament. Rhoda was the least helpful. She couldn't decide whether or not she actually wanted to move. Her indecision was based on her ever-changing speculation that the boys in their new town would either find her more or less attractive than those she already knew in Earswick.

Being the youngest, much of the grunt work fell on Clodagh, which she accepted with stoic resignation. Clodagh found it helpful to stay busy as a way to numb her feelings. Her childhood was ending with a sharp finality. Most ages of life shift gradually like the seasons with harbingers of the future blending with lingering pieces of the past. Not so for the childhood of Clodagh Clott. Her childhood had slammed into adolescence as dramatically as if a summer thunderstorm had turned into a blizzard. That morning she put her dolls in a corrugated cardboard box and fastened it with packing tape. She hadn't played with them for years, but they had been ever visible in her room, silent witnesses to her slow evolution from a little girl to a young woman.

Now, however, they were sealed up, and with it an era. Clodagh studied each carefully, caressing a lock of hair here, smoothing a ruffle on a dress there, as she laid them softly in the carton. A strong dread, a sense of finality hung over her. She somehow knew they would not be unpacked at the new house. Instead, the box would be stored in a new attic or a new basement and forgotten. She imagined that someday, perhaps in fifteen or twenty years, for some reason, she would reopen the box, perhaps with her own daughter by her side. She imagined her telling that little girl the story of the day she packed them up those many years ago. Clodagh lifted the tape for a moment, peeking back into the box at the most tangible vestige of her girlhood, and she suddenly felt older than her own mother. With a deep sigh, she pushed down on the tape, uncapped a black Magic Marker, and wrote "Clodagh's..." She stopped; her hand poised above the cardboard. She had almost written "Dolls" next, but that didn't seem quite right. "Dolls" seemed too adult. She almost wrote "friends," but that seemed too babyish. Finally, she wrote: "Stuff," though "Childhood" would have been the most accurate description.

Feeling like an accomplice in a crime against her youth, Clodagh fled the scene and retreated to another bastion of her childhood, the tree house. Lately, Clodagh had been a solitary visitor to the tree. Chesney had been nearby, but he too had been packed away with the same sense of finality as other pieces of her childhood. At least the old Chesney was gone, the soft, physically pliable, mentally inquisitive boy whom she had half-tolerated, half-admired, and of whom she had always been very fond. In his place was a boy she half-feared and was oddly attracted to by more than half. The decisive, focused boy – no not a boy, he was now a young man – had grown so much in the last few weeks that the comfortable old Chesney also seemed sealed up forever. Unlike the dolls that she imagined rediscovering someday, Clodagh could see no revisiting of the old Chesney.

"No, no, that's not it," she heard Chesney bark with the authority of a drill sergeant, "how many times do I have to tell you? Head down! Elbow out...no, no, your right elbow! If you're not going to follow my instructions, why am I wasting my time? I'm sure I can find another pupil."

"I'll get it right, wait, I will. Don't go," the other voice was oddly submissive. It belonged to Stosh.

Clodagh peered over the wall of the fort, through the screen of maple leaves and into the Potoski's backyard. Though he was at least a head shorter than his brother, Chesney now seemed to tower over Stosh. Their body language alone made it clear who was the master and who was the pupil.

The change in Chesney was remarkable. He was a different person. She was glad when, after years of being a foil to Stosh's cruelty, Chesney finally struck back. This new decisiveness offered hope that the hesitant, cowering boy would become a man who would stand on his own two feet. That was what she had anticipated, but not what she had gotten.

In the past month, Chesney had grown almost unrecognizable. It was both frightening and exciting in a sensual way. He might look the same in a photograph, but in action and in the way he carried himself, he was different, even dangerous, at least compared to his old self. As she peered down through the branches, Clodagh saw a young man who not only knew what he wanted, but he was hell-bent on getting it. Even standing still, as he was at the moment, he seemed imbued with an alarming vitality.

"Now, that's better," said Chesney directing his brother's golf swing. "Practice that swing ten times – with the follow through – and then maybe – maybe – you'll be ready to hit a few plastic balls."

Suddenly Stosh rose to his full height. Clodagh retreated half a step, as she watched.

"Plastic balls!" bellowed Stosh. "This is a lot of crap! Swinging at nothing and then at plastic. I think I'm going…"

She detected a moment's hesitation in Chesney, but it quickly evaporated.

"You think? *You think?*" Chesney threw back his shoulders, puffed out his chest, and pulled in his stomach in one assertive thrust. "You don't think. *I* think. *You* think, and *you* lose. Golf is a matter of physical skill coupled with acute mental acumen." He said this last line almost by rote as if he were reciting a sacred text. "You've got the physical skill…"

"That's right…"

"But so do half the baboons in the jungle! They could be taught to play a winning round of golf with enough repetition and a strategic caddy behind them."

"Who you calling a bab…" Stosh drew back his arm as if cocking it for action. Chesney didn't flinch.

"I don't need a baboon," barked Chesney. He confidently turned his back on his brother just as Stosh was poised to strike. "I'm certain that if I gave half of the coaching I'm giving to you to any one of your competitors in this tournament, they would be the odds-on favorite to win…"

"Look, I've had about…" Stosh's arm coiled tighter, and Clodagh could see his sinews tensing from up in the tree fort.

"…like Caprice Clott!" Chesney bit off the words sharply, and then paused for a moment, looking away as if he were observing the local fauna. Stosh's arm deflated as if punctured and fell limply to his side. "I'm sure Caprice could easily win with just a few minor refinements to her game." Chesney turned another quarter turn as if he were making his observation to a nearby tree. By the time he turned back to his brother, Stosh's head was down, his elbow out, and he had already made two of the prescribed ten practice strokes at the air.

Chesney looked at him and nodded as if that quelled the rebellion once and for all. Stosh kept his head down, submitting to strokes four and five, intimidated, as if each stroke were an act of self-flagellation, beating himself into submission.

Up in the tree house, Clodagh exhaled and put her hand to her heart.

– 46 –
The First Kiss
Is the Deepest

It was all coming together perfectly. Nothing to be done had been left undone. The long wait was finally over. Chesney savored the perfection of the moment as he chased the last Cheerio around in his morning cereal bowl. He corralled the errant oat morsel with his spoon, lifted it to his lips, and swallowed it with a slurp of satisfaction: a minor triumph in what would be a day of satisfying outcomes.

He looked up and noticed his mother puttering around the kitchen, humming a little song. It was a discordant little tune that she'd cobbled together over the years from a variety of sources that included bits of Rachmaninoff's *Piano Concerto Number 2, Mairzy Doats,* and an old Chevrolet jingle. The resulting tune, such as it was, made her cooking seem harmonious by comparison.

As she emerged from behind the refrigerator door, Chesney noted her expanding size. She was approximately seven months along now and was just entering into a phase which he would learn was called: "nesting." For his mother, this phenomenon was marked by more than just the usual urge to clean and rearrange items in anticipation of the impending newborn. In her inimitable way, Prudence Potoski had begun cleaning things that even nature didn't intend to be cleaned, least of all by a pregnant lady. The phase had started with her changing every bit of shelf paper in the house no fewer than three times in ten days. From there, it only got worse. The previous week, for example, Mr. Potoski had come to discover that his wife was overhauling the motor on the washing machine. It is a testimony to the sheer power of motherhood that she did so without any previous mechanical experience armed with only a screwdriver, a flashlight, a toothbrush, and half a dozen hairpins. Not only had she completed the job in four hours, but the washer now ran more quietly.

Across the breakfast table, Stosh slumped over his food, wearing his lucky golf outfit: a red polo shirt over black slacks. Stosh was even more hunched over of late, particularly in the presence of Chesney, his golf mentor, and taskmaster. At the moment he was grazing on an English muffin, generously slathered with strawberry jam. Chesney couldn't resist the urge to comment.

"Muffin, eh?" He barked.

Stosh peered upwards from beneath his brow like an abused dog anticipating another swift kick up his backside. He nodded.

"Muffin's okay," said Chesney. "Carbohydrate for endurance, slow burning. Jam? Sugar for quick energy....eat your germ?"

Stosh made a face. The reference was to his daily dose of wheat germ. Chesney prescribed two heaping spoonfuls of the stuff, not because it would help Stosh's golf game, but merely because he could get away with doing so. At this point, Chesney could have ordered Stosh to eat a pile of dead leaves soaked in dog drool, and he would have obeyed. If Stosh balked at any of Chesney's dictates, he would remind him of the golfing skill of Caprice Clott.

"Did you eat your wheat germ?" Chesney repeated with a tone that threatened terrible consequences if the answer was in the negative.

"Yes!" said Stosh. "Yes, I did!" His response was so violent that a generous blob of jam plopped on to the crotch of his trousers. Stosh's eyes grew to twice their size as he stared down at the jam and then up at Chesney.

"My lucky pants," he gasped as if the tournament had just been lost. "I've got jam on my lucky pants."

Chesney smirked. "Wear something else," he said calmly, knowing Stosh would sooner golf in his underwear than give up his lucky outfit.

"These are my lucky pants..."

"Don't worry, dear," said Mrs. Potoski scurrying around the counter with a damp washcloth and a spray bottle of household cleaner. She was beaming at the opportunity to clean something, anything, even her son's crotch. "I'll spritz you right up. Good thing that your trousers are black; a quick wipe and they'll be as good as new."

Mrs. Potoski held her washcloth in the ready and took aim at her eldest son's groin with the spray bottle. Stosh, always sensitive to any physical assault to his manhood, craned his neck away from the bottle as if it had been a semi-automatic pistol.

"Just a quick..."

Phht, Phht, PHHT the nozzle of the plastic bottle wheezed asthmatically, but without delivering any cleanser. Mrs. Potoski looked at the label, then took fresh aim and fired.

PHHT, PHHT, PHHHHHT! The plastic bottle tried valiantly to comply with her earnest pumping, but it hadn't the wherewithal to deliver.

Prudence Potoski lifted the bottle to her ear and shook it for any signs of life, then fully convinced it was indeed empty, took the final step of aiming the nozzle at her own eye and giving it one last pump. Fortunately, it was empty and wasn't a more lethal weapon.

"Huh!" She said as if she expected the cleaning fluid to have been manufactured by the same vendor as had supplied Elijah's widow woman her bottomless flour barrel. "It must be empty. Never mind, I'll go get another one." With that, she waddled toward the pantry.

Chesney was about to drill his brother on the essential components of the effective backswing when he looked at the clock. It was 7:29. Glancing out the kitchen window, he saw Clodagh Clott. She was loitering as nonchalantly as she could without being accused of lurking. Fortunately, Stosh had his back to the window; besides which he was preoccupied with his lucky trousers.

"I'll be back in a few minutes," said Chesney rising from his chair. Stosh raised his hands in mute appeal and then pointed to his soiled crotch.

"I'll be right back. I, uh, I have to check on your supply of tees."

"But…"

"Don't worry, Mom'll clean you all up."

As if on cue, they heard the garage door shut and Mrs. Potoski call out that a fresh bottle of cleaner was on the way.

"Sorry I'm late," said Chesney sliding out the side door and joining Clodagh behind the arborvitae bush. "There was a minor crisis. Stosh spilled jam on his lucky golf slacks."

She glanced at her watch. "Thirty seconds," said Clodagh. "I wouldn't exactly call that late."

"You're right. We don't actually get on the clock until everyone leaves for the tournament. How's Caprice?"

Clodagh shrugged her shoulders. "About the same as she always is."

Chesney nodded. "We need her to be her normal self. I mean, she needs to have a good golf game. I can keep it close, but if she's playing poorly, it means I'll have to adjust Stosh to play even worse than usual."

"You don't think he suspects, do you?"

Chesney twisted his lip. "No…no, not really. He's so worked up about this stupid tournament that he'll do anything I tell him to do and believe anything I say. That's why I had to read that stupid book, so I could improve his game. I hope I never see another stupid golf ball after today. Still, it will be worth it when he loses." He looked wistfully into the air, imagining the look on Stosh's face when he had been publicly beaten by a girl.

Clodagh cleared her throat, disturbing his daydream. "Uh, I've got a schedule to keep, remember?"

"Oh, right," he said. "You've got your routes set, check?"

Clodagh pulled a piece of paper from her back pocket. "Check! I've got all the trails mapped out, just like we said. I'll start with the trails around the neighborhoods leading to the central gathering point, and then I'll lay down the scent from the 18th hole…"

"The 18th *green*," Chesney interrupted.

"Well, the 18th *hole* is where the 18th *green* is," she answered in a voice nearly as testy as the one with which he had challenged her.

"Sorry," he said, "yes, go on, the 18th…"

"Yes, the 18th. I'll lay down a trail from the 18th hole or green, or whatever, working back towards the town."

"What time?"

Clodagh glanced at her wristwatch and then at her list. "I estimate that to be around 10:30."

Chesney nodded. "Good, no one will be that far along the course yet, so you won't be seen. Fortunately, only four foursomes are playing, and they're teeing off in reverse order of their ranking…"

"So, your brother is in the last group to go off, and so is Caprice."

"That did work out well." He paused, savoring the situation he had created before realizing that Clodagh was staring at him. "Sorry, sorry. Yes, no one will see you when you lay down the trail from the end of the course back into town. Sorry, go on."

"Then I just have to wait and connect that trail to the gathering point."

"You'll wait, won't you?" he said anxiously. "You won't complete the trail to the golf course until they're well up the fairway. I'd say at least half-way up it."

"Yes, I know," she said. "We've been over it a dozen times."

"Have you got your binoculars so you can tell when they're up the fairway?"

"Yes!"

"Just want to get it right," he said anxiously. He took a deep breath. "Just think, Stosh, afraid of dogs, afraid of losing to your sister, on the verge of winning, needing perhaps one last putt to clinch it all, when every dog in town comes swarming up the course, barking like mad, surrounding him, ruining his shot, running all over the 18th green, driven out of their happy little skulls by, what'd you call it?"

"*Pimpinella anisum*," she said.

He smiled. Anise seed: guaranteed to drive dogs to ecstasy. Chesney had scraped together all of his saving and his allowance, plus the income from any odd jobs he could find to buy all the anise seed he could from Mr. Acton and the local supermarkets. For the past week, he and Clodagh had been secretly mixing the seed into a solution that would be undetectable to humans while still remaining irresistible to the local canine population.

"Every dog in town will be there when Stosh tries to finish the tournament."

"Almost every dog," said Clodagh.

"Oh, yes, that's right: almost every dog."

He had considered whether or not to include Fritz the Horrible in the day's events, but he concluded that it was too harsh a punishment, even for Stosh and his lifetime of nastiness. Besides, there were too many problems involved with Fritz's appearance, not the least of which was how to get a humongous dog over a ten-foot chain link fence. No, hundreds of ecstatic dogs and Stosh's defeat would be enough.

Chesney led Clodagh to the back of the garage. There, under a drop cloth, was their trove of anise solution. The mixture was stored in an odd assortment of bottles they had managed to scrounge together over the past month from various sources. About half of it was in gallon jugs previous used for bleach and detergent, cleaned to remove any traces of their previous contents. These were the supply vessels. The rest was held in smaller containers, mostly squirt bottles, used to deliver streams of the liquid in precise amounts for maximum effect. The last container, of which there was but one, was a new two-gallon metal can, the type used to carry gasoline.

Chesney helped Clodagh load the front basket of her bicycle with the various jugs and bottles, which she then covered with a cloth to hide them from inquisitive eyes. Next, he strapped the gas can to the flat rack situated over the rear wheels. Once secured, the conspirators knelt beside the can.

"I think we can fill it now," said Chesney, fingering a piece of electrical tape attached to the bottom of the can. "But remember..."

"...Don't take the tape off till I'm out of the neighborhood," said Clodagh sharply. "I'm not stupid. I'm as much responsible for the plan as you."

"Yes, sorry." He removed the tape to verify that the small holes they drilled in the bottom of the can had not healed up since he last checked them. This was at least the third time in the last few days he had done so.

They stood up, Chesney taking a step back to view their handiwork one last time. Clodagh climbed on the bike. He looked over the bike and its contents from front to back, stopping to look at Clodagh's legs sticking out from her shorts. He'd never noticed before how long they were. He looked up at her face and then blushed and looked away, wondering if he had been staring. When he looked back, she was still standing there.

"Well," he said, "Good luck. I'll see you when it's all over."

She nodded for him to come a little closer as if she were going to whisper something in his ear, but as he did so, she did the most extraordinary thing. In one swift motion, Clodagh grabbed his chin, swung his head around to face hers, and then kissed him hard on the lips.

So unexpected, so unusual, and in some ways so pleasurable was the experience that before he could recollect his wits, Clodagh was up the block, pedaling towards the events of the day.

– 47 –
The Battle of the Century!
Subcard: Batman vs. Napoleon Solo

When he returned to himself, Chesney was standing in the middle of the international departures terminal at Kennedy Airport. It was as if he had been on a playground merry-go-round while someone twirled it faster and faster. The events of the day were smeared like finger paints on paper. He looked up at the large clock in the terminal – six hours. He sat down on a plastic bench and exhaled. It was only then, with hundreds of people rushing by, ignoring him as they bustled off to far-flung corners of the globe, that Chesney could recall, let alone reflect on, what had happened.

It had all gone wrong. Things had happened. His family was all in the hospital. All of them scarred – some physically, all emotionally. One was...

He recalled getting on the girl's bicycle and pedaling. He pedaled furiously, mindlessly, harder than he had ever pedaled before but not feeling any exertion. He rode guided by an unknown impulse. He had read stories of abandoned pets that had instinctively traveled thousands of miles to reunite with their owners, or of migratory birds that flew between continents directed only by some inborn sense, but he never knew such intuition resided within him. He was three-quarters of the way to the airport before he realized it. Even then, he was cognizant only long enough to confirm the destination and continue. Then instinct took over again. Instinct released his mind once he was in the terminal, and he was astonished. He had hardly ever pedaled more than three miles before. Now he was over twenty miles from home. He had rarely ventured out on to the town's main artery for fear of the traffic, but he had just held his own against the traffic of the Belt Parkway. It just proved what a person could do when their mind shut off, and they ran on raw emotion.

The sun was shining as their father dropped them off for the golf tournament. The crowd was smaller than he had imagined. In his mind Chesney had pictured a throng of at least four deep lining all 18 holes, following breathlessly along as Stosh and Caprice Clott matched swing for swing, putt for putt, divot for divot. In reality, there were only five of them most of the time, the four golfers and Chesney. The other players didn't even have their own caddies. Every few holes they would meet one of the club officials who would ride by on an electric cart, asking how it was going, before hurrying off again to check on another foursome. Even Mr. Potoski hadn't stayed around. He had to finish wallpapering the baby's room. He promised to be back later in time for the end. Still, Mr. Potoski was proud of Stosh and even seemed to see Chesney in a new light. Chesney recalled a pang of guilt at winning his father's approval while plotting his brother's downfall. Chesney would have to bear that guilt in order to free dead authors and unborn babies from the threat of Stosh.

Aside from Stosh and Caprice, the foursome was completed by an overstuffed seventeen-year-old named Wesley, and Warren, a gangly sixteen-year-old with a bad case of acne. Wesley had signed up for the tournament because he hoped that everyone would receive a trophy merely for participating. Warren was equally unenthusiastic, having entered to avoid attending his cousin's tenth birthday party.

The first nine holes were played in silence, except for Warren and Wesley talking about their favorite television shows. They argued over whether The Man From Uncle could beat Batman in a fight. There were also some salacious remarks about giving My Mother the Car a lube job. The debate came to an abrupt end on the eighth fairway when their chattering distracted Stosh, and his shot landed in the rough. Stosh told them to shut up or get lost. The boys decided on the second option and left to go to the movies.

At the half-way point of the match, both Stosh and Caprice were playing according to expectations. What Stosh gained by sheer muscle on his drives, Caprice made up through finesse on her short game. Chesney's advice to his brother kept the contest close. He didn't want either of them to get more than three strokes ahead or behind the other.

Behind the ninth hole was a snack bar which provided the players with hot dogs and sodas. With a two-stroke lead, Stosh approached his hot dog with cautious optimism, chewing with wary confidence. He didn't want to be too aggressive either with the frankfurter or with remaining nine holes lest he choke on either. Chesney, sipping on a can of orange soda, was pleased with his brother's demeanor. Stosh was now concerned with not losing his lead. The tactic of not playing to win, but rather playing not to lose was a pitfall of many competitors. Chesney could use this if…

"It's good that you brought your little brother along," he heard Caprice taunt.

Stosh looked up, a half-eaten piece of meat dangling in his gaping mouth.

"I would have brought my little sister along," continued Caprice Clott, holding her frankfurter casually as if she didn't care whether or not she ate it, "but my little sister doesn't know anything about golf."

Stosh's jaw tightened. Caprice noticed this and smiled.

"It's a good thing your little brother knows about golf. He's been such a help to you today."

"I don't..." Stosh began to answer, but not before a half-chewed chunk of meat caught in his throat.

"Careful, careful," said Chesney hitting Stosh between his shoulder blades. "You don't want to choke!" He only realized his poor choice of words after it was too late.

"Oh, yes," said Caprice feigning concern, "I wouldn't want you to choke on your lunch...or anything else."

Chesney glowered at her. He wanted to tell her to shut up. He wanted to tell her that he could win this stupid golf tournament for her without her help. He wanted to say that, but all he could trust himself to do is keep patting Stosh on the back and offer him the rest of his orange soda.

Chesney rubbed Stosh's back in an attempt to calm him down. For her part, Caprice stood there, smiling sweetly, as if she were genuinely glad the color was returning to Stosh's face. Then she looked at the hot dog in her hand as if she has studied under Freud, before casually flipping it into the trash can. Then she arched her back as if she was stretching, but the main result was to thrust her well-formed chest in Stosh's direction. Then, with a provocative pivot of her hips, she announced she had to "freshen up" before they continued, and disappeared into lavatory facilities around the back of the stand.

As he watched her leave, Chesney was distracted by the thought that Caprice bore a passing resemblance to Clodagh, if not in their features or coloring then in the way they moved. His mind raced back to Clodagh's kiss. He touched his lips as if doing so would help him understand why she had kissed him and the sensations it had provoked in him. He wondered if Clodagh's body would continue to develop along the lines of her older sister's and if he would ever see her again after this week. Had he wasted too much time with this elaborate scheme instead of spending the last month with Clodagh?

"Stupid twat!" Stosh snapped, jerking Chesney from his reverie.

"Huh?" Chesney turned to see Stosh pacing like a caged puma. He forced himself to regain his concentration so he could restore Stosh's focus as well.

"Don't worry about her," said Chesney. "You're the one who's winning. She's just trying to get in your head. She's trying to psyche you out. You're ahead. Forget about her..."

"In my head!" From his reaction, it was apparent that Caprice had successfully pierced Stosh's thick skull and had struck an active cluster of brain cells. Still being Stosh, he tried to deflect her mental attack in the only way he knew how: crudely. "In my head? Sure, she can get in my head, but I'd like to get in her…"

"Golf," said Chesney, "Concentrate on the golf. It's your match. You're in the lead right where I want, uh, right where you want to be. Now finish it off."

Moments later, after a strident but insincere pep talk from Chesney, they waited on the 10th tee. Caprice soon joined them. She indeed looked "freshened up" and had a smug air atop her tanned complexion. Chesney wondered what she, two strokes back, had to be so confident about. Did she know about his plan?

Chesney selected a three wood from the bag and muttered a few words of advice on the approach to Stosh. Caprice drove first, from the ladies' tee, and sent a rocket up the middle of the fairway. Stosh pretended not to notice, but it was evident from his reaction that he envied the shot.

"Driver," he mumbled, handing back the club.

Out of the corner of his eye, Chesney noticed Caprice watching them. "You're not good enough," he said under his breath. "You haven't practiced with…"

"Driver!" he repeated, brandishing the three-wood like a weapon, the implication being that if he had to use the wood its first stroke would be off the side of his brother's head.

Chesney sighed and gave him the balkier club and stood back to witness what he believed to be a foregone conclusion. Stosh and the driver did not disappoint. The club gave him greater distance but proved as unwieldy as it had for generations of amateur golfers. Stosh's tee shot went at least 100 yards farther than Caprice's had, but in the wrong direction. Stosh sullenly flung the club back at his caddy and trudged off in the direction of his ball, somewhere in some undergrowth.

"You're away," said Caprice sweetly, indicating that despite his more powerful shot, its inaccuracy had left him further from the green, and, by the rules of golf, Stosh had the next shot.

Chesney followed, annoyed by the interference in his plot by its main participants. Though Caprice was doing everything to win, and Stosh was trying his hardest to lose, both were doing so without his help.

Stosh lost that hole bringing Caprice within one stroke. Similarly, ill-advised play made him falter on the 11th and 12th holes, leaving Caprice with a two-stroke lead with six holes to play. This wasn't the plan. The final result would be okay, sort of, but it wasn't what Chesney had planned. He preferred his fantasy ending: Stosh up by two strokes approaching the last hole, and then Chesney steering the victory into disaster. He envisioned looking Stosh in the eye as Caprice sank the winning putt and giving him a subtle look that would reveal that his crushing defeat had been preordained by his younger brother. He would have to pull Stosh together. Stosh had to taste victory before it was yanked from him at the last moment. His normal coaching hadn't worked on the previous two holes. The 13th hole did not bode lucky either. Off the tee, Caprice's drive pulled to the right but was still in the fairway. Stosh, trying to correct for his recent wildness to the right, overcorrected and went wide to the left.

As his brother trudged off in pursuit of his errant ball, Chesney caught sight of Clodagh across several fairways standing on the edge of the course. Clodagh tilted a subtle nod in his direction, the signal that all her responsibilities were proceeding according to plan. Chesney glanced at his watch. She had done it with time to spare. He started to say "Good old Clo" to himself, but stopped and recalled that kiss. That had changed everything. She wasn't "Good old Clo" any longer. She was enticing Clodagh Clott, alluring Clodagh Clott, even sexy Clodagh Clott. If only she didn't have to leave, he thought, if only…

"Fore! FORE! HEY LOOK OUT!"

Chesney heard the warnings, but in his romantic reverie, they failed to register. While the shouts from Stosh hadn't got his attention, the golf ball ricocheting off his right ear more than did the trick. Chesney went down like a sack of potatoes dropped from the rear of a station wagon. The impact left Chesney dazed, lying in the tall grass of the rough. Then he saw a familiar face hovering over him.

– 48 –
Jaws of Defeat; Jaws of Victory; and, Just Jaws

"A re you okay?" she asked.

"Kiss me again," he said dreamily.

A scowl darkened the face. "Kiss you? Why you horny little pervert!"

The girl who he thought was Clodagh turned out to be her sister Caprice. Stosh appeared by her side.

"Didn't you hear me yelling?" asked Stosh.

"No," said Chesney rising up on one elbow. He felt his ear swell from the golf ball's impact. His face glowed red from asking Caprice for a kiss.

"It's okay. Look!" Stosh pointed up the fairway. "The ball bounced off your head and landed on the green. A lucky stroke, I'd say. Get it? Lucky stoke!" Stosh laughed heartily, as he did whenever he thought he'd perpetrated a random act of wit.

"That's not legal," protested Caprice, "that was an accident."

"Exactly," said Stosh, "an accident, not planned. It's just like he was a tree or something . . . a natural hazard."

The two bickered for several minutes until one of the tournament judges came by to settle the dispute in Stosh's favor.

"In match play," the judge explained, "if your ball hits a caddie, you may play the ball as it lies or replay the shot."

"Replay it?" Stosh snorted. "Listen, if it got me closer to a hole, I'd whack the ball off his head like that all day!"

So, Chesney was just another dumb obstruction on the course.

Stosh strode up the green; Caprice pouted as she followed after him; and, the judge slid away for a drink back at the clubhouse. Chesney stood there rubbing the side of his head. Despite the pain, he realized that it had been, as Stosh put it: "a stroke of luck." Watching the body language of the two competitors as they walked away told him that the momentum had shifted once again.

Stosh won that hole, along with the next two and regained the lead. With his confidence restored, only Chesney's subtle misdirection kept Stosh from routing Caprice. Even then, Stosh almost overcame the sabotage. It was like a crooked jockey trying to hold back a determined thoroughbred as they neared the finish line.

By the time Stosh one-putted on the 17th green, he was two strokes in the lead. Chesney had planned he'd only be up by one at that point, but controlling two individuals, neither of whom had any idea they were being manipulated, was more difficult than he had imagined. Still, to get within one stroke of his schedule was quite an accomplishment. It would just take a little more effort to make Stosh lose on the final hole, and that would make his defeat that much more crushing.

As they approached the 18th tee, a crowd had gathered to watch the finale of the stupid tournament. As crowds went, it was small, though by Earswick standards it was large, certainly the largest crowd Chesney had ever seen outside of school assemblies and Fourth of July parades. Stosh and Caprice were the last contestants to finish and also the leaders coming into the final hole. And while he had always envisioned a huge audience to view to Stosh's embarrassment, Chesney had failed to realize that he would also have to execute Stosh's downfall in front of them without it being too obvious. Apart from the other golfers and club officials, Chesney noticed his father standing towards the rear of the group, his face beaming with pride. Mr. Potoski kept glancing up the hill towards the 18th green and the clubhouse, though Chesney couldn't tell why.

The spectators were murmuring in that odd way golf galleries do. They hushed their already muted tones, however, as Caprice approached the tee. She drove an excellent shot off the tee straight up the center of the fairway. The crowd responded with that polite applause that made it sound as if they were all wearing woolen mittens. Stosh hardly took notice of her drive. Instead, he approached the ball with the swagger of a young man who had not only already won this tournament, but the next five or six as well. He smiled at Chesney as he flicked one finger his way, indicating he wanted his club. The cowed subservience that he had worn during the weeks of coaching had all but evaporated, and vestiges of the old Stosh reemerge on his face. Their eyes met and for a split second Stosh's seemed to convey a promise to short-sheet his bed as soon as he had completed the formality of winning the golf tournament. Chesney blanched from reflex, but he regained his composure and adopted a submissive look that fed his brother's rapidly expanding ego. Overconfidence spewed from Stosh's every gesture, and that was perfect for Chesney's next move.

He handed Stosh a club. Stosh took it with an attitude that seemed to say: "thank you, I'll deal with you later," and then strode to the tee. He swished the clubhead back and forth, waggling it over the ball perched on the wooden tee, adjusted his feet several times in a rocking motion, put his head down, and then stopped. He looked up, a glimmer of self-doubt crossing his face for the first time since the 13th hole, and looked back at Chesney with a plaintive expression. Chesney, knowing precisely the reason, scurried to his brother's side. Not wishing to show weakness in front of the spectators, Stosh muttered out of the side of his mouth.

"It's the driver." His eyes cast down at the head of the club frozen inches behind the ball.

"Yes, I know," whispered Chesney.

"I-I can't hit a…"

"Yes, you can," interrupted Chesney. "You're the champ. You've already won this. You couldn't lose now if you tried. You can do anything."

Without lifting his head, Stosh looked sideways at his younger brother.

"Show all these people how it's done. You're the champ. You're the winner. You're…you're my hero!"

Chesney almost choked on these last words. The compliment swelled Stosh's ego to an even greater size. With a nod indicating that he fully believed every bit of malarkey just fed to him, Stosh jutted out his arm almost shoving his brother from the tee.

Then with the assurance of his invincibility, Stosh lowered his head, drew back his driver, and with all the strength in his body, swung down and continued on with a mighty follow through. The ball rocketed from the tee, which was pulverized to splinters from the blow. The crowd gasped much as crowds of old must have groaned in awe at the power of Babe Ruth's home run swings. For a second, Chesney's face dropped and then lit up again, and then adopted a false expression of horror. Stosh had indeed driven the ball further than anyone could remember a ball being hit on the course. If it had gone straight, it probably would have hit the green. As it was, it landed just in front of the green, though the green in question was on the 16th hole. Still frozen in his follow-through as if he were posing for his statue in the Golf Hall of Fame, Stosh had no idea where his mighty clout had landed. At first, he was buoyed by the excited gasps of the gallery, and then bewildered by whispers heavy with disappointment. It was only after he dropped his arms down from his Herculean stance that he asked a tournament judge.

"Where'd it go?"

"Looks like you're over on 16," said the judge. Many shook their heads and more than a few teeth clicked "tsk-tsk's" at yet another would-be hero who filled his golf shoes with feet of clay. Stosh glowered at Chesney waiting with the golf bag on his shoulder. Chesney grabbed the club from Stosh before it could be used as a weapon, and then hurried up the course. Stosh caught up with him several yards along as they separated from the crowd in search of the errant ball. Apparently, the gallery had counted out Stosh as soon as his shot had sailed over the adjoining hole. They were following Caprice, she of the straight and true drive, she who now would undoubtedly overcome her two-shot deficit and win the tournament. Everyone loves a winner. Losers walk alone, save for the company of their caddies.

"Driver! F**kin' driver!" Stosh kept repeating as the trudged across the empty fairways.

Chesney walked as quickly as he could ahead of his irate brother.

"Can't lose? Can't lose? Can't f**kin' lose? Is that what you said?"

"How was I to know?" whined Chesney. This wasn't going at all well. He had hoped that Stosh would shank the ball with the driver; enough to erase his two-point lead. He didn't think Stosh would launch the ball into orbit and end the match with them alone in the wilderness. It would have been perfect to see Stosh lose with an audience around with only a vague suspicion that Chesney had been the architect of the defeat. For Stosh to lose two holes away with no witnesses and with all the fault landing on Chesney was suicidal.

Chesney reached the ball first with Stosh hot on his heels still muttering profane epitaphs and threats. Chesney swung around using the golf bag as a shield.

"Look," he said weakly, "you're on the green."

Stosh snarled at him, the ball, the green, golf, and life. He thrust out his hand.

"Gimme a club!"

"Which one?"

"You tell me, golf genius. Which one can I do the most f**kin' damage with?"

Chesney winced, not only at the menacing situation but at the fact that the sentence had ended with a preposition.

"Language, Stosh."

Though he had been thinking of something along those lines, the words didn't come from Chesney's lips. Instead, the voice came from a clump of pine trees from which emerged Mr. Potoski. Most of the murder drained from Stosh's coiled muscles, with only a residue of grievous bodily harm remaining. Chesney exhaled. At worst he would be maimed for life, but he would live.

"Dad..." said Stosh.

Rodney Potoski looked at the ball and then turned his back and looked back towards the direction of the 18th green.

"It's difficult but not impossible," he said studying it with the calm logic he displayed when pondering a problem not his own. He was quite sage, Chesney noted, if he wasn't personally aggravated by a difficulty.

"Dad, I woulda won if this little shit hadn't given me a driver..."

"Not the best choice of a club," agreed Mr. Potoski, "but you didn't have to take it, and he didn't swing the club, you did." Almost as an afterthought, he reminded Stosh that Chesney was not a small bit of excrement.

"But I lost..."

Mr. Potoski reminded him in severe fatherly tones that he had not raised any quitters and the tournament was not over until he finished playing out the hole, which was the least that good sportsmanship required under the circumstances. Then, he advised Stosh on the shortest line of approach back to the 18th green and suggested Stosh use the highest iron he could accurately control.

"He can swing a two iron, Dad," said Chesney just loud enough to be heard.

His father's eyebrows shot up. "Really? A two?" His lower lip folded over, indicating that he was impressed but skeptical. "Okay. Give it a shot. Aim over those trees, those ones there, the ones I just came through. I walked it off, that's the most direct shot. Chesney, you run ahead so you can spot the ball."

Chesney gratefully escaped through the trees. Ten seconds later the ball came zipping through the trees over the 17th tee and nearly halfway back to the 18th hole. It was a great shot. As he hustled after the ball, he came to a stop. There, in the loneliness of the empty hole, he heard the ruckus. The first sound was of people shouting. He wondered why until he heard the barking of dogs.

The dogs! He completely forgot about the dogs. The canine cacophony brought it all flooding back. Clodagh had done it. The dogs had arrived on time, only Stosh wasn't there to be the victim, let alone to see, their assault. Chesney dropped the golf bag and started running towards the small hill that hid the 18th green from view. As he reached the crest, the full panorama of chaos unfolded before his eyes.

It was magnificent!

There were at least 30 dogs of all shapes and sizes, and all of them having a wonderful time. The humans were enjoying themselves far less. In fact, none of them seemed to be enjoying themselves at all. It was perfect. It was all he hoped it would be except for one thing: Stosh wasn't there. Turning around, he saw Stosh and his father approaching the spot where his last shot had landed. Mr. Potoski had the golf bag and was selecting a club for Stosh. Stosh might be able to land back on the 18th hole with one good shot. That would put his ball in the middle of the canine pandemonium. Neither Stosh or his father heard the uproar. Chesney stood there, looking back and forth with a full view of both scenes. Then another familiar voice called out.

"Stop! Don't shoot! DON'T SHOOT!"

He wheeled around to see his very pregnant mother waddling up from the side.

"I thought I told you to wait up at the 18th green," shouted his father. "I don't want you walking around so much!"

"Don't shoot!"

"Nobody's shooting," said Mr. Potoski, grabbing the end of Stosh's club. "What are you doing?"

Mrs. Potoski bustled down the hill. Chesney met her at the bottom.

"Don't shoot," she panted.

"You said that," said Mr. Potoski. "Why?"

"Dogs!"

Both his father and brother repeated the word. Chesney didn't since he already knew all about the four-legged invasion. A moment later, he realized that he also should have acted surprised to avoid suspicion.

Leaning on the golf bag, Mrs. Potoski described the scene taking place just over the hill. It seemed that Caprice had just made her second shot when the flood of pooches came spilling on to the course. The dogs were running all over the fairway, including the area where Caprice's ball had landed. A judge had tried retrieving the ball so as not lose its place, but a playful Pomeranian had reached the spot just ahead of him and carried the ball off in his mouth. From that point the tournament had devolved into a free-for-all with people trying to secure dogs, dogs trying their damnedest to stay unsecured, club officials trying to find the protocol for such an occurrence in the rule book, and everyone else trying to offer advice. When some semblance of order was resumed, Caprice was allowed to drop another ball at the spot where her last shot had come to rest. Unfortunately, her next shot went wide to the left and hit an excitable borzoi. The interference caused the ball to bounce back and land even further away from the hole. It also caused a renewal of the mass confusion.

"So," panted Mrs. Potoski, "you can't shoot."

"Come on," Mr. Potoski motioned to Stosh and started up the hill to the green. When Chesney began to follow, he was told to stay with the ball. Though it was a bit annoying to be excluded from a riot he had engineered, Chesney folded his arms in silence. Still winded, Mrs. Potoski remained behind with Chesney. After ten minutes, during which they heard even more yelling and more barking, Mr. Potoski and Stosh returned skipping as they crested the hill.

"It's the damnedest thing, the damnedest thing!" shouted Mr. Potoski.

Mrs. Potoski placed her hands on either side of her massive belly as if that marked the location of the baby's ears. "Watch your language, Rodney!"

He ignored her and proceeded to retell the account of the dogs as if she hadn't been the one who first related it to him. Throughout, Stosh kept trying to interrupt, though he was repeatedly waved to be quiet by his father.

"So, the upshot of it all," said Mr. Potoski, slowing down as he came to the climax of the story.

"I'm winning!" Blurted out Stosh, finally getting a word in edgewise.

"Winning?" Chesney said, feeling his jaw droop.

"Yeah, that same rule," said Stosh, "the one that worked for me when I bounced that shot off your head..."

"Oh, Chesney, my baby!" Mrs. Potoski cried. She had been standing on the other side of Chesney and hadn't seen his welt, but now spun him around and smothered him with motherly affection.

"It's okay, Ma," assured Stosh, "that shot worked out real good. It got me nearer the hole. But the same rule worked against her. She kept hitting the dogs, and her balls kept going further from the hole! So now I'm winning."

Mr. Potoski then explained how the dogs had finally been removed from the course, and Caprice was allowed to finish out the hole. Between the various canine setbacks and her totally ruined concentration, she had quadruple bogeyed the hole. Stosh just needed to get down in three to win the hole and the tournament.

Mr. Potoski selected a club and advised Stosh on his approach over the hill. It was clear that Chesney didn't matter anymore in events. He felt his mother take his hand, and suddenly, he was a little boy again. These last weeks he had been almost grown up. For a brief time, he had been an expert. He had authority over people and events. Now that was all gone. He looked at his father directing Stosh and felt just as he had when he was very small; when he had enjoyed some activity until the big kids showed up and took over the game. He sighed inwardly and wondered if that was life. Just when things were going his way, would there always be "big kids" to come along and push him aside?

Stosh, the fresh scent of victory in his nostrils, executed a perfect shot over the hill. From the applause, it was clear the ball's landing had been as good as its take off.

He walked over the hill, with his mother. His father and Stosh were ten yards ahead of them. There was Caprice Clott, standing off to the side of the green, an unflattering combination of anger and misery spoiling her healthy beauty. Around her were officials from the golf club, some with clipboards. A few feet back was a table holding trophies, ribbons, and certificates and some prizes. There were still a few dogs around, but those that remained were being restrained. Towards the clubhouse the greenskeeper and some boys were herding the rest of the dogs into a shed. Over a quarter of a mile away, standing on the edge of the road, straddling her bicycle, he saw Clodagh. Her bike was free of the incriminating cans that had delivered the anise solution. She looked like a girl disinterestedly watching from a distance. Chesney tried to move away from his mother, but it was no use. He felt like a fat, dumb kid again and doubted if Clodagh would ever want to give him a second kiss.

Chesney looked down. There was the ball on the green, not more than fifteen feet from the hole. Stosh only needed to two-putt to win. Putting wasn't Stosh's strength, its finesse was lost on his raw power, but even he could make up fifteen feet in two putts... couldn't he? For a moment, Chesney imagined diving in front of the ball to give the match to Caprice. It was a tantalizing thought, but only briefly entertained. If he ruined Stosh's victory now, it would be obvious. He would have to admit everything and would be punished by his parents and tortured by Stosh. No, Stosh would win the match and his reign as the biggest bastard – youth division – in Earswick would not only continue unchecked but reach new heights of dastardliness. Perhaps he thought, that was the way life was too. There was no justice or at least no satisfying revenge.

Stosh one-putted. He would. Everyone was cheering. In his exultation, Stosh was hugging everyone, even a few of the dogs...especially the dogs. He gave the dogs more credit than he gave Chesney. Caprice shook Stosh's hand more graciously than he would have shaken hers had the circumstances been reversed. Then the president of the golf club was holding the impressive trophy with Stosh standing next to him. The president was speaking, a bit too much for Stosh's liking, his fingers twitching to clutch his prize. The president was waxing eloquent on the importance of golf in molding good character in the youth of America. He seemed to be reaching the climax to his remarks when it happened.

At first, no one recognized it. It began with the low barking of a dog. With so many barks, woofs, and yips over the last half hour, such sounds had faded into the background. As the bark neared, it grew louder, deeper, more robust, less playful, and more menacing. The father of one of the other contestants first put up the alarm, though it wasn't much more than an observation.

"Hey, that's that really big dog, the one in the yard with the really big fence..."

Every head turned down the empty 18th fairway, empty that is except for the massive, powerful, bounding form of Fritz, the really big dog who lived behind the really big fence; only now he was the really big dog who was out from behind the really big fence. Ironically, it seemed to register with Stosh last, absorbed as he was with the large silver-plated loving cup about to be delivered into his mitts. His brain finally processed who was coming to his ceremony uninvited and what it probably meant, but by then it was too late. Fritz, employing the strong leg muscles that had so long been constrained behind ten feet of chain link fence, was tearing through the green, past the hole, past the rough, up towards the table where Stosh stood. The dog's nostrils flared as they kept low to the ground, following the anise trail laid out to attract more congenial pups. While his head was tilted down, Fritz's gaze was pointed dead ahead. The dog's ear perked up, and his eyes glistened as he caught sight of his longtime tormentor. Then, ten feet from Stosh, Fritz executed one mighty spring from his powerful back haunches and flew the remaining distance, his fierce jaws locked in the attack position, and he didn't come down until he had clamped them directly on Stosh's crotch.

There were groans from men, screams from women, and cries from children; even the other dogs present didn't enjoy the sight. But these collective expressions of agony and woe paled in comparison to the hellish, blood-curdling shout of pain that issued forth from Stosh's heaven-raised mouth. Though it was but one syllable, Stosh held it so long as to be the envy of tenors at the Metropolitan Opera. Though it was an incomprehensible collection of letters, it was more profane than a year's worth of cusses from the mouths of the most blasphemous sailors.

Chesney watched in horror, trying to look away, but unable to do so. Fritz's jaws remained clamped on his brother's groin, as intractable as a steel bear trap. His mother fainted. His father tried to simultaneously minister to both her and Stosh and so helped neither one. Finally, the scene which seemed to have been played out over hours, but in reality, had only taken less than 30 seconds from the first appearance of Fritz down the fairway, came to an end. The president of the club raised Stosh's trophy high over his head and after repeated blows managed to fell the devil dog. Still, unconscious or dead, it wasn't certain which, Fritz's jaw remained clamped on Stosh's nether regions. While first aid was administered to all who needed it and the ambulance was called and came, Chesney stared at it all without moving.

Slowly, like a photographic print emerging in a darkroom chemical tray, Chesney began to realize what had happened. Overlaid on the current moment, he saw Stosh spilling jam on his lucky trousers; his mother trying to clean them; leaving the room to get some more cleaner; and then... She had inadvertently picked up a bottle of the anise concentrate. She had unwittingly saturated her son's crotch with a liquid designed to attract dogs and drive them wild.

He watched as the paramedics attended to Stosh, and then felt a nudge at his elbow. He turned to see Clodagh standing there.

"I can explain," she said softly.

For a split second, Chesney thought of the kiss and how under different circumstances they would be celebrating their coup and then perhaps she would be explaining other things. He shook his head to dispel any residual thoughts of what might have been.

"About what?" he asked.

"Fritz," she said, "how he got here."

He turned and looked at her crossly. "You didn't..."

"Of course, I didn't!" Her eyes flared. He bit his lip. "I think I know what happened."

Chesney was about to angrily ask her why she would take a container dripping a concentration to attract dogs past the yard of the most vicious dog in the town. He was about to ask her how she could be so stupid when he realized that he had designed the routes, and he had made the maps that she had followed. Then she spoke.

"I got a flat tire in front of Fritz's yard."

"A flat tire..." he said hollowly.

"Yes," she continued. "I had to stop and patch it and then pump it up again. It couldn't have taken me more than two or three minutes, but in that time..."

He raised his hand, silencing her. In that time, he thought the anise-filled receptacle continued to drip an irresistible pool of the liquid. He almost asked why she didn't close up the hole on the container, but he told himself he wouldn't have thought to do it either. Besides, Fritz was behind a ten-foot fence. Whether he got over it, under it, or through it didn't matter. The dog had never had such a powerful incitement to escape before.

"I feel horrible, your poor brother," she said. He tried to wave her quiet, but she continued. "It's my fault. I shouldn't have gotten a flat. I shouldn't have thought of the anise. I shouldn't have kept telling you to stick up for yourself..."

"No," said Chesney, "it's not your fault, it's all..."

He froze and looked over towards the ambulance. A second gurney was being loaded, this one transporting a distended silhouette of his mother. He saw his father clamber into the back of the vehicle, and then stop as if he forgot something incidental. Then after scanning around, he spotted what he was looking for: his other son.

"Chesney," his father called out, "go... find... go over to the neighbors..."

With that ambiguous command, he hopped into the ambulance. An attendant shut the door behind him, sealing his family inside, then they drove off.

Chesney stood staring at it until it was well out of sight and then looked at the girl standing next to him, yes, Clodagh, that's who she was. His mouth opened as if he wanted to say something, but too many thoughts clogged his brain, and nothing came out. Finally, he looked down at the handlebars of her bicycle, then back up at her. He grabbed the bicycle from her and said: "Yes, thank you," as if he were responding to an offer of the bike that she had never made. Then he climbed on and began to pedal.

– 49 –
Family Subtractions

A baby girl.

She would have been his sister.

No, Chesney thought, he had a sister. That's what he would say. "Yes, I have a brother, and I had a sister, but…"

Even then, moments after he heard the news from a nurse, he couldn't imagine ever finishing that sentence.

"…but she died."

She had hardly been alive. She hadn't really been alive, had she? She had never seen the light of day. She had never drawn a breath on her own. She had never known the love of her older brother. She had never… she had never killed a member of her own family.

He was in the hallway of the hospital. He wasn't supposed to be there. There was a hospital rule about not allowing children younger than thirteen as visitors. He tried explaining why he was there to the nurse at the desk, but most of his words came out in wavering sobs. The nurse took pity on him and sat him down. She brought him a half-pint of milk in a wax container, and he spasmodically slurped it down through a paper straw. After the milk and the soothing of the nurse, he explained his mother had just been brought in and the surrounding circumstances.

"Oh, yes," said the nurse softly, "and your brother too…"

He had forgotten about Stosh. He admitted that was his fault too. The nurse looked at him askance and assured him he was not to blame. She wasn't there. She couldn't know. Still, he felt enough guilt without having to convince anyone else of it.

"You sit here," she said. "I'll see what I can find out."

A few minutes later, the nurse came back and explained that his "Mommy" had lost the baby, a baby girl.

He wanted to cry. His eyes felt full of tears, but something inside of him wouldn't release them, not there, not then. He was glad he hadn't started crying again because a few minutes after that, his father staggered out into the hallway. He walked like a man who had just stirred from a nightmare and wasn't yet fully awake. Mr. Potoski looked blankly at Chesney for a moment and then offered him a wan smile. He sat down next to him and patted him on the shoulder more as a comfort to himself. It was as if he were confirming that at least one member of his family was intact. He sat there for several moments; his eyes seemed to be searching the air for the right words. Finally, Mr. Potoski spoke.

"Your mother will be fine," he said. Chesney nodded. "She lost…"

"I know, Dad," he whispered.

Mr. Potoski jerked his head to the side as if he was trying to shrug it off, but he oversold the attempt.

"Those things happen. Miscarriages… it means something wasn't right. It's nature's way of taking care of something that's not right. You understand?"

Chesney nodded. He wanted to confess about the golf tournament and the dogs and everything but didn't know how.

"Dad, I'm sorry…"

"I know." He patted Chesney's knee. "Your brother's going to be okay, too."

"He will?"

"Well, yes, eventually…"

"How is he?"

Mr. Potoski exhaled. "He's had what's called an orchiectomy, well, that's what the end result is."

Chesney looked at him for clarification.

"That dog started it. The doctors finished it. He's lost one…uh…one testicle. They said he'd be normal with one. He can be a fa…uh…have children." Mr. Potoski almost broke down, then drew a sharp intake of air and thought for a moment. "I doubt you remember it, but we had trouble with that same dog before. He attacked your brother when he was little. The dog was little back then, as well. It's a long story, but they kept that dog behind a big fence. He must have gotten out somehow. Funny how that dog would remember your brother after all those years." A faraway expression seemed to cloud his face. "Funny how some people just become natural adversaries. There was this guy back in school…" He caught himself and snapped back to the present day. "Anyway, everyone…" He paused. "Your mother and brother are going to be okay…" He stopped there, excused himself, and disappeared around the corner. A moment later, Chesney heard the most frightening sound he could ever recall. He heard his father, the strongest person he had ever known, sobbing uncontrollably.

Rather than face him, or his mother, or his brother, Chesney walked out of the hospital as if he were in a trance. He got on Clodagh's bicycle and started pedaling.

Now, hours later, sitting in the international terminal, surrounded by a multitude of strangers, Chesney stopped, buried his face in his hands and burst into tears.

– 50 –
The Aubergine Sandals
and the NoDoz Deity

He wasn't sure how long he'd been crying. But there was comfort in the emotional release, and he continued. For an impassioned breakdown, one can't beat a crowded terminal in a busy airport. Such a public locale is perfect for maintaining a sense of privacy. For at least ten minutes, Chesney vented his conscience with the rest of the world content to ignore him.

It was a surprise then when Chesney felt a gentle hand rubbing his back. His tears slowed as he composed himself in preparation for telling his comforter to mind their own business and get on the next flight to Kuala Lumpur or wherever they were going.

He looked down and saw a familiar pair of purple sandals. Then he looked up and instead of seeing a meddling stewardess or some old busybody, he looked into a pair of warm eyes of mismatched color. His mouth dropped open.

"Hello, Chesney, my love," said Aunt Elinor, still stroking his shoulders.

He didn't speak, though he looked her up and down to verify it was really her. Then he buried his face in her shoulder and cried even harder than before. After several minutes questions began to form in his mind. Why hadn't she pushed his head off her shoulder, stuck a handkerchief in his hand and told him to stop crying? Why wasn't she asking a lot of questions about what he was doing there, where he was going, or what had happened? His tears slowed to a sob, then dried up in a series of spasms, and finally, he lifted his head. She merely smiled at him.

He looked down at her shoulder. Her dress was soaked from his tears, but she seemed to take no notice of it.

"I got your dress all wet," he said.

She didn't even look down, instead shrugged. "I've got other dresses. I've only got one nephew."

"You've got two," said Chesney, while thinking: and a little less of him.

"Oh, yes," she said, looking up as if a tally of her relations was listed on the giant flight tote board. "Yes, two nephews... but I've only got one you."

"Don't you want to know what I'm doing here?"

"When you're ready to tell me...."

He looked at her askance. By now, every other grown-up he knew would have shaken his story out of him and had him half-way home for more scolding. Gratefully, he hugged her again for several minutes before releasing her with a sigh.

"Are you hungry?" she asked.

He hadn't thought of it, but the suggestion made him ravenous. She led him to a nearby restaurant, found the most secluded table and ordered him a sandwich. He was three-quarters of the way through it before he started to answer the questions that she had not yet asked.

"I... I was going to see you, I suppose," he said, wiping his mouth with a paper napkin. She smiled but said nothing. "I mean, in London. I suppose I was running away."

She nodded. "I suspected we were two of a kind, but I had no idea it extended to going half-way across the globe."

His puzzled expression encouraged her to continue.

"A long time ago," she began, and then paused as if she were gazing through a portal of time, "I ran away, too."

"Just like me!" He was consoled by the fact that he had reacted in the same way as his favorite relative.

"Well, I was a little older, but yes, the outcome was similar. We must be cut from the same cloth, you and me. Li Gao once said the wind scatters the seeds of the lotus tree far, but its offspring are unmistakable."

"That's when you went to Tibet," said Chesney.

Elinor looked surprised. "Who said I went to Tibet? Oh, you probably heard that from your father."

Chesney nodded. He had heard it from his father, but he didn't want to admit that he had been crouching in the closet at the time.

"I never went to Tibet. Your parents thought I did," she added as if to preserve his parents' reputations. "But I never did. I meant to..."

"Then who is that Chinese guy you're always quoting."

She laughed. "Li Gao runs a takeaway restaurant. It's right next door to my friend Mr. Postlewaite's shop in London. Did you think he was a Tibetan monk or something? Oh, Postlewaite will have a good laugh at that. It's a logical conclusion, but you'd need to see Li Gao to get the joke. He's a lovely man, just not a monk." Her smile lingered on her lips, then it slowly faded.

"No, Chesney dear," she continued, "I didn't go to Tibet. I was involved in a terrible accident a long time ago. A man died. He wasn't a particularly nice man, and he wasn't particularly nice to some people I cared about, but

still, he didn't deserve to die. But it was an accident, and I was involved...
it probably wouldn't have happened if I hadn't been there. But I was there.
And that was no accident."

"I thought you said it was an accident."

"What happened was an accident, but it wasn't an accident that I was
there."

Chesney looked at her for a moment, trying to understand. "But you
ran away, right?"

"Yes, dear, I ran away," Aunt Elinor nodded, stroking his hair, and then
wiping a bit of lettuce from the corner of his mouth.

"But not to Tibet?"

"No, I meant to go to Tibet. Things happened along the way."

"Accidents?"

"Accidentally, but not by accident," she said. "There really are no
accidents. This must sound very confusing, but let me explain. A long
time ago, when I was in college, I was up in the attic of the house where I
was living. I was moving some trunks and boxes around so I could get to
the open floorboards..."

"Open floorboards?"

"Yes, well, I wanted to poke a hole in the floor so I could see into the
room below. I needed to know what was going on, so, well, it's all very
complicated. It's not really important why I was moving things around,
but I was. While I was up in the attic, I shoved a heavy crate off the finished
part of the floor on to an unfinished part. It went through the floor and fell
on a man in the room below."

"But you didn't know he was there."

"Well, I was pretty sure he was there, but I certainly didn't want a crate
to crush him. The police called it an accident, but I still felt very badly
about it. You see, I hadn't wanted him harmed, well, not physically, but
I still felt responsible for his death. I wanted him to stop doing the bad
things he was doing, but I certainly didn't want to kill him. But after
all, getting crushed by that crate stopped him from doing all the bad
things he was doing, didn't it? And he wouldn't have died if I hadn't
been up in the attic moving things around. I explained all that to the
police, and they were satisfied that it was an accident. They cleared me
of responsibility, but unfortunately, the police can't clear a person's
conscience. I left as soon as the official business was all settled. No one
in my family understood, and I guess I really didn't try to explain it
to them. I was in too much of a hurry to run away. I'm not sure if I
was running away from something, or to something. That's one of the
reasons I decided to go to Tibet. Back then, a lot of people thought if
you were looking for some great insight or enlightenment, you went to
Tibet or India, or someplace far away and exotic. It's pretty silly. I often
wonder if people in Tibet go to Upstate New York for the same reason. I
suppose it's just human nature to feel that you have to wander half-way

around the globe to search inside yourself. In my case, I only had to go a quarter of the way around the world."

"To England?" Chesney guessed.

"Yes, dear, to England. Back then, very few people went to England for much of anything, least of all enlightenment. They didn't have mod fashions or the Beatles or anything like that. It was actually a pretty drab place then."

"Then, Aunt El, why did you decide to go to England instead of Tibet?"

She smiled awkwardly. "Because that's where I ran out of money on the way to Tibet. I actually knew I didn't have enough money to get all the way to Tibet. I planned on getting to England and then working to earn the rest of the money. I got a job as a waitress, not a very good one."

"It wasn't a good job?"

"No, it was an okay job; I just wasn't a very good waitress. I wasn't used to the language."

"But it's English."

"Exactly," she agreed. "The English and the Americans call things by different names. For example, what we call 'jelly' they call 'jam,' but if they talk about jelly, they mean what we call 'Jell-O,' and what we call 'cookies' they call 'biscuits.' Even my favorite color, dark purple, what we call 'eggplant,' they call 'aubergine.' Anyway, it made for some odd looks and orders when I first was there. Despite that, I did manage to start saving for my trip to Tibet. That's when I went to the travel agency and met Li Gao."

"I thought you said he worked in a restaurant."

"He did. His restaurant is next to the travel agency. The travel agency was closed, but the restaurant was open, so I went in there to wait."

"And you met Li Gao…"

"No, I met Mr. Postlewaite first. He was in there having a cup of tea. We got to talking, and then he introduced me to Li Gao, and that was that."

Chesney scratched his head. "What was what?"

"That's where I stayed, and that's where I've been since then."

"But what about your quest for spiritual enlightenment?"

"Oh, I picked that up in Li Gao's takeaway and Postlewaite's knickknack shop in London."

She took a sip of tea and continued.

"We have some fascinating discussions, we do," she said. "Li Gao is something of a philosopher…"

"Buddhist," injected Chesney.

"No, actually Congregational," she said. "He's a lay minister. His family left China when the Communists took over. And Mr. Postlewaite has an excellent record collection… mostly old funny recordings. That's where I get all those silly records I send you. Between the two of them, I suppose I learned to trust in a power greater than myself and not to take the rest too seriously – especially myself."

"But you said there aren't any accidents."

"No," she said, taking another sip of tea, "at least I don't think there are. Some cultures call it 'fate,' others 'Kismet,' or 'happenstance.' Whether you believe in God, or the Politburo, or the Great Wood Nymph, it's clear that we're not the final say in what happens. I was planning something, but all my plans were pretty weak. Oh, I was doing all I could do in my power to bring about an outcome, but really, look at me. I'm just a girl from Upstate New York. Even on my best day, if everyone else on Earth took the day off, what could I hope to control? I can't make the world spin, or the tides go in and out. And neither can anyone else. Other people might have more power and influence, but still, they couldn't stop the rain from falling or make time stand still. So, whether you acknowledge it or ignore it, all our little hopes and schemes are at the mercy of someone up the ladder. I'm convinced that's an intelligent and benevolent being, but that's something everyone has to decide for themselves. Dessert?"

Chesney couldn't help thinking of his stillborn sister and his mutilated older brother. "But what about…"

"…Bad things that happen?"

"I was trying to do something…" Chesney stopped. Had he been trying to do something good? What had his whole plan been for? He thought a moment while his Aunt watched him patiently. "I was trying to get back, no, I was trying to stick up for someone, and it didn't work out. In fact, it went very, very badly."

Aunt Elinor nodded. "Yes, you're a Potoski. We always get it wrong, don't we? You've been born into a fine tradition. We're always trying to right the wrongs of the world, whether it's our job to or not. It rarely is. Your grandfather…well, no, that's a long story. You'll find out about that someday…"

"The trunk…" Chesney began then stopped himself. He only knew about that by eavesdropping.

"You've heard about that, have you? Hmm, he's more hung up about that than I thought." Elinor leaned over. "You must promise me something, Chesney. Someday you will most likely inherit your grandfather's trunk, as I did. If and when you do, promise me that you'll never let your father see inside of it. Or maybe I'll just destroy it, I don't know. It would help explain our family curse."

"Curse?"

"No, not a curse, I just mean Potoskis always seem to be doing right things but getting them all wrong, or doing the wrong thing and having it work out right."

Chesney nodded.

"Still it always seems to work out in the end, sort of. It never works out how we planned it, but it does work out all the same. I suppose we should give up, or at least make sure our motives are pure before we launch into another of our classic cock-ups."

"Cock-up?"

"Oh, sorry," she said, "another Briticism…it means a fiasco, a mistake."

Chesney nodded and then thought for a moment. "But they work out okay in the end?"

"They seem to," she said, "Of course, we should make sure we're acting from the right motives."

"Motives? How do you mean?"

"Are we doing something because it's the right thing to do; because we're trying to help someone else; or are we just being selfish?"

"Does that make a difference?"

"I think so. You see, dear, we can do an awful lot of things through selfishness."

"You mean like being greedy?"

"Well, yes, greed is a very selfish thing, but that's pretty easy to spot. No, I've found, usually the hard way, that the bad things that have happened to me and to other people around me, usually happen when I'm being selfish, when I'm chasing what I want most of all. I've used people to get what I wanted with very little regard for what was best for them."

"But you're not like that… you're Aunt El…"

She smiled. "I'm glad that at least one person sees me that way, Chesney, dear. I wish your… But, never mind, that. I guess what I'm trying to say, from my own experience, is that when I've been looking out for what I wanted regardless of everyone else, it's turned out wrong and ultimately I've been unhappy."

"Even when you got what you wanted?

"Especially then," she said. "We think we're pretty clever, hiding our motives, especially from ourselves. We can fool ourselves into thinking we're doing some very great thing when we're actually being perfectly wretched. It's the difference between justice and revenge. If we're doing something just to get back at someone, then all sorts of horrible things could happen."

He sat there staring at the crusts of bread on his plate for several minutes, trying to sort out the thoughts running through his mind. Had his motives been pure? Had he been trying to do something good? And if so, how had it all turned out so badly? Was there a higher power who would make it all work out? Then he thought again of the baby and then put his head down and started to cry.

His tears were interrupted by the soft voice of Aunt Elinor and her arm around him. "Chesney, my love, the baby wasn't your fault."

The shock of her words staunched his tears as if a faucet had been suddenly shut. He looked up at her.

"I know about it," she said. "I know, and it wasn't you."

"But…"

"I called," she said in soothing tones. "When I saw you, sitting there, I called home. It took a few times, but finally, I talked to your father. I didn't tell him where you were or why I was calling. I just pretended as if I were calling to chat. I explained that I was calling from the airport during the layover."

"But she lost the baby when she saw Stosh get..."

"That wasn't the cause," said Aunt Elinor, "it was a difficult pregnancy from the start. Your mother is older, and, well, there were other circumstances, but none that you caused or made worse. So, it's not your fault."

He tried to smile a moment and then recalled his brother. "Stosh is my fault."

"Oh, yes, something about a dog biting him?"

Chesney took a deep breath and then gave the full explanation including the book that had been glued together, the lifetime of practical jokes, the anise seed, all culminating in the arrival of Fritz and his assault on Stosh's nether regions. Throughout it all, Aunt Elinor listened judiciously.

"So," he said, reaching the end of the story, "what do you think?"

"From what I heard, he'll be okay," said his Aunt. "He should even be able to father children. His pants might not fit quite right, but then there are worse things in life than baggy trousers."

"No, I mean, what about my," he searched for the word, "my motives?"

She shrugged. "That's between you, your conscience. You'll have to search your own heart. I can't really do that for you, dear. And I don't really think you'd want me to."

Crestfallen, he stared at his feet beneath the table.

"Not many people," she added, "would have done what you did."

"They wouldn't?"

"No, they would have let that big dog out on purpose. Come on," she stood up and extended her hand to him. He took it. It was warm and comforting.

As they walked hand in hand through the terminal, he squeezed her hand, and she squeezed back a little harder. As they walked through the busy concourse, Chesney wondered how anyone could possibly sort out all the plans and intents of the human heart and somehow work it all out to a greater good. Then, through that special bond that seemed to exist between them, she answered the questions of his heart.

"It boggles my mind," she said as much to herself as to him, "I've come to believe in God, but yet I can't help wondering when I see more than five people together how it could possibly be."

"How one person could keep all this straight?" he asked.

"Not just that, but why there's so much that actually goes right. I mean, everyone making plans and having them bump up against everyone else's little schemes. Do you have a favorite Christmas carol?"

He stopped. That was an odd question to ask in the middle of summer in a busy airport. For some reason, the only one that came to mind was *Santa Claus is Coming to Town*, but that didn't seem appropriate, no matter what she was driving at, so he merely shook his head.

"I like '*I Heard the Bells on Christmas Day*,'" Elinor said. "It's from a Longfellow poem. I like it for the verse that goes:

Then in despair, I hung my head,
there is no peace on Earth, I said,
For hate is strong and mocks the song
of peace on Earth, goodwill to men.
Then pealed the bells more loud and deep,
God is not dead, nor does he sleep,
The wrong shall fail, the right prevail,
With Peace on Earth, good will towards men...

She stood in transfigured reflection for a moment in the middle of the bustling airport, then gave a quick shake of her shag hairdo, and then looked at her nephew.

"Anyway," she said almost apologetically, "that's what I believe. No matter what else happens, no matter what anyone does or doesn't do, God is not asleep. Everything will work out for the best; perhaps not our idea of what's best, but for the best just the same."

When they reached the entrance, she turned to him again. "Tell me, do you have much money?" He confessed he hadn't really thought about it and had less than two dollars. She nodded, then frowned, and finally smiled.

"Definitely cut from the same cloth. Fortunately, you didn't have to go all the way to England to start working out these things. Perhaps there's hope for the Potoskis after all. You figured it out just a few miles from home."

They walked out to where he had left Clodagh's bicycle. Miraculously it was still there, and Chesney took it for a sign that perhaps his motives weren't totally selfish after all. Aunt Elinor hailed a cab. The driver loaded the bike into the trunk, while Elinor loaded her nephew in the backseat. Then she gave the driver enough fare for the ride back to Earswick and instructed him to leave Chesney off a block from his home. Then she kissed him once on each cheek and squeezed him nearly as hard as he squeezed her.

"Please come and visit me," she said, her eyes wet but bright, "but not as a fugitive, okay?"

He laughed and agreed while fighting back his own tears. Then with a wave, he was off. He sat up on his knees on the back seat, looking at her outside the terminal. She didn't move, nor did he, until they had finally lost sight of each other.

– 51 –
A Fresh New Day Dawns on an Old Familiar Face

Lorraine Innis shed a tear for Aunt Elinor as she closed the old suitcase. Mr. and Mrs. Potoski recovered from the loss of the baby, confirming Aunt Elinor's assertion that they had known the pregnancy was fraught with risk. In true Potoski fashion, they never discussed it before or after; especially afterward. Chesney missed the sister he had never known more than anyone, though he never mentioned her either.

The Stupid Golf Tournament left Stosh scarred physically, though it had subdued his reign of terror. Chesney could never be sure if Stosh knew he was behind it all, or if Stosh was less aggressive due to running on only one testicle, or if he was merely growing up. Whatever it was, Stosh seemed to be a better person – slightly – by having his manhood divided by half. Still, he was always quick to throw a punch when someone called him "One-Nut," or "Half-Sack," or any other derisive nickname. Stosh retained fond memories of the Stupid Golf Tournament. He kept the battered trophy, the one they had used to beat Fritz senseless, prominently displayed.

The night-long reminiscence brought the current situation into sharper focus for Lorraine. While Mrs. Potoski thought Lorraine was a dead-ringer for Aunt Elinor physically, perhaps his mother had been correct. Maybe Lorraine didn't have Aunt El's wisdom or her moral clarity.

Lorraine recalled the look in Peter Liverot's eyes as he lay dying. His confession, or rather the lack of one, echoed in her mind: Liverot hadn't been responsible for Martina's death. While her plan to bring Liverot to justice wasn't an exact parallel to Chesney plan to get back at Stosh, one constant remained: they had both ended tragically. Another recurring fact, the most troublesome of all, was that both plans were designed and executed by Chesney.

Lorraine shook her head. Chesney always seemed to get it wrong. No matter how right he thought he was, no matter how he scrutinized his motives, ultimately, he always got it wrong. She opened the front of the leather-bound volume of Dickens. There, in between the pages, she took out a photograph of Aunt Elinor. If only Aunt Elinor were still alive. She would have a ready answer. Where else could she turn? To Valerie? It was Valerie who was certain Liverot was responsible for Martina's death. Lorraine couldn't ask Valerie to take a second stab at blind justice by helping her go after Albrecht Eckner; if Eckner were indeed accountable. No, Lorraine thought, this was her responsibility. She wouldn't risk putting any more innocent blood on Valerie's hands. She would have to take her next step alone. But how could she, given Chesney's penchant for ill-fated schemes?

Lorraine carried the suitcase downstairs and returned it to the closet, resting it atop the trunk that had also been a legacy from Aunt Elinor.

As Lorraine entered the kitchen, dawn's first purple streaks were appearing in the sky. In the early morning light, she caught sight of her reflection in the mirror across the room and stopped to stare at the image. Apart from the color of the eyes, she looked even more like her Aunt than usual. Maybe it was the dim light, or perhaps her night-long waking dream was affecting her vision.

"If only you were Aunt El," she said to the reflection. "You could tell me what to do so I don't mess up this any more than I already have."

Lorraine put the kettle on for tea, and out of habit turned on the small television that sat atop the counter. She stood there, leaning against the counter, looking into space, thinking a dozen different thoughts, while not focusing on any single one. Suddenly a voice on the TV forced itself on her consciousness. There was something about it. She turned to look at the screen. It was an early morning cable news show. There was something familiar about the person being interviewed.

Lorraine Innis stood, mouth agape, ignoring the kettle's shrill whistle. By the time she closed her mouth and turned off the burner, she knew exactly what she needed to do.

The End
of

The Girl in the Aubergine Sandals

G.C. Allen

The story of Lorraine Innis will continue in

The Girl in the Lime Green Wellies

Visit www.iLorraine.com